THE FOREST WITCH

THE SIBYLLINE SAGA: BOOK ONE

ANNA CACKLER

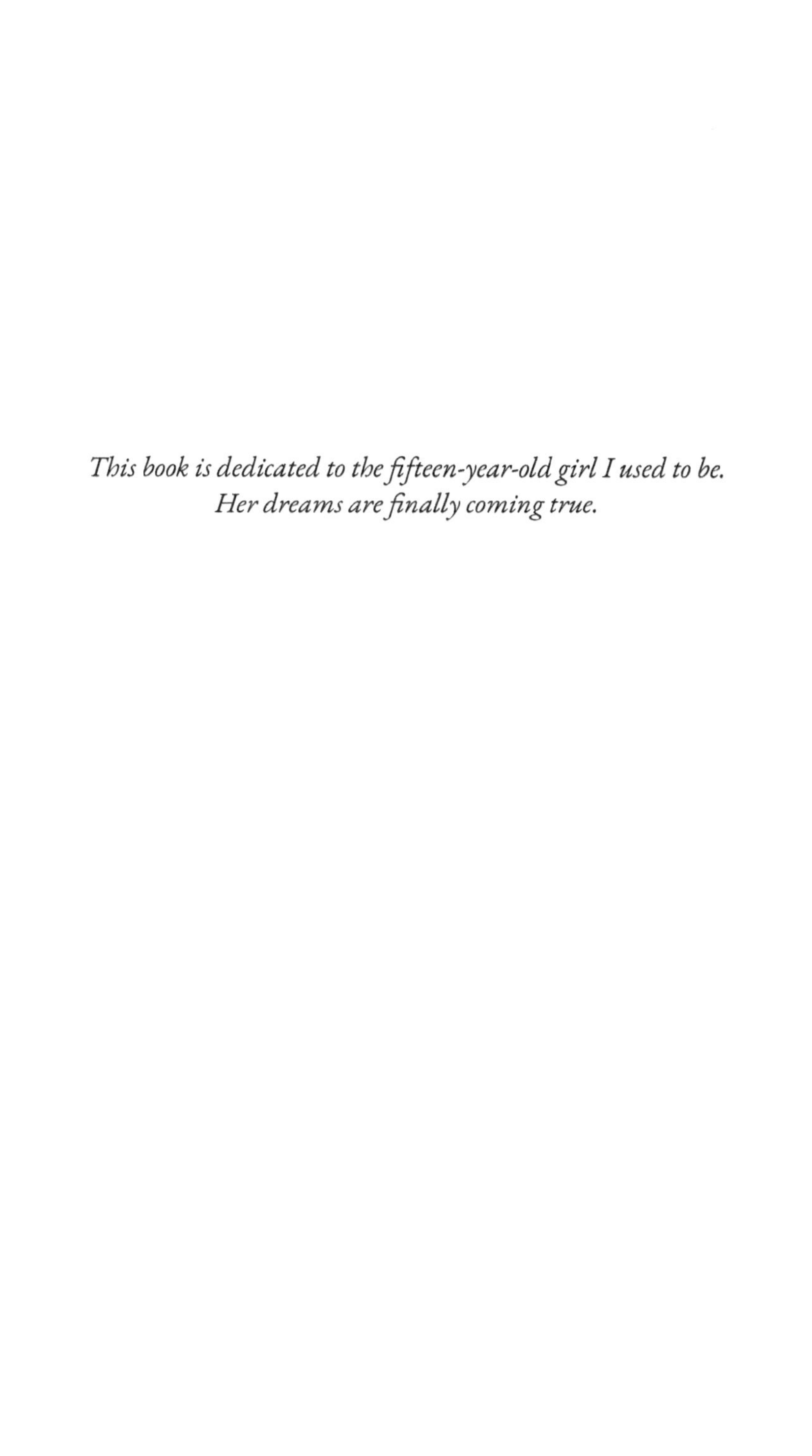

This book is dedicated to the fifteen-year-old girl I used to be.
Her dreams are finally coming true.

Contents

Author's Note

This book includes scenes that may be distressing to some readers. Please refer to the appendix at the back of this book for a complete list of these sensitive topics, or visit my website: annacackler.com

Take care of yourselves, loves.

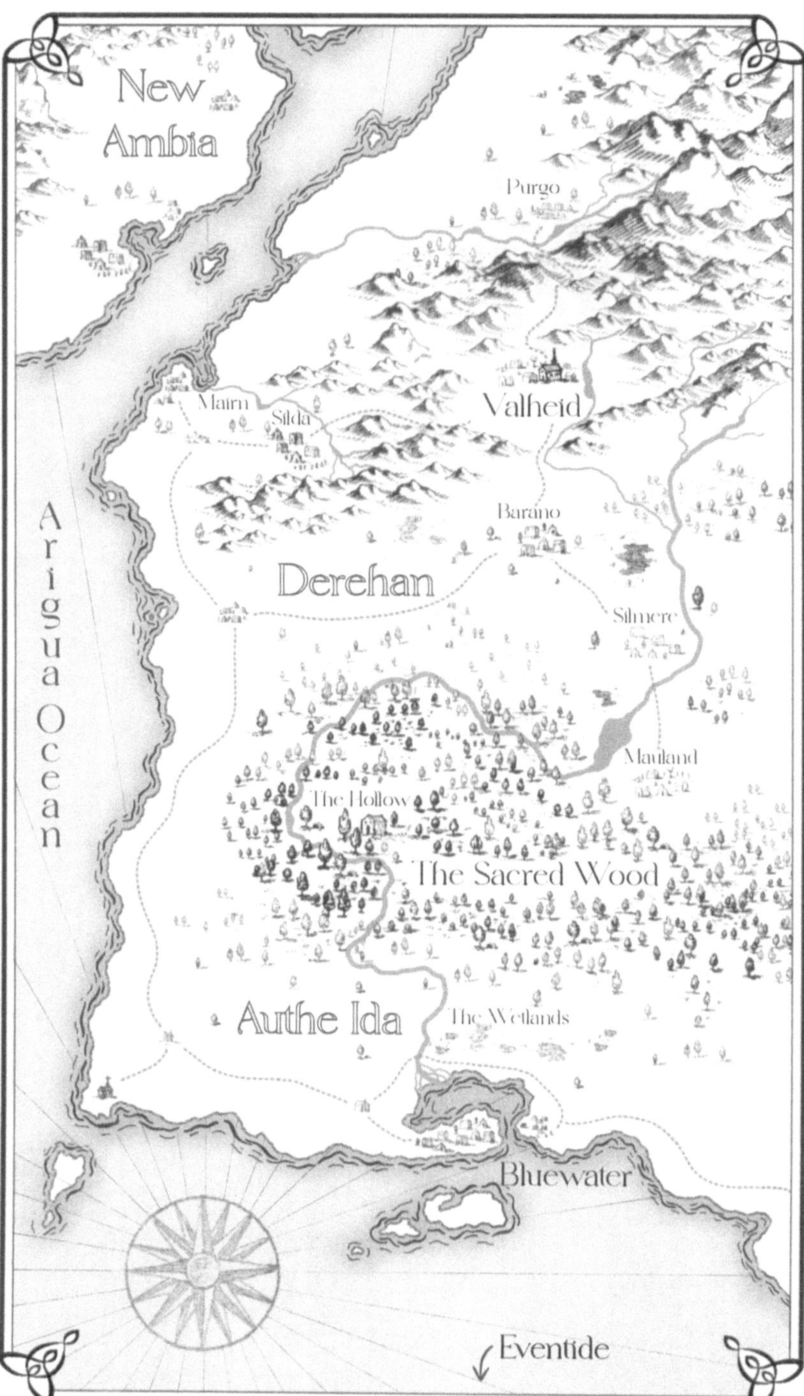

New Ambia
Purgo
Mairn
Silda
Valheid
Barano
Derehan
Silmere
Mauland
The Hollow
The Sacred Wood
Authe Ida
The Wetlands
Arigua Ocean
Bluewater
Eventide

A Warning

Beware, beware the Crone,
    who whispers in your ear.
    She spins her tales of woe,
    that she might draw you near.

Beware, beware the Child,
    who has no need of tales.
    She'll turn your hand and smile,
    the wild thing unveiled.

The pair, they live in Dreamland,
    where ne'er a wind shall blow.
    The fates, the gods, the laws of man,
    there, none dare to go.

The Crone, she draws the stitches,
    the Child, your heart to give.
    So hide yourself from witches,
    and suffer them not to live.

PART ONE
THE BLACKBERRY CRONE

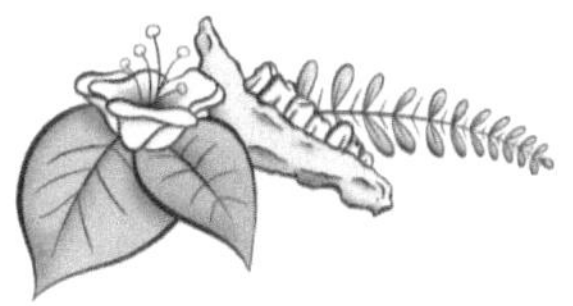

ONE

I crouched on a high branch of the sycamore, silent as the shadows, and peered down at the intruders.

Two men and a woman, dressed in thick traveling clothes against the early autumn dawn, strode through the underbrush toward my tree. They didn't carry weapons, only utility knives, hunting bows, and line for snares. The younger man pulled a stout pack mule behind him, loaded down with parcels, furs, and supplies for living rough.

I tightened my fists on the branch below me, crumbling the papery bark under my fingers.

Trappers in the Sacred Wood. How could they dare?

Most of those who cut through the Wood were refugees, sibyls like myself, though much weaker. They often gathered up their families to flee the hatred of their neighbors and head for the relative safety of the north. Those people I could understand.

But trappers? Profit seekers? They did not belong here.

This was divine land, a relic of the before-times, when the Old Kind lived amongst these great sprawling hardwoods. The old magic still hummed in the dark places, in crevices between rocks and in the hollow oaks. I'd never seen it, but I'd felt it in the dark recesses of my mind. And when I would look closer, I'd find a tiny clay pot in the crack of a tree or a bone talisman under a mossy stone, long forgotten and brittle with time.

The intruders felt the old magic too. They hunched their shoulders and kept their eyes on their feet. The younger man hauled the mule's lead rope, urging the animal to move faster over the uneven ground. The noise of their passing assaulted me: crashing, blundering, cursing. They hissed at each other to move faster as they trampled through underbrush.

I hunkered down on my branch, trying to make myself as small and still as possible. So long as I kept myself hidden, so long as I didn't have to interact with them, I wouldn't be tempted to hurt them. I wouldn't have to find out if my nightmares were real.

The invasive noise grew louder as they drew closer to where I squatted among the dense foliage of the sycamore. Its leaves, already turning yellow at the edges, hid me well.

Michael and I had no flax or sheep, so we wore leather. I had made my tunic and pants from a doe hide I harvested the year before and trimmed in soft rabbit fur. My dark hair hung to my elbows in a tangle of knots and scavenged feathers, and my bare feet were more mud than skin.

Compared to these efficient travelers, I was a wild thing. A creature of the woods, as at home on that tree branch as any bird or scurrying rodent. So when the trappers passed under my tree and the woman glanced upward, she didn't see a young woman crouching in the sycamore. She saw an animal. A faerie. A *thing*.

My heart stopped in my chest when we locked eyes.

The woman froze, causing the younger man to clamber into her.

"What is it, Marta?" the man asked, following her gaze upward. He found me after a few seconds of confused searching among the lower branches, and he paused as well.

The first man continued a few more steps before he realized his companions no longer followed him. "What are you two gawping at?" he called. "I want to get out of this forsaken place. What's the hold up?"

I unfolded my body and stood sure-footed on the smooth bark, looking down at the trio on the forest floor. Their mule nosed around, unconcerned, for something to eat.

"You should not be here," I said, my voice low.

The woman and the younger man trembled, but the other became angry. Tall and strong, he trampled back to get a clearer view of me.

"What's this? A little forest witch?"

"Nate, no!" Marta hissed. She clutched at a rope of seashells around her neck. They must have been Authe Idans, possibly from Bluewater or Iolde, which were the closest cities on the southern border of the Sacred Wood.

That explained why they dared come into the Wood at all. Authe Idans had forgotten the Old Way. To them, we sibyls were scapegoats or scary stories told to frighten children. Mindwalkers, they called us—people who could flit into their minds and lay their very thoughts bare. Sometimes, they called us witches or blamed us for cursing cattle, children, or the weather.

And maybe such creatures *had* existed in the world once. If so, then they had disappeared centuries ago, along with the giants and the faeries, driven out of the world by the fear of man.

The ruler of Bluewater, a terrifying man called Eustis Metaxas, used sibyls as fodder for his fires. And though their shores and sunsets and silks were famed across the continent, Bluewater was one place I never wished to see.

Nate ignored his friend's warning. "Come down here, girl! If we don't belong, then neither do you. What are you doing all alone in the woods?"

I tried, truly I tried, to hang on to my reservations. But the shells around their necks and Nate's leering tone drove away all thoughts of caution. The mental image of the monster I could be slipped away, like mist through the trees. I was only Gwenna, facing intruders who had dared to enter the Sacred Wood without fear.

"I am not alone," I said.

A conveniently timed gust of wind roared through the trees. Branches heaved their loads of foliage and hanging moss, as if to shoo the trappers away.

But perhaps it wasn't a coincidence at all. For in the rushing wind hid the faintest whispers, the slightest thrill of half-remembered magic. The Wood had not abandoned me.

I swayed on my branch, undaunted in the uproar. The feathers in my hair fluttered wildly in the gale as Marta and the younger man cowered. They turned and fled to the north with gasps of panic.

But Nate was not afraid. He, like most Authe Idans, had forgotten what it meant to fear.

"It's just the wind, you idiots!" he yelled after his two companions, who pressed onward with renewed speed. Their long-suffering mule plodded along behind them.

Nate turned back to me and sneered. "I'm not scared of you, witch. Come down here, or I'll come up to get you."

It wasn't an empty threat. He had a lithe body, strong and capable. He could probably climb a tree as well as I, and my branch wasn't particularly high off the ground.

Now what was I supposed to do?

Hiding had failed. Intimidation had failed. I was not strong enough to fight this man physically. I could run, but his legs were long and powerful. He wore sturdy boots, and though my feet were tough, it wouldn't be wise to run barefoot through the brambles. I would only weaken myself with every incautious step I took.

There was no alternative. It was against the rules, but I had no choice. There was nothing for it.

Besides, I could not allow this fearless man to walk away from the Sacred Wood thinking it was nothing at all. The Wood had helped me scare off two of the trappers. Now it was up to me to get rid of the third.

I slipped from the tree branch and landed noiselessly on the mossy earth in front of the man.

Nate was very tall. The top of my head came only to the middle of his chest. He leered down at me.

I was only eighteen, but that was woman enough for most. Despite growing up in isolation, I had not been sheltered from the hard truths of life. So, I didn't need to hear Nate's thoughts to know them.

My hair could be combed, the mud washed from my body. My wildness could be tamed.

I was a toy to him, nothing more. Something naïve and pretty to look at and to warm his bed.

By far, the worst thing was his arrogance.

"That's right," he said in a smug tone. "Very good. Why don't you come with me, little witch? We'll get you a proper meal, some real clothes. You'd like that, wouldn't you?"

He held out one grubby hand to me—and stopped. He hovered, expression frozen, hand extended without moving.

Right at the very core of all people, there was a little life-string. A tiny, glowing link from mind to body. It called to me in a tenuous, lilting vibration. I only needed to wrap my mind around his life-string and take control.

A thrill of joy spread through me. This was easy, far easier than I had expected.

I had only ever tried to coerce Michael before, and then only in controlled situations. Educational. This was real. Nate did not want to freeze, but he had no choice. Only I could decide.

Nate lowered his hand to rest at his side. This was simple too. I controlled his body in the same way I did my own. The thought passed from my mind to his, as light as a breath of wind, and his body obeyed me. I only had to will it, and he complied.

Though I could not control his thoughts, I could feel them all as they passed by.

Witch! I can't move! Just move, Nate! One finger. Blink! Fuck!

I did not enjoy his rising panic, but it meant I had succeeded. He was entirely my puppet. And that realization drew a smirk of satisfaction to my face.

I stepped closer, inhaling his sour body odor. He hadn't washed in days.

"When you wake up, you will leave this place," I said. "You will not look for me. You will only remember. And next time, you will take the road around the Sacred Wood. You should not be here." Then, using a trick I had perfected with Michael, I forced his mind into unconsciousness.

Nate crumpled to the ground, fast asleep.

I turned toward home and started walking, holding my grip on Nate's mind until I was half a mile away. There I paused and monitored his thoughts while he regained consciousness.

His confusion at waking up alone in the forest melted into terror when he remembered our encounter. He wondered briefly if I was still around but decided it would be best to simply flee. Nate trampled off through the brush toward the north, where his friends had gone before.

Michael had been sitting on a smooth boulder in front of our hut when I arrived back at the hollow, shelling dried peas into a bowl to be stored for the winter. He was an older man, lean and limber, with fly-away white hair and a beard tamed with simple braids and leather thongs.

His wrinkled hands moved gracefully over the pods, slipping a yellowed thumbnail inside and scooping out the green peas, which plinked into the bowl between his knees. He paused his work when I approached, my words already gushing forth in a rapid confession, and listened with a concerned expression.

"I shouldn't have used that man's body against him like that," I said in a trembling voice. "I shouldn't have done it. But what else was I supposed to do? Why even have gifts like these if I am never to use them? He wasn't hurt! I only made him sleep and sent him away! He wanted to take me away, Michael!"

He frowned at my desperate rationalizing. "He was not hurt," Michael confirmed in his usual, steady tone. "But that does not make it right, Little Owl."

"So, I should have let him take me? Hurt me?"

"It would have been better to injure him with your knife than do what you did. You took his body away from him. Even though it was only a few seconds, you took his most basic animal right to his own body. No one should have that power, Gwenna."

I crouched on the ground and buried my head in my arms. The shafts of several feathers dug into my arms and scalp when I squeezed. I welcomed the small pain. It drew my attention away from the wrenching guilt in my gut.

Beware, beware the Child, who has no need of tales...

The words of the old nursery rhyme echoed unbidden through my mind.

It was true. I was the Child. The entire world of men had been warned against me. Not some phantom or distant threat, but me.

I clutched my hair even tighter. No! It wasn't true. That verse wasn't a prophecy. It was only a nursery rhyme. It was nothing. My nightmares and childish imagination had magnified it. Nothing more.

Michael set aside his abandoned bowl of peas and wrapped me up in a tight hug. We sat there for several minutes, and he patiently waited for me to relax.

"That's it, little one," he said, when my breathing slowed and my fingers relaxed their hold on my hair. Then he pulled my arms away from my head. Michael sat me on the ground next to his rock and passed me a handful of dried pods to split open.

Work. There was nothing better than work to ease the mind.

"Have you been having your nightmares again?" he asked softly.

I tightened my fingers on the pea pod and squeezed my eyes shut. Images of blood, fire, and terror pierced the blackness behind my eyelids. "Always," I replied.

Michael shifted his weight on the boulder and resumed shelling peas. "I have not told you why we came to live in the Sacred Wood, have I?" He opened a pea pod with a faint crackle. Seven hard, green peas spilled out and joined their fellows in the bowl. "I brought you away from the world, and you never questioned it."

"I was too powerful," I said without hesitation. And deep inside, unbidden and unwanted, a fundamental truth whispered in my mind: *Because I was the Child*.

Michael nodded, unaware of my internal struggle. "Yes. I lived my whole life in a small village in the southeast of Derehan, pretending to be like everyone else. But when you were born, you displayed such power. You pushed into every mind around you, even as an infant. They could not hide what you were."

I poked into a pea pod, eyebrows furrowed, and said nothing. This explanation matched my long-held assumptions.

"Your family asked me to take you away," he continued. "To teach you control. To provide protection from those who would fear you."

A daunting idea occurred to me, and it burst out of my mouth without a thought. "Will we ever go back? Now that I have mastered myself, will we go back there? To my family?"

"Do you want to go back?" His lined face remained calm, but the question lay heavy behind his eyes.

I thought hard about this while I stared into the pile of peas in the bowl in front of me, thinking of the life I knew and the freedoms I had. The silence of the Sacred Wood was something I loved, the connection to the earth and to the steady life of the forest. Could I bear to live in the stone of a town or a city? It would be like an owl living in someone's bedroom.

And then there were the nightmares. I'd always thought I would never hurt another person with my abilities, that those horrors would only ever be confined to my dreams.

But today, I had hurt someone. I had violated his body and his mind, and I'd enjoyed it. Just like in my nightmares.

And then I'd tried to rationalize it afterward.

"I like it here," I said in a stern voice.

TWO

In my dreams, I am always Death. Not the kindly Death who welcomed a person to peace and rest after a long life well lived.

No, I am horror, despair, and pain. And I am very efficient.

I don't know where the nightmares came from. Everything was as it should have been, secure and safe. We lived alone, Michael and I, under the high canopy of the Sacred Wood. We worked hard to maintain our lonely home: hunting, cultivating, preserving. I ran wild through the mossy leaf litter in bare feet, my dark hair adorned with fluttering feathers of every color and species.

We were earthbound and good, and my whole life was ahead of me.

Then at night, the nightmares came again, and I was Death.

Sometimes, I dreamed of cities and battles, of men and women tearing into each other with grim determination. Other times, I dreamed of a great fire—a woman stranded on the roof of a burning building. Her curls were pulled back into a tattered braid, but I never saw her dark face. There was always someone standing next to me when I had this dream, another faceless presence. I didn't need to look at him, though. He was safety, an anchor in the chaos of flames and horror.

That dream came often, and I would wake, choking on phantom smoke and sweating through my clothes.

The night after the trappers, I dreamed of myself as a little girl. I watched her warily while she walked between simple houses with steep, thatched roofs. My dark hair—no, her dark hair—hung limp and dirty, her feet bare.

A few people followed her, walking with bland expressions, puppets under her complete control. One by one, more people joined her crowd, exiting their homes to trail dutifully behind.

She entered the town square. Then, when the entire town stood gathered about her, two hundred people or more, the carnage began. The little girl who was and was not me didn't even flinch when the village people bashed themselves against walls or plunged knives into bellies.

I felt her boredom as if it were my own. Maybe it *was* my own. Either way, this was too easy. She wreaked havoc among the villagers using only a fraction of her ability. No one was safe, not the young or old, strong or weak. They were all hers to do with as she pleased, and no one could stop her.

Next time, she should try a city. Maybe that would be a real challenge.

This was so much worse than with Nate. So much more violent. This could not be me. I would never do such a thing. *Could* never. But there was no denying that this little girl, this monster, was me. Because when she suddenly turned and looked me in the eye, only my own face gazed back at me.

I jerked awake with a gasp, my heart pounding. Michael cried out from his cot across the room and glanced around wildly.

"What is it?" he asked in a bleary voice. "What happened?"

I sat on my cot, unable to speak or think. My lungs heaved in and out, in and out. I clawed at my shirt with sweaty hands, desperate to ease the invisible weight on my chest.

Michael hauled himself out of bed and came to crouch next to me. He wrapped me up in a tight embrace and shushed into my hair. "Hush, Little Owl. It's just a dream."

"It's not!" I rasped. "How can it be a dream? It must be real! It was a premonition, Michael. I don't care that I was a little girl in the vision. It was a premonition!"

"Visions are rarely exact, my child." He looked me in the eye. "Even if it was a premonition, it was only one possibility out of thousands. Maybe it could have been you in a different life. But you are here. You are good and safe. You would never hurt anyone."

"But I did, Michael. I hurt that trapper. I hurt him. I shouldn't have made him freeze or sleep. I should have just run."

"What's done is done," Michael said. "You made a choice, and you have learned from it."

I nodded frantically. "Yes."

"It was only a dream." Michael had said this line to me nearly every night for as long as I could remember.

"Only a dream," I responded in a whisper. My breathing slowed. "Only a dream."

A month later, while I picked wild blackberries in the dappled sunlight of a cool autumn morning, it happened again.

The first crackling of trampled leaves, I dismissed. There was no one around for miles. I had checked. It was probably only a small animal, a fox or a squirrel snuffling through the undergrowth for its breakfast.

But there was something wrong about the sound. It wasn't a searching, turning-over of last year's leaf litter. It had the suddenness of a footfall, sharp and quickly silenced.

When this realization hit me several seconds after the fact, I whirled around in alarm. The blackberries had stained both of my hands purple, and a half-filled basket swung from my forearm.

An old woman stood about ten feet away. She stared at me without a hint of fear or alarm, clicking her tongue.

A torn, baggy shirt dwarfed her bent figure, and she wore old leather leggings, black with filth from the knee down. She clutched a simple staff decorated with tattered fabric and rattling strings of beads, feathers, and bones, which clacked against the worn wood near the top. Her knobby fingers worried at it in apparent delight. Her fist opened and closed, opened and closed, over the gnarled shaft.

A limerick danced through my mind unbidden, that old nursery song everyone knew. An old warning from centuries past meant to frighten children away from strangers. *"Beware, beware the Crone, who whispers in your ear..."*

A thrill of fear went through me, but I squashed it down. Just because this woman was old didn't make her the Crone from my childhood nightmares. And I was no longer a child. I was nearly grown and too old for nursery tales.

"Hello, my darling," said the old woman in a cautious tone. Her voice was high-pitched and scratchy, like the hiss of an angry badger.

I stared at her, too afraid to move or speak.

This was no trapper, no traveler. She wasn't passing through, nor had she found me by chance.

This woman was sibylline, like Michael and me. Her mind pushed against me like an intimidating granite shell in a show of confidence and arrogance that baffled me.

"What? Nothing to say?" she continued in her raspy voice.

"Where did you come from?" I asked.

She held out one arthritic hand to me. Her sleeve pulled back on her arm as she reached, revealing three ancient, soft scars in parallel lines on the back of her arm. It must have been a nasty wound, once upon a time. Violence, ugliness, destruction. Scars like that didn't happen to nice people.

"Would you like to see?" the old woman asked.

My gaze flitted from her face to her shaking hand, then back again. "Just tell me."

The woman dropped her hand with a humorless chuckle. "He's told you nothing. I thought as much. That old fool has kept you here, alone, for far too long."

The opposing desires to flee or to attack warred inside me. She should not be here. In all my life, I had never seen anyone besides the odd traveler, and only once had they ever spotted me. Yet there stood this old woman, with her tattered clothes and knowing smile. What could it possibly mean? Where had she come from?

"Either speak plainly or leave." I stood as straight and tall as I could. "I have no interest in hints or riddles."

The woman took a single step closer and leaned forward on her staff. She held out her hand once more and smiled. "Take my hand, darling, and you'll see the truth for yourself."

"That's enough," I said with a disgusted scowl, then turned and stalked away from the little meadow. My basket of blackberries tumbled its contents over the leaf litter as I slipped between the trees.

Half of me wanted to stop and gather the fallen berries so they wouldn't be wasted. But my other half vibrated with anger. Whoever this woman was, she had come to me deliberately to play games. I didn't care why anymore. I wasn't playing.

"Can you spot a lie, little one?" The woman's voice followed me with an amused laugh.

"You shouldn't be here!" I said over my shoulder.

"Neither should you! Not anymore." She tried to follow me, but I was sure-footed. The noise of her hesitant trampling through the underbrush quickly halted behind me. "Michael is lying to you! Mark my words! He's lying! Look under what he says, and you'll see."

I paused and turned halfway back to face the old woman, my chin raised. "How do you know his name? How do you know me? Who are you?"

She did not offer her hand to me again. "Ask him," she said. "Run along home and ask him, little one. And look for the lies. Come here again tomorrow, and I will tell you the truth."

I scowled at her. More riddles. Was this how all people spoke with each other in the world? If so, then I'd gladly spend the rest of my life in the Sacred Wood.

"Michael does not lie," I said flatly, then sprinted away before she could reply.

I slipped under the high, twisted branches, swift as an owl gliding on the night wind. These woods were my home, every stone, every branch and turning, so it did not take me long to find my way back to the hut.

I didn't stop running until I passed through the protective ring of runestones which guided people away from the hollow where our hut sat. Small and hard to spot, the stones had been nestled in the ground, often covered in moss and leaf litter. But I felt them when I passed. I ignored the overwhelming urge to turn away and stepped over the invisible line.

I entered our sheltered garden at a trot, my heart pounding from the exertion. Michael stood near the warmth of the stove, just visible through a narrow window. He busily braided onions for the upcoming winter, his white hair tied back with a bramble cord I'd spun myself that summer.

He went about his work like any other day, and the old woman's words rattled through my head. *He's told you nothing.*

No. Michael wasn't a liar. He always answered every question I'd ever asked.

Not that I had ever asked any.

A large quartz stone propped open the door to let in the fresh air, so Michael didn't hear when I stepped quietly inside.

"Good morning, Michael."

He jumped visibly when I spoke. "Gracious, Gwenna." The loose skin around his jaw quivered. His eyes crinkled with a smile in greeting. "You startled me, child. I didn't expect you back for some hours yet. Did you find anything good in the Wood today?"

In answer, I sat my basket of blackberries on the rough-hewn table, where Michael oohed over the ripe berries. He popped two in his mouth and closed his eyes in delight.

"My favorite. Were there many more, do you think? We can cook them down into a jam."

"Yes, there were more. I'll go out again tomorrow."

He ate two more before returning to his onions.

I stared at the back of his head. This man had been a scholar before he brought me to this place as an infant. He spoke of it often, of the studies he'd done and the books he'd read. Michael had taught me everything he knew and was often wistful about the grand libraries he had left behind.

And now here he was, his day filled with mundane tasks, which mostly involved preserving food and repairing leaky buckets and torn shirts.

"What city did you say we came from?" I asked, lowering myself into the solitary upright chair by the table.

His long fingers didn't falter on the long onion greens. Over, under, over, under. "A small town in the west. A place called Mauland, near the border with Authe Ida."

That was when I saw it: the lie.

No, I didn't *see* it. I didn't feel it or hear it. It had no substance, only a broad sensing.

It was a combination of many things. First, it was the slight increase in his heartbeat and breathing, which I could feel as easily as my own. But it was also in the adjustment of his mental shields. He didn't block me out completely, which would have drawn my suspicions. But he erected them in just the right way to deflect my notice. And when I looked around those shields, it was in the way his thoughts turned just a little to the side.

It was in the way his thoughts became deliberately repetitious. *Over, under, over, under.* I could only hear what was on his mind in the moment, so he deliberately thought of innocuous things.

This earth-shattering realization hit me in the space of a breath, between one sentence and the next.

"Why do you ask?" he continued, unaware of what I now knew.

I kept myself outwardly calm. He could not feel me as acutely as I felt him. No one could. But even an ungifted person would notice agitation in another's breath or tone of voice.

"I've just been thinking about what you told me a few weeks ago. About how you took me away as an infant. Who asked you to do it? My family?"

Michael's hands finally stilled at their task. He turned to face me with a somber expression. "Your mother died giving birth to you, I'm afraid."

This was the truth. I pressed on.

"And my father?"

"Gone before you were born."

"But alive?"

"I don't know."

Another truth. These things I believed.

"So, I have no one? Nowhere to go?"

He shifted his weight from one foot to the other. "Why do you ask, Gwen? Do you want to leave the Sacred Wood?"

"No," I said sharply. "No, I don't want to go anywhere. I was just curious." I stood up, feeling guilty and confused. For the first time in my life, cracks had begun to appear in my own solid understanding of the world.

Michael gave a comforting half smile. "We are safe here, Little Owl."

I nodded and moved toward the door. "I'll go get water."

But as I snatched up the buckets from their spot by the door, my gut churned.

He's told you nothing.

~

The next morning, before Michael woke, I left with my blackberry basket in one hand. I looked for the old woman behind every tree and around every mossy boulder, but she was nowhere to be seen. I kept my mind open, a mental net cast over the Wood for a mile in every direction.

Nothing. Aside from the usual undercurrent of life pulsing through the trees, I was alone.

The blackberry bramble overwhelmed a small, natural meadow. The thorny bushes thrived in that small pool of bright sunlight, so rare in the deep parts of the Sacred Wood. And as I glanced over the wild tangle, I began to wonder if it had all been a dream. There had been no woman, no confusion. No lies.

With a frown, I began industriously picking the berries. It was slow work, but with cautious, deliberate movements, I was able to avoid the worst of the thorns.

"I told you he'd lie," said a high, throaty voice behind me.

I jumped, earning a line of painful, shallow scratches along my forearm in my carelessness. Fine lines of blood immediately appeared on my skin.

I ignored the pain and turned with hard eyes to face the old woman.

"Who are you?" I asked.

"Straight to the point, I see," she said with a chuckle. "I like a little fight in a young person. I have had many names over the years, but most call me Theo now."

"And who are you, Theo? How do you know me?"

A sly smile spread across her wrinkled face. Much older than Michael. Her skin was like antique paper handled too often by careless hands. Her knuckles bulged in giant, painful-looking knobs, and she was so thin she might blow over in the wind.

"I have known you all your life. And Michael too," she said. "He fears me, what I can teach you. That is why he lies. Why he keeps you hidden away in this old place."

"And what can you teach me?"

"Your power goes deeper than any magic the world has seen in centuries. There is no limit to what you can do, and yet he has leashed you. Tamed you. Lied to you. He has you here, picking berries, like you're nothing." She held out her hand to me like a claw. "But I can show you another world. Help you see your true potential."

I knew my potential, had seen it many times in my nightmares. Blood-soaked and terrifying. A death god let loose on the world. I did not want that life.

"Why now?" I asked. "If you've known me all my life, why only come to me now?"

She smirked and lifted her chin. "I didn't know where to find you, girl. Until a few weeks ago, when a few trappers in a grubby bar started spreading tales. They talked about a forest witch who could use a person's body like a puppet."

I froze, squashing the instinct to curl up on myself in shame. I felt seen. Not just by Theo, but by the whole world.

"You scared them proper," Theo said with a chuckle. "And you were right to do so. Authe Ida has lost all respect for this sacred place. They have forgotten who we are, and that makes them dangerous."

"No." My mouth screwed up in determination. "I made them afraid. The fear of man is what destroyed us. Sent us into hiding."

"Wrong again, little one." Theo wagged a crooked finger. "It was our own fear that drove our kind away. Imagine what the world could have been if our foremothers had stood their ground against the fear of mankind? If they had stood tall and demanded their rightful place in the world? As you did with those trappers?"

Theo's words held no hint of a lie. Despite her tantalizing

string of non-answers, she spoke only the truth. Or what she believed the truth to be.

Where Michael told only half-truths, Theo offered something more substantial. Real information. Real change. Real answers.

So I dropped my half-filled basket of blackberries and stepped closer to her. I took Theo's bent hand and marveled at the softness of her withered skin.

She grinned once, a twisted, satisfied smile, and yanked me out of the world.

An irresistible vacuum sucked the very breath from my lungs, and my heart ceased to beat. I tightened my hand around Theo's, but she had gone.

A brilliant, white light blanketed the world around me, making it hard to keep my watering eyes open. I was a mass of contradictions, falling and landing at the same time. My body felt heavy, but it moved more easily than usual. Everything was backward, upside down, wrong in every way.

But then it stopped, just as quickly and unexpectedly as it had begun.

I opened my tightly shut eyes and looked around. The white light was gone, and the bony fist of the old woman once again clasped my own. She peeled her fingers away as if it were extremely difficult for her to separate herself from me. The slyness had disappeared from her face, replaced with a pained look.

"It's not so easy as it once was to cross the void. I'm getting too old for this," she said.

I stumbled away from her and braced myself against the rough bark of the closest tree. My breath came in shaky gasps, and I stared around at my surroundings.

The forest had changed. The trees were much too large, too old and gnarled. Dry, dead grass and dusty earth made up the forest floor. No flowers, no weeds, no moss. Only thirst.

The woods were free of underbrush, making it possible to see for long stretches between the trunks. But there was nothing else. Only more trees. On and on they went, forever apparently.

I shivered. There was something wrong with this dead forest. I couldn't quite tell what it was, but I hated it. Something was missing, something important.

I swallowed hard and forced myself to focus on Theo's words. "The void?" I asked.

She rolled her shoulders. "The nothingness between the worlds. It is a rare gift to pass through the void unharmed. Only the sibyls can do it and survive."

"Between the worlds? Where are we? Is this another world?"

"A place of hiding. A sanctuary," she said, still sounding pained.

Small drops of blood fell from my scratched forearm, and the parched earth absorbed it immediately, like water on dry sand. "Hiding from what?" I asked, hauling myself upright.

Theo shrugged. "Everything. People. Fear. Time itself. Here, we are safe."

Michael had said the same thing. *We're safe here, Little Owl.*

I stared around at the empty place, and my heart hammered in my chest. "This isn't a sanctuary. It's just another prison."

I kept a firm grip on my own mental shields, but that didn't stop Theo from trying to get inside. The granite of her mind melted and conformed to my own, looking for any crack to slide through.

"I'm not your enemy, girl," she said, annoyed. "I was Michael's teacher, and he carries on my work, now that I am too old to continue it myself. I will not steal your secrets, what few inconsequential ones you may have."

Inwardly, we danced. She slipped to the side; I redoubled my defenses.

"Why did he hide me from you?" I asked.

She shrugged. "We had a bit of a falling out several years ago. He didn't agree with some of my methods." Theo studied me carefully for a moment or two while she tried and failed to break through my mental shields. "Nice to see he's going on with my work, though. Finishing up what I started. He's taught you a few tricks, has he?"

"I thought you said he tamed me. You're speaking in riddles again. Answering questions without answering."

"You're just not listening properly." Theo thudded her staff on the dry earth for emphasis. She was getting angry and tried in earnest to get past my blocks. Theo managed to skirt around a few and concentrated very hard on my sense of direction. She wanted to know where I had come from.

She was trying to find the hollow.

"I don't think so." With one mighty mental heave, I shoved her out of my mind. The relief was instant, as if I had dusted a mass of cobwebs from between my memories. Everything grew clearer.

I no longer had any desire to listen to this woman.

Theo threw her head back and laughed, raspy and harsh. Her horrible cackle echoed between the trees, and I wrapped my arms around myself to ward off the chills wracking my body.

I realized what was wrong with our surroundings.

Theo's laugh reverberating amongst the trees had thrown the deafening silence into harsh relief. There was no noise in that place. No birds sang in the branches. The wind did not rustle through the leaves. There was no chatter of squirrels or rabbits in the underbrush. The forest was entirely deserted. Utterly empty.

"I want to go home." I wanted out of that awful, lonely place.

The woman's expression faded quickly from shock, to confusion, to anger.

"You horrible, ungrateful girl," she spat. "Don't you realize the amount of knowledge this place holds? Don't you recognize the gift I am giving you? The gift of time itself!"

"I don't care!" A cold sweat broke out all over my body. I stared around in a panic, searching for any kind of exit. I wanted more than anything to run to Michael and hide under my blankets, where she couldn't find me.

But there were only more trees. More and more, forever.

"I want to go home!"

Her eyes blazed with fire, and her control over her telepathy wavered for just an instant. The anger consumed her.

In a moment of heart-stopping panic, I returned to the white nothingness and then to the familiar hardwood forest I called home. I collapsed onto the hard earth and vomited. My throat ached with the stale taste of bile, but I was home.

I staggered up and ran to the hollow, leaving the blackberries behind. I expected to find the old woman waiting for me behind every tree, over every hill. I could almost see her craggy face and feel her rancid breath on my neck as I raced home. The very thought of her terrified me.

Michael! I sent the mental message as soon as I was close enough. *Michael!*

"What is it, Little Owl?" he asked, looking concerned, when he exited the hut to meet me.

The relief of seeing his familiar, kind face slammed into me like fresh, life-giving air after too long under water.

I did not try to explain it in words; I showed him instead. My tight control over my thoughts melted away. Images of Theo and the dead place flooded freely from my mind to his. Michael staggered under the weight of them at first, not ready for such a load so suddenly.

"Theo," he told me. "Her name is Theo, and she was my teacher, so long ago." He put his arm around me, still a little wobbly from the unexpected rush of emotional memories.

I suddenly noticed how frail Michael had become in the failing light as he leaned on me for support. Dark circles shaded his eyes, as if he hadn't slept for days. He looked so very tired.

"Come inside," he said. "Come inside and I will explain everything."

THREE

He told it to me like one of his stories. First he made some tea, and he didn't rush the process. He prepared the cups while he boiled water over our clay stove, scooping in chamomile and lavender in precise amounts.

I waited patiently, quite used to this routine. Once the tea was poured, we settled near the heat of the little stove, me on the mat and him in his armchair.

Finally, Michael spoke, still unhurried. "Theo was a wise woman in the village where you were born," he said through the steam rising from his tea. "She lived in the forest outside of town and attended to those who sought her out, in exchange for coin or food or supplies."

Despite his calm tone, I couldn't quite settle. I stared out the rough window, on alert, scanning the darkened trees for any sign of movement that didn't belong.

"I've told you before, about when you were born. How you pushed into every mind in the area. People could feel you four houses down. Everyone knew what you were. They were frightened and angry.

"Your mother died giving birth to you, as you know. You had

no one else, and none of your neighbors wanted anything to do with you. I took you because there was no one else and because I was able to block you out, and—"

He paused, pressing his interlaced knuckles to his mouth, as if to keep the words in.

"And because Theo took an unnatural interest in you. She wanted you, Little Owl. She wanted to take you and twist you into something like her, something that scrounges at the edge of town for scraps, something manipulative and hated and feared. She saw your power and coveted it for herself. She would make you her puppet, Gwen."

Michael leaned forward in his chair and sat down his cup, only half-drunk. He took my hands and squeezed, putting as much love, comfort, and apology into the gesture as he could.

"I could do better for you, give you a life of freedom and peace. I could teach you to live close to the earth and the trees, teach you to revere the Sacred Wood as the sibyls of old have done throughout history. I brought you here to keep you safe from other people who would fear you, and to keep you safe from her."

He stared at me when he finished speaking, clearly wanting me to say something to assure him he had done right. And indeed, I could think of no alternative course of action in the circumstances.

Had Michael done right? I had no family left, no one in the village where I was born. I had been saved from a crone who I personally knew to be manipulative, manic, and cold-hearted at best. And I had grown up happy, healthy, and free in the Sacred Wood that I loved.

But I couldn't reassure him. Something didn't feel right about his story. I didn't believe him. And why not?

Because it was too innocent.

If the only threat was from Theo, why hadn't he told me about her voluntarily before this? Why did I need to ask? We were safe from her in the hollow. As long as the old magic of the runestones protecting this place endured, she could not find us here. That magic was older than us, older than our hut, older than Derehan itself. It was strong and lasting. We were safe.

So why hadn't Michael told me about Theo? Why keep me in the dark about my own past? Why lie?

I looked up at him. For the second time, I understood what it felt like when a person lied to me. It wasn't in his looks or his tone, but in his mind. Michael blocked me out very carefully, but his heart beat faster, his breath came too short, and his thoughts turned to the side, just a bit.

This history was half-truth, half-lie.

"Gwen," he said upon an exhale, his expression both despairing and pleading.

I was never one to play games. I looked him directly in the eye, my mouth set in a firm line. "Will you tell me the whole truth?"

"I have told the whole truth," he said.

Lie.

Michael studied my face for a long moment. I couldn't make out what he was thinking, but it was obvious he was trying to decide how to proceed.

"You are nearly grown. You are old enough to take charge of your own life. You are strong enough to keep control of your mind, and you are capable enough to fend for yourself. The time is coming soon, Gwen, for you to decide if you want to stay here in the Wood or leave."

I leaned away, baffled. Why was he bringing this up again?

"I cannot stop you from leaving me," he said quietly, almost begging. "But please wait just a little before you go. If you go. Wait until the spring, when you can be sure the weather will hold for traveling."

"I'm not leaving, Michael," I said. "I'm not going anywhere. This is my home."

This caused him to frown even deeper. Now it was his turn to disbelieve.

"Do you want me to leave?" I asked, alarmed. Even now, my voice remained low and calm, but he could feel my hurt.

"No! No, I don't want you to go. You and I are family. I don't want you to leave."

"If I left, then you could too," I said, the ideas coming to me slowly. "We could both leave, together or separately. We could both live among people."

Michael closed his eyes and made no answer. "I am tired," he said, rising from his hard chair. "I'm sorry for all of this, Little Owl. I'm so sorry."

I stood as well, my lips parted and my breath coming fast.

Would he say nothing else? Would he leave it at this? These half-truths and unanswered questions? Was he going to bring up my deserting him, then leave me to fret alone?

Michael smiled and went to his cot in the corner. He settled down onto the straw mattress and closed his eyes. Discussion over.

I stared at him for a few moments. The conversation had lasted less than a half hour, but those few minutes had changed everything. More than simply knowing more of my own history, now I saw someone entirely different laying on that cot. He was not the Michael I had known.

He had been lying to me for my entire life, and he would go on lying for as long as he could. Forever, maybe. He had been this person the entire time, a liar. A keeper of secrets.

And I had been fooled.

I hovered there in the hut, unsure of what to do or say. Michael knew I stood there, yet he remained turned away, feigning sleep. Eventually, I went outside and resumed sewing a new pair of fur boots on the bench under my favorite willow tree, like it was any other day.

Whatever Michael's reasons, whatever the whole truth was, I would find it eventually. If not, then maybe it really was time to consider leaving. The spring seemed ages away, but Michael was right about the weather. The winters could be devastating in the north, and I would need time to find a home.

And so I forced needle and thread through the tough hides and thought about what my life could be, how it might change if I set out on my own. In the end, I decided I didn't want it to change. I loved the Wood, I loved my home, and despite everything, I loved Michael too. In time, I would find a way to forgive him. Not today, not now, but soon.

After that, Michael and I developed a sort of distant friendship. It was nothing like what we had before, but it was livable. We did not speak of Theo or of Michael's lies. We pretended nothing had happened, that nothing had changed.

But something had changed. A small tension existed between us, as if neither of us were quite comfortable with the other anymore.

I hated it. All I had to do was talk to Michael about it and tell him I was all right, that I had forgiven him. And I wanted to, so badly, but I never could. He was still keeping something from me, and that hurt more than anything.

More than a week passed away before I could bring myself to venture beyond the protection of the runestones, and even then, I refused to go far.

Michael and I tended our small garden and reaped a decent harvest. I went out and picked a good number of apples to save for the winter, foraged a wealth of mushrooms and berries, and brought down several rabbits. The meat would dry well, and the furs would serve as a new blanket to replace my ratty old one.

I did not see Theo again, though I jumped at every small noise while walking through the woods. I hated myself for being so afraid. I should be vigilant and alert, but never afraid.

But the nagging dread ran deep, and I could not completely shake it.

Before I knew it, autumn bloomed fully in the Sacred Wood. The trees exploded with color—dusky reds, oranges, and yellows—and my breath hovered in a cloud of fog in the mornings.

I worked tirelessly to make sure there was enough wood for our squat, clay stove and decent stores set away to last us through the winter. Michael did as much as he could, but he tired easily. In a few years, he wouldn't be able to contribute much at all. He would hate that.

Michael was always so happy to be out of doors, doing good, honest work with his hands. He must have been a very strong young man, but his muscles had grown softer. It made him sad. I could feel it.

"Gwenna," he said, on one of the last warm nights of the season. "Come to the river with me tonight. I need the constancy of the stars, and I cannot see them in the forest."

"You know I hate the ravine." I looked up at him with a small frown on my face. As a child, I had nearly fallen into the gorge once, when the earth gave way at the edge. I had avoided the place ever since.

"You're going to have to return to it someday," he said. "You haven't had a proper look at the sky since you were eight."

"So give me a memory."

"It's not the same," he said.

"But—"

"But nothing." There was a finality to his tone that he rarely had to use with me. "Get your cloak. You need to see the sky for yourself. Now, let's go."

I stood from the table, frowning. Michael cast his eyes downward and left the little hut. He was up to something, and he almost seemed ashamed.

I wanted to read his mind, but he had shields up. They weren't strong; I could break them if I wanted, but that would go against the rules. No listening in.

Even after all he'd kept from me, I still did not press him for answers. Call it trust. Call it habit. Whatever it was, I didn't break through his shields.

I followed Michael out of the hut, pulling my leather cloak over my shoulders and drawing up the fur-lined hood as I went. He had already reached the edge of the little valley where we lived, moving steadily in the direction of the Lily River and the deep canyon it had carved. I took a calming breath and followed him without a word.

The deep quiet of the forest bid us to silence as well. Our footsteps barely made a sound on the soft undergrowth. An owl hooted in the distance, a soothing sound. I shivered and pulled my cloak closer about my body.

I couldn't quite put my finger on it, but something was wrong. Something was present which should not have been. It was very faint, very distant, and Michael and I were headed directly toward it.

Michael?

Yes?

Where are you taking me?

To the river.

My heart raced in my chest, but I didn't press the issue. I listened hard for any sound that did not belong, but the crickets, frogs, nightbirds, and our own footfalls drowned out everything else.

We reached the edge of the cliff just as night began to fall. The moon was bright, but not too much so to blot out the stars. I gave the sheer drop one wary glance and then looked up at the sky.

I did not venture too close; I didn't have to. The tree line stopped well before the earth dropped down to where the river raged, making the sky easily visible. Michael had been right—his memories couldn't compare to the beauty of the heavens at night.

I retreated further from the edge and settled into the grass next to Michael. We both lay back, and after a few quiet moments, he began pointing out constellations, communicating mind to mind like we used to.

There you see the Firefly, the last of the magical creatures. And the Sprite on its back. Do you see those five stars in a line?

Where?

Just there, to the right of the Crow? That's the tail of the Scorpion, who tricked the Sprite into giving up its sword.

On and on he went for nearly half an hour, reciting the old tales I had almost forgotten. And all the while, that strange feeling in the back of my mind grew, formless and unrecognizable, making the hairs stand up on my arms.

Finally, I sat up and looked to the west along the ravine. Whatever it was, that's where it came from. And it was moving in our direction.

Michael! There are people nearby!

A great crowd of people moved in the distance, their lives shining brightly in my mind's eye. I began to hear their thoughts as they drew ever closer. I hadn't recognized the feeling because I had never before sensed so many people at such close range. Not three or four minds, but dozens and dozens. The sensation wasn't at all what I had imagined it to be, and it threw me.

I scrambled toward the underbrush where we could hide, but paused when Michael didn't follow.

Michael! Hurry! We must hide! I don't think I can control them all at once!

He gazed over at me. His face changed a little, as if puzzling over a complicated decision.

My disorientation grew while dozens of other people bounded about freely in my head. Their thoughts and feelings were very clear now. Many of them snuck in, climbing nearby trees and looking for advantageous hiding places. They all had one thing on their minds: Kill the enemy.

It was a small army moving into position to ambush someone.

And I knew who that someone was.

A smaller group—just five men and one woman—traveling light, approached the ravine from the southeast, seemingly unaware of the danger awaiting them. They strolled through the darkness, sure-footed, tired, and unafraid.

My head ached. It was getting very hard to pay attention to my surroundings. I had no control over my telepathy, and it began to rule me.

The smaller group stepped into the clearing near the edge of the ravine. Six travelers. Six against fifty.

Michael's inner voice broke into the haze my brain had become. *Down here. There's going to be an ambush, I think. We have to hide.*

I took his hand and let him lead me, half-blind in the night and confusion, to the edge of the underbrush. We squatted down and made ourselves completely still. We would be entirely hidden between the darkness and our clothes of leather, feathers, and fur.

I fidgeted in the dirt, lost in my own mind, while dozens of thoughts belonging to other people jostled me about. Michael gathered me close to him and squeezed, trying to keep me quiet.

A bit further.

Kill them all!

They may talk!

I could not block them out, could not control it. I even went so far as to forget where I was entirely, so immersed in forced thoughts and feelings as I was.

Gwenna.

Michael's inner voice rang through the din. I caught hold of it and clung on for dear life.

"Not yet," one man said to his companion. His voice cut clear and sharp through the darkness, though he didn't speak loudly.

"It's past dark," another replied. "We should have stopped an hour ago, at least. This is madness, John."

"Not yet," the first man said again. "A bit further. I know a place where we can rest that will be safe."

"Nothing's safe here," another man said.

No, he didn't say it aloud. He thought it.

I clutched my head, desperately muddled. Too many thoughts from too many sources. They jumbled in my mind, incomprehensible.

Just breathe.

It's been so long.

Michael?

We'll just leave them here.

Kill!

Michael! Make it stop!

Just breathe, Little Owl. Michael latched onto me, mind to mind. He threw me a lifeline of sorts, pulling me out, helping me handle the sudden load. *You must take control. Remember who and where you are. Focus on the present. Remember what is yours and what belongs to others. Block them out! Get control!*

His advice was all well and good, but it was extremely hard to do. I knew who I was. I was Robert, a middle-aged man with two grown girls and a wife who had died three years before in a raid in a village in the south. I came here to kill the Derehanis. To get revenge. I would taste blood tonight, even if my own was mixed in.

I had almost rushed in the direction of the Derehani men with revenge on my mind before I realized that, no, that wasn't right. I was a young boy, ready to prove himself, not a widower. There was a girl waiting for me at home. She was small, with a long face, wide eyes, and a smile that made my heart jump.

No, that wasn't it. I was a lithe woman creeping around a tree, looking for a clear shot.

Michael?

Focus!

On what? What was there to focus on?

Remember who you are. Where you came from. Repeat the familiar things to yourself until you have control.

The six people in the clearing at the edge of the ravine argued calmly. They were the Derehani. What were they doing here, out in this deserted stretch of the Sacred Wood? Even stranger still, how could the Authe Idans dare to attack them? The two nations had no love for each other, but there was no war. Even if there had been, the Wood was a no man's land. Battle was forbidden here.

I tried to ignore the men. Instead, I focused on remembering that I was Gwenna and had grown up in the hollow. I thought of the little vegetable patch near the window by my bed and remembered the constellations. *The Firefly and the Sprite, tricked by the Scorpion. The Maned Goat and its horns, forever chasing the sun.*

Good. Good. Michael's voice came clearer now. Much easier to distinguish.

As I retold the stories to myself, the jumble began to clear. And with a final effort, I erected a spherical shield around my mind. Thin and transparent as glass, but there, and the voices faded to a distant muffle.

Now, I could think. I could make a plan. Michael's white beard and bright eyes came into focus in the dim moonlight. The travelers stood nearby. So close. If the nearest man reached out, he would brush my nose.

They had no idea they were surrounded by their enemies. Unseen. Deadly. Waiting.

Then a blinding pain rocketed through my left eye, and I screamed.

I fell forward into the bare dirt broken only with small, prickly patches of sticker weed, which clung to the rocky soil.

A man had been shot. The one who could have touched my nose if he'd known I was there. He fell, an arrow plunged deep into his eye.

"Connor!" someone cried out in shock and disbelief.

Another man only a few paces away dove toward his fallen

friend. His hands hovered over the body, his mouth gaping in shock.

Then he looked up and locked eyes with me. To him, I was a witch girl looming out of the darkness, dirty and covered in feathers, horror written plainly on my face. We both froze in fear.

"Ambush!" cried one of the travelers.

His companions melted into a fighting stance.

The enemy darted into the open with shouts of war. Swords and knives flashed in the moonlight. Blood flew. Screams rang between the trees and ruined the serene rushing of the water in the ravine nearby. The man who had spotted me cast me one last wary glance before he drew his own sword and stepped into the fray.

That archer had had a keen aim, even in the dark. But then again, it could have been pure luck. Either way, a dead man lay in the dirt inches from where I clutched my aching head. I stared at his bloodied, ruined face, unable to move or think. My lungs heaved air in and out, in and out.

Too fast, too much air. Too much noise. Too many people. And the blood. So much blood. Just like my nightmares.

Had I done this? Had I coerced that woman to loose her arrow?

No, surely not. I would never.

My head threatened to burst, but I managed to crawl away from the dead man. I struggled back toward Michael through the dirt, the feathers on my hair catching in the underbrush.

But as I got close enough to reach his outstretched hand, I clenched up.

A sickening pain exploded through my entire body, originating from an arrow sunk deep in my left breast. I gasped, unable to draw breath into my ruined lungs. I looked down, shocked to see no arrow protruding from my chest.

It was pain, but it was not *my* pain.

I looked up to where Michael crouched, still half concealed in the underbrush a few feet away. It was his pain I felt. The long shaft of the arrow protruded from his chest, a gruesome confirmation of someone else's good aim.

His emotions flowed freely to my mind, like they had the long habit of doing. Flashes of his distant past swam before my vision, too many to sort out. A woman. A huge horse, too big to ride. A feeling of desperation. A baby. Fear. A book. A young woman, different from the first. My laughing face. Love.

Everything happened so fast, and I barely had time to comprehend it all. I lunged toward him, though the pain in his chest stopped the breath in my own, but I couldn't reach him before he fell. His consciousness tore from me like a limb ripped from its socket.

With a strangled gasp, I felt him die. I felt his terror, his desperation, the animal need to survive being stripped away, bit by bit until he was gone. A hole opened up inside me, gaping and senseless. I couldn't breathe around it. I couldn't think. I couldn't get up to hide from the chaos around me.

My fingers scrabbled over the front of his shirt as I struggled to take a breath. Finally, it came as a gasp of new pain. This time it was my right leg, just below the knee.

Yet another arrow.

This time, it was real. This time, it was me.

The air rushed into my desperate lungs, only to be pushed out again when a strong arm looped around my middle. I was hauled off the ground and slung over a man's shoulder, but I couldn't tear my eyes off Michael's body in the darkness. The unknown man bore me away from the carnage.

One moment, we had been telling stories. The next, everything was shredded. I finally lost the battle to stay conscious. The last thing I heard before losing myself was the voice of the man who carried me.

"Damn it. Stay with me."

PART TWO
THE LITTLE KNIFE

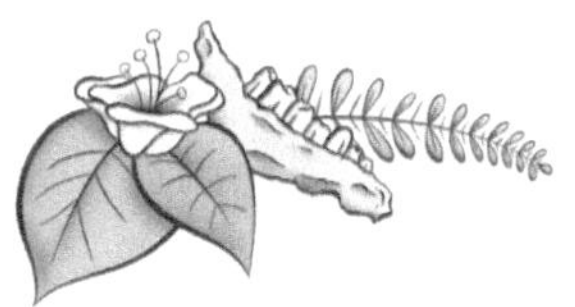

Four

The sun sat high in the sky and filtered through the trees in a dull, green glow. Piercing golden shafts of light slipped between the leaves to tear through my aching head.

I squeezed my eyes shut and tried to breathe slowly in a desperate attempt to keep down the nausea. Had I slept the morning away? Why were the trees visible from my bed?

The realization that I wasn't in my bed came to me in a rush. I'd slept outside. Why?

I was a mass of pain. My right leg throbbed with sharp, unendurable stabs of agony with every beat of my heart. My stomach rolled, not with sickness, but with the pain itself.

More than that, though, a deep, wrenching in my chest bewildered me. I had never felt this before. I couldn't find the edges of it. I couldn't tell exactly where it came from, or if it was a burning or a freezing or a spasm. Breath came shallowly. My heart beat too hard. The world spun behind my closed eyes.

The stabbing pain in my right leg gave a particularly sharp throb, and I had a vague memory of an arrow striking me there, just below the knee. That made sense. That pain was identifiable.

The wrenching in my gut was different. It existed everywhere and nowhere.

An arrow in my leg. I had been shot. There had been brigands with bows. Michael had been shot as well.

Michael.

The pain in my chest solidified into an identifiable shape. Michael had died. He had died afraid, in pain, and helpless, and I had experienced every bit of it. His telepathic connection with me had been torn away. Only a rip was left—a bleeding, invisible wound in my very self where he had been. The only family I had ever known.

Voices sounded from a little way off, close enough to keep an eye on me, far enough to let me sleep.

Right. After Michael's death, someone had plucked me off the ground and carried me away. A man, judging by his voice. But had it been the attackers or the victims?

Carefully, oh so slowly, I turned my head toward them.

Three people sat on logs or stones around a neat little fire. They were an impressive sight. A man and a woman, broad, dark, and well built. The third, another man, was leaner, lighter, and fairer, but still intimidating in his confident posture.

The two Derehani looked very much alike. Possibly brother and sister. The man wore a short beard, and the woman's thick hair fell in elaborate, messy braids down her back, but their builds, their black hair and warm skin, and the way they held their heads mirrored each other. He stirred the fire while she did something with her hands that I couldn't see.

The third was a strange sight: fair, sun-kissed skin, with golden hair tied efficiently in a short tail. He wore a thick fur cloak, at odds with the lighter linen of his shirt and trousers. An Authe Idan man wearing borrowed Derehani fur against the chill of a late autumn morning.

They spoke to each other in voices too low for me to make out clearly. Disjointed words floated on the wind and had no meaning, their tones somber.

These were the travelers who had been ambushed on the cliffside. The siblings were earthbound, like all Derehani. Michael had raised me in his own Derehani culture, but these people weren't like me. Their hair was long and dirty but tied back securely. Their clothes were soiled and plain but constructed with wool that had been woven with care and great skill.

Even the Authe Idan man, though oddly matched with the rest of the group, carried his culture with pride, right down to the bright seashell hanging from a cord around his neck.

Looking at them, I suddenly felt small and dirty. The pride that came when Michael had called me Little Owl shrank to nothing. I wasn't a Little Owl. I was a scrawny, untamed foundling, more feral than human.

These people were earthbound, but I was a wild thing. From the animal hides that I wore to the feathers in my matted hair, to the thick soles of my bare feet, I was a wild thing. I didn't belong with civilized people like this.

But here I was, and I had no way of knowing where they had brought me. The trees rose tall and straight in this part of the forest. The sun cut through airy foliage in bright, golden shafts, and the wind rushed through the high canopy in a distant *shhh*.

We had left the Sacred Wood behind, and with it, all the places I had ever known. The Wood was south of Derehan, but that was all I knew. It might take me days to get home.

Did I even want to go home? What would life be like, truly alone in the hollow? Michael was gone forever.

The great ache in my chest gave a throb. Tears pooled in my eyes and slid sideways down my temple.

The life I had known, the life I had assumed would go on forever, was over.

It didn't take them long to notice I'd woken up. The woman

turned to glance at me, saw me watching them, and immediately alerted the other two.

"Run and tell John, brother," she directed the Derehani man, confirming my suspicions.

Her brother got up, downed the last of whatever was in his cup, and took off to the east. The sister knelt down next to me and put a hand on my shoulder when I tried to sit up.

"Just lie still." She tossed her fraying braid over her shoulder. The woman spoke with a bright smile. "There's no rush, so just rest while you can. You're with friends now. I'm Sinead. That's Aris."

The Authe Idan man approached when Sinead gestured at him.

I didn't like lying still while they towered over me. It made me feel even smaller and more vulnerable. But there was sense in what she said. My head still ached, and my stomach swam. Every movement sent stabs of pain through my right leg, which had been neatly bandaged by someone while I slept. It was easier to lie still.

The Authe Idan fetched some water, and Sinead helped prop me up to drink it. It was tepid and tasted of dirt, but it was clean enough, and I needed it. I drank obediently, then lay back down.

"She's up?" said another voice. "Has she said anything?"

I turned slowly. The man they called John was striding out of the trees, with Sinead's brother right behind.

John dressed the same as the others, in wool and leather. His short, brown hair curled around his ears, and his beard was trimmed close. He moved purposefully through the sparse underbrush toward us, his powerful legs eating up the distance between us in great, sure steps.

This man was at home in the forest. He was at home anywhere.

John turned his hard eyes on me when Sinead spoke.

"She hasn't said anything yet. I'll fetch something for her to eat."

John knelt next to me and continued to stare. The siblings stood back a little, their interest caught. The Authe Idan lingered next to them, peering down at me with deep blue, curious eyes.

"What's your name?" John asked in a gentle voice. "Can you sit up?"

Sit up was exactly what I wanted to do. I didn't like the way he loomed over me, even kneeling. I struggled to my elbows, but I winced horribly when the muscles of my right leg flexed.

John noticed my difficulty and reached out to help me all the way up. As soon as I was able, I pulled away from his touch and crossed my arms over my chest.

He allowed me to pull away and didn't attempt to touch me again. "What's your name?" he asked again.

I stared at him, terrified.

"Can you hear me?" he asked when I didn't answer. Then, after an unsure glance at his companions, he tried in another language I didn't know.

"There's no way she's Ambic," said the brother, whose name I still hadn't caught. "How could she have gotten here?"

"She's just frightened," the Authe Idan man offered. What had Sinead called him? Aris? His voice sounded different than the others, caressing his vowels until they shone golden and smooth.

John turned back to me and tried again. "Can you understand me? Just nod yes or no."

I gave a small nod, not taking my eyes off him.

"Can you speak?"

Another small nod.

"What's your name?"

I didn't want to speak to him. I wanted to bolt and hide in the forest. I wanted to slip away and disappear. I could make them all sleep and be gone long before they woke up. Just like Nate.

But that wasn't possible, not with my leg injured. And it wasn't right to invade their minds anyway. I was stuck with them and incredibly dependent. So, I had to talk to him and make a place for myself amongst them. I had nowhere else to go. There was nothing else to do.

"Gwenna," I whispered, my voice barely more than a breath.

"Gwenna?" he asked in confirmation.

I nodded.

"Okay." He settled down into the dirt in front of me. "I'm John. We're going to help you, all right? I'm sorry to have to tell you this, but the man you were with...Your grandfather?"

I closed my eyes.

I had to answer him. I couldn't close up.

I gave a small nod of confirmation. It was easier to let them believe Michael was my grandfather.

"I'm sorry, but he was killed in the attack," John said. "He was shot in the chest. We couldn't save him. One of our own men died as well. Connor."

I glanced around at the four strangers watching me. They all wore pinched expressions at these words. Clearly, they had been close to the man who died. Sinead's brother crossed his arms over his chest, a muscle flexing in his jaw.

"We can—" John broke off, then paused. He half glanced to the side, where Sinead stood with her brother, but caught himself before looking at them fully. John turned to me again, his brow furrowed.

If he had been Michael, I would have simply slipped into his mind. Not to pry, but to save him the trouble of searching for the right words. Meaning was so much easier mind to mind than when it was put to words.

But that was wrong. It would be an invasion to slip into John's mind, just to spare him the trouble of speaking aloud. Besides any of that, people feared gifts like mine. I couldn't afford to have these people be afraid of me. I needed them.

So, I squashed the instinct, the urge to enter his thoughts. No listening in. No coercion. No lies.

Finally, John found his course. "We are traveling home now," he said to me in a lower tone. "We are eager to end our journey, but we can't just leave an injured young girl in the wild on her own. Especially not after encountering a band of criminals like we did last night. We can take you home. Where do you live?" He narrowed his eyes and looked at me meaningfully before adding, "Not in the Sacred Wood, surely?"

I stared at him, wishing more than ever that it wouldn't be a violation to look into his thoughts. A lifetime of speaking mind to mind with Michael had made me dependent on it, but John was sending a very clear message with his eyes: *Do not admit to having lived in the Sacred Wood.*

"I have no home," I whispered. "Not anymore."

"What do you mean, not anymore?" Sinead asked.

"You lived alone with your grandfather?" John raised his eyebrows.

I gazed back at him. He seemed to have already decided my story. That was just fine. I was not an accomplished liar.

I nodded in confirmation.

Aris frowned in sympathy. Sinead's brother shook his head.

"You'll have to come with us, then. At least as far as Barano," John said. He watched me for three seconds of silence, then stood. Relief flooded through me when his attention moved away. He continued to speak as he moved toward the fire. "Rest that leg as much as you can today. We can't wait longer than that. We set out at first light. I'll get supper." Then he swung a bow and quiver over his shoulder and disappeared into the trees.

He'd come and gone in under five minutes.

The siblings helped me get up and limp nearer to the fire. They propped me up against a young tree and passed over an apple and some roasted meat that had gone cold. I ate it all without complaint and wished for more.

"I'm Dan," the brother said once I had been settled.

I stared at him. Closer to, the resemblance between brother and sister was even more pronounced. They had the same wide eyes, sharp nose, and full mouth, but the brother's beard accentuated his more angular jaw. The same face twice, but in different genders.

This was the man who had spotted me last night. The man who had lurched after his fallen friend in the Sacred Wood, dead from an arrow lodged in his eye socket.

If he grieved now, he hid it well. "You've met John, of course. And this is my sister, Sinead."

Sinead cast me a lopsided grin and a wink. "She knows me, brother. We're best friends already."

"And I'm Aristeidis." Aris sat across the fire from me with a broad smile. His accent caught my attention again. He sounded like sunlight—bright and mellow. "You scared us. Thought you might never wake up."

All three of them wore knives and bows strapped to themselves like jewelry. These were more than soldiers. I could tell by the way Dan sharpened his short sword with easy care that came from expertise and much practice. In the way Sinead handled her small knife, whittling at the head of a tall, pale staff of ash wood. By their organization and how muscular their bodies were. They moved heavy logs like they were nothing. The group obviously lived rough and were perfectly comfortable. These travelers were a dangerous, well-oiled machine.

Even Aristeidis, leaner and a bit cleaner than the other two, handled himself with extraordinary grace and strength. He perched comfortably on an upturned log as if it were a cushioned stool.

"There was someone else with you," I said, adjusting the placement of my right leg. No position gave me complete relief, so I gave up and bore it. "There were six of you before—" I paused, unsure if I should mention the man who had died.

"Yes. Connor was killed," Dan said, eyes cast downward toward the small fire. "And Paul is on watch now. He won't come back until after we've eaten. Then I'll take watch."

"I see."

Sinead cast a wary glance at her brother and changed the subject. "You'll have to walk on that long before you should." She nodded toward my leg. "But this staff should help. It's a barn owl." She scooted closer and showed me what she'd whittled on the top of the ash wood staff. "What do you think?"

I took the knobby staff from her. As tall as I was and strong, it would certainly make it easier to walk with an injured leg. The owl on the top was fine work, though only half finished. She had carved out the rough shape and was in the process of adding detail to one wing. Each feather was finely wrought, and the large eyes followed me as if they were alive.

I ran my fingers over the smooth wood, and a wave of longing came over me. "That's what Michael used to call me," I said quietly. "Little Owl."

"It suits you," Dan said, his eyes on the fire. "Was Michael your grandfather?"

I nodded and passed the staff back to Sinead. "You are very skilled."

She smiled with pleasure. "It's a hobby of mine. I don't get much time for it most days."

"You should see our house," Dan added, stirring the fire. "She's carved every inch of it. There isn't a stretch of wood in the entire house that doesn't have a deer or a girl or a vine carved into it. Even the stair rail is a snake."

I turned wondering eyes to Sinead. "Really?"

She shrugged and dug the tip of her small knife into the detail of another feather. "We've lived there our whole lives. Started when I was a girl. And I didn't do all of it," she said. "Our father's the one who showed me how. He made the stair rail. And this handle too. See?"

Sinead passed me her own short sword, intricately carved, with the head of a wolf as the handle. The fur near the grip had been worn smooth with much use, but even so, it was beautiful.

I passed that back as well. "May I ask?" I hesitated, unsure.

"Ask anything," said Dan. "What is it?"

"Why were you passing through the Wood?"

"We could ask the same of you," Sinead said with a sly smile.

I opened my mouth to form some excuse, but nothing came to mind. Fortunately, the Authe Idan saved me the trouble.

"Because of me," Aristeidis said. "It's a pilgrimage."

I stared at him. "A what?"

Something passed between the siblings, and I was desperately curious what had made them uncomfortable. But I could guess it had something to do with the fact that there was no such thing as a pilgrimage through the Sacred Wood. At least, none that I had ever heard of.

"Aris here is on his way to Valheid, the capital," Dan said, still staring at the fire. "He means to ask Our Lady Josephine for a marriage alliance to unite Derehan and Authe Ida. We're escorting him there for the Festival of Wheat."

"He's a prince of Bluewater," Sinead said.

"I'm not a prince," Aris said with the tone of a man who had repeated this phrase many times over the past few days. "My father is Milhail Metaxas, who rules Bluewater."

"I thought Eustis Metaxas ruled Bluewater," I said, remembering the endless lessons Michael had taught me about the two countries that bordered the Sacred Wood. Eustis was known for his agenda against sibyls like myself. People running from his pyres made up the bulk of the people cutting through the Sacred Wood.

I vaguely recalled learning about his younger brother, Milhail, but I had never given him much thought. And here sat his son, right across from me.

"My uncle disappeared six weeks ago," Aris said.

"And good riddance," Sinead muttered.

Aris eyed her, but I broke in before he could respond.

"He disappeared?" I asked. "Where did he go?"

"My uncle had many enemies," Aris said with a shrug. "My

father among them. He never approved of the lynchings and the witch hunts."

"Even so," I said. "The lord of a grand city like Bluewater doesn't just disappear."

"That's what I said," Sinead added. "But again, good riddance. Hopefully he's rotting at the bottom of Bluewater Bay."

"That's enough Sinead," Dan said.

Aris resolutely changed the subject. "My father, Milhail, immediately sued for peace with Derehan when he took power. That's why I've come. To make it official."

I stared between the three travelers, unsure of how to respond. This was certainly a new development. After generations of an unsteady truce, could Authe Ida and Derehan truly call themselves allies?

"I still don't see the fascination with marriage." Sinead rotated the staff slightly in her hand to gain better access to the next feather on her owl carving. "I don't understand why you Authe Idans bother with it."

Aris grinned at her. "It's official. It lets you share the event with friends and family."

Sinead waved her knife conversationally. "I still say it's a bloody great waste of time. It's nobody else's business who you partner with."

"For Aris it is, Sinead," Dan said. "He's a prince, remember? And he wants to whisk off our Josephine and turn her into a princess by the sea. You can't do that without a whole ceremony."

"I'm not a prince!"

Sinead's expression melted slightly, some signal passing between them that I didn't know how to interpret. She elbowed her brother and laughed.

But her laughter died quickly when Dan's expression sagged again. He got up without a word, patted her on the shoulder, and settled himself down further away.

Had they been close? Friends, or maybe lovers? The rest of the group didn't seem to be hurting so badly as Dan.

"So, Aris..." She forced brightness back into her eyes. "Tell us all about your princess sisters. At last count, I heard there were at least fifteen of them."

"Five," Aris said, accepting the change of subject. "And they're not princesses."

My eyes flicked back and forth as the conversation bounced between them. I had never considered myself to be lonely, but for the first time in my life, I began to understand what it meant to be among people—among friends, maybe.

But I could not share in their laughter. My chest still ached with the loss of Michael. More than my injured calf, the place in my heart where he had been ripped away ate at me.

And when I glanced back at Dan, his expression was a mirror of my own. He sat against a tree, arms crossed, legs stretched out, eyes closed, mouth pulled down in a frown.

We had both lost someone important that night.

FIVE

John came back before long with several rabbits on a stick. The others immediately set about preparing the coals and setting up the spit Aris had been improving while he chatted with Sinead. John skinned the rabbits with a practiced hand. Before long, they were roasting over the efficient bank of coals, and the smell of fresh meat set my stomach to grumbling.

To further distract myself, I offered to flesh the pelts. John looked at me askance but passed them to me, along with a small knife I could use.

This I could do while sitting, though awkwardly. I scraped them down and rinsed them with some of the water left in my cup. The others talked amicably while I worked, and soon the pelts were clean enough to carry to the nearest settlement for trade and tanning.

It felt good to be helpful, and it passed the time.

More than once during the evening, I caught John looking at me. They all watched me, but John's gaze drew my attention. Every time I glanced up at him, he would turn away with no reaction whatsoever. What did he mean by it?

Once we had eaten, Dan got up and disappeared into the trees.

Shortly after, another man appeared and sat down to the remaining rabbit that had been set aside for him. This was Paul. He was very tall and much younger than the siblings, though old enough to have a full beard.

His eyes shone clear and bright in the firelight, but he spoke very little. After John introduced us, Paul nodded his head in acknowledgement before settling to his meal. Then he immediately tucked himself under his cloak and went to sleep.

The rest of us followed suit not long after.

As difficult as it was for me to be among these strangers, it was far worse when quiet fell and they all went to sleep. I lay for a long time under my cloak. My leg throbbed. My chest ached. I could feel every twig and stone beneath me. But what really kept me awake was the expression of shock and terror on Michael's face in my memory. It was the ripping, the animal desperation to cling to life. Over and over, the image came to me.

But sleep must have come eventually, because suddenly I was being shaken awake.

"Wake up, Little Owl," Aris said. His hand was gentle on my shoulder. "We'll be moving on in a few minutes."

My eyes dragged open to find the early dawn filtering through the trees. The others were industriously packing up camp and dousing the fire. They gave me some rations and water, and Sinead helped me to the edge of camp to relieve myself. Then it was time to go.

I had no pack, no possessions, aside from the cloak I wore and the feathers in my hair. But the others carried large packs on their backs. Even burdened as they were, I still held them up. The staff Sinead had whittled for me helped greatly, but it wasn't enough. The arrow had gone straight through my calf muscle less than two days before. It had not damaged the bone, but the wound was large and fresh. In under an hour of limping, fresh blood ran down to my ankle in rivulets.

They noticed, though I didn't complain. Dan stopped the

group and called John from the front to come look at the state of my leg.

"What is it?" John's tone was short, impatient with the fact that we had barely left our camp.

Blood soaked through the woolen bandage. Someone had roughly stitched my wound while I was unconscious, but it hadn't been enough. John hissed his disapproval as he examined me, and Dan started digging in his own pack. Soon they had the bleeding stopped and the strip of wool changed for a clean one, tied tighter than before.

"She can't walk on that anymore," Dan said to John while he repacked his bag. "Not over this terrain."

"Can we make a stretcher?" Aris suggested from the front of the group.

John wiped his bloody hands on his pants and stood. He looked around at the others, calculating. "Sinead, Aris, take my pack and divide it between you." They moved to obey, and John turned to face me. "You'll have to get on my back."

I stared up at him, appalled. I cast about for some other option, something that didn't require me to cling to him, body to body. "Couldn't we...A stretcher?"

"The easiest way to carry your weight is on one person's back, not shared between two people and held by hand," John said. "It's rough terrain. A stretcher would slow us down too much."

He held out his hand to help me up, which I allowed. Then he turned and knelt down in front of me. When I hesitated too long, he took my wrist and pulled my arm around his neck to his front. This forced me to bend down and press myself against his back. He hooked his arms around and under my thighs and hauled us both up.

I clutched at his shoulders and gasped when we rose abruptly. John took a few seconds to steady himself and adjust his balance to account for my weight, then off he went.

We moved much faster after that.

John was tireless. I was small, but I weighed easily twice his pack. Still, he went on without even breathing hard. Occasionally, he would hike me up a bit higher on his back, which sent a jolt of pain through my leg. He must have heard my hiss of pain the first time because he warned me before he did it again.

We traveled quietly. The others spoke barely a word to each other during the entire day, and Dan said nothing at all. We stopped a few times to rest and eat, which was when they made plans and prepared. After every rest, John would kneel before me so I could wrap myself around him again. Then we'd be up and gone, as if we had never stopped at all.

It was strange to be walking so steadily in one direction. With every step, this group took me further and further away from home. Would I ever see the hollow again? Certainly not any time soon, but maybe someday I could go back. Would I be able to find it?

Paul was rarely with us, though the others always seemed to know where he was. He appeared from time to time, sometimes from ahead, from behind, or the side. Paul was constantly running, always on the watch for movement or danger. Once he came from ahead and guided us further east to avoid a gulch in our path.

When we finally stopped for the night, it was at a spot Paul had found for us. He had scouted far ahead and located a small, high clearing concealed by a ring of trees and thick underbrush. It was close enough to an overlook to keep an eye out for danger. A large boulder took up most of the clearing, but it provided a substantial overhang to protect us from dew.

John eased me to the ground near the mass of rock. Dan set himself to piling up kindling for a fire.

"How does it feel?" John asked, unwrapping my calf.

"The same." I winced when he pulled away the last of the bandaging.

My leg looked horrible. Purple, throbbing flesh surrounded the jagged tear where the arrow had pierced me. The entire area was swollen and hot to the touch. The rough stitches held the wound closed, but only barely.

"It was a clean shot, but it's going to be a long time healing," John said. "It looks infected, but not too bad yet. We should make it to Barano long before it gets dangerous." He changed my bandage for another new one and looked up at me, his bright eyes suddenly dark.

"What is it?" I asked.

He blinked once and scratched under his beard, then stood up. "It's nothing. Rest your leg. We'll check it again in the morning."

That night, Paul sat with us, and John manned the first watch. I thought I might see what sort of person Paul was, but he spoke only when necessary, took very little notice of me, and minded his own affairs. He sat quite still and watched the fire while Aris and Sinead talked.

Dan brought me a hunk of stale hardtack and a bowl of stew to soak it in, then to my surprise, he sat down on the log next to me to eat his own portion.

"Thank you," I said.

"No problem."

"I'm..." I hesitated, unsure how to broach the subject. But my heart broke for him, so I had to say something. "I'm sorry about what happened to your friend. Connor."

"Thank you," he said.

"Was he your partner?"

"No," Dan answered with a sniff. "But he could have been. One day."

But now he never would be. The words hung between us, unspoken but sorely felt.

"And I'm sorry about your grandfather," he said after a minute.

I nodded, taking a small bite of soggy bread. The fatty broth from the soup filled my mouth with flavor, but I couldn't savor it. Maybe someday, but not today.

We sat in companionable silence after that. The others chatted across the fire, oblivious to the little link we had forged between us.

That night was worse than the one before. During the day, the ache in my chest had dulled to a low burn, but at night, I had nothing but the crickets to distract me. I lay curled under my cloak with my arm for a pillow and stared at the glowing coals for hours, trying to forget the jolt of pain that had come when Michael was shot.

The next morning, John and Dan examined my leg again. The wound was still closed, but only just. Without a word, John knelt before me, and I wrapped myself around him once more. With a lurch, he hauled us both up, and off we all went.

"How far is it to Barano?" I asked while John strode along through the trees.

He looked around as if to judge where we were, his breath loud at such close quarters. The woods all appeared the same to me, but he seemed to recognize them well enough.

"Another two nights at least before we come to the road. After that, it will only be a few hours to the town. Depending on where we come out of the forest."

Sinead turned and added, "We'll stop there for a night or two and have a real doctor look at your leg. It'll be safer to hang around there. Not like in the woods."

"Are travelers often attacked in the wild?" I asked. "We're not at war."

"No, we're not at war." John grunted as he stepped up and over a small boulder. "But the truce has never been easy with Authe Ida. The men we met at the ravine the other day were just a band of outlaws. They're common enough, and they have no love for us northerners."

"They probably just wanted our supplies." Aris said. "But they ran off so fast...Clearly, they weren't ready to pay for it with their lives."

"They would attack in the Sacred Wood?" I asked. "They would steal?"

"They don't remember like we do," Sinead said, her breathing steady despite the demanding pace. "They forget the Old Way, and they will pay for it in time."

I adjusted my arm on John's shoulder and rested my chin on my hand. One of my feathers tickled his ear, and he flinched away a bit. I pulled it aside and settled back down.

"Apparently, there's some festival coming up in the next couple of weeks," Aris called from the front of the group. "I've heard of your wild northern parties. I've always wanted to see one."

Michael and I had been planning for the equinox holiday back at the hollow before—Well, before. I swallowed hard against the idea that our quarterly celebrations for the World Mothers and the World Fathers would never happen again. "I expect it's very grand in a big city like that."

Sinead grinned. "Oh yes. We do it up right in Valheid. You should see it. Roast pigs and pies and tarts. And they get the best musicians. I mean, of course they do. Big audiences like that? Of course the players come flocking in at feast times."

Sinead's enthusiasm dragged a smile out of me, and she spent the rest of the morning regaling us with stories from past holidays in the capital.

When we stopped for a rest, John rolled his shoulders and stretched. My weight on his back was harder on him than he let on.

"You want me to carry her for a bit, Johnny?" Dan asked.

John simply said no and knelt before me again.

I still didn't care for being carried, but I no longer cringed away from John's bulk. And I was glad he didn't let Dan take a turn. At least John was familiar.

Paul continued to be a mystery. We saw little of him, and when he was present, he had nothing to say beyond the necessary. I watched him, my curiosity piqued, but I didn't know how to talk to him.

That night, while Aris, Sinead, and I all sat around the cook fire, I leaned back against a small tree, trying to smooth out a number of tangles in my long hair. John and Dan had already curled up a few feet away to try and rest, and Paul kept watch just out of sight, as usual.

"Look," Aris said. "A firefly."

"It's too late in the season," Sinead said without glancing up.

"No," I said. "He's right. Look." Sure enough, a single, tiny, yellow light blinked unceremoniously amongst the underbrush. "You know the story about fireflies."

"What story?" Sinead asked. "They're bugs."

"They're more than that," I said. "They're the last reminder."

"Of what?"

"Of magic." I said it without thinking, but their expressions of interest jolted me back to attention.

Sinead leaned forward. "This promises to be a good story. Don't leave us wondering."

"You've never heard this? About the fireflies?"

They both shook their heads.

"It's a story Michael used to tell me when I was little. Long ago, before the time of kings and queens in Derehan, the Old Way was the New, and magical creatures lived side by side with men." A corner of my mouth tucked up in a nostalgic smile. "That's how he started all his stories."

Sinead nodded. "My mother was the same. Go on."

"Fairies, giants, sibyls, witches, and even dragons walked the earth for centuries. But as we all know, the most destructive force in the world is the fear of men. And in their fear, mankind drove away all that they could not understand. So, over time, one by one, the magic in our world receded to nothing so that now all that remains of them are the very deepest of magics and relics. The fireflies are the very last of their kind, and even their small magic goes unnoticed."

Sinead watched the solitary bug flash by. "Do you really think they're magic? Or just bugs?"

"Just bugs, definitely," Aris said, stoking the coals.

"What do you think, Gwen?"

I shrugged, watching the little light as well. "I suppose we'll never know."

"You know, they say Queen Lily was sibylline. A telepath," Sinead said.

"That's just a myth," Aris replied. "Just because she was particularly loved and just because she was the last great queen doesn't make her a sibyl."

"It wouldn't be unheard of," Sinead insisted. "Mindwalkers crop up from time to time. Tell him, Gwen."

"What?" Aris said with a sneer of disbelief.

"I've heard that before about the queen," I hedged, suddenly desperate to change the subject. "But again, we can't know for sure. It was so long ago."

Aris laughed derisively. "You can't be serious, either one of you. You don't actually believe the sibyls are real."

My eyes landed on him, and he faltered.

But Sinead didn't notice. "Of course they're real! Who do you think your precious uncle Eustis burned alive for all those years?"

"People," Aris answered shortly. "Just people. Victims of hysteria. Scapegoats. And it was people like you who burned them. People who actually delude themselves into believing mindwalkers are a real thing."

Sinead sat up a little straighter. "Oh no. Not people like me. It's your people, Aristeidis, who burned people alive. People who refuse to see the truth and then panic when it slaps them in the face. The first time you see something you can't explain, you destroy it. You let fear take over."

"You don't know the first thing about me, Sinead," Aris said calmly.

"I know you bury your head in the sand," she powered on. "How can you possibly come into Derehan and claim the sibyls aren't real? Where do you think all the Authe Idan sibyls go? We have mindwalkers to spare in the north. Most of them hide what they are, or at least they try. And we look the other way, and nobody has to die."

"Name one," Aris said, eyebrows raised.

"What?"

"Name one sibyl that you know personally."

I hunkered down under my cloak and wrapped my arms around my knees. My eyes bounced back and forth between them as they argued, silently begging them to both forget I was there at all.

"Easy!" Sinead said, casting around for names. "Uh, well, there's..." She paused, thinking hard. "I mean, shit. There's always Theo. She's been around forever. Since I was a kid. And they say someone else was identified as a sibyl in Rideout just last year."

I stared at her, my mouth dry. No words came. Theo? She knew Theo? How far did the old woman's reach extend? I forced myself to look away, to hide my surprise.

"But you don't know either of these people personally?" Aris asked.

Sinead waved his objection away. "Everyone knows Theo. She's the Crone."

I looked up again, unable to stop myself. "The Crone?"

Sinead turned her attention to me. "Yeah, of course. She's been old for decades, and she definitely whispers."

"What in the hell are you two talking about?" Aris asked, but we both ignored him.

"But how can you be sure?" I asked. "That prophecy is so old, so long passed. It could be anyone. Why Theo?"

"So, you know her? Did anyone in your village ever see her?"

My hands shook. I clasped them together. "Once," I answered.

"Well, maybe we can't know for sure that Theo is the Crone," Sinead said, "but everyone has accepted it as truth. She is too well known. She has been old for so long. My grandfather was the one who first told me she was the Crone. Had to be. He's been warning me to watch for the Child since I was a kid. Now that the Crone has finally made herself known, it's only a matter of time before the Child comes."

I glared at my hands, which had begun to shake.

She'll turn your hand and smile...

"That's just a children's story," I said.

"It's not," Sinead insisted. "Maybe it's just a nursery song now, but it started out as much more, and everyone knows it. This warning has been passed down, generation to generation, for as long as anyone can remember. The Child will come. The Wild Thing will come. And when she does, we'll all wish we had paid heed to the warning passed down to us. Derehan remembers."

Sinead ended this passionate speech with a particularly savage stab into the cook fire, sending sparks spiraling up on the hot air.

Aris huffed and continued to argue, but I had stopped listening. As I watched the sparks rise into the air, they became stars. Clear, sharp points in the sky. It meant nothing that the canopy of trees overhead blocked the constellations from my view.

I wasn't seeing through my own eyes, but through someone else's.

Then a sharp, dreadfully familiar pain in my chest. It stopped the breath in my throat. I looked down. An old dagger protruded from my torso, its hilt shining in the moonlight.

I tried to breathe, tried to focus, but I couldn't. The world tipped on its side as I fell off the tree branch where I'd been keeping watch. I barely felt the jolt of hitting the ground.

The world went slowly dark, winking out around me.

Six

"Gwenna!" someone shouted.

Sinead shook my arm, trying desperately to get my attention.

My eyes focused on her, but that didn't ease her worry.

Aris knelt next to her. "What's the matter? Are you all right?"

Sinead narrowed her eyes at me. "Did you see something, Gwen?"

I couldn't answer her. It may already be too late. I scrambled to my feet, injured leg and all, and hobbled off into the dark to the north where Paul was keeping watch. The distance and the trees made no difference. His mind was as visible to me as the faces of my companions, and I knew exactly where to find him.

He hadn't gone far, just to the edge of a rise where he could climb a branch or two to observe the valley below us.

When I burst out of the underbrush on unsteady legs, Paul sat up on his branch, immediately alert. He dropped easily to the ground to meet me.

"What is it?" he asked.

I stared at him, confused. How could this be? I had seen Paul with a knife in his chest. He should be lying half dead in the grass.

Then a movement from behind sent my senses flying out.

An anxious man stood behind me, hidden by the shadows and the shrubbery. Paul hadn't noticed him yet, but he saw the look of horror on my face. That was all the warning either of us had before the stranger slipped out of the dark and grabbed my arm.

A thin man, reeking of sweat and waste, pulled me roughly against himself. He gripped my arm painfully and pressed something sharp against my neck. That knife, probably.

"Gwen! Wait!" Sinead called through the trees. With a crash of underbrush, she appeared in the small clearing next to Paul, followed immediately by Aris.

It took all of two seconds for them to recognize the danger, and they instantly melted into the warriors I knew them to be. Blades appeared in their hands, and they focused all attention on the strange man holding me hostage.

Aris became something distinctly different: lithe, sure-footed, and focused. He hadn't been raised in the mountains like the rest of us. Aris had grown up on sea-tossed fishing boats, with spears instead of swords and bows. And the thin, sharp blade he now held looked more suited to cleaning fish than defense, but it would certainly do the job in a pinch.

All of my focus narrowed onto the point of the little knife at my throat. The man took little care, and it dug painfully into my skin.

"Let the girl go," Paul said. "She doesn't need to get hurt."

Aris sidestepped to our left, causing the man to dart his gaze from one danger to another.

The man's fingers dug painfully into the skin of my arm, but his trembling body and rasping breaths belied his terror. His grip on my arm amplified his thoughts, making it difficult to focus.

The man was a thief, nothing more. He couldn't believe his luck when he'd spotted Paul, inattentive in the tree. An easy mark. But then I had appeared and ruined everything. And now three large, powerful fighters, fully armed and angry, bore down on him. All he had was the little knife and a hostage.

"Stay back!" The thief turned us to keep the two Derehanis and Aris in view while the latter continued to maneuver. "Stay back or I'll kill her. I won't hesitate."

His voice was strong, but he quivered with adrenaline. He pressed his knife even harder into my neck and punched through the skin. I tried not to wince, but hot blood ran down to my collar bone in a sickening stream.

"Just let her go and you can walk away," Sinead said.

"She comes with me!" the man shot back, darting his focus from one to the other in quick succession. "I need assurance that you won't shoot me in the back! Stop there! Stop moving!"

Aris halted, but he kept his knees bent, ready to take another step the instant the thief looked away.

"You have our word," Paul said in an attempt to draw the thief's attention away from Aris.

The thief gripped me tighter, sending shooting pain up my right arm. "She comes with me. I'll let her go at the bottom of the hill, and she can come back free and clear."

Lie.

"He's going to kill me," I said as loudly as I could through the panic. "At the bottom of the hill. He plans to kill me and run."

"She's injured, man. She can't walk that far. Just let her go."

"This is your final warning!"

Aris took another silent step, nearly behind us now.

The thief dragged me around, trying to keep eyes on him. "Stay back! I swear I'll kill her right here!"

I was losing track of the exchange. Instead, I allowed myself to fall backward into his mind. Maybe I would be able to find some information that would be useful, some detail I could exploit.

But a telepath could only hear the thoughts passing through a mind in a specific moment, and just then, the thief's consciousness was erratic, focused solely on getting out, getting away, and hiding.

Get to the bottom of the hill. Kill the girl. Run. Kill the girl, then run. Just get to the bottom of the hill.

"He's going to kill me!" I said again, this time more of a cry. Too loud, too shaky.

If they didn't act soon, time would run out. If he got me out of sight, it was over.

"Gwenna!" John shouted. He thundered into the clearing, with Dan only right behind. His youthful face was hard and calculating.

Had he called my name aloud, or had he only thought it? John didn't even look at me. He stared down my captor, like a great cat awaiting his chance to strike.

But still, he did not act. Nobody did.

Aris circled behind, and everyone else did their best to keep the thief's attention away from him. But even that might have been a mistake. The instant Aris attacked, the thief would probably jerk his knife a few inches to the right, and I would be dead.

"Please let me go," I begged, my voice barely audible.

"Shut up!" He jerked my arm hard, shaking my head around on my neck.

The knife pierced a little deeper, and I screamed.

On reflex, I reached for the only solution I had. I closed my eyes and prepared to take control of the thief's mind. The shining glow of his life-string called out to me.

It would be easy. I could end this right now. The danger would pass. I would be safe.

But I forced myself to hold back. I shouldn't do this. It was wrong. I should allow my new friends to save me in a human way. They would attack, get me free. I wouldn't have to hurt anyone.

Again, I was jolted out of his mind. A stab of pain throbbed through my leg when he forced me to take a step backward.

"Stay there, all of you," he cried.

"If you leave her and go, we will have no reason to follow!" Dan said. A last-ditch effort.

John watched me now. There was no fear in his face, only hardness.

The man dragged me back another step. Then another. He had very little patience for my limp and yanked me roughly backward. I cried out in pain, clutching at his filthy arm to gain any support I could. Every one of my friends flinched at the sound, muscles bunched and ready to spring at the first opportunity.

There was no room for hesitation. If he managed to get me out of sight of the group, he would kill me and run.

I pulled against him, but my fingers scraped ineffectually against his grip. So instead, I curled my fingers into claws and dragged my nails through dirt and skin. He flinched hard but did not release me. And when he forced me to take another step, I stumbled, knocking him off-balance.

"Stupid girl!" the thief howled, wrenching my arm behind me with a sudden jerk.

This was it. The time had come. He was going to kill me. The thief would punch that little knife into my neck, and he would flee. What was skin anyway? Nothing to a sharp little blade.

All reason fled my mind. All sense, all logic. All I could think was *Get him off of me! Get away!*

With a shriek of terror, I drove my focus down into his mind. The shining link called to me as before, raw, exposed, and shaking with fear. Without a pause, before he could force me to take another painful step, before I could think too hard about right and wrong, I took control.

Because if I had control, then he couldn't hurt me anymore.

The thief made two quick movements. First, he removed his knife from the bleeding cut on my neck. Then he deliberately jabbed it into his own jugular.

For an incredulous five seconds, nobody moved. My protectors stared at the thief, who calmly withdrew the knife and began to bleed profusely.

Everything happened at once.

The man slumped backward to the ground. Blood burbled from the wound and soaked into the moonlit grass in a widening pool around his head.

John lunged forward and lifted me clear off the ground and away from the man, back to where all our companions bristled.

Dan, Sinead, Paul, and Aris charged the fallen thief, still not comprehending the truth of what had happened.

John examined the cut on my neck where the knife had pierced me. It wasn't dangerous, but it was deep enough to cause a fair amount of blood to spill down my neck and smear along the leather collar of my tunic. I pawed at the runnels of blood with numb hands, thinking to wipe it away, but my shaking fingers wouldn't obey me. I just rubbed it around my neck and collarbone uselessly as even more blood welled from the cut.

John took both my hands and held them tight to stop the shaking. "Are you hurt?" he asked. "Are you okay?"

The others all stared down at the man I had killed. Their faces were masks of confusion when they turned to look at me. Sinead's expression was closer to fear. Aris's was of pure incomprehension.

I stared up at John with wide eyes. "I'm sorry," I whispered.

"What? Why?"

"I had to. I'm sorry. He was going to kill me at the bottom of the hill. I had to." Tears fell down my face, and my throat closed up on the words.

Comprehension dawned visibly on his face. Whatever the others might have been thinking, John didn't seem to care. One look at my grief and he took my face in both of his hands.

Vaguely, I knew he was rubbing blood on my cheeks now too, but that knowledge was distant.

"Listen to me," he said. "Listen carefully. If a man is willing to take another person's life, he forfeits any rights to his own. You had to kill him."

I couldn't make any words come out, so I just nodded between his hands.

He turned to the others. "If he had anything of value, we'll put it to good use. Dispose of him. Dan, with me."

Dan hesitated for half a second, his eyes narrowing on me, then he obeyed. Sinead spoke half a protest, but she also complied.

"Wait!" Aris said, his thin knife still clutched in one hand. "What just happened here? She didn't kill him. He killed himself. Why did he kill himself?"

"Just move, Aris," Sinead said in a growl.

"She didn't do anything!" Aris insisted. "I saw it. He did it to himself!"

"We all saw it!" Sinead hissed.

John bent, picked me up bodily, and carried me away from the others while they continued to argue. He strode with purpose through the trees and back to camp until the voices of the others faded to incomprehension.

Seven

I had undone several days of healing in my mad dash through the trees. The rough stitches had torn and needed to be cut away. My flesh, which had already been swollen, was angry and oozing. Dan had no more thread to restitch it, so they had to be satisfied with clean dressing alone. I didn't think I could endure the stitching anyway, so I didn't complain.

They tried to get me to drink something. But my hands shook too badly to hold the cup, and I was too nauseous to keep it down. They just sat me by the fire.

Then John asked me something that shocked me greatly, though it probably shouldn't have. "Is there anyone else around, Gwen?"

Dan froze in the act of putting away the dirty bandages and stared at us.

"What?" I asked.

"Is there anyone else around at all?"

"I-I don't know." I shook my head. "I don't know."

"Yes, you do. Close your eyes. Cast out. Concentrate."

I stared at him, fear growing in my chest. He knew about me, about what I was. John had to know after what I did to that man in the woods, but to outright ask me to use my gifts? I had expected him to look the other way, to pretend nothing had happened. That's what Dan was desperately trying to do.

After a few seconds, during which I did not need to close my eyes, I confirmed there was no one else around for several miles. John accepted this as truth and moved to help Dan clear up.

It didn't take the others long to finish their unpleasant task. They filtered through the trees all at once, all of them. Paul came as well, abandoning his watch for now. They had collected a few coins, the little knife, and some other small items from the man's body. These were noted and carefully stowed.

They all stood near the fire, blatantly staring from me to John and back again. The three Derehanis were grim, but Aris downright bristled. The silence was complete. Even the owls went quiet in the trees.

They wanted answers.

I curled up under my cloak and tried to make myself as unobtrusive as possible without causing myself more pain. John, on the other hand, returned their gazes calmly across the fire.

"I suppose you want an explanation?" he asked bluntly.

"We think that's fair." Dan kept the anger in his voice reined in, but only just.

Aris opened his mouth to speak but decided to wait instead. I couldn't imagine what he was thinking about all of this.

John nodded, then began. "We weren't in the Sacred Wood by accident. We were sent to retrieve Gwen and Michael. The mission to meet with Metaxas was a cover."

Sinead hissed in disapproval, and Dan crossed his arms over his chest, breathing hard. He bounced back and forth from one foot to the other, his anger barely contained. His sister glanced up at him, worry plain on her face.

I, on the other hand, felt as though the world had dropped away.

And Aris was floored. "What did you just say?"

John returned his gaze. "Josephine never asked us to bring you on a pilgrimage through the Wood. I lied. We had to return home by that route, and you insisted on coming with us. It was the only way."

Aris waited a few seconds, turning incredulous glares from one Derehani to the next, possibly for some sort of apology, but none came. Before the Authe Idan could speak again, John continued addressing the group as a whole.

"Of course, we couldn't have guessed that we'd be attacked by a gang of criminals at the crucial moment. We were supposed to come away with everyone. Michael was supposed to return to Valheid with his granddaughter and resume his life there."

Dan turned and growled into the night. He shook out his arms, pacing.

"Resume?" Sinead said, brows furrowed. "You can't mean—"

"Yes, I do mean Gwen's grandfather is Michael Gray, who was a scribe at the Greathouse for Kerric's grandfather years ago. He has been living rough these eighteen years, but last month he sent a message asking for an envoy to bring him and his granddaughter home."

Too fast. The conversation moved too fast for me to follow. I stared from one to the other, panic surging in my chest.

"But why?" Dan's voice rose in anger. "Why all the secrecy? Why has he been in hiding and why come back now?"

"Why not tell us outright?" Paul added, his wary eyes on Dan.

"You should have *told us*, John!" Dan yelled, his fists clenched. "If we had known, maybe Connor wouldn't have—" He broke off and resumed pacing. "Why didn't you just tell us?"

My heart constricted at the sight of his pain. "Because of me," I said breathlessly, more to myself than to them. Of course it was because of me. Michael's lies stretched out before me, an endless and empty sea.

Five pairs of eyes turned in my direction, and I immediately regretted speaking at all.

"Because of Gwen," John confirmed, his gaze steady on my face.

I tried to focus on him alone. At least John didn't seem to be afraid of me.

Breathe, Gwen. Just breathe.

"Why her?" Aris asked. His voice shook with accusation and anger.

It was his turn to be stared at by the whole group.

"He left to hide in the Wood because of what Gwen is," John said. "Because she was extremely powerful, even as an infant. She had to be isolated until she learned control."

"Control of what?" Aris asked. "Why did that man kill himself? What is going on here?"

"Eighteen years ago?" Dan asked, ignoring Aris completely. He scrutinized my face, as if trying to find a resemblance to the man he had apparently known in his younger days. "I didn't know Michael had children, much less grandchildren."

"He did," John answered, and said no more about it.

I knew, and possibly John did as well, that Michael had been childless. If John knew that, if he was telling this lie on purpose, did he have some idea of my true parentage?

"What is she, then?" Aris took a step forward, looking at all of them for answers but never at me.

None of us knew how to reply. People like me weren't spoken about in Derehan. Where we couldn't blend in, we lived on the margins—feared witches who couldn't be trusted and wise ones who would sell you prophecies for coin.

But in Authe Ida, in Aris's city of Bluewater, we were evil to most people, a myth to everyone else.

"Gwen is sibylline, Aris," John said. "A mindwalker. And very powerful, as I'm sure you saw tonight."

Aris stared from one man to the next, waiting for someone to speak sense. They all returned his gaze calmly, patiently.

"Maybe this pilgrimage *was* a lie," Sinead said at length, "but it seems like it was for the best. If you want to join hands with Our Lady Josephine, there are some things you'd best understand about the place she comes from. Derehan doesn't forget. We never forget. This"—she pointed right at me—"is why we remember."

"Easy, Sinead," John said, seeing how I flinched under her finger.

But Sinead didn't back down. "We remember precisely for nights like tonight. So when a child forces a grown man to kill himself, when she turns his own hand against him, we know what to do. What to think."

John stood up, fists tight. His voice remained calm, however. "And what is that, Sinead? What is it that you think we should do?"

Dan took a step forward, unsure how to rein in his sister. Sinead turned to John, less calm.

"We listen," she said, voice trembling. Not anger, not fear, not violence. Passion, though. She was *passionate*. Sinead turned her back to John and faced Aris once more. "I see the fear in your face, Aris. It was the fear of man that changed this world forever. That is what we remember. Not what was, but what destroyed it. So whatever it is that you are thinking now, remember this...

"While you are here in Derehan, keep your ears open. Not just your ears, but your heart as well. You've passed through the Sacred Wood. You've seen things that you cannot explain away. You will continue to see and hear things that do not make sense to you. Authe Ida has forgotten, but *you* can remember. You can see for yourself what the fear of man has cost us. And you can start by looking at that girl's face."

"Hear, hear," Dan said.

Aris glanced reflexively at me when Sinead pointed again. It was the first time since I'd run away from camp an hour ago. I couldn't read his expression, and I refused to dip into his mind.

"You want me to listen?" he asked, his face red with consternation. "Well, I listened earlier today, when you were telling me about the Crone and the Child. *'She'll turn your hand and smile, the wild thing unveiled.'* That was the line, right? What do you call that, then? She turned a man's hand against himself. You said it just now."

"He has a point," Dan said with a pained expression.

Sinead turned to look at me.

I ducked and wrapped my arms around my head. No, no. Not this. Anything but this.

"She's not a child," John said sternly.

"That's just a story!" Sinead replied, despite her ardent speech earlier that night about warnings and prophecies. "Are you going to let nursery rhymes turn you into a monster?"

"Theoretically, she could make any one of us kill ourselves at any time!" Aris argued.

"And you could use your knife to kill any of us in our sleep," John said. "We've all killed people. We all have weapons. What's so different about hers?"

Aris stared around at the group who had become his friends, incredulous. "But—"

"She used her sibylline abilities to save my life and then her own," Paul said flatly, unimpressed with Aris's attitude. "What more could you ask of any of us?"

Aris gaped once, then closed his mouth and crossed his arms over his chest. He wasn't convinced, but he now recognized he stood on the losing side of the argument.

Dan came forward and put a hand on his sister's shoulder. "Sinead's right. We cannot let fear rule us. But what is she?" he asked in a low voice. "I've heard of telepaths and seers. I've seen people have premonitions before. But to force a man to kill himself like that? That is not like any sibyl I've ever heard of."

"She had to kill that man." John sat back down on the log. "He was going to take her life. She was defending herself." And he offered no other explanation on that subject. Again, he seemed to have already decided what my story was and didn't press me for any other information.

Dan was right. Coercion was unheard of amongst the sibyls. John should have been as shocked as the rest of them, but he wasn't. He was unconcerned, and he clearly wouldn't encourage the others to question it either.

This was not the time for pressing him, however. He had made that clear enough. John had presented facts to the group about their mission and kept the details about me and Michael vague. He knew something. He did. Most importantly, though, he kept that something away from his people.

"We will bring her home with us, to Valheid," John said. "It was Michael's wish, as well as Kerric and Josephine's." He turned to me before continuing. "I don't know how much Michael told you about his home, but you have a place there. Will you come with us?"

What else could I do? Where else could I go?

I nodded.

"Who else knows what she is?" Sinead asked.

"How much do we have to lie?" Aris's voice was just a shade too aggressive.

John rounded on them all, but his tone remained calm and clear. "This girl is not dangerous. She is the same girl that you all considered a little sister not two hours ago. She is hurt. She is alone. She is afraid. Michael vouched for her, and that's enough for me. Dan, Sinead, I know you remember him. You can't doubt his judgment."

Dan nodded, catching my eye. "We were young, but the Michael I knew was a good man. An honorable man. He wouldn't put us in danger."

"A good man," Sinead agreed.

John turned to the others. "The rest of you may be too young to have known Michael well, but his word is good enough for me. It's good enough for the twins. And what's more, it's good enough for Kerric and Josephine Moore, who rule Derehan itself. The very land you stand on. What say you all?"

Paul, Aris, Dan, and Sinead stood undecided. They continued glaring at John defiantly, trying not to glance at me too much. The group didn't want me there anymore, that much was clear. They were afraid of me, despite Sinead's words. Even Dan was unsure, though he seemed to have decided to ignore that instinct.

John remained seated while the others stood over him, but somehow he still commanded the high ground. He stared them down as they decided their loyalties, and none of us questioned for a minute that he was the authority here. They all glowered, even Paul. This was not a decision any of them ever thought they'd have to make.

A decision about me. A judgement.

That silence was among the worst I had ever known. I had lived in dread the last few days, thinking they would discover what I was and abandon me. These warriors were the first friends I had ever known. I couldn't bear the idea of them casting me out. And what was worse, I wouldn't survive on my own, not with my leg so badly injured.

Finally, Paul spoke. "She saved my life. She killed that man cleanly. And even though it was right, she regrets it. I never knew Michael Gray, but I learned a lot about his granddaughter tonight."

A glimmer of hope, and from Paul of all people. Silent, distant, watchful Paul. He trusted me, at least.

Dan looked over at Paul and, after a grim hesitation, nodded. "Paul speaks the truth."

Then Sinead, maybe a little reluctantly, added, "Aye."

Aris said nothing, and we all took that as acceptance enough.

And that was the final word on the subject.

Relief flooded through me. The group stepped away without saying anything or even looking at me, but at least they had agreed to let me stay.

John turned to me. There was no fear in his eyes. None at all.

But I was afraid. These revelations had left me with even more questions, even more uncertainties. They had also taught me to be cautious. John was hiding something about me and about Michael. I hadn't known this man long, but I recognized the wisdom of following his lead.

"Did he not tell you about us?" John asked me.

I darted my eyes toward the others. They weren't quite out of earshot. I had to be careful.

"He told me *nothing*," I said with a cracking voice. Hot tears pricked my eyes as I realized just how true this was.

John pursed his lips. He leaned down and pretended to examine my fresh bandaging. Spots of blood had already appeared through the wool. He spoke very quietly so only I could hear.

"We'll talk later," he whispered. "Earn their trust. You'll need it."

He began to rise, but I grabbed his sleeve to stop him. "What about you?" I asked. "Why are you helping me?"

John's blunt gaze softened with uncertainty. "Because—" He hesitated. "Because it's you." He frowned at me, unhappy with his answer. He clearly wanted me to understand something he didn't know how to say.

His answer didn't make sense. Because it's me? He didn't know me. Did he?

John stood and moved to stand next to Dan by the fire. The pair of them spoke in low voices, their heads close together, then John wrapped Dan up in a tight, comforting embrace.

Dan slapped his back twice, then turned to settle next to Sinead, who put an arm around his waist.

Between the renewed throbs of pain in my leg and the labyrinth of secrets and revelations that would surely keep my mind spinning through the night, there was no way I could settle. I had known Michael kept things from me, but his lies only grew with every step I took away from the Sacred Wood. I was lost. I couldn't find the edges of the lies, of the secrets. There was no end to them.

What was this place we were going to, and how did I fit into it? What was John's role in this? Why was he hiding who my family was?

And through it all, I kept picturing that man jabbing a knife into his own neck. I had killed a man. I was a murderer, and it had been so easy. Because of me, that man's life was over. Gone. Irretrievable. Of all the time I'd spent on the earth so far, this was the one event that had split my life between before and after.

Before tonight, I was just Gwen. Afterward, I was a murderer. It hadn't been discovering Theo and the strange place she called a Sanctuary. It hadn't been learning that Michael was a liar. It hadn't been his death or my journey with these people, my only friends now.

No, it was the knowledge that I could kill a person with half a thought and no effort. I could, and I had. I had done it. I had killed him.

Murderer.

It was my nightmares come to life.

A movement on my right made me jump, sending a spasm of pain through my leg. Paul sat next to me in the dark and watched the fire. We were too far to feel much heat, but the light was reassuring.

I swiped at my eyes and tried to appear strong, but I didn't know what to say to him.

After a minute, Paul broke the silence. "I fell asleep."

I looked over at him. He was very young, more so than the rest. Maybe early twenties. Paul wore his black hair pulled back neatly with a leather tie, and he'd trimmed his beard short, though it was untidy after several weeks of traveling. He was thin and strong, a runner, and his voice came quiet when he spoke. I almost didn't hear him speak at all.

"You were watching the stars," I said.

A corner of his mouth twitched up. He nodded. "Yes, I was. I was watching the stars, but I must have fallen asleep because you woke me up when you came running." He turned his head to look at me. "You saved my life."

I nodded, but tears filled my eyes again, and I had to look away. I had saved him, but I had damned myself.

"You did the right thing, Gwen," he said.

My breath caught in my throat as I nodded, and a small sob escaped me.

"It helps to think of better things," Paul said. "I know it's hard, but try. Think about a time when you were happy. Think about the smell, the sounds, what you were thinking."

I nodded again and closed my eyes, wanting so desperately to stop feeling that man's death, to pretend it hadn't happened. I would try anything.

So I tried to recall the innocence I'd had as a child. Life had been so easy. Take care of the house and garden. Study with Michael. Clamber through the twisted old trees. Living, breathing, being the forest. The Little Owl.

I tried. I really tried to put myself into it like Paul had said. To cast away my uncertain future and the horror of what I had done. I wrapped myself in the Sacred Wood, and I hid there.

EIGHT

My leg woke me the next morning. It worked itself into my dreams, taking the form of a rabid raccoon digging into my flesh while I slept. When I awoke fully, the pain was far worse than it had ever been.

Dan was too quiet as he checked the wound. True infection had finally set in. My mad dash through the woods the night before had done it, there was no doubt. My entire calf had swollen, and the skin around the wound flamed an angry purplish-red. The leg would bear no weight at all.

"How much further to Barano?" Dan asked softly.

"If we push, we can make the road before nightfall," Paul said.

Nobody liked this answer, me least of all. But John was all grim determination.

"How long before fever sets in?"

"A day at most," Dan answered. "Probably less."

"Paul, you run ahead," John said. "Make the road and flag down a horse or a cart for us. Leave a trail for us to follow behind. Go now."

Paul didn't hesitate. He snapped up his pack and disappeared between the trees to the north.

"We move quickly today," John continued. "We're not losing anyone else on this damned mission."

We barely stopped that day. John finally felt the strain of carrying my weight without rest, but he pushed on.

My leg was aflame. Every step John took was agony. I clutched his jerkin and tried not to complain, but he noticed my hisses of pain. He allowed a five minute stop to brace my leg better, which helped. The swelling was noticeably worse, but Dan said nothing.

By noon, I was shivering. John's body warmth disappeared, and the air hit my skin like ice. He noticed that too. John didn't call for a stop, but Dan came and walked beside us to check on me. He put a hand to my face, and his glower deepened.

"The fever came fast," Dan said to John with a huff.

They powered ever onward. Aris and Sinead glanced back but didn't slow their pace. They pushed ahead, clearing the path and watching for the broken branches and scraps of fabric Paul had left behind to guide us.

"Gwen," John said to me, his breathing rough with exertion. "Gwen, how do you feel?"

"Tired," I said. "The pain is worse."

"Listen," he said. "You have to tell me if it gets hard to focus."

A low dread filled my gut. I hadn't thought of that before. "I can keep control," I said with more confidence than I felt.

"I know you can," he replied.

After another couple of hours, I couldn't hold on to him anymore. He hiked me higher and higher on his back as he went, trying to make it easier for me, but it was no good. I begged him to let me lie down. We all could have used a break, and I just needed to lie still for a bit.

John refused. No stops.

They used some spare shirts and paired a strong, green branch with the staff Sinead had carved for me to make a stretcher. They laid me out on it and covered me with their bed rolls to help with the shivering. John and Dan lifted me together, and we pushed onward. The bouncing and jerking movement was uncomfortable, but finally, I was able to sleep.

The next few hours passed in a blur. Sleep came and went so sporadically that I began to believe I had spent my entire life being carried on that damned stretcher. I caught a few words here and there while the men negotiated their awkward burden over the rough landscape.

At one point, I realized I was lying on something hard rather than in the makeshift stretcher, but we were still moving. True night had fallen, and the stars shone brightly overhead. For the first time in my life, no protective ceiling of tree branches obstructed the view.

I glanced over and found John sitting up next to me, sleeping. His chin bounced on his chest as the cart we rode in rolled over a rough road. Someone else's leg pressed against my thigh, but I couldn't tell whose it was. Maybe Paul or Dan.

I should wake John up. He should know I was having trouble focusing. He told me to let him know.

"Get under her knees."

A collective cry of pain filled the air when someone jostled my leg.

The cart had stopped. A house loomed overhead, with a steep thatched roof that came nearly all the way to the ground. People gathered around me, trying to lift my body out of the cart. They all winced as I lashed out. Dan's leg gave out and he nearly went to the ground.

"Gwen, focus!" John called out of the dark. "Can you hear me?"

"Yes," I replied, breathlessly.

"Focus on me," he said. "Paul, get the door. No, I've got her. Gwen, are you with me?"

He hoisted me back into his arms, and I cried out again. But this time, I kept the pain isolated to myself.

Or did I? John staggered for a second before he could take a step.

"I'm sorry," I whispered.

"Just focus on me."

He jumped down from the cart, and his own leg buckled. Someone reached out to steady him, but he pushed past them. John carried me inside a house and ordered everyone else out.

"Get away from this house," he ordered the others. Sweat gathered on his brow. "Do not come back here until morning. Do you understand?"

They must have understood because no one argued. The house was empty except for a woman I didn't know. I couldn't look at her or even think about her much. John laid me out on a large table under her appraising eye. She unwrapped my leg, sending spasms of agony through it that made the world waver before my eyes.

"Hold her down," the woman said.

John limped to my left side to do as he was told. "Listen to my voice, Gwen. Put all your focus on me. I can take it. Mariah has to be able to work, so don't think about her."

But Mariah spoke at the same time, as if John weren't talking at all. "I can't clean this wound if she's thrashing about. I'll have to give her something to knock her out."

"No!" John and I both called out at once.

"She has to stay focused," John added.

"Then let me give her some whiskey, at least!" Mariah insisted stubbornly. "This will be extremely painful."

"No! No liquor!" I hissed.

"No whiskey. She'll have to take the pain," John agreed.

"But—"

John rose to his full height. "She must remain conscious," he said sternly. "If she loses control, she takes the rest of us out with her. Do you understand me?"

Mariah stared at him, fear plain on her face. Clearly, she understood what he was insinuating.

"Don't tell me you're going to be a coward now," John said in a low voice.

"If she's a danger to us, then I can't risk it," Mariah replied, but I couldn't get a good look at her through the dizziness. "You'll have to find someone else."

"You'd rather I took her to a house in town? With neighbors?" John asked. "Or are you suggesting that I murder her here and now and be done with it? A eighteen-year-old girl who was injured through no fault of her own? Who put her own life at risk to save one of my men?"

Mariah hesitated for a second but still appeared uncertain.

John bent down so he could look her in the eye. "She can handle it. I can keep her focused. You can save her life."

She closed her eyes and took a deep breath. "You keep her focused. Keep her still. I'm going to have to cut some of this away before I can clean it. Then I'll have to stitch it fresh. It will be extremely painful." She gazed down at me and continued. "Did you hear me? Extremely painful. Prepare yourself. You have to keep very still. Don't tense up."

I nodded, gripping John's hand for dear life.

"Cover her up. Stop the shivering."

John did everything she instructed as Mariah prepared to treat my leg. He gathered blankets, fetched water, stoked the fire. John limped with every step, and I knew it was my own pain. I tried to seal it off from him, but I couldn't. It was too much, and my head was too foggy.

My leg burned. Not just my calf, but my whole leg, my hip, my trunk. The throbbing radiated up my body in hellish waves. My leg was no longer flesh. It was fire only. Not coals, not embers, but wild, hot flames.

John returned to my side, holding both of my hands in his. "Are you ready?" he asked.

I nodded.

"You give everything to me, do you hear? Let me take as much as I can so you can keep still."

I nodded again, my eyes closed.

"That's right," he said.

No, he didn't say it. He thought it. *Focus on me.*

Mariah set her sharp little knife to my inflamed flesh, and we screamed.

It didn't take too long, as bad as it was. John stayed with me the whole time, his forehead pressed to the table, his hands cold in my own feverish ones. Neither one of us tried to keep quiet or dignified, though I did manage to keep my leg still enough that Mariah didn't complain. I cried and sobbed, and he grunted and shouted. We both felt every slice, every swab of ointment, every stab of the needle and drag of the thread.

And finally, *finally*, she began wrapping my leg in fresh, soft cotton. The pain dulled to a tolerable smolder, and I was able to focus on my surroundings.

I was lying on what appeared to be a kitchen table in a comfortable room. Mariah, an older woman with a generous amount of gray streaking through her dark hair, busily cleared up her tools. She was a local doctor, maybe, and very practical. Red coated her hands to the wrists, and her eyes were hooded with the strain of what she had just done.

She said nothing and continued to clear up.

John sat next to the table where I lay, his head resting on my shoulder. His breaths came as ragged as my own, and he continued to grip my hand tightly.

"The wound wasn't so bad," Mariah said, making us both jump. "I mean, it was *bad*, don't get me wrong. But you got her here early enough for me to do something meaningful about it. Let her fever run its course. If it breaks by morning, she'll live."

John nodded against my shoulder, then he raised his head to

look at her. "I hate to ask," he said with a hoarse voice, "but can we sleep here tonight? Just tonight. We can pay."

Mariah pursed her lips and wiped her hands on a clean towel. "There's a guest room upstairs. Extra blankets in the wardrobe."

"Thank you."

John stood and hauled me up again, his face a mask of exhaustion. He carried me up the narrow stairs and into a small bedroom. The open window showed only blackness beyond. He lowered me onto the small bed and helped me ease my leg under the blankets. Then he pulled out more bedding and set himself up on the floor.

"John?" I whispered, my voice harsh from overuse.

"Hmm?"

"Thank you."

"Hm."

NINE

Mariah's voice woke us the next morning. She yelled at someone downstairs, which echoed through the small house. I couldn't quite tell what she said, but her tone oozed annoyance.

John jumped at the commotion and sat up, groping in my direction. His hand found my face clumsily, then pressed to my cheek and forehead. His skin felt pleasantly warm against mine, which I took for a good sign. My fever had broken.

John seemed to come to the same conclusion.

He pulled away, leaned back against the wardrobe with a sigh, and rubbed his eyes miserably. He hadn't gotten enough rest, considering the strain of the day before, but he was never one to complain.

John shook his head once to clear it, then got up. "Stay here," was all he said to me.

As if I could get up on my own. No way in hell would I put any weight on my leg for the next several days, if I could help it. I had learned that lesson well.

I pushed the heavy blankets off and reveled in the cool air of the room. My bedding was soaked with sweat, and my clothes stank with it. I hadn't had a proper wash in a week, and now that we had left the only life I'd ever known, I wasn't sure how to handle myself. Water was something I had gotten from the stream, or I'd climb directly into the stream itself on a warm day. People in villages had wells and tubs.

Several of these questions were answered for me almost at once. Mariah herself came charging into the room with a bucket of heated water and various supplies.

"Those men have no sense," she grumbled, helping me peel off my stinking leathers. "They barge into my home like it's a public house and start ordering me about like I'm some sort of-of, I don't know. A barmaid." She tossed my clothes into a pile in the corner and began undoing my braids and pulling the feathers from my hair. These she stacked neatly on a small table by the window.

Mariah gave me a bar of soap, which smelled of berries. Michael and I had always used lye soap, if we used soap at all. This was delightful. She helped me wash my hair over the bucket, and I wiped myself down head to foot.

Between the dirt, sweat, and blood I had accumulated on my journey, the water turned nearly black before we finished. Mariah took it out, grumbling, and came back with fresh water, cold this time. I got another rinse that raised gooseflesh on my skin.

I was still exhausted, but it felt wonderful to be clean.

Finally, she helped me navigate a new dress. It was plain, brown homespun and a little big for me, but I marveled at it. I'd worn skins my entire life. This woolen work dress felt so strange to the touch. It moved and stretched with me and clung in ways I didn't expect.

Mariah studied me, hands on hips. "Well? You feel up to going down? I'm sure your bodyguards are very anxious to see for themselves that you're alive."

She called Dan to help me downstairs. He lifted me as easily as John ever had, but it was awkward. Dan carried me downstairs and sat me at the large table where Mariah had cleaned my leg the night before.

General cries of relief and welcome met me from everyone. Sinead patted my back affectionately while Paul moved to sit next to me. He gave a rare smile and passed me some dried meat from our supplies.

"We'll get something better to eat once we make it to town," Sinead said when I took the jerky.

"You're looking much less wild this morning." Dan sat down opposite me. "I barely recognized you."

"I had a good wash," I said. "And the fever broke in the night."

"She is not to walk on that leg for at least a week," Mariah announced, entering the room with the sheets from my bed. "Tie her down if you have to. I swear, if she goes and tears out those stitches again after all that ruckus last night..." She threw the bedding into a pile in the corner with a huff. "I swear, I'll chop your whole damn leg off next time and save us all the trouble. And you need to drink something after that fever."

"We hired a cart last night." Sinead passed a pitcher of water in my direction. "She won't be walking anywhere anytime soon."

"She'd better not be." Mariah disappeared back up the stairs.

Aris came inside. John followed him in, wiping his hands on his pants.

"Since we have a cart, I don't want to stay in Barano longer than we have to," John said. "We'll take today to resupply and let Gwen recover, but we need to move on in the morning."

Then he noticed me sitting next to Paul, clean and wearing real clothes and alert for the first time in more than a day. I gave him a small smile. He hesitated for half a second, then returned the greeting with a polite nod.

John didn't seem to know what to say to me after the night we'd had, so he simply moved on to other practicalities. He and Paul went outside to check the donkey and the cart they had hired while the others scowled over how little I was eating. Aris stood silent by the door, watching us, until Sinead goaded him into joining the group.

"Don't be so standoffish, man," Sinead said when Aris sat down next to her. "You Authe Idans can't seem to take a little excitement."

Aris cracked a smile. Sinead pounded him good-naturedly on the back. The sight of it eased something in my gut.

A few minutes later, John announced it was time to go. I thanked Mariah at least four times, and she squeezed my hand with a grim smile.

"Remember what I said now," she said. "At least a week before you try and walk on that. The stitches can come out in two. And try and find a real doctor to do it, would you? Don't let whoever stitched you up the first time take another crack at it."

"Hey!" Sinead admonished her for the sake of her brother's work. "It was better than nothing!"

Mariah pointed a wooden spoon at her. "Like hell it was! I've never seen such butchery in my life! It's a wonder she made it as long as she did!"

"Leave it, Sinead." Dan moved toward the door. "Thank you for your help, Mariah."

Mariah harrumphed and leaned on my chair. "That's the one who did it, isn't it?" she asked conspiratorially. "Yeah, I'll bet. You can always tell." She frowned while the rest of them cleared out. "Don't tell him I said so, but it wasn't so bad, really. If you hadn't torn the stitches out, you'd have probably been okay. Nasty scar, though. Big stitches like that?" She sighed and patted my shoulder.

John came in when Mariah moved away. Only the three of us remained inside.

"Thank you for helping us," he said to her. He dropped a small purse onto the table. "That's for letting us stay last night. We appreciate it."

"Keep your money. I don't need it."

"Then spend it on someone who does," John said. "And I hope we can count on you to keep some...details to yourself."

"Hang your secrets and hang yourself," Mariah grumbled, but she pushed a loaf of yesterday's bread into my hands as she said it.

"Thank you," I said again.

"Stop it now. Off with you."

I nodded, and John helped me stand.

"You take care of her, you hear me?" Mariah said sternly to John. "I'll know if you don't."

"Yes, ma'am," he answered seriously. "I will."

John carried me out to the cart and helped me settle into the back of it with their packs, which were tolerably comfortable to sit against. It was a very small cart, the sort one didn't drive but led the donkey with a rope.

It was an easy walk for the others, who no longer needed to carry their packs or me. They talked and occasionally laughed as we moved down the narrow track in the cool morning air with the open sky above. It was a strange, exposed sort of place to be. I had lived my entire life under a canopy of trees and had never seen so much sky. We passed field after field, some with grazing animals and others lush with crops nearly ready for harvest.

Sinead and Aris talked my ear off about that breed of cow or how this farmer had taken advantage of the creek to build crude irrigation. A part of me wanted them to leave me to try and sleep, but mostly, I was curious. I had never seen such huge swaths of crops or even a single cow or goat in my life. Here were more than I could count. They ambled about in herds of black and brown and white, tearing up grass with blunt, yellow teeth, without paying us the slightest attention.

The closer we got to Barano, the more people we passed on the road. Soon we were joined by other travelers and carts laden with goods for sale. John and Paul grew quiet, but a pretty woman leading a pair of young goats drew Sinead into a bubbly conversation.

Aris and I attracted more attention than anyone: he for his exotic appearance, and me for my injury. And though it was disorienting at first, I quickly found the shape of so many minds at once and was able to enjoy the company I had been starved of my entire life.

Children trotted alongside the cart, asking Aris question after question about the sea and Bluewater while their parents eyed him suspiciously. One young man passed me a wildflower with a shy grin, and his friend elbowed him. They trotted away, laughing.

I glanced around at John. He returned my amused grin as I tucked the little white flower into my tidy braid.

But my night had been spent tossing and turning, in pain and feverish, and my morning had been full of new people and places. So when we finally reached an inn on the main road in Barano, I was exhausted.

As soon as the rooms were paid for, John collected me from the cart and carried me upstairs. The innkeeper's wife led us to a small room barely big enough for two single beds and the space to walk between them.

John thanked the woman and lowered me gently on one foot. I sank gratefully onto one of the beds. It wasn't as soft as the one in Mariah's house, but the room was quiet and warm.

John knelt by the bed and felt my face again for fever, finding nothing to worry him there, he said, "Are you going to be all right alone?"

"Yes. I just want to sleep."

He placed Sinead's staff on the floor next to my bed with a clunk. "Use this if you need to get up. Don't walk on that leg. One of us will stay downstairs, but I'll hear you if you call."

I nodded against the rough pillow and pulled the blanket up over my head. I didn't hear him leave.

Several hours later, I woke to the sounds of the boisterous pub on the ground floor. I sat up and rubbed my eyes, feeling better than I had in days.

I picked up my staff and studied the owl on top. Sinead had finished it beautifully, adding the hint of vines and leaves down the head of the staff. Every feather was perfect, every leaf unique.

My leg ached horribly, but it no longer worried me. The swelling had gone with the fever, and the pain no longer lanced halfway across my body. This would heal.

But only if I allowed it to.

I used the staff and took a couple of trial steps to see if I could move without putting any weight on it. My toes were necessary for balance, but the staff bore my weight well.

It took a while to get downstairs to the public room, but I managed. It felt good to move and use my muscles, to be a little less dependent.

Paul and Aris sat at a table near the back wall, playing a game with cards. Sinead sat with them, whittling as usual.

"You're awake!" Sinead got up to help me sit. "You've been in bed most of the day. Are you hungry?"

"Yes," I said with feeling. "Very hungry."

"Just wait here. I'll see what they've got for you." She left to find the kitchen girl.

"Shit!" Aris hissed when Paul played his hand.

Paul gave me the tiniest of proud grins while Aris reshuffled the cards for another game.

"You're not walking on that, are you?" Aris asked me, dealing the cards again. "Is the staff helping?"

"Yes, but it's slow." I settled myself more comfortably in the chair. "I won't be going anywhere far."

"You'll be leaving for Valheid tomorrow," Paul countered, "but you won't be walking, that's true enough."

"I'm glad you were able to find someone willing to lend you a cart and a donkey for such a long trip."

"We bought them," Aris said. "Traded for them, more like. He took all our furs off of us and most of the money we had left."

"And one of my figures." Sinead appeared with a plate of food for me. Her black hair fell clean and straight down her back, freshly braided. I wasn't the only one who'd had a bath. "I was making it for our cousin, but I'll just make another. Here you go—bread and butter and some stew from lunch. It's a bit cold now, but it's good."

"And Paul and I each gave up a knife," Aris said. "Good ones too."

I turned to Paul, who was studying his cards. "Thank you. I'm grateful to all of you, I am."

"None of us are complaining," Sinead said. "Now we don't have to carry the supply packs anymore. The donkey can do it."

"We're happy to do it," Paul added. "You've already proven you'd do the same for us."

I smiled at him, then turned to the food Sinead had brought me.

It was a quiet afternoon, though fascinating to me. People came and went all day, some of them staying to talk, have a drink, or join a game.

Sinead was popular with the young women and drew nearly all of them into long conversations by the bar. Paul seemed to be friends with every rough looking man who walked by the pub. When Dan came in a little later with a load of supplies, he and Sinead attracted even more attention. All the young ladies who hadn't been charmed by Sinead flocked to Dan instead.

Aris's fair face drew many furtive looks, but soon his obvious good humor soothed every worry. It wasn't long before he was just as engaged as the twins.

John came in once or twice to check in with Dan or take a new pack up to our rooms. Paul left with him before dinner, and the pair didn't return until after dark. It was raining by then, and I had made my way out to the wide front porch to find a bit of quiet.

"You all right out here?" John asked, climbing the steps.

"Yes," I said. "It's just crowded in there, that's all."

He nodded and went inside. Paul followed him, but he dropped his cloak around my shoulders when he passed. The material was very warm and only a bit damp, so wherever they had been must have been safe from the rain. I pulled it close and leaned against the pillar next to me, my injured leg stretched out on the wooden decking.

After a while, the front door opened again, and John appeared with two mugs of a hot drink. He passed me one and sat down next to me, his back against the wall.

I sipped, finding it a little bitter but warm and rich with spices. "What is it?" I asked.

"Mulled wine."

I frowned at it. "You think I should?"

"One mug won't affect you." He took a drink of his own. "It'll warm you up."

Reassured, I tasted it again.

"We should talk while we can," John said after a minute. "The men are inside and occupied. Paul will make sure they won't come out and bother us."

I glanced at him, then turned back to my mug of wine, my hands shaking.

The time had come, finally, for answers.

TEN

"What did Michael tell you? About where you came from?"

I inhaled a long, steadying breath. "The same thing you told the others. That I lashed out as an infant and had to be taken away." I set down my mug, then picked it up again, just so I could have something to do with my hands. "He told me he was our neighbor, that we lived in a small village in the south of Derehan. He said I had no family, that my mother died giving birth to me, that no one in the village would take me."

I turned to face him, spilling a few drops of my wine in my carelessness.

"I never once thought to question it. It seemed reasonable enough, but I was young when he told me this. That was before I knew how to see a lie. He lied to me many times, Johnny. More times than I can even say. Bigger lies than—I can't find the edges of them! I can't find where his lies end!"

"Shh." He took my wine and gripped my shaking hands. "Slow down."

I held on to him, drawing comfort from his familiar warmth.

Had I really only known him a few days? After a lifetime of knowing no one at all?

"I didn't know how much he kept from me until you came. Until that night with Paul, until you said you had been sent to collect us. I had no idea. His lies keep growing. And he's gone now, and I can't even be angry with him for it."

Hot tears came suddenly to my eyes, and I swiped at them uselessly. As hurt as I had been by Michael's death, as painful as it had been, I had not cried for him yet. I hadn't allowed myself to. Now that I had begun, it seemed impossible to stop.

A bout of raucous laughter floated out of the open pub windows behind us, making me jump. I leaned against the pole and turned my face away.

"But you say I come from Valheid. From the capital. You know who my family was?"

"Yes, I know your family," John said. "I'm taking you to live with them."

I swiped at my eyes again and took a long drink from my quickly cooling mug, wiping my mouth with trembling fingers. "They're alive? My parents?"

"No," he said. "Your father left before you were born. We don't know where he is or if he is even alive. Your mother, Ellen, died giving birth to you, as Michael said."

So, there was one truth, at least.

"I'm taking you to your brother and your sister," he continued. "Kerric Moore is the lord of Valheid, and Josephine acts as one of his advisors. You were named Sasha Moore, after your grandmother, but Michael must have changed that when he took you away. The three of you were born from kings, Gwenna. That is the real reason you were sent away. Because someone like you, gifted as you are, could not be given authority."

I covered my face with my hands. Panic rose in my chest. Lords and ladies. This was absurd. I was no lady. I was the Little Owl.

And Sasha? The name sounded foreign in my mouth. That wasn't my name. That wasn't who I was.

"There were riots," John said. "We were only children, but I remember it. I studied with Josephine and Michael every day, and a mob came to the Greathouse while I was there with them. You were just a baby, not even sitting up, but you woke the entire city every night, crying for the nursemaid. They were terrified of the time when you would learn to throw tantrums, as every child does. Any toddler with that kind of power would be…They were terrified of you, and it made them violent." He took a deep breath. "Michael took you away after that, and the people were told you had died."

I sat in silence, trying not to picture the horrific event that must have come with the mob to the Greathouse. People did drastic things when they were afraid.

"So, though I'm taking you to live with your brother and sister, the official story must be that you're Michael's granddaughter. He was well known. The people there will accept you in that role."

"If he was so well known," I said, "then won't it also be known that he had no children?"

John hesitated. "People may doubt the story. They may suspect who you are, especially because you look very like Josephine and your mother. But Michael's been gone a long time. Eighteen years. They may whisper to each other, but no one will argue with the Moores. Not outright."

I stared at my mug, now mostly empty. I wished I could have more to dull this hammering in my heart.

After a minute of silence, John tentatively said, "Gwen?"

"Why now?" I asked. "Why did you come for us now?"

"We were told to wait for Michael's call. We heard it about six weeks ago."

"We?"

"Josephine and I."

I closed my eyes, gripping my mug so tightly my knuckles went white in the darkness. "You're like me?" I asked in a low voice.

"Josephine is like you," he answered, his voice just as quiet. "I don't know if you've ever met someone like me, though. Michael used to call me a passive."

I bowed my head, my lips pursed.

A passive telepath. Of course, he was a passive. He wouldn't be able to flit from one mind to the other like I could, but he was able to connect with a telepath. That was why his voice had been so clear in my head. Most people wouldn't even realize I was in their mind, much less be able to answer back. That was why I'd been able to pour my pain into him while Mariah cleaned my wound, how he knew so much about my gifts and how to focus them.

I let out a heavy sigh and looked out through the rain. "I should have known."

"No one knows, except for Kerric and Josephine," he said. "It's been easy for me to hide. Not like you."

"And what about my...sister? Josephine?"

"It's hard for her to hide as well as I can, but the people love her. It's not spoken of out loud. She's very sweet-natured. Like you."

"They accept her in power but not me?" I couldn't hide the bitterness in my voice, though I tried. "If I'm so much like her, why was I the one who was sent away?"

He scowled down at his own mug, which was growing cold with the chilly evening. "Because she was never as powerful as you, Gwen. Because she can hide who she is for the most part. She could blend in with everyone else. And because—"

John hesitated. His mouth clamped shut.

When he didn't continue, I pressed. "Because what, John?"

"I–I don't—"

"What is it? There have been too many lies already. Too many secrets. Don't you add to them. Not you."

"I don't know!" He threw out his hand in exasperation. "I

don't understand it. Josephine said something to me once, back when we were children. She was protecting you from something, Gwen, but she would never tell me what. Whatever it was, it scared her. It scared her more than the mobs, more than anything else."

I frowned. "And she never told you anything about it?"

"I was just a boy. Neither one of us were old enough to understand, not really. She said something about a prophecy. She said there was a place where no one could get to, right out of the world. Something about that place scared her badly. She never spoke of it again, no matter how hard Kerric or I tried. But she told your grandfather, who was lord at that time, and she told Michael. And then you were gone."

I stared at him, horrified. He couldn't mean...He couldn't have been talking about Theo's Sanctuary—that sickly, brown, dead place she had taken me to just a few months ago.

He noticed my expression and knew immediately that I understood. "You know the place?" he asked, leaning forward eagerly. "You know what she meant?"

"No," I said. "I mean, maybe. But I don't know what scared her about it. I don't know about any prophecy."

"What is the place? How did you get there?"

"I don't know," I said in earnest. "I don't know what it was or where it was. It was a dead place, too quiet. Too still. There were trees, but there was no life. No wind even."

"But how did you get there?"

"I don't know! She took me!"

"Who?"

"Theo did. It was Theo. Just a couple of months ago."

John stared at me, his dark eyes narrowed. He drew back slightly. "Theo?"

"Yes," I said. "Sinead mentioned her the other day. I gather she is well known in Derehan."

John opened his mouth to speak, then closed it. He tried again. "She is very well known, though she uses many names. She appears all over as a wise woman, selling fortunes to anyone who will speak to her. You said two months ago?"

"Maybe a little less."

"Maybe six weeks ago?"

I looked up at him. Six weeks? "Maybe?"

"Did you tell Michael?"

I nodded. "She scared me."

He sat back, grim. "That's why, then. That's why he called us now. It has to be."

"Why? Because of Theo?"

"It has to be something to do with that dead place, whatever it was. He knew about Josephine's prophecy. That was why he hid you away in the Sacred Wood in the first place."

"Will she tell me? Josephine? Will she tell me what it was that scared her?"

He shook his head. "I don't know. She's never kept anything from me. Nothing but that."

I sat back against the wall and stared out into the darkness. The rain kept everyone off the street, so we were well and truly alone.

"But why did Michael keep all of this from me?" I asked in a whisper.

"I don't know that either." John lifted his mug, found it empty, and put it down again.

I tried to picture the brother and sister who waited for me at Valheid, but it was difficult. In my mind, Josephine was just another me. Small, dark, brown-haired, quiet. But Kerric, I couldn't imagine. I could only conjure up a faceless man standing in a grand, stone house. In my mind, he wore the same sort of clothes as my companions. Leather, wool, weapons. I had nothing else to go on. They were both an enigmatic, empty something looming before me.

"There's something else," John said quietly.

I glanced over at him. He sat staring at his hands, knotted together in his lap, his brows furrowed. His breathing came a little faster than normal. His posture created an odd juxtaposition with the thrum of the gentle rain on the roof and the croak of the frogs in the darkness.

"What is it?"

It took him a long time to continue.

"It's not..." He hesitated. "It's not important. It doesn't have to be. But I don't believe in keeping secrets unless I have to."

John stopped again. I turned to face him fully but said nothing. I just needed to wait for him to find his words again. That much I understood.

"Josephine told me...She said...she saw something else. About you." He looked up at me, suddenly resolute. "She said you and I would...be close."

I stared at him, utterly taken aback. This was not at all what I had expected.

What did he mean, close? Lovers? The way he had hesitated certainly inferred that. He was a grown man, and I was barely a woman. Only eighteen years old. I knew how it was between men and women, but that was the furthest thing from my mind now. Not now.

But I had to know. So, out of curiosity alone, I reached out to lay my fingertips on the back of his bare forearm. I needed to understand what he meant, what had been foretold about him and about me.

I shouldn't have done it. I should have left well enough alone.

But I had to know.

The instant my fingers made contact with his skin, I was overwhelmed with images and emotions so strong I lost all connection with the here and now. I was me, but not me. I was older, and I didn't have to stretch too far to kiss him. My body fit so neatly against his chest, my arms tight around his neck, his hands on my waist. A passion and a heat flowed through me, one I wouldn't have even known to expect.

We walked through the trees on a warm afternoon. He teased

me, and I laughed. *Laughed!* I genuinely felt the giddiness rise in my chest. He grabbed my hand and pulled me close in a shaft of bright sunlight.

John carried me before him on a horse. My face was pale, and rain and blood soaked us both to the skin.

I pulled him by the hand into a secluded corner, sneaking a kiss in a grand house built of stone.

I yelled at him, brandishing a sheaf of papers in a library, and he rubbed his eyes in frustration.

He rolled over in his sleep and pulled me close with a sigh.

Fire, smoke, and desperation. A faceless woman in a green dress on the roof of a burning building. The faceless presence next to me had to be John. It felt like him. I knew him. I knew that place, that fire. I'd seen it before.

But too fast, the vision changed, and we were at supper in a great hall. John squeezed my hand under the table at a large dinner.

We made love in our bed, with the window open, the night air cooling the sweat on our bodies.

Each vision lasted a lifetime. Each emotion, passion, and connection flamed real and alive.

When I finally came back to myself, my face flooded with heat. My breath came in heady gasps. I yanked my hand away from his arm and stared down at my fingers, shocked to find myself a teenager again. We had lived a lifetime together in the space of a second.

John's expression reflected my own. His lips parted as he exhaled. He had seen it too, every damned second. John had witnessed it, felt it, and lived it with me. He was a passive telepath. John could connect with me if I let him, and I certainly hadn't stopped him then.

"Gwen," he said breathlessly.

"No," I whispered. "No."

I scrambled to my feet, forgetting for an instant to favor my right leg, and stumbled before righting myself against the wall. John was up in a flash to steady me.

I hobbled back. He reached for me again, clearly wanting to catch me if I fell, but I pulled away, crossing my arms over my pounding heart.

No.

I couldn't take it.

Johnny was my guide and my friend. I needed him. But now I couldn't bear to touch him. I couldn't even look at him. Didn't know how anymore. Every bracing hand, every word, was a potential loss. I had loved Michael too, had relied on him just the same, but the only thing left of that love was a gaping hole in my heart.

Once more, I felt death. I felt Michael's life ripped from my chest. His last breath, his last terror, his last pain. I felt the emptiness in myself, still aching, raw, and unbearable.

I wouldn't survive it. Not again.

"Pass me my staff, please," I said, my face burning in embarrassment.

John did so immediately. I took it and limped another step away. The old boards of the porch creaked under me. He remained where he was, utterly helpless. It broke my heart, even now.

It felt as though my closest friend had been taken away from me. My only confidant. But I couldn't think of anything to say or do that wouldn't make everything worse.

"Is there anything else that I should know about myself?" I asked.

"Not that I know of," he said. "Gwen, please—"

"I don't know who the other bed in my room is for. But I'd prefer it wasn't you. Thank you for being honest with me tonight. Please don't follow me inside."

And with that, I limped past him and into the noise and heat of the pub. He didn't try to stop me.

Sinead ended up helping me upstairs later that night, and she slept in the other bed in my room. Dan was the one to lift me into the cart the next morning. John took up the donkey's lead rope and never ventured to the back of the group, where I rode.

Neither of us spoke to the other, and neither of us said anything about it to our companions.

And as I rode in that cart, watching the road lengthen behind us, I wished bitterly that I didn't know.

PART THREE
OF TRUTH AND BLOOD

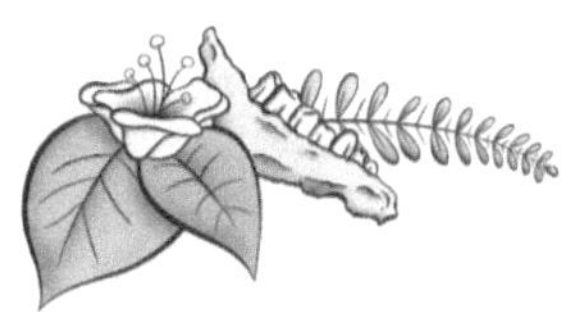

Eleven

The journey to Valheid took most of the day. More and more travelers crowded the road around us, causing dust to rise in shafts of morning sunlight. They dragged carts and mules like us, rode horses, drove sheep, or simply walked with wagons overloaded with furs, fabrics, fruits, rattling bottles, and grain. We passed through four villages and saw countless farms and settlements along the way.

My friends were never without some acquaintance or a friendly stranger to chat with as they walked along. They didn't seem like soldiers that day, not really. Their swords and bows were all packed in neat bundles next to me in the cart, so we were just travelers, like anyone else.

No one noticed me. I made myself small and pretended to be just another pack among the rest. Even my own companions seemed to forget about me. Paul came by once or twice to pass me the water skin or a bit of salted beef to chew on. Dan checked on me a couple of times, not quite believing I was truly on the mend.

But otherwise, they left me to my thoughts, which swung wildly between the life I had left, the family of strangers I was throwing myself into, and John.

I half wished he would come speak to me, force me to deal with the vision we had shared. But I was too embarrassed. I wasn't the tall, confident woman wearing my face in that vision. I had never dreamed of taking a man's hand, much less kissing him. I wouldn't even know how to go about it.

Surely, John wouldn't expect anything to change between us.

But it didn't matter. Whatever he expected, he was thinking about it. If I was, then he was too. He had seen me naked. I had seen him.

Would see.

Had seen?

It was too twisted, backward. There was no right way to react.

I squirmed uncomfortably in the cart, wishing I could tuck my injured leg under my body.

That woman in the vision wasn't me. I didn't know how it ever could be. Sure, I'd had a wash and wore a tidy homespun dress, but that was just a costume. I was still a little wildling, an owl caught indoors.

My own pack sat crammed against my thigh. I pulled it out and dug through it until I found the little pile of feathers Mariah had taken out of my hair. They were old and rumpled from being tied up in my hair, most of them gathered just this past summer. Closing them up in my pack had only made matters worse.

I smoothed them out, one by one. They were a mess, but they were mine. This was me.

I began braiding the feathers back into my hair where they belonged, discarding the withered wildflower a stranger had given me the day before. When that was done, I pulled my leather cloak out and put that on as well. Looking out from under the hood, I felt more like myself. Whatever was coming, I wouldn't pretend.

And so, when we finally came to the outskirts of Valheid, I was the Little Owl again. I stopped hiding from our fellow travelers and received several disconcerted looks when they noticed me. We passed farmhouse after farmhouse, and more and more people crowded the road.

Sinead called out to a man walking in the other direction and actually left the group entirely. She said a few words to John, then came back and hauled her pack out of the cart.

"Chin up, Little Owl," she said. "I'll come into town tomorrow and check in on you."

I smiled and nodded, but it hurt to watch her walk away with some man I didn't know. She had a life and people who were closer to her than I had ever been. I had known that about her, about all of them, but it was starting to feel real now. The few days we'd had together felt like my whole life, but it wasn't the same for them.

I'd seen pictures of the Wall, the protective barrier that surrounded the capital city of Valheid. Michael had even shown me visions of it from his own memories. But when we passed under an enormous iron gate set in rough stone walls, six feet wide at least, I couldn't help but gape at it.

Guards stood on top, watching the crowd surging below them. Dan shouted a greeting out to them, and one man grinned and called him something foul. Dan only laughed and returned the favor.

The city itself was all stone, dirt, and thatch. The roofs pitched at an extreme angle to shed snow in winter, but vivid designs blossomed across doors and windows. Bright green stags, blue skeletal trees, swirling reds, purples, and yellows.

And then there were the people.

I stared around in awe, and my nerves faded. People of all sizes and colors milled about. Aris was no longer the most exotic person in sight, with his golden skin and light clothing.

A hub of activity, Valheid hosted merchants from all over the world. A woman's bright red hair caught my eye when she held up a swath of patterned fabric to show a customer. A small man with night-dark skin and hair drove a cart past us, filled to capacity with dried corn stalks. Two girls with flower crowns darted among the crowd, hocking bouquets to anyone who would listen.

There was so much to see. I'd had no idea.

Another soldier ran up and walked with John. They spoke quietly together for several minutes before he darted off again, disappearing into the noise and bustle.

"I'm off, Gwen," Paul said, making me jump. I hadn't noticed him approaching the cart. "I have a room at the Ullman house, just down that alley."

"You're all going," I said. "I expected you all to come to the Greathouse."

"John will speak to Lord Moore for all of us. I don't know what we would say about you anyway. What's supposed to be said..." Paul strapped on his pack with a huff. "Don't worry. I'll see you soon. We all turn up at the practice yard or on guard duty when we're not in the fields. The twins both live at the barracks right by the big house."

He held out his hand to me, and I took it, unsure. Paul squeezed once, then let go. I lost him in the crowd as he disappeared down a small side street.

My heart pounded. With a determined frown, I twisted around in the cart to look forward.

The buildings loomed larger and closer together the deeper we moved into the city, to what was clearly the city square. We wove our way through a crowded market, which filled the wide, cobbled square, surrounded by two-story buildings.

Towering above them all was the most massive structure I had ever seen: a stone monstrosity with turrets, towers, and wide-open gates. Smaller, squat buildings crowded around it, probably bake houses, stables, storerooms, and breweries. People milled about, shouting about their harvests of apples or their best mohair fabrics. It was chaos.

John and Dan led us into the courtyard of the massive house without pause, though many tried to hold them up. We had accumulated a small crowd of onlookers, most of whom seemed to be more interested in me than in welcoming the men home. And though many stared, none tried to speak to me, which was just as well. What would I have said back?

"And here I thought I would draw all the attention," Aris said in an undertone.

Eyes followed me down the road. I wasn't ready. It was too fast. The sky was too open, the people too close. I was torn between a desire to explore every market stall or hide to catch my breath.

But we had arrived, whether I was ready or not.

The cart came to an unceremonious stop, and Dan disengaged from his friends to help me down. He had barely a moment to spare for me.

"Take care of yourself, Little Owl." Dan said with a quick squeeze on my arm. "I'll see you soon, I expect." He grabbed his own pack with a grim expression and disappeared.

"Gwen," said a low voice on my left.

I jumped.

John appeared beside me, Aris on his other side. The Authe Idan's eyes were wide in his golden face as he took in what must have been strange and exotic sights.

John's face was entirely unreadable but still comforting. As always, he was an anchor in a raging river.

Then I remembered the vision we had shared the night before, and I couldn't think how to answer him.

"Can you walk?" he asked.

I nodded. "Slowly."

He looked over my shoulder. I followed his gaze toward the great stone steps of the manor house. Several people stood by the hulking wooden doors, and even more emerged from the darkness inside.

"Remember the story," he said without looking away from the people in the doorway.

I swallowed and nodded.

He glanced down at me. "There are some here who must believe the lies."

"Johnny!" someone called from the top of the stairs.

John gripped my arm, refusing to answer the call just yet, and whispered so Aris could not hear. "Whatever passed between us last night, it must stay between us for now. Do you trust me?"

I stared at him, my heart pounding. "Yes."

"Johnny! Come inside!" The man bounced down the steps with the eagerness of an old friend and embraced John, even as the latter continued to grip my arm.

"Hello, old friend," John said with a smile.

"Yes, yes! We weren't expecting you for another week, at least! And this must be Aristeidis! It's good to meet you finally. Welcome to Valheid." He shook Aris's hand warmly.

"Thank you for having me, Lord Moore," Aris said with a formality that didn't quite suit him. "I hope this will be the beginning of a true peace between Derehan and Authe Ida. My father sends his respects."

My heart stopped. Lord Moore?

This was Kerric, the brother I'd never met. When I looked again, it seemed obvious. His tawny skin matched mine, as did his thick, brown hair. And something about his eyes, the way they landed on one person at a time and did not falter—it felt familiar.

Was this how I looked at people? Steadily, unreserved?

Kerric laughed at the awkwardness on the Authe Idan's face, causing Aris to crack a more natural smile. "Come now, man. Enough with all that. Come inside and we'll talk business later."

John turned to me again while the two men spoke.

"I don't know if you mean it when you say you trust me," he said earnestly, "but make *them* believe it. You need them, and they do trust me. Use that."

Kerric caught me staring at him from behind John's arm and faltered for the barest of seconds. His face immediately formed itself into a friendly, polite expression. "And who is this you've brought home?"

A small scuffle erupted at the great wooden doors, and someone else appeared amongst the onlookers. A young woman, wearing what appeared to be a dressing gown thrown hastily over herself, spotted me instantly in the heavy crowd. Her hair swung in a heavy, dark braid. She gripped the arm of an older woman next to her and stared at us, trying to catch her breath.

"Kerric," John said, his eyes on the breathless woman who had just appeared on the steps. "This is Gwenna Gray. We came upon her in the Sacred Wood, alone and injured. Let's go inside and I'll tell you how we came to bring her home with us."

"Yes, of course." Kerric furrowed his eyebrows. He gazed directly at me and held out a hand. "If you're unwell, you should come inside. We'll call for a surgeon immediately."

I glanced down at his hand, then back up at his face.

This was my brother. This tall, strong figure who knew his place and knew it well. And that woman, the one with the thick, dark hair, she was my sister. That was Josephine.

She stared back at me, her eyes wide and her mouth set with determination.

John gently pushed me in the direction of Kerric's proffered hand. I forced myself to reach out and take it, limping just a bit to reach. Kerric put out another hand and steadied me.

"Is it your leg?" he asked. "Can you walk?"

"Thank you," I said, then again more clearly. "Thank you, yes. I can walk with my staff."

My eyes found Josephine when a small presence made itself known in my mind. Carefully, oh so carefully, I opened a tiny corner of my thoughts to her.

Welcome home, sister. Only that and nothing more. She gave me a small, hopeful smile over the heads of the crowd.

I didn't know how to respond, so I closed off my mind, but I did give her a quick nod of acknowledgement. That woman, sister or not, had me sent away as an infant.

"We won't make you go far." Kerric took my arm and helped me up the steps.

John followed behind. We left the cart and donkey for various servants and groomsmen to handle.

"You must be tired," Kerric said, gesturing to a serving woman on our left. "Rest first, and we'll send Gregor up to look at your leg. We'll talk at dinner. Johnny, a word before you go?"

And in a flurry of activity, he handed me off to two serving girls. Every face I knew disappeared into the crowd, and soon I was engulfed in the darkness of the wide-open doors of the Greathouse.

The two girls led me slowly up one flight of stairs to what appeared to be a guest chamber. It was simple but quite large compared to Mariah's accommodations, which had been the sum of my experience so far. A squat little iron stove nestled in the corner, and two large windows with thick, wavy glass let in plenty of light. A small tub had been positioned behind a screen on the far wall. The bed was bare, but a chest under one window sat open, revealing stacks of bright quilts and furs.

The two girls introduced themselves to me, but I forgot their names immediately and was too ashamed to ask again. They showed me around the room while still more people brought in fresh linens and a bucket of warm water for washing.

After they left, I made good use of the water and more lovely soft soap. I undid my braids and used my fingers to comb my hair, putting it into a single plait over my shoulder to get it out of my way, leaving my three best feathers tucked into the tail end. My dress I took off to air by the open window, and I put on an old but clean dressing gown I had found in the wardrobe.

I sat in a wide armchair by the window and let the autumn breeze chill my flushed skin, feeling fresher and glad to be alone. From there, I had a pleasant view of a quiet alley between the

Greathouse and an outbuilding, the bustling market visible on the left, where the alley entered the courtyard.

Judging by the appetizing scent of baking bread wafting up from the alley, I guessed the outbuilding to be the bakehouse.

How did I get here? How had my life changed so much in just a couple of weeks?

I felt like a piece of driftwood being dragged by a current I couldn't see. I'd always felt like the master of my own life, but that last night with Michael had changed everything. I had no control, no voice, no nothing.

I didn't even know my own story anymore.

My home and my only parent had been taken from me. I had been swept up by John and his men and carried far away. And now here I sat, thrust into a family I didn't choose and didn't know, in a city I'd never even thought of, in a Greathouse made of stone.

TWELVE

Someone knocked on the door, making me jump.

"It's just me and the surgeon, miss!" a woman's voice called.

"Come in," I said, simply because it would have been too difficult to limp to the door.

In came one of the serving girls who had helped me settle in earlier. With her was an elderly man with flyaway white hair and a cane. He wore thick gray and brown robes, with a wide leather belt cinched tightly across his middle.

I stood awkwardly on one leg, and they both paused at the sight of me.

With dawning worry, I realized what I must have looked like. Earlier, I had been dirty and wearing a leather cloak and hood. But now I wore a dressing gown, with my hair swinging in a heavy dark braid. John had said I looked very like Josephine. Had the surgeon and serving girl seen the resemblance as well?

"Feeling better, miss?" the girl asked hesitantly.

"Yes, thank you."

"I was told you needed an injury looked at," the man said. "I'm Gregor. What's your name, young lady?"

"Gwenna."

He eyed me for half a second, then decided not to pursue it. "All right then, Gwenna. Let's see it. Is it your leg, then?"

Gregor examined my wound and cleaned it very carefully, but he pronounced Mariah's treatments to be perfectly acceptable. He showed me how to keep it clean and bandaged, then promised to come back and take out the stitches in a week or two.

"The master's asked to see you as soon as you're ready." The serving girl fetched my dress down from where I had draped it over the window sill. "Would you like some help getting dressed?"

"Um..." I didn't need help, but if I let her leave, how would I find her again? "Yes, all right. Thank you."

She smiled and set about the clearly unnecessary task of pulling the simple gown over my head. I didn't mind, though. Once I was dressed, she immediately offered to take me down to Kerric's study.

In Authe Ida, they built houses and towers that stretched to the sky. Michael had shown me gorgeous prints of an Authe Idan city called Bluewater, and I'd spent hours poring over them. Great swaths of cement buildings rolled along the steep hillsides. They were beautiful but strong enough to withstand the tempest storms blowing in from the sea. Open and airy, the great arches funneled in the ocean breeze to cool the wide courtyards and soaring turrets. One could get lost among those rooms.

But Derehan was not like that. In the north, they used stone and mortar. Our homes were small and squat, with thatched or sod roofs. This Greathouse was little different. It was larger, grander, and had a stone roof supported by great wooden beams, dark with age and smoke. The structure grown in fits and starts, with rooms added as they became necessary. Doors and stairs appeared in strange corners, and the halls made odd angles. Lamps sat unlit in alcoves, useless in the daylight.

The serving girl, Mary—as she reminded me—led me slowly back down to the main hall and to a door set just behind a large column. Low, insistent voices came through the heavy wood, but their meaning was lost in the general noise of the great hall.

Mary knocked and waited for a call to enter before turning the latch. "Miss Gwenna, my lord," she said. With a bob of her head to the room and a quick, reassuring smile, she disappeared into the steady flow of people moving through the main hall.

I hesitated only for a second, but it felt like forever. My heart pounded in my chest. I didn't want to go in. Once I met them, there would be no going back.

But my hand had already pushed the door open. I limped inside and shut it behind me, unable to back out now.

Only three people waited inside. On my left, Josephine and Kerric stood near a large table littered with papers and books. They stared at me, both simultaneously hesitant and anxious. John sat on a wide window seat on my right, staring out at the pleasant garden outside. He didn't look in my direction even once.

Josephine broke the silence first. She came forward and made an abortive gesture of reaching out to me. Ultimately, she had to force herself to take my hand in greeting, but once she did, the warmth in the gesture felt genuine enough.

"Gwenna," she said. "Welcome home. Please, come sit down. Rest your leg and we can talk."

Kerric, set in motion by his sister's example, helped me to the chair. "I'm so sorry that I couldn't greet you properly outside," he said once I was settled.

He sat down opposite me, and Josephine took the chair next to mine. John never moved from the window.

"John has told us some of your journey and that he explained as much to you as he could. Is it true Michael told you nothing?"

Some of our journey? Did he tell them everything? Did they know about the man I had killed?

It was all too much to take in at once. All I could do was nod in confirmation. I glanced over at John, wishing he would say something. I had already gotten used to him handling these things for me.

"I'm sure you have many questions," Josephine said. "But we have had a long time to prepare for your return, and we have a plan in place. The official story is that you are Michael's granddaughter. He lived here in the Greathouse, so you will do the same. He taught you his skills in scribing, so you will join the scholars that work here, in the records room."

I couldn't help but scowl at all this. If Michael had been so well known, if he had lived and worked in this house only eighteen years ago, everyone would know it was impossible for him to have a granddaughter. Who would believe it?

Josephine misunderstood my expression. "It is an honored position. It comes with a seat on the council, which is the main reason why we thought of it for you. You can't live as our sister, but it is your right to have your voice heard."

She paused, possibly giving me time to say something. But when I remained silent, she pressed on.

"There is only one other scribe here in the Greathouse. His name is Wallace. He wasn't—"

I held up my hand to stop her, frowning. She paused, hands clasped in her lap, fingers tight. Kerric didn't wring his hands, but he sat forward, tense all the same. I didn't look at John, but I felt him at the window. He kept his mind open, a pool of still, cool water on a warm day.

I looked from brother to sister, then back again. The time had come for me to take control of my own story. No more lies, no more decisions made for me. They had already chosen where I would live and what job I would do. They had uprooted me as a baby, and now they dared to lay out this tidy path? Eighteen years too late?

"Why?" I asked.

Kerric blinked. "What do you mean?"

"Why was I sent away?"

He turned to Josephine, who looked me squarely in the eye, though her clasped hands shook in her lap.

"You were too powerful. The people were afraid," she said.

"You would lie to me? Still?"

Her eyes widened just a little.

"My whole life has been lies," I said. "I didn't realize at first, but over the past few weeks, I have begun to see them. Michael—" I stopped, suddenly close to tears again. *Damn it.* I blinked them back stubbornly. "It is time for the truth. The whole truth. What did you see about me? John told me that much. You saw something that scared you so badly that I was sent away for it. What was it?"

Josephine stared at me. "Don't ask me that."

"Jo," Kerric said softly. "It's time."

"I have a right to know," I demanded over him.

Josephine couldn't take her eyes off mine. Even she, gifted as she was, even Josephine was afraid of me. "The danger is past now." Her voice trembled. "It doesn't matter anymore."

"It matters to me." I stood up, leaning heavily on my staff, and limped away from my chair. With one hand held out to her, I said, "If you can't say it, then show me."

She didn't get up. "You don't want to see it. It's abominable."

"You're right. I don't," I said firmly. "But I must."

Josephine gazed past me to where John sat in the window. Still, he said nothing. Slowly, hesitantly, she stood up and came to stand before me. I held out my hand to her, but she didn't take it yet.

Her dark eyes bored into mine. "No one can know," she said softly. "No one can *ever* know. After this, I will never relive it again." She took a deep breath, then held out her own hand.

"Wait," John said, getting up. "I want to see it too."

He crossed the room in four steps. John took my staff from me and passed it abruptly to Kerric, then held out his hands to us. He had washed since we arrived, but dirt still clung stubbornly under his nails and in the creases of his palms. His hands probably always looked like this: never quite clean. Working hands.

Josephine turned to me, her eyes questioning. This she would leave to me to decide.

I glanced over at Kerric, who made no move to join us. He sat gripping my staff where it lay on the tabletop, his face a grim mask.

Kerric had no sibylline gift. He couldn't see this if he wanted to.

"Gwen..." John held his hand out to me.

The last time I touched him, I had learned things I would have given anything to unlearn. But when I brushed my mind against his, he was still that cool, calm pool of water. It didn't matter what we had shared the night before. It didn't change who he was. It didn't have to. And no matter what happened, he was a part of this already. He deserved to know.

I took his calloused hand and Josephine's too. She closed the circle by grasping John's other hand.

Josephine spoke directly to our minds, her inner voice smooth as warm tallow.

Come with me.

THIRTEEN

Together we fell, not through the air, but through time itself. Whiteness filled my vision, and a dull roaring drowned out every noise. Only the two hands gripping my own—one slim, one rough—existed in the void.

And then there was screaming.

Not just screaming, but whimpering, begging, sobbing. Many voices rose and fell in agony and loss. Men and women alike, even children. They shrieked in shock and pain.

We still stood in the study, but Kerric was gone. The sun shone brightly through the broken windows. The agonized voices came from the main hall, just outside the door.

Josephine closed her eyes, close to tears already.

"Can I let go?" I asked her.

"We should stay together," she said. "Don't let go of Johnny, at least."

"Wait. What's out there?" he asked.

"Death," she whispered.

The word hit me hard, and I squeezed John's hand hard. Visions of my childhood nightmares flashed before my mind's eye.

They're only dreams, Little Owl.

But the screaming outside Kerric's door made Michael's old reassurances seem as flimsy as wet paper.

"Are we in danger?" John asked.

Josephine sniffed and shook her head. "No. We are like ghosts to them. They won't see or hear us."

"Either way..." His voice was very low. He adjusted his grip on my arm first. He let go of my hand and we grasped wrists instead. He did the same with Josephine.

It probably wasn't necessary, but I felt much more secure.

"Okay, you two can let go now."

"You go first, Gwen," Josephine said. "We'll follow you."

My left hand now free, I limped toward the door, using John's arm for support. I hesitated on the handle and looked up at him. He squeezed my wrist and nodded.

The handle was difficult to turn. John had to lean his shoulder against the door to force it open for me. Something had been in front of it, wedging it shut.

The thing, whatever it was, twitched.

Upon closer inspection, it was clearly a goat, its left horn tied securely to its back leg with a fraying rope so it couldn't stand up straight. Blood and intestines oozed from a large wound in its side. It stared up at nothing, unable to see us, eyes wide and mouth panting. It couldn't get up.

It wouldn't matter soon anyway. The wound in its side was fatal.

Slowly, we all stepped around the pitiful thing on the floor.

The screaming and sobbing was much clearer since we had left the study, and when we rounded the large column blocking the view of the main hall, I understood why Josephine hadn't wanted to return here.

It was my nightmares come to life.

Dozens of people lay sprawled in pools of gore in the main hall, not all of them dead. Some were soldiers, but most weren't.

This wasn't a battle. This was torture for the sake of it. Not even the children had been spared.

I couldn't bear to gaze upon their tiny bodies, and the sobs of those left clinging to life tore at my heart. One woman, her leg ripped mostly away, clung to the body of a small girl. The child seemed uninjured but dead, nonetheless.

It was sickening. Again and again, I reached out to help a woman sit up, to comfort a crying child. But every time, my hand passed through them like vapor. There was absolutely nothing we could do for any of them.

They weren't real. Or possibly, the three of us weren't real.

Of all the people in the hall, only one appeared unhurt—another child, a small girl with long, dark hair and light brown skin. She couldn't have been more than eight or nine years old.

The girl stood with her back to us, focusing on disemboweling a great longhorn bull one piece at a time, as if trying to take apart a large puzzle to figure out how the parts went together. She held a large carving knife in one hand and pulled out ropes of intestines with the other. The girl sang while she did it, a jolly tune children usually recited while playing tag.

"What are you doing!" a harsh voice barked, then gasped. Theo, of all people, pushed her way inside through the open front door. She looked just the same as when I'd seen her during the summer, ancient and bent, with ratty, muddy clothing and a staff adorned with fabric, beads, and bones. Her face contorted into a mask of fury and horror as she took in the scene before her. "What did you *do*?"

The child barely glanced up from the dead bull. "I was bored."

"Bored?" Theo croaked. "*Bored*? If you're bored, we will find something to do! Why did you kill everyone? What sort of message do you think that sends?"

The few people still alive cringed away from Theo when she passed. They didn't even bother asking her for help.

"I didn't kill them." The girl tossed a chunk of liver to the floor. She dug in her knife to try and dislodge the rest. "They killed each other. That woman over there killed her own sister with a hammer."

"Fuck you!" moaned the redheaded woman by the wall, her voice little more than breath.

"Because you made them!" Theo said, ignoring the woman.

The girl threw a piece of flesh to the floor in agitation and finally turned to face Theo. "What do you want me to say? Huh? It's too late now! It's done! Just go home!"

"You stupid girl!" Theo hissed, then froze in a look of strain.

The girl stared at her, focused. She had become the master, and Theo had become a puppet.

"I said to go—" The little girl stopped mid-sentence, but she held Theo frozen in place by the door.

Someone whimpered in fear near the stairs.

The girl looked around, showing us her face for the first time. My heart stopped in my chest.

No.

It couldn't be.

But at the same time, what else had I expected?

Blood covered her face, soaked her clothes, and dripped from her hair. Even so, under all the viscera, we all recognized her. There was no question.

It was me.

The girl searched the empty air where we stood. Younger, corrupted, beautiful.

John's hand tightened on my wrist, and Josephine whimpered. No wonder she feared me. No wonder I'd been sent away. This was what she'd seen about me. This was the me Josephine had been expecting. A monster who tortured others out of boredom.

The girl's face was untouched by the evil she had done, though a permanent frown creased her brow. She was sweet-faced and angelic, even with the blood. The bright red only made her skin glow warmer.

"Who is here?" the girl asked softly in her musical voice.

Josephine sucked in a breath behind us, and I gripped John even tighter.

The girl turned back to Theo, who remained frozen by the door. "Who did you bring here, Theo? Speak!"

"I didn't bring anyone, you little shit!" Theo spat.

"Someone is here! Someone who shouldn't be!"

She turned around again, looking in our general direction. I flinched when her eyes passed over us, but there was nothing for her to see. We were not real.

Weren't we?

The girl dropped the knife with a clatter and climbed barefoot over limbs, slipping on blood. She moved toward us a few steps, then seemed to recognize someone on the floor.

"You!" she hissed. "Brother of mine. What tricks are you playing on me?"

The man she spoke to choked and sputtered on the ground. He shook his head. "Nothing. I don't know." He coughed and tried to edge away from her.

Josephine wept behind us, though only the three of us could hear her. Her sobs came heavy and unrestrained as she watched the little girl's progress.

I couldn't blame her. The man on the ground was Kerric, decades older than when we had left. He had a full beard streaked liberally with gray. He'd lost the trimness of youth, though he held himself with strength, even with blood oozing from the wound in his gut.

The girl stared down at him, her eyes bright. She wasn't bored anymore.

"No," she said. "No, I think it's not you after all." She looked up, again in our direction. The girl reached out with her mind, searching for people who were not there. Her probes felt like wire, light, precise, and sharp.

My heart pounded in my chest. Could she feel us? Could she

feel *me*?

The girl stepped on Kerric's chest, pushing a groan out of him, and kept coming toward us.

Everything in me screamed to run and hide, but I moved a pace toward her anyway. I had to know more. This might be my only chance.

John's grip stayed firm on my wrist. I clung to him as well, but he didn't hold me back. He and Josephine followed behind as I approached the girl.

She stopped just a few feet in front of me, staring into the empty space where I stood.

I knelt down to get on her level, with John clinging to my wrist like a lifeline.

A tear slid down my face. I took in her familiar features. "Is it me that you feel, little one?" I asked, voice shaking.

She perked up immediately. "Who said that?" she asked.

"Who do you hear, Sasha?" Theo asked, still frozen in place by the door.

"Who are you!" the girl shouted in my direction, making me jump. She clearly wasn't used to going unanswered.

"Gwen! Let's go!" Josephine pleaded.

"How can she hear you?" John asked in an urgent whisper.

"You've seen it all! Let's go!" Josephine's voice cracked on a desperate sob.

"Gwen!"

"Gwen, please!"

"Who are you! Where are you!" the girl called Sasha screamed. Her face distorted with rage until even the beauty of youth vanished. "You're tricking me! You can't trick me! Answer me!"

In a flurry of her childish temper, people around the room began screaming and writhing in pain. Those who could stand threw themselves against walls. Those who could not simply tore at their own eyes or thrust fingers into open wounds.

"Gwen!" Josephine screamed.

Only one seemed able to resist the little girl. One man had kept control of his own body, and now he saw his chance. He hauled himself up to his knees while she was distracted, a knife in his hand.

But it was no use in the end. No one could resist her, not fully.

The girl sensed his intentions at the last second. She pivoted to him and glared when he lunged for her. He turned his knife on himself, jamming it into his own throat with a finality that stunned me.

I stared at the man, dread filling my heart. "Wait!" Tears streamed down my face. "Josephine, wait!"

It was too late. She pulled John, and he hauled me back in turn. Not to the broken study, but back to the real world.

"Answer me! Who are you! You're tricking me!"

The horrible little girl's screams followed us and continued ringing in my ears, even after I sat in a huddle on the floor of Kerric's study.

"Are you okay?" John asked. He wrapped me in his strong embrace and helped me sit up.

I couldn't answer, trembling so violently I could barely breathe.

Kerric helped his sister into a chair. She cried quietly and accepted the kerchief he offered.

"Too young, too young," I found myself whispering. "Too young."

"Breathe, Gwen," John said into my hair. "It wasn't real. It can't have been."

"What did you see?" Kerric asked.

He stood next to his sister, just a few feet away. Kerric was young and strong again, with no trace of gray in his thick, dark beard. No gushing wound marred his abdomen.

"Too old." I stared at him over John's shoulder. "I should have been older. Too old."

"Shh," John said. He shook too and squeezed my hands desperately. "Come back to us. How do I help you, Gwenna? What do I do?"

I looked up and found John's face. He was agitated, but he was still that cool, clear pool of water. If I wasn't careful, I would pink that water with blood.

With a cry of alarm, I pushed myself away. I scooted one-legged toward the wall, hands up to keep him away. "Don't!" I sobbed. I was going to be sick. "No! Don't! Stay back!"

"Gwen!" Josephine said miserably. She stood and came toward me as well, but I begged her to keep her distance.

I clutched at the wall from where I sat huddled on the floor. Vomit rose in my throat, but I gulped and forced it down.

Then I couldn't hold it and threw up on the floor. The room spun around me, and I closed my eyes, desperate to stay conscious.

Someone dabbed at my face with a clean cloth. Small hands, a light touch.

"Shh," Josephine said softly. "It didn't happen. We stopped it. It'll never happen."

I looked up at her, my eyes streaming and my mouth sour with vomit. "I'm a monster."

"No!" she said firmly. "You're not."

"I am. Look what I did!"

"You didn't do that. We stopped that from happening!"

"I killed that man!"

Her voice shook, but she set her jaw against the rising panic in her eyes. "It didn't happen, Gwen. It was just a vision that never came true."

She didn't understand. Josephine thought I meant the man in the vision who had tried to stab the little girl. But I meant the man in the woods who had taken me hostage. I had used his own hand against him and ended his life. It had been so easy. Just as easy as it had been for that child in the vision.

Just the same.

Murderer.

Monster.

"She was going to take you." Josephine's voice came thick through the fog in my brain. "Theo was going to take you and turn you into that thing. That is the real reason we sent you away as a baby. To save you from becoming what you saw just now. And we succeeded."

She sat back, gripping my hands in hers.

"We won, Gwen. You never became that monster—that Child. You grew up in the Sacred Wood, close to the earth. Michael taught you to control your gift, and now you are ready to come home. We won. It's over."

I shook my head and covered my face with my hands, surprised to find they weren't covered in blood. How could it possibly be over? As long as I was alive, as long as I had this terrible power, it would never be over.

"No, no!" I begged with my eyes for them to hear me. "You don't understand!"

"Help us understand!" Josephine said.

"That was me! It is me! I am the...the Child of the Prophecy. I've always known it, deep down. No matter what you did to stop it, I am still me! It will never be over!"

"Gwen, it's not—"

"No!" I screamed, clutching at my head. I couldn't get the visions of that little girl covered in blood, of the dismembered bodies, of the crying, terrified children, out of my head.

"Focus, Gwen!" John rubbed at his own temple.

"Focus?" I hissed at him. "Focus! You want me to focus?" I hauled myself to my feet, glaring at John. They weren't listening. They didn't understand. I clenched both fists at my sides, blood roaring through my ears. "Fine! I'll focus!"

All three of them collapsed. They fell into crumpled heaps on the floor so suddenly that, for a moment, I didn't comprehend what had happened.

My heart stopped. Oh hell, what had I done? Were they dead? I'd done it again! Murderer. My only family...My only friend who knew what I was and never feared me.

Not again.

"No," I said breathlessly. "I'm sorry! I'm sorry!" I hobbled to Josephine in a panic and felt her pulse.

Her heart beat steadily under my fingers, and her chest rose and fell in easy breaths. I reached with my mind, confirming that Kerric and John were both alive as well.

Sleeping. I had made them sleep, that's all.

With sobs of relief, I slid down the wall and huddled there on the floor, as far from the pool of vomit as my injured leg would allow. I wrapped my head in my arms and cried for several minutes, alone in that silence and misery while I waited for them to wake up.

Only sleep, sure, but still monstrous. It was still an invasion. I had overstepped so badly, had lost control so completely. What would Michael say? He'd be so disappointed.

And then I remembered Michael was dead, and he was a liar, and I loved him, and he was gone.

I was a monster, and I was alone.

FOURTEEN

Kerric woke first. He sat up, rubbing his eyes like he'd just had a nap and was confused why he had done it on the floor of his study. Kerric looked around, noticing his sister and John still sleeping next to him, and me in a huddle by the wall, crying.

He dropped his hand, expression wary. "Gwen?" he said cautiously.

"I'm so sorry," I whispered between sobs. "I didn't mean to."

He got up and went straight to Josephine. Once satisfied she was only sleeping, as he had been, he turned his attention to me. Kerric came over to where I sat, knees drawn up and face streaming, and knelt by me.

He reached out tentatively to grip my arm, not aggressive, but comforting. I stared at his hand, then back up at his face.

Now that I looked, his features strongly favored Josephine's. Probably mine as well. We each had the same wide, brown eyes, dark hair, and fine mouth. His features were much broader, and his beard obscured his jaw, but we were, all three, essentially the same.

"Are you okay?" he asked.

My breath came in violent hics while the hysteria subsided. "I don't...know."

He nodded, then helped me get up and sit at the table.

About the time Kerric placed a cup of water in front of me, John sat up with a jerk. His violent movement caused Josephine to gasp and open her eyes.

Kerric glanced at his sister before turning back to me. And it hit me.

Josephine wasn't his only sister.

She wasn't the only person in the room he was concerned about and felt responsible for.

He had two sisters: her and me.

I knew this, of course. It was something John had told me two days before. But it hadn't felt real until just now. Not until Kerric pushed the cup of water into my shaking hands and sat next to me to make sure I drank it.

I took a sip simply because I didn't know what else to do with myself. It felt like nothing in my mouth. I only swallowed it because I couldn't spit it back out.

Josephine came and sat on my other side. She put her hand on my arm and squeezed. Maybe it was just to prove to me—or to herself—that she wasn't afraid. Maybe it was to comfort me.

Perhaps it was both.

"I'm so sorry." I looked up at Johnny so he would know I was speaking to him as well. "I didn't mean to do it. I'm sorry."

"We know." With determination, Josephine pulled me into a tight hug.

I froze in her arms. This woman was a stranger, regardless of any blood ties we had. But she hugged me like we had grown up together, as sisters should. "We'll figure it out," she said into my hair before pulling back to arm's length. "Whatever it is, we'll figure it out. I know that was a shock, but try and remember...it didn't happen."

I closed my eyes and shook my head. She still did not understand.

Maybe I hadn't tortured dozens of people out of boredom, but I had killed a man. And I had just rendered all three of them unconscious by force. I was still that little girl, just on a different path.

I was still that *thing*.

"There's someone I'd like you to meet," Kerric said from my other side. "My son. Will you come outside?"

Josephine frowned up at him. "Not now, Kerric. Surely."

"Now," he said firmly. "Will you come, Gwen?"

I rubbed my face with my sleeve, which was tear-streaked and dirty. It felt like I had been in this room for days, clawing to keep my own sanity. I didn't want to meet anyone else just now, but I also didn't want to tell him no.

"Kerric, let the girl recover a bit," Josephine insisted. She handed me a kerchief to use in place of my sleeve.

He wavered. "What if I called him here, to this room? Would you meet him here, Gwen?"

"I don't think now is the best time," I said, scrubbing at my eyes. "I would like to go back to my room. I need time to think."

"Of course," Josephine said. "We'll introduce you to Garreth another day. Here, let me help you."

She passed my staff to me when I stood, but I wobbled. John appeared at my side, as I knew he would. He put a hand to my elbow to steady me.

"Can I help you?" he asked in a low voice.

I passed a hand over my face so I couldn't look him in the eye, endlessly tired and uncertain. Here he stood, so reliable. John didn't pick me up or insist; he just asked.

I didn't want him to touch me, but at the same time, I didn't care anymore. I just wanted to sleep. My legs ached: one from the slow-healing wound and the other from overuse. My head burned with the visions we had shared. My heart throbbed with fear.

At least John wasn't afraid.

"Yes," I said. "Thank you."

"I'll take her upstairs, then I'll be back to discuss Metaxas," John said to the others, to my siblings. Then with a gentleness I had come to expect, he lifted me and stepped outside.

He said nothing while he carried me back up the stairs to the room I had been given. A large potted plant stood sentry in an alcove to the left of my door, a welcome landmark in these twisting halls. I pointed out the door with the staff.

He stood me carefully in front of the door and opened it for me. I hobbled inside and sat on the bed. John hovered by the open door.

"I'll have someone bring up a tray," he said. "I know you're not familiar with how a Greathouse runs, but the people here are happy to help. If you need something, ask anyone."

I nodded, unable to look up from the floor.

"And if you ever need anything from me, just call out. I'll hear you."

"Thank you," I said.

He hesitated for half a minute, silent. Then he stepped into the hallway, closing the door behind him.

A short time later, someone knocked and let themselves in. It was Mary, the serving girl from before. She set a covered tray on the table by the window. I watched her from the bed while she straightened a chair and tied back a curtain, which had come loose. She bobbed her head to me politely and left.

A savory and salty aroma wafted out from under that cover. My stomach growled, but I couldn't will myself to crawl out of bed. I burrowed in the heavy quilts and drowsed the rest of the evening, trying desperately to make sense of what I had seen and learned in Kerric's study.

There were so many unanswered questions. Why had Kerric been so old when Sasha was still a child? How had Sasha heard me speak? And what of the dead place? John had said Josephine knew about Theo's sanctuary, but I neither saw nor heard anything about it in that vision. Had she seen something else as well? Was there *another* vision? One she did not wish to share?

The questions chased each other about my head, but I kept coming back to that one thing Sasha had screamed over and over.

Who's tricking me! You can't trick me!

How? *How* had she heard me?

FIFTEEN

I woke the next morning to the sound of timid knocking and peeled my eyes open in confusion. Michael and I lived in a one-room hut in the hollow. There were no doors to knock on.

My bed was too soft and too large. Thick, down pillows obstructed my view of the room, which was stuffy and bright at the same time, the air still. This wasn't home.

"Gwen? It's Josephine." Her voice came muffled but clear through the heavy, wooden door.

And with her voice came the rushing memories of all that had happened in the last two weeks.

This was my new home. My new bedroom in the Greathouse of Valheid.

I sat up groggily and rubbed my face to clear my mind. The heavy glass windows were closed, and the thick air lay over me like another blanket. The sun streamed in, illuminating too-bright patches on the wooden floors, which had been worn smooth over the years.

When I didn't answer, Josephine called again. "Can I come in?"

Come in.

She turned the knob and peeked around the door. When she saw me dragging myself out from under the covers, she came the rest of the way in.

Josephine wore a thick, cream-colored bolero over her simple work dress to ward off the autumn chill. It looked soft, like fuzzy wool. I wanted to touch it, which was an odd thought to have in that moment, considering the circumstances.

"I'm sorry to wake you," she said. The door latched behind her. "I'm sure you're exhausted. Visions take a lot out of me too. Especially ones that intense."

I hung my feet over the edge of the bed but did not stand, just stared at the floor. What did you say to a person after screaming at them, vomiting on yourself, and forcing them to sleep against their will? After seeing what we had seen together?

What could she possibly think of me?

"Are you feeling better?" she asked.

That was easy enough. "Yes. I slept most of yesterday and all night."

She nodded. "I'm not surprised."

A short silence followed. Josephine seemed comfortable to be quiet, but I was in knots over the events of the day before. She stepped over to the window and pushed it open to let in a little air.

"I'm sorry, again," I said. "About yesterday. I lost control."

She smiled. "Don't worry. No harm done."

I turned away. She still didn't understand. No harm? How could she say such a thing?

No, I couldn't stay silent.

"You don't seem to understand, Josephine." I put everything into my voice to keep it from shaking. She absolutely *had* to believe me. "You did save me. You did. That—" A memory of blood and screaming made me falter.

And for a few seconds, I thought maybe I could still feel that girl, like she stood right there in the room with us. My eyes fell on a spot by the window, but there was nothing. Only dust motes floating in the bright beams of sunlight.

Was this what Sasha had felt in the vision? An unknown presence standing just over there, in the empty air? Another me?

But no, she was not real. She was simply a vision that never came true.

I powered on. "That disaster was averted. You stopped me from doing so many terrible things when you sent me away. But you have not changed who I am."

"And who is that?" she asked.

"I am still the Child of the Prophecy, just on a different path. I am still that thing that can take over a person's body with half a thought."

"I disagree," she said.

"How can you possibly say that?"

Josephine pulled the armchair away from the window so she could sit facing me. The sleeves of her bolero came right down over her hands, with only her slim fingers sticking out to tangle together. It looked cozy.

"That vision has plagued me for years, Gwenna. Years. I have watched it and many others just like it, over and over. I have lived it. I have become very familiar with Sasha. I forced myself to come right up next to her and watch her face as she did these heinous things. I've made it my purpose to understand her, and I have lived in dread of the day you came home. I was..." She paused, looking for words. "I was terrified, Gwen, that I would see her in your face."

I didn't speak or move. Josephine gathered herself, twisting a loose thread from my quilt around one finger until it hurt.

"But I don't see her in you. I don't." She leaned forward and took both my hands in hers. "I see *you*, Gwen. I don't see the monster from that vision. And do you know why?"

I shook my head.

"Because you still feel shame. John told me what happened with the thief in the woods that night. He told me what you did, and that scared me. But he also told me that you were horrified by it. And after you made us sleep, you were truly sorry. That's the difference. Don't you see?"

My eyes began to fill. Her words made sense, but they were still hard to believe. I didn't know how to convey the ease with which I had killed that man. Not just the ability, but the willingness. It was a truth I tried not to think about.

If I were in that position again, if it was my life or someone else's, I would do the same thing. It felt right. It was a solution.

But maybe Josephine was right. Behind the ease came shame and horror. I didn't want to be a monster. But that girl that I could have been? Sasha? She didn't care.

"So maybe you still have the same abilities, and maybe that's power one person shouldn't have, but we sent you away so that you could learn to control that power with morality. And in that, we were successful. Michael did what we asked of him."

When I still could not respond, Josephine continued.

"Let me ask you one thing, and maybe that will convince you. Could you ever imagine yourself doing any of the things Sasha was doing in that vision?"

Again I saw the blood, the manipulation, and the dead eyes of that little girl I could have been. "No," I said immediately. "No, never."

But even as I said the words, I thought of that man in the vision, the one who had rushed Sasha and had been killed for it. I had done that. There was no hypothetical about it. I had killed a man who had threatened me. I had done exactly the same as Sasha.

But that was different. That had been reasonable.

Right?

"There you go," she said, unaware of my continued doubt. "You are not Sasha. You never will be."

I nodded. Yes. Maybe if I was determined, I could believe it some day. It made sense. It did. It just didn't feel like the truth yet.

Josephine smiled a little too kindly. "I'm so glad you're home," she said.

It was a half-truth. She knew I could tell, and she'd said it anyway.

"There's something I don't understand," I said.

"What's that?"

"In the vision, Sasha was still a child, but everyone else had grown old. Kerric had gray hair. But he's only, what, ten years older than me?"

"He was fourteen when you were born and sent away."

"So that means Sasha should have been middle-aged as well, but she was still a child. Not even ten."

Josephine was nodding. "Yes, I've seen that as well. I didn't understand it for a very long time, but I have a theory. Have you been to the dead place? Or seen it, maybe?"

"Theo took me there a few months ago. And John said you knew about it."

"Yes, I know about it. I haven't been there, but I've seen it, and I've seen Sasha and Theo talking about it in my visions. From what I can tell, it's right out of this world. Entirely separate. I think Theo lives there, and I think she would have taken you to live there, had she gotten her hands on you as a baby."

"And?"

"My theory is strange, but considering the evidence, I think it must be true. Theo has been old for decades, maybe longer. Our grandfather knew of her when he was young, and she always looked the same. And he wasn't the only one. It's common knowledge that she does not age the same way the rest of us do. There are stories about her passed down through the generations, and yet she does not die. I think it's because of the time she spends in the dead place. I think either there is no time there or maybe she has found some magic there that stops her aging."

"That is strange," I said. "How could such a thing be true?"

"I don't know. As I said, it's only a theory. But these visions about Sasha only support it. She never grows up, even though everyone else does. And I think this may be part of what makes her so vicious. Her formative years were poisoned by Theo, and those years were stretched on and on until she lost all concept of humanity. Combine that with the ability to do anything and everything a child could ever want, and you get a monster."

I stared at her in astonishment.

"And that only supports what I was saying before, Gwen. You are not the Child. You were not poisoned the way Sasha was. You have the abilities, but we saved you from that corruption."

"I could believe it," I said, almost to myself. "There is no life there. The dead place, you call it? Yes, it is dead there. Theo called it a Sanctuary. But it felt wrong."

"It's the silence," Josephine said. "Maybe it's different being there for real, but in my visions, it is so quiet and dry."

I nodded. "No weather. No life. It makes sense that there would be no time."

After another minute of silence, I spoke again. "So, what now?"

Josephine heaved a large breath. "Well, you're home. Now you settle in. Did you give much thought to our ideas about making you a scribe with Wallace?"

Just the mention of the offered position lay on my shoulders like a load of grain. "I'm so tired."

She nodded, getting up. "Of course you are. You've been through so much. You should rest. We'll talk about this later."

"No," I cut in. "Not physically tired. I'm tired of the lies and the secrets. I'm tired of being afraid, Josephine. I'm so tired."

"You don't have to be afraid anymore. Not here."

"No, there will always be fear." I shook my head and rubbed my eyes with my palms. "I'm no good with words. I never had to use them much, so forgive me if I'm not clear."

"It's okay. Just take your time."

I closed my eyes to help me think. It was the same sort of thing John would do when he searched for the right way to say a thing. He'd screw up his eyebrows and wait patiently for the words to come.

I forced myself to slow down and allow the words to come out. After a long, quiet minute, they came. "I've lived a lie my whole life," I said finally. "I didn't know it, but I did. Michael lied to me from the beginning."

Josephine nodded, but she didn't interrupt.

"And then when I left the Wood, I lived a lie then too. I pretended I was normal and that Michael had been my grandfather. That was harder because I constantly worried they'd figure it out. And that night with the thief..." I stopped, carefully negotiating my thoughts around that subject. "John told the men a different lie about me, and I had to pretend it was true. And now that I'm here, Josephine, what am I supposed to do? Continue lying about who and what I am for the rest of my life? Is that really what you want me to do?"

Her face fell slowly into a frown while I spoke, but still she did not interrupt.

"You want me to live here and be a scribe so that I can be on the council while pretending I'm not your sister."

"You don't have to be a—" she began.

"I won't do it," I said. "I won't lie to everyone here and live in dread of the day they figure it out. Because it won't go well when that day comes. It will start as a rumor. People knew Michael. They knew he was childless. They knew he left the same time Sasha 'died.' And then his granddaughter, who looks exactly like the lady of the house, comes back eighteen years later? How can people not know?"

"They won't argue with the official statement," she insisted.

That was what John had said as well. Had he been parroting Josephine, or did he believe it as well?

"Maybe not," I agreed. "But they will talk amongst themselves. It will be unspoken knowledge. And the first time something goes wrong or I slip up, they will say it out loud, and we will be blamed. They will call us all liars. You will lose any trust you had. And when you lose the trust of your people, you lose your rule. And me? I will lose everything."

"You can't know that will happen."

"And you can't know it won't," I said sharply, causing her mouth to snap shut. A pang of regret stopped the words in my mouth.

I continued with a deliberately calmer tone.

"We can't know how any of this will turn out. We can't. All we can do is our best right now, and I refuse to live a lie. I won't do it, Josephine. And if you or Kerric can't abide me living here as myself or if you think the people won't tolerate it, then I'll leave. As soon as my leg is well enough for me to walk, I'll go where no one cares who my family is or what my abilities are. At least that way I can live in peace."

My sister studied my face for an endless moment. Her forehead creased in a deep frown. "If you live openly as our sister, the people will know that you are sibylline. It's common knowledge."

I nodded once, fear creeping into my chest.

"The people already know about me. They think they're sly about it, but I've heard the whispers. They're not afraid of me, but they pretend not to know."

"So you're saying if I live openly, that means I'm forcing you to do the same."

"Yes."

"Are you asking me to hide so that you can continue hiding?"

She pursed her lips.

"Will there be unrest?"

Josephine shook her head quickly. "There will be scandal, I think. But Derehan has long been a place of safety, a place where the sibyllines are allowed to pretend and blend in. If there were ever a place or a time to live openly as a mindwalker, it is here and now."

"If you don't want me to claim my birthright, I won't," I said. "But I won't stay here and live a lie either. I'll just move on."

She put a hand on my arm and squeezed comfortingly, but her expression betrayed her worry. "What about Aris?"

I raised my eyebrows. "You think he'll run? You think he'll rescind his offer for a marriage alliance with you?"

"He's Authe Idan. They don't look so kindly on the sibyls."

"You want him to look kindly on you?"

"I want—" She broke off, suddenly looking like a girl with a crush. And for a moment, we didn't feel like grand ladies deciding the fate of our country. We were just sisters talking about a wedding and a man. "I want to be able to consider it," she said carefully.

I laughed. "Well, he saw with his own eyes what I am, and he stayed."

"He doesn't know you're my sister."

"If he's going to be your husband, he should know."

Josephine sat back in her chair and stared at the floor. "I should tell him, shouldn't I?"

"Yes, you should," I said without hesitation. "Before this goes too far, he should know what he's getting into."

She smiled at me and nodded. "Yes, you're right. Of course, you're right. We have a council meeting tomorrow. I had planned to bring up the alliance to the council before I made my decision. I should speak with Aris before that."

"Yes."

"And I don't want you to move on either," she said seriously. "This is your home. You should stay here with us, if that is what you want."

"Thank you," I said, and I meant it.

"That means you'll be at the council meeting as well. Kerric will have to claim you as his sister. And you will need to meet everyone, let them see that you're real."

I nodded my understanding and ignored the flash of anxiety that accompanied her matter-of-fact pronouncement.

"It's high time I stopped pretending anyway," she said, moving toward the door. "Maybe you're right. No more lies."

"No more lies."

Sixteen

The council room was less grand than I expected: long and low, with a huge table dominating the room. Fruits and finger foods had been laid out on the table, along with pitchers of various jewel-colored drinks. Additional chairs had been lined along all four walls to accommodate the bloated roster of council members.

I wasn't the last person to arrive, but neither was I the first. The room already buzzed with more than a dozen people. They had grouped into twos and threes, talking amongst themselves.

No one noticed me slip in behind Josephine and claim a seat under one of the great, open windows, where the fresh air washed in over my shoulders.

Jo had spent most of the day before helping me gather up a bit of a wardrobe. I had come to the Greathouse with nothing at all. No underthings, no work pants, nothing. The only thing I owned was the too-large homespun Mariah had given me after tossing my ruined leathers.

"If nothing else, you must have something appropriate for the council meeting tomorrow," she said.

And after many objections, alterations, and requests from me, I now owned a "best dress."

I had never thought much about clothes before. They were just a way to keep warm and protect your skin. But here, appearances mattered. Josephine insisted I wear a full skirt belted low on my waist. Though my linen shirt was plain and efficient, elaborate vines and flowers crawled along the hem of my skirt—a traditional style for highborn women.

And after noticing how my eye kept falling to her bolero, she produced a second one from her own room.

"I couldn't," I protested, even as my fingers itched to reach out and stroke the fuzzy, soft wool.

"Of course you can," Josephine said with a smile, pressing it into my hands.

This one was a muted bluish gray and had some cabling along the sleeves. I wore it to the council meeting as well, my hands buried within, cozy and warm.

She selected a skirt to match mine out of solidarity, though hers was dyed a brilliant, eye-catching blue.

My sister did not usher me or hover. She smiled when I took my out-of-the-way seat, then off she went to speak with someone on the far side of the room.

I looked around and was grateful to have taken Josephine's advice. At least half of the women gathered there wore clothes very similar to my own. Even with my feathers, I disappeared into the background, and no one looked at me twice.

The council meeting wouldn't begin for several minutes. More and more people entered, calling greetings to each other, grasping hands, and clapping backs. This didn't feel like a council meeting. It felt like some kind of reunion.

They were an odd and varied bunch. Many of them I would expect to see at such a function: military, wealthy landowners, scribes, governors. But those were the minority. Most of the men and women surrounding me wore simple clothes, many of them still filthy from the fields. They were rough, hardy-looking people. Laborers, tradesmen, and farmers.

"Do you mind if I sit with you?"

I jumped and turned to find John standing a few paces away. He'd finally had a proper wash and a good rest. John wore a well-fitting wool sweater, worked over with great skill to create intricate cables and knots down the front, paired with comfortable pants and simple, clean boots. Gone was his bandolier of knives and the healthy layer of dirt I had grown accustomed to. The sun bounced off his short curls.

So, one person had noticed me, after all. The discomfort curled in my chest, but I chose to ignore it. John had only ever been a friend to me—maybe my first friend. It wasn't his fault there was a prophecy about us. It wasn't anyone's fault. It just was.

"No, I don't mind," I said.

He sat heavily in the chair next to mine and leaned forward, elbows on knees. John didn't speak at first, so I returned to watching the growing crowd. After a few minutes, I forgot he was there at all, so when he did speak at last, I jumped again.

"Is your leg healing well?" The corner of his mouth turned up when I startled.

"Oh, uh, yes. I suppose. I'm afraid to even try to walk on it now. I don't want to tear the stitches like I did that—" I cut myself off, unwilling to mention that terrible night the week before. I didn't know if I ever could.

"I don't blame you." John pulled down the shoulder of his beautiful sweater and showed me a nasty scar that blotched his upper arm. "I won't go into details, but I know what it is to tear a stitch out. It's not an experience I'd like to repeat either."

He pulled his shirt back up before I'd finished looking, but it didn't feel right to press the topic. So I changed the subject.

"I didn't expect to see so many laborers and tradesfolk here today."

John nodded. "Yes, Kerric is very much a man of the people. Do you know much about how the Council is selected?"

"Yes. Michael made sure I understood how the government of Derehan was run. Only recently did I understand he was preparing me"—I gestured broadly at the room—"for this."

John smirked again but did not comment on that. "So you know there are some positions that are entitled to a seat on the Council. Scholars, governors.I got one as an emissary. The military gets three seats: one for the general and two for captains. There's Cynebald, the general."

He pointed out a broad, graying man with a battle axe strapped to his belt. The man was talking with Kerric, his expression serious.

"And the two captain seats are elected, correct?" I asked.

John nodded. "Elected by the soldiers every four years. There's Graham there, but I don't see Editha yet." He pointed out Graham, another rough-looking man but leaner than his general and much younger. "And then, of course, you have the landowners. If Kerric wants to make use of their resources and fighters, he has to make nice with them. But they're not all bad. That's Nanette there. She has extensive landholdings north of Valheid, in Purgo. She rarely misses a Council because she lives so close. We rarely see Leland, on the other hand, which is probably for the best. He's a pest. Oh, damn. There he is, actually."

I followed his gaze to a robust man with a colored jewel on each finger and a goblet of wine in one fist. He spoke animatedly with two men, who both appeared desperate for an excuse to leave the room.

"Just a pest?" I asked.

John nodded. "Usually. Sometimes, he says things that can start an avalanche, though. His lands are near Silda. Three days' ride. Five if you're bringing an entourage. Come to think of it, he's probably only here for the feasting this weekend."

"And the laborers? Kerric appointed them all?"

A young woman sat in the corner, spinning thread on a drop spindle. She couldn't afford to stop working, not even for a council meeting.

John nodded. "He makes liberal use of that particular power. It seems like he appoints someone new every month. I admire the sentiment, but it's getting crowded in here."

"And this month it's me?"

He glanced at me, eyes wry, and rested his chin on his clasped hands. "You're not appointed. You have a right to be here, as a member of the ruling family. You're a Moore."

My brows drew together. A member of the ruling family? It still didn't feel real. I was just the Little Owl. I should be in a tree right now, watching a snare set out to catch my dinner.

"Are you really going to tell everyone?" John sounded worried.

I took a deep breath and nodded.

"Are you sure that's wise?"

"It's the only wise thing to do. It will be hard, though."

"What do you mean?"

I pursed my lips, considering, and dug my fingers into the plush sleeves of my new bolero. "You said Leland can start an avalanche with just a few words. Well, it's the same with me. Lies beget lies. If I start lying now, the avalanche will come. Maybe now, maybe in a few years. But it will come." I forced myself to turn toward him. "No one should have the power I have, Johnny. But I do. I have it, and there's nothing to be done about it. I have to be careful, or people will get hurt."

He watched me with pensive eyes, nodded, then looked away. John said nothing more about it.

I opened my mouth to speak, to change the subject again. I wanted him to point out more people, tell me more names. And I wanted to move past this dense feeling between us. But a loud voice cut across the growing din of the crowd.

"Oi! My lord! I don't see as anyone's missing!"

Another voice called out, a woman this time. "Aye. Are we ready to get started?"

People began moving toward chairs, either at the table or beside John and me along the wall, before Kerric could call out his agreement and start the meeting.

"Yes, yes!" Kerric strode toward his chair at the head of the table, with Josephine on his right. "Everyone, settle in. We have a lot to talk about today!"

When someone tried to sit on Kerric's left, he stopped them with a soft word and a shake of his hand. He then took the chair, pulled it out, and tipped it forward to lean against the tabletop: a clear sign that no one was to occupy that particular seat. Though this earned him several pointed looks and a few whispers, no one asked him about it.

"Right!" Kerric said, standing at the head of the table. "Is everyone present and ready to begin?"

A rumble of agreement reverberated from the Council, and a few people banged plates, goblets, and fists on the table. Kerric smiled, raising his hands for quiet.

"Welcome everyone! I'm glad to see some of our far-flung members have made it in today. Thank you for taking the time. I am especially glad to see such a full room today, of all days, for there are some unusually important items to discuss. There is more tension in the south, but that's business as usual. We have some trade items with New Ambia and Authe Ida to talk over. Shall we start with old business? Bethanne? What came of the talks with New Ambia last month?"

And so, the meeting began. The discussion went smoothly, considering how many people were present. Such a crowd should have invited chaos, but people waited their turn and rarely spoke over each other. A matter was introduced, discussed, then voted on by a show of hands.

From my studies with Michael, I knew Kerric had the power to enact laws in any way he liked, but in every matter, he chose to follow the majority will of the Council. Everything was carefully recorded by the scholar sitting next to Josephine, who John identified as Wallace.

"Nervous, but honest," John said of Wallace. "He hardly ever speaks up, but he's worth listening to when he does."

John kept up a running commentary during the discussions, telling me names when people stood to speak. It was difficult to both keep an ear on the meeting and focus on what John said to me, but it was valuable information and worth the effort. If I was going to stay here, these people would be my peers.

After about two hours, the old business concluded. Kerric announced a break, but very few people left the room. Mostly, they just stood up and resumed talking amongst each other.

I drew more and more sidelong looks. Very few people recognized me, and those who did knew I had just arrived from the south only a few days before, and nothing else. What business did I have in a Council meeting?

The woman John had identified as Nanette, one of the wealthier landowners from just north of Valheid, came and introduced herself during the break.

"Hello, my dear," she said, stalking right up to me with a welcoming smile. Her own full skirt swished gracefully around her legs as she strode forward. "I don't believe we've met before. I am Nanette Graves."

"Gwenna," I replied, taking her hand without standing.

Nanette was a tall, middle-aged woman with striking gray hair swept up at the nape of her neck. I imagined it was quite long, to be able to swirl the way it did. She wore very little jewelry, in sharp contrast with Leland the Pest, who had on far too much.

"And where do you hail from, my dear?"

"Here, actually. I was born here in Valheid. Though I have been living south of Barano most of my life."

"I was under the impression that there wasn't much directly south of Barano. Aside from the Sacred Wood, I mean."

"There isn't, ma'am," I said, then quickly changed the subject. "John tells me you live quite near here." I turned to have John confirm it, but he had disappeared. The sight of his empty seat sent a small jolt of panic through me.

"Quite true. My estate is only half a day's ride from here, and I have a regular room here in the Greathouse. Kerric is very accommodating. But then again, he is likely only so for the sake of our grain reserves and chattel." She laughed slyly and winked, which prompted me to smile back. *Truly* smile. She was funny, this woman. And kind as well.

"Oh really, Nanette," Kerric said, coming up behind her and squeezing her shoulder. "As if I could ever tell you no. Even if you had nothing to your name, you could still charm anyone out of house and home."

"Only you, my boy!" she countered with a laugh. "Only you are so easy to charm. Tell me, why have you not introduced our new member to us? She seems quite nice, though I've only just met her."

Kerric smiled. "All in good time, my friend."

"Oh, nonsense," she snorted, then raised her voice to catch everyone's attention. "Our lord and master is keeping secrets, my friends! Come now, Kerric! Introduce our new member to the Council."

"Hear, hear!" someone shouted over the growing quiet.

The crowd's attention was captured.

Kerric scowled at Nanette for half a second, clearly put out at having his plans derailed.

He caught my gaze next, eyebrows raised in a silent question.

I took a deep breath and nodded. The time had come, and there was no sense in putting it off any longer.

SEVENTEEN

Kerric strode to the head of the table, addressing the whole room as he went. "I had hoped to introduce Gwen near the end of the session, but I see you cannot be put aside. Everyone, please resume your places."

I stayed where I was and dug my nails into my thighs in agitation. Nanette gave me another wink before returning to her own chair.

John reappeared and slipped back into the seat next to me, eyebrows drawn together. "Are you ready?" he asked in an undertone.

I nodded. After all, I didn't have any choice. I had to be ready. The time had come.

With shaking hands, I gripped the fabric of my skirt, and John noticed.

"If you start to panic, remember, you can focus it on me."

"I'm not going to do that again," I said.

"Just the same."

"Friends!" Kerric called out, smothering John's soft words. "My honorable Council, I have something very strange to tell you today. As I said, I'd hoped to hold this until the end for fear it would disrupt our discussions, but I see that's not to be. I ask that you please listen to what I have to say and hold all questions until I have finished."

This last request was entirely ignored by one man halfway down the table. "Is this your way of announcing another child on the way, Kerric? By the Old Kind, this is a lot of preamble!"

There were a few chortles down the table, and even Kerric smirked. "No, Mark. It's nothing like that. Please listen."

When attentive silence finally fell, Kerric took a deep breath and began.

"As many of you know, Josephine and I are not the only two children in our family. For those of you who aren't aware—or for those who may have a distorted version of the story—let me tell you about our sister, Sasha."

I closed my eyes at the sound of my given name. But I was not Sasha. That thing, *she* was Sasha. Not me.

A different kind of silence descended on the crowded room. The smiles and smirks disappeared. People sat straight forward in their seats. Even the spinster in the corner stopped her spindle in her hands, the loose thread butterflied between her pinky and thumb.

Enough of my story had already been whispered about for the past eighteen years. Everyone had at least heard of it. Whispered, but never spoken aloud. This was a subject none of them had ever thought to hear of again.

"She was born nearly nineteen years ago, and our mother died giving birth to her," Kerric continued into the stillness. "As many of you know, her sibylline gifts were quite strong, even as an infant. Her abilities were like none any of us had ever heard of before. Everyone was affected. She touched everyone for miles. It was not well tolerated amongst the people, and who could blame them?"

He hesitated, taking a shaky breath.

"There was a mob. Good people, driven by fear, were killed. I was still a boy then, only fourteen years old, but I remember it well. Many of you remember the event. Some of you were there."

Josephine sat stone-faced in her seat. She wasn't the only one. Several people squirmed in their chairs or looked away from Kerric's steady gaze.

I crammed my fists around wads of the soft sleeves, which fell over my hands. My fault. The mob had been because of me. My fault.

John watched me, but he didn't try to touch me. Maybe before Barano, I would have welcomed a comforting squeeze of the hand, but it wasn't so easy anymore.

"Shortly after that," Kerric said, "Sasha died. I know there were several rumors about her death. Some said we killed her to save the city from further unrest. Some said her mental gifts were too much for her infant body to cope with. Some said she simply died from an illness. Coincidence."

More silence sucked up these words. The room was stagnant with it.

Kerric stood straight, bracing himself for the final truth. "I am here to tell you that all of it was a lie. Our youngest sister did not die that day eighteen years ago. She was sent away with Michael Gray, to live in solitude and master her gifts in peace."

A murmur rose amongst the Council members. It was the sound of a high wind blowing through pines. As one, every person in that room turned to stare at me. Every last one of them understood what Kerric was driving at.

Kerric said the next part quite loudly to be heard over the gust of voices. "I would like to formally introduce the Council to Gwenna Moore, born Sasha Moore, my youngest sister and lady of this Great House of Valheid."

And then he took the chair on his left, the one he had leaned against the table so no one could sit in it, and sat it upright once more. Then he waited, watching me.

I stared at the empty chair. Everyone stared at me, their voices a low rumble in the big room.

"Come, sister, and take your place at my side," Kerric said.

John nudged me with his elbow. When that didn't work, he all but pushed me out of the chair and onto my feet.

I stood wobbling, grasping my staff.

Walk, Gwenna. Just move your feet. Just move. The rest comes later.

My feet began to move. Everyone watched my halting limp across the room. Everyone watched as I approached the chair. Everyone watched as Kerric pulled that chair out for me and helped me sit.

I looked across the table and caught Josephine's eye, her expression set. She knocked politely at my mental walls, asking to speak with me. I let her into a corner of my thoughts.

So far so good, she said. *You're doing well. Now face them. Show them who you are.*

I swallowed, then did as she recommended. I turned in my seat, willing the fear out of my expression, and faced the council.

They all stared back at me with a wide range of expressions, from stern to agape to outright fear, but every one of them fell silent again. Several people near the far end of the table actually stood up in an attempt to see me better.

"Thank you for your attention," Kerric said when it was clear the entire room had stalled. "This is a shock, I know. We invite your questions."

"Yeah, I have a question," said a gruff man halfway down. John hadn't mentioned his name yet, but he wore heavy working clothes still filthy from the fields. "I see you've set the girl on your left, in a place of honor. You've called her a lady of the house. Why was this decision made without consulting the Council?"

Kerric set his mouth. As impertinent as the question was, he seemed resolved to answer it calmly. "No decision has been made, Stephen. Gwen is a lady of this house, regardless of any Council.

She is my sister. And I am sitting her here on my left as a show of my support."

"So, then what's the point of introducing her to us, if her place here hasn't been decided? When will you make up your mind? Cause it seems to be made up already."

A few mumbled assents rose around the room.

"You seem to be mistaken, man," Kerric said through his teeth. "The decision is not mine to make. The lady is not my property or my servant. She is my sister, and she must decide where to make her home. That is why I brought her here today, so she can make that decision."

The room rumbled while the councilors digested this new perspective.

"I have seated her on my left," Kerric called over them, "to demonstrate my desire for her to stay and advise me, as Josephine does. If she chooses to stay as a lady of the house, she will have all the rights and privileges that position holds, as well as taking her place in the line of my inheritance, after my son, Garreth, and my eldest sister, Josephine."

More rumbling at this pronouncement. Even I took exception. In line to inherit the rule? Me? Never before had I felt more like a ruffled bird stuck in an attic. The panic John had mentioned reared its head. I looked over to where he sat under the window, my former seat still empty next to him.

He had offered to take the panic for me, but I remained firm in my resolve to bear it myself. John returned my stare, however, and his cool, steady gaze was enough to stall the uncertainty.

I wasn't alone. I had a friend here. More than one. I turned to Josephine across from me. She, too, had confidence to spare.

Show them who you are.

I stood then, surprising myself as well as Kerric, who hurried to help me get out from under the table. Once I stood steady on my feet, tall enough to be seen by everyone clearly, the rumble of voices died down.

"My brother speaks the truth." My voice came clear and loud, which only served to make me feel stronger. "I have not yet decided if I should stay here or not. I know my presence here can be distressing. I know it was before. I do not wish to make anyone here uncomfortable. If I am not welcome here by the people, then I will leave this place and live my life elsewhere. I would like to hear your questions, then maybe have a vote?"

I turned toward Kerric, unsure if I was entitled to call a vote. He nodded once.

"Yes, we'll have a vote. But first, your questions."

They came without hesitation now. A few people were rude, some were curious and probing, and others were fascinated. A couple of them refused to speak at all and only glared at me.

They wanted to know where I'd been, how I had gotten back, why I was injured, where Michael was, and a thousand things besides. I answered their questions as honestly as I could, though I was careful to never mention anything about that night in the woods with the thief.

Murderer.

But then the questions got harder.

"Just what sort of gifts do you have?" someone asked with a scowl.

Another person shouted out on their heels. "I remember back when you was a baby. You was in all our heads at once! I remember!"

I balked at them. This question felt too personal. Intrusive. I glanced at Josephine, but she was baffled. She shook her head at me.

"I—" The words didn't want to come.

"How do we even know she is the lady?" someone else popped in. "How do we know she's not an imposter?"

"She is my sister," Kerric said sternly. "I know this for a fact."

"But how?" one of the council members asked. This man I knew. It was Leland, the pest who started avalanches. "How do you know this, my lord? With Michael gone, there is no one left to confirm it."

Several voices murmured agreements. The metaphorical snow started to quiver near the peak.

"How can it be proven?" Leland pressed.

"I can testify to its truth," John said, standing. "I witnessed Michael's murder and Gwen's injury. I swear to all here that she is who she says she is."

"But that proves nothing." Leland's voice was very high-pitched and melodious. It rang clearly through the hall, calling others to join him. He sang to them, a piper with his rats. "It only proves that the girl was with Michael when he died, nothing more."

"Aye!" another person agreed, standing as well. "You're a good man, Kerric, and a good master. But who's to say you haven't been lied to as well?"

Kerric slammed his fist onto the tabletop, causing several people to jump. "How is this even a question?" he asked, indignant. "I can understand your hesitation to accept her, but to question her identity? Can you not see the resemblance, at least?" He gestured to Josephine, who did look very much like me.

A few people stumbled in their suspicions, but Leland was not satisfied. "There must be some way, my lord, to alleviate any doubt. A way to stop any nasty rumors before they even have a chance to begin. You must see that my only aim here is to ensure the lady is accepted fully by her people." He smiled graciously and bowed to me. "Should she choose to stay, that is."

Everyone seemed to agree that this view was sound. I should prove who I was for my own well-being.

John's glower was of deep annoyance. Abruptly, he stood and stalked straight to the head of the table. He gestured for me to step closer so he could speak softly to Kerric and I both. "It's up to you, Gwen, but I know how you can prove it. You can show them your gifts."

A jolt of panic ran through me. Show them? Outright?

"And how do you expect me to do that?" I hissed.

"Show them something. A vision, maybe."

When I continued to stare, incredulous, John shrugged.

"You're the one that wanted to be honest, Gwenna. Here's your chance. Show them what you're capable of."

Such a thing had never occurred to me. I had never even thought of showing another person, much less the full council, a vision. My plan was to live like any other person and hopefully never use my gifts at all.

"It could work," Kerric said. "But if you're going to do it, show them something nice. No horrorscapes, please."

My eyes danced from one to the other. The pressure to make a decision was immense. Dozens of eyes were focused on the back of my head while I debated, and the seconds felt like minutes.

Do something!

"Okay," I said. "I'll do it. I'll try anyway."

John gave a curt nod and started back to his seat, calling out for the whole room to hear. "I ask the lady to prove herself by displaying her sibylline abilities to the Council. Because we all know for a fact that the infant Sasha had gifts beyond all measure, will such a display satisfy you all that this is the same woman?"

There was a smattering of agreement, mostly born of intrigue, but when Leland piped up, it was settled. "I believe a sufficient display of power would be proof enough. What says the room?"

"Aye!" called several voices at once.

Every head turned toward me, expectant. I returned their gazes, eyes wide, like a startled deer. How the hell would I show a room full of people a vision? I had only ever connected with other telepaths. Was the connection the same? Was it almost the same, at least?

No, I wasn't entirely without experience. I had a vague memory of being lifted out of a cart and every man around me crying out in pain. Though I had been fever-addled at the time, I had done it then. It wasn't so different, maybe.

But even if I did manage to connect with the councilors—all forty-two of them—what was I supposed to show them?

Something nice.

I thought back to a time when I had known what nice felt like. Back home in the hollow, with Michael pulling weeds in our spring garden, me running barefoot over the moss and leaf litter, with feathers in my hair.

The vision came to me easily once I thought of it. I could almost hear the laughter in Michael's voice calling after me.

Let them hear it too.

My mind was a great sprawling oak tree in a glass sphere. When Josephine had asked to speak with me, I allowed her a peek inside. I let her see a single leaf or maybe a twig. In that way, we were able to speak to each other, mind to mind.

When I had passed John my pain, he had been given an entire branch. But when we had shared that damned vision in Barano, the sphere had come away entirely, and he had come right in among the roots.

I didn't need to go so far with these people. I needed only to stretch out a limb, a branch for each mind, and let them feel it. Let them see what I saw and hear what I heard.

They needed to sit under the shade of ancient trees and have the cool breeze caressing their faces. They needed to be surrounded by the smells of the earth, the bark, and the rotting leaves. To be cushioned by the moss under their feet.

I ached for these things, for the life I'd had before. And I needed them to ache for it too.

A very real chorus of gasps and exhalations registered at the back of my mind, but mostly, I only heard Michael calling after me. The wind in the wide trees shushed past me as I ran, and Michael laughed again.

"Get back here, Gwenna!" he called. "These weeds won't pull themselves!"

I peeked at him from behind a tree, a giggle rising in my throat. Several people in the real world laughed with me. They couldn't help it. I had given them the giddiness of a child.

"What are you playing at, Little Owl?" Michael said, a smile in his voice.

"I want to go exploring! Can't we go swimming, Michael?"

He threw up his hands, slinging dirt. "What am I going to do with you? There is work to be done, child."

I scampered down the rise toward him. "Okay. We'll pull the weeds, but then can we go? Please? We haven't had a swim in ages!"

"The faster we pull the weeds, the faster we can go." Then Michael cried out in protest of my motivated work. "Not the tomatoes! Those we need!"

That should be enough. Slowly, I let go of the trees, of the moss, of the wind, of the earth, of Michael. Slowly, I came back to the council chamber, and so did everyone else.

The room fell silent once more.

Sounds of life outside the Greathouse floated in through the windows. Horse hooves clopped on the cobbles. A kitchen maid shouted something. Someone walked by directly under the window and laughed.

It felt separate now. Everything outside this room and outside of the vision I had just given the Council...Everything else was separate. It was them and us, even if just for a few moments.

My heart felt empty. The vision had been so real I had forgotten that my life in the hollow was gone forever. Vaguely, I could tell that everyone in the room felt the same emptiness. I wasn't the only one with damp eyes.

Their gazes were too heavy now, and no one had any idea what to say. Not even Leland the Pest.

I started down at the table.

Kerric reached out and took my hand. The sudden contact

made me jump, but I let him do it. This was my brother. My own family. Finally.

"I understand," I said, my voice low.

People leaned forward, straining to hear me.

"I understand if you do not wish me to stay. Perhaps we've had enough questions. Enough proof. It's time for a vote, I think."

Silence met my words, but it didn't last. Someone spoke from halfway down the table—was his name Mark?

"With all due respect, my lady," he said from his seat, "I don't think a vote would be appropriate. This is your home, same as it's ours."

A mumbled assent rolled around the room. Not everyone, but most. They had voted, whether they meant to or not.

"Welcome home, Lady Gwenna," Nanette said, loud and clear. She wore a little frown between her eyes, but she smiled through it.

"Thank you," I said.

"All right," Nanette continued. "Now that's taken care of. What's next on the agenda, Kerric?"

Kerric stared at her for several seconds, taken aback.

Hadn't the entire world just stopped? How could we continue with a council meeting after the revelations about me and my visions?

"Well, there is the question of Aristeidis Metaxas," Josephine said dryly.

Eighteen

It was decided that Josephine would agree to marry Aris in four years' time. She would go and make this offer to him personally after the council, but no one had any doubt he would accept. It was a reasonable response. She'd be twenty-eight by then and ready to start a family of her own.

"You would really leave this place?" I asked her afterward. "You've lived here your whole life."

"Yes, I would," she said, chewing her lip. "I think I'd even be excited to see the seaside. Can you imagine it?"

"How did he take it when you told him about us?"

"Better than I expected. I think I have you to thank for that. He was very glad to know I can't control people the way you do. A little telepathy and foresight is nothing in comparison."

I laughed, which set her giggling. And for the first time in weeks, I began to see the light at the end of the tunnel.

Both the marriage alliance and my arrival would be announced at the Feast that weekend.

There were four feast days in Derehan, one for each solstice and equinox. Long ago, these were holy days of worship, but now they had become little more than tradition and holidays. We followed the Old Way, though, to some extent. We still gave thanks, we celebrated life, and we competed, drank, and ate to excess.

Because it was the autumn equinox, it was time for the Festival of Wheat. Everyone brought food, drink, and supplies. No one bought or sold, only shared. Our own smokehouse had roasted ten pigs the night before. Everyone was able to have their fill and then some.

Musicians played here and there in the crowd. A troupe of actors entertained children during the afternoon, then switched to more tawdry tales when the night fell and drink flowed. Everywhere there was food and laughter and ale. Both highborn and low sat together, just like at the council meeting.

The World Mothers and World Fathers were gone, lost to the myths of time, but they had not been forgotten. This year, a tailor called Mark was honored with playing the Father of Wheat. He moved through the crowd in his bright costume, laughing while he gave people sips from his wine skin and stuck stalks of wheat in their hair or their buttonholes.

Feasts were held in every major city. Even Michael and I had always observed the holidays in our own way. But the feasts in Valheid were far grander than anything I had ever imagined. Candles, bunting, bouquets, and garlands of wheat and flowers bedecked the courtyard. The Greathouse had the resources and manpower to create a true spectacle.

Though I knew almost no one, I did see one familiar face. Mariah had left her home in Barano to celebrate with us, though clearly she had only come to check up on me.

"You're looking well," she said with a tight hug. "I'm glad to see you're taking it easy on that leg. Is that captain taking care of you like I told him to?"

I smiled. "Yes, he is looking out for me very well. I can't count how many times he has personally carried me from one place to another so I wouldn't have to walk."

She scratched her nose and lifted an eyebrow. "I can't say as I'm surprised to hear that. I'd never say it to his face, but he's an honorable one. Word gets around about the highborn folk that run about the country all the time."

"Why wouldn't you say that to his face?" I asked.

"Give him a big head, that's why," she answered without ceremony. "People are like that, you know."

"Not John, I think."

A great guffaw of laughter from across the table drew our attention. A crowd of friends surrounded Sinead, all of them hanging on her every word.

"Sinead, on the other hand," I said. "She knows exactly how attractive she is."

Mariah had a good laugh at that.

Kerric called Josephine and me to stand beside him in the early afternoon. He made the announcements about Josephine's marriage and my return home, though it was only a formality. The council had been instructed to spread the word so that the city was ready to hear the announcements without incident.

Josephine's news was horribly overshadowed by mine. The entire courtyard went silent, and everyone craned to get a better look at me. The seconds ticked by, and yet Kerric waited. Just like in the Council room, it was time for the people to have an opinion.

Finally, a familiar voice called out from the back of the crowd. "Three cheers for the Ladies Moore!"

And as the crowd followed suit, I sent my mind searching for the owner of the voice. I found John raising his mug with the rest of them.

For the entire day, I was never without friends. If Josephine wasn't introducing me to people, Sinead and Paul were carrying me from one group to another.

And to my joy, when he noticed my wistful glances in the direction of the dancers, Paul hitched me onto his back and set off to join them by the bonfire. I couldn't dance long on one leg, even with Paul there to help hold me up. But I reveled in every second I could.

Aristeidis came and went, as conspicuous as my sister and me. The novelty of being Authe Idan notwithstanding, he planned to wed the lady of the house and take her away to the seaside. Everyone wanted to form an opinion about him, so he was passed from group to group and interrogated under a thin veil of polite curiosity.

"May the Old Kind save me," he muttered to me after one such interrogation. "If I have to explain marriage one more time, I may combust. Yo! Sinead. Pass me that ale."

"What did you expect?" I asked. "Marriage isn't common here, aside from political alliances like yours. Everyone seems to feel entitled to their opinion."

"Uncommon as it is, you all understand the concept." Aris took a hearty drink from the mug Sinead had given him.

"They just want an excuse to talk to you."

"And what's more, they all seem to think they're Josephine's keeper!" he barreled on. "I've been threatened by no less than six farmers to take care of her properly. Six, I tell you. You all had better hope my father never visits here. He would have no patience for such treatment."

I laughed as he traded out his newly empty mug for another. "He'd do better here than your uncle Eustis would have done."

"Aye, that's true enough."

"I can't say I'm sorry he's gone. He did cruel things to people like me. But I am sorry you lost him. Were you close?"

Aris climbed up to sit next to me on the table and scrubbed his eyes. "No, not really," he said. "He was a cold, distant man. And my family didn't grow up in the capital. We only moved in once he disappeared."

"Even so," I said.

"Yes, even so." He swiped his hand through his blond hair. "But no more talk of sad things and missing uncles."

After a pause, I worked up the courage to bring up another subject, which had been weighing on me for several days. "Aris?"

"Yes, my dear?" he asked jovially.

A corner of my mouth perked up. "Are you sure you're okay with Josephine and me? What we are, I mean? After that night in the woods, I wasn't sure you'd ever talk to me again."

"Oh, you mean the fact that you're a pair of witches?" He smirked into his mug. "I'm not going to lie. The past week has been a trial. We don't believe in ghost stories where I'm from."

"No," I agreed. "You don't."

He caught sight of someone in the crowd. "But witches? Sibyls, you call yourselves? Now, that's something worth seeing."

The odd look on his face had me following his gaze. He was watching my sister.

Her hair was loose and black as night. Sprigs of wheat crowned her head, like a harvest goddess. The heavy tresses swung around her as she danced barefoot with the rest of the crowd.

For a moment, I saw what he saw. Adventure, delight, and dark beauty. That's what Josephine Moore was. And when he'd asked, she had said yes. Ghost stories be damned.

Then she looked up and caught us watching her. With a flash of mischief, she darted toward us.

"Come. Dance with me, Aris!" she said with a broad grin.

"I don't know how!" he replied with a laugh.

She came right up to us and pulled on his shirt. "I'll show you. Take your shirt off and come on!"

"My shirt?"

"You can't dance looking so proper!" Josephine tugged on his sleeve again.

"Okay, just a minute!" He grinned. "Let me catch my breath, woman."

She laughed and allowed herself to be carried off by a crowd of friends toward the bonfire.

Aris stared after her. "I know it was a ruse—the pilgrimage through the Sacred Wood. But I suspect Sinead was right that night. I needed it. This place is a different kind of wilderness, only pretending to be a city. I don't think I would have made a good first impression on her otherwise."

"Are you glad about the alliance?" I asked.

"Yes, I think so."

"And the wedding?"

"I think so," he said again with a smirk. Then he downed the last of his ale and moved off toward the bonfire to find my sister.

Paul scooted over to fill the space Aris had vacated on the table-top. We both watched Josephine haul Aris's shirt off over his head. He was the only one at the bonfire fully dressed, and clearly, that wasn't going to stand. His pale chest stood out in high contrast against the deeper skin tones of the Derehani all around him. Aris tolerated it begrudgingly, accepted the stalk of wheat Josephine stuck in his pants pocket, and then began the arduous task of learning to dance like one of us.

"That man is done for," Paul said.

I huffed out a laugh. "There are worse fates, I think."

We watched the dancers in companionable silence for a while, until Paul noticed me yawn.

"It's too early to be getting tired," he said.

"Not too early for me."

"It's a holiday," Paul said. "Many people stay out until dawn most times."

I laughed without humor. "I won't be staying out that late. In fact, if I could convince you to help me up the stairs, I'd go to bed right now."

Paul grinned into his mug. "Sorry, Little Owl. You're not getting out that easily. What you need is some strong ale. Or maybe a little whiskey. That'll warm you up."

My smile fell to chagrin. "I can't."

Paul nodded once. "Right. I suppose not."

"What can't you do?" Josephine asked breathlessly. She was approaching us again, pulling a young boy along with her.

Another woman accompanied them with a welcoming expression. She had deep red hair and fairer skin than most in this part of the world.

I turned to answer, but the words died in my throat when I saw the boy holding Josephine's hand. I leapt to my feet and backed away awkwardly over Paul's knees. He caught me before I fell, and I clutched at his arm for support as I stared at the boy.

He was about thirteen or fourteen years old, though he was tall for his age. The boy was dark-haired and dark-eyed, like many in Derehan, but something about the way he held himself spoke strongly of Kerric. Steady, tall, and sure.

This must be my brother's son—the one Kerric had wanted to introduce me to a few days earlier.

The boy tucked his chin to the side, wide-eyed and clearly startled by my reaction.

But Josephine wasn't surprised. She watched me with grim acceptance and knew what I had realized.

"Gwenna, this is our nephew, Garreth, and his mother, Elana," Josephine said. "Garreth, this is your Aunt Gwen."

Garreth said nothing, only stared at me, unsure.

It wasn't because of who I was or the power I held. No, he was scared because I had acted so incredibly afraid of him. His mother's expression had hardened into wariness.

Propriety dictated that I take his hand and say something kind. He was just a young boy and my own blood. But I couldn't do it, even while the silence stretched between us.

"Gwen?" Paul said, uncertain.

I could only stare at Garreth.

He was just a boy, but someday, he would grow up strong and brave. My nephew would be the only man in an entire city with the strength to resist The Child that I could have been. He would be the only man who could get close enough to try and kill her with a knife.

But in the end, it hadn't been enough. She had sensed him at the last moment and killed him where he stood.

This boy, he was the only one who could keep me out. The only one. I would never see him coming.

It terrified me.

NINETEEN

"It's good to meet you, Garreth," I said finally, though my voice was strained with the effort it took. "And you, Elana."

He watched me, wary. "You too," he replied after a minute. "Aunt Jo has told me a lot about you."

I forced myself to breathe, to smile. "Yes, you as well."

"Are you all right, dear?" Elana asked. The power of her voice belied the kind words. She clearly didn't like the way I had greeted them.

And when I really looked at her, I was thrown once more. I knew this face as well, though now it was round and full of youth. When I had last seen this woman, she had been middle-aged, graying, and cursing at Sasha. Elana had been made to kill her own sister with a hammer.

"Gwen was just asking me to help her upstairs," Paul said, by way of excusing me.

"So early?" Elana asked, one eyebrow raised.

"No," I said. "No, I'm sorry. I'd like to stay. I'm sorry for being so startled. This has all been a lot to take in. I never had any family before last week, you know."

"And now you've got it in spades." Josephine gave a hostess's grin.

"Is it true you grew up in the Sacred Wood?" Garreth asked.

"Yes, that's true. We lived in a hut surrounded by runestones in the very heart of the Wood."

"Runestones?"

"Yes. They kept travelers from seeing us when they passed through."

Garreth ventured a little bravery. "I'd love to see that. Did you really show a vision to the whole council room? Will you show me the stones?"

"Garreth," Elana said, but her son ignored her.

"Please, Aunt Gwen? Will you show me?"

"Not now, Garreth," Elana said with a bit more authority. "Let the poor woman breathe!"

"Maybe Gwenna can join us for our lessons next week," Josephine said. "Maybe we can all practice together."

"Lessons? For what?" I asked.

Josephine spared half a glance at Paul, then shrugged with resignation. "Garreth is gifted, like us. But in a different way."

"Is he a passive?" I looked down at the boy, as if I could see signs of it on his face.

"No, a block," Josephine said. "His mind is a vault, but I can sometimes break through. Can't I, little man?"

"Not for long," Garreth said stubbornly.

"A block. Yes, of course," I said.

Elana looked at me sharply but said nothing.

"I've never met anyone like you before, Garreth. I would love to join your lessons, if your mother approves."

I looked to Elana to await her answer, but she hesitated.

She didn't look to Josephine or to anyone else before finally saying, "Of course. So long as Josephine is with you, I don't mind."

My smile hardened on my face.

She didn't trust me. That was fair. The only thing she knew about me was that I was dangerous. Elana could only hope I was well-meaning toward children and family, and that even though I could hurt her son, I would choose not to.

But really, that was all anyone could hope for.

"Will you show me the Sacred Wood?" Garreth asked. "In our lesson, I mean? Have you ever seen a real fairy hole or giant's bone?"

"Garreth!" Another boy burst into our circle and grabbed Garreth by the arms. "Garreth, you won't believe what Charlie's found. Come look."

"Okay. Bye, Aunt Gwen!" And they both disappeared into the crowd, like only children could.

Josephine laughed. "Boys have no attention span. You must forgive him, Gwen."

I smiled as well, but we were interrupted almost immediately by Aris.

"God's sake, woman! You take me off to dance with you, then you abandon me? I'll teach you manners!"

He bent to scoop her off her feet. She yelped in surprise when he threw her over his bare shoulder like a sack of grain.

"Ladies," Aris said politely to Elana and me over Josephine's backside. He gave Paul a friendly nod before carrying a laughing Josephine back toward the bonfire.

"You know him better than I do," Elana said to me, her eyes on the dancers. "Is he a good sort of man?"

I stared at her in surprise for half a second before answering. "I think so. I haven't known him long, though."

"Longer than me," she said.

I gazed back to where they danced: Josephine with wild grace and skill and Aris with enthusiasm, at the very least.

"What do you say, Paul?" Elana asked. "You've known him longest."

"I saw something of how he was in Authe Ida," Paul said. "I wasn't impressed at first, but he's learning."

"Learning what?"

He hesitated a moment before answering. "How to listen."

Elana nodded once. "Good. I'm glad to hear it. It was good to meet you, Gwenna." She patted Paul's arm and moved off into the crowd.

Relieved, I turned back toward the table to resume my seat. Paul moved to help me up, but I stopped him and froze.

"What is it?" he asked.

I turned and scanned the milling crowd, searching for John. For a few confusing seconds, I couldn't comprehend why.

Then I felt it again—the tiniest tapping on my mental shields. It was very weak compared to Michael or Josephine, but it was unmistakable.

"Gwen?" Paul asked again.

"It's nothing," I said, my eyes still moving over the masses of people. "Will you pass me my staff, please? I need to take care of something."

"Let me help you." Paul hopped down and reached for my staff.

"No, that's okay." I smiled up at him. "I won't go far."

I didn't reach out to John. That seemed too cold. Instead, I went and found him.

He sat on a low rock wall overlooking a moonlit bean field, just a block away from the brightly lit festival square. I would have found him much faster if I had let Paul help me walk, but I wanted to talk to John alone. Something told me he felt the same way.

Why else would he reach out to me the way he did? He could have just joined us at the table, like everyone else had.

John heard me coming; my staff was noisy against the cobblestones. I thought at first he would get up to come help me for the last few yards, but he didn't. He just waited.

I sat a few feet away with a sigh.

"It's much quieter out here," John said, by way of greeting.

It was true. The music and the roar of the revelers floated over to us, muffled by a building or two between us and them. The lights of the party glowed over the rooftops and peeked through the alleys, visible on the outskirts of where we sat.

"I love it." I glanced back toward the noise of the party. "Never thought I'd see a night like this."

"A bit different from where you came from, I suppose."

"Hm," I agreed. "It's the people, I think. I love the quiet as well. It was—" I swallowed hard, thinking briefly of Michael and my silent, magical wood. That part of my life was over, but it had been such a good life. "It was beautiful. But there are so many people to talk to and all of them different. It's beautiful too. A new kind of beauty I didn't know I'd been missing."

John scratched his nose and gave me a small smile. "I suppose it is. I grew up here, and I guess that can make it feel a bit mundane after a while. The same hustle and bustle day in and day out."

I snorted. "Mundane? Hardly. Aris called it just another wilderness, only pretending to be a city."

John laughed. "He's not wrong, I suppose."

We both looked out over the bean field.

A cloud scuttled across the moon, sending total blackness sweeping along the ground for a moment. It was so dark out there, and there were so many lights behind us. I used to belong out there, but now I had to stay with other people, in this new wilderness.

"I think they will do well," I said after a moment.

"Who?"

"Aris and Josephine."

John nodded. "Yes, I think she likes him. It'll be good for everyone too."

"Sometimes I forget you're a politician."

"Just being practical," John said. "Authe Ida has been after this alliance for a while. Metaxas won't be happy that she's pushed it off for four years, but he'll be glad it's agreed to, at least."

"Authe Ida's been pursuing it? Is that strange?"

"Maybe. But at the same time, we can't find any reason to reject them. There are only benefits to this marriage. Trade, peace, military aid if we need it. We don't have a true military, you know. Only the Guard. Maybe we'll finally see an end to the skirmishes near the border. Maybe we'll—" He broke off and shook his head. "This isn't why I called you out here."

"Why did you, then?"

John finally looked over at me, but as usual, he found it hard to speak. I got up and scooted a little closer, near enough that I could rest a hand on his arm.

"What is it?"

He glanced down at the place where my fingers lay on the soft fabric of his sleeve. Finally, he said, "I'm leaving in the morning."

"Oh." I returned my hand to my lap. Despite all the discomfort between us, his short statement had caused a deep pang of disappointment. "So soon?"

"Much of my duties as emissary involve traveling. I do it most of the year while the weather holds."

"And where do you winter?"

"It depends on where I am when winter comes," he said.

"Oh." The disappointment solidified. I didn't quite know what to do with it or how to interpret it.

It wasn't that I needed him here, and the vision between us was a near constant source of stress. Having him gone would make things so much simpler.

Nonetheless, my gut wrenched.

"So, you wanted to say goodbye?" I asked.

"I'll be gone by dawn. I'll accompany Nanette back to her estate in Purgo, then I go east to Silda. I'll be there for a few weeks with your aunt, Heidi, who governs that city."

"My aunt?"

"Your mother's sister," he said. "I'll have plenty to discuss with her, even without your and Josephine's news. Then I'll be back in a few weeks to take Aris home."

I nodded. Back in a few weeks, but likely not for any real amount of time. My perceptions of life in Valheid subtly adjusted. John would not be a fixture, after all.

"I wanted to clear the air between us before I went," he said. "After Barano—"

"There's no need for that."

"But there is. I need to make something clear to you."

John waited for me to respond, to accept. I turned more toward him, tucking my good leg under me so I could sit sideways on the low wall.

"I have known about that prophecy for a very long time," he said.

I waited.

"I'd never seen it before, not until that night with you, but I knew about it. Josephine told me years ago. I was a teenager with —" He hesitated. "To tell the truth, I had feelings for her."

"For Josephine?"

"Yes. We had grown up together, had taken lessons together. She was my best friend. Of course I had a crush. But she just laughed at me." He closed his eyes and shook his head with a small smile. "She thought it was the funniest thing in the world, which made me so angry. So, she told me about you, about the visions she'd had. And even though she shouldn't have laughed"—he emphasized that point by jabbing his hand into the air, scolding someone who wasn't there—"I understood."

"And so, what? You've been waiting for me this whole time?"

John pursed his lips in frustration. "Yes and no. I haven't stopped living my life. I've had my lovers. But I've always known you were out there, That when I found you, that would be it."

I stared at him. I should say something, but now I was the one who couldn't find words. How did a person respond to something like this?

"But then I did find you, and of course, real life is rarely how we imagine it. You were hurting and wild and afraid. And so young."

"You knew how old I was."

"Yes, I knew. I *know*. I remember when you were born, for hell's sake."

I held out my hand to stop his rambling. "I understand. You had been skipping ahead in your imagination."

"Yes, I think that's it," he said. "In my mind, when we met, that would be it. I hadn't counted on meeting you so soon, I think."

I nodded, chewing my lip, but still my gut turned in on itself. Not in disappointment, but in fear. This was a feeling like that night in Barano again, when I had been confronted with things I wasn't ready for.

"John—"

"But that's not what I wanted to tell you either," he said over me. "I mean, I did want you to know those things. I won't pretend I didn't expect things. I won't lie to you."

"Then what is it?"

"You don't owe me anything." He screwed up his face. That wasn't what he wanted to say either. "I'm sorry. I can't find the right words. Give me a room full of angry lords any day, but sit one girl in front of me, and I lose all capacity to speak."

"That can't be true," I said.

John shook his head, laughing at himself. "It's not! It's just you, Gwen. You make me stumble! I suppose it's fitting!"

He turned to face me on the rock wall and took both of my hands in his. It was the first time he'd touched me skin to skin since Kerric's office, and I tensed up at first. He had to have noticed, but he ignored it.

"So, I'll just get it out. Forgive me if I say it wrong, but I know you'll understand me. Gwenna, that prophecy doesn't have to mean anything. Nothing. Not if we don't want it to. It does not take away your choices or mine. You do not have to be my woman, now or ever. We can't pretend we didn't see it, and I can't pretend I haven't lived with it half my life. But it doesn't have to rule us. Am I being clear?"

I nodded, unable to reply properly.

"I care about you, it's true. But I had expected to love you right away, and I just don't. But I do care, and I want to leave knowing that you and I are friends. I can't leave you here thinking you owe me something. Because you don't."

My eyes filled, and I nodded, squeezing his hand. "You're wrong about one thing," I said. "I do owe you something."

"No, you don't."

"You saved my life, Johnny. More than once. And you got me here, and you've helped me again and again. So, I owe you something, even if it's just gratitude."

"Gwen—"

"And you *are* my friend." I squeezed his hand. "My first friend, I think, and the only one who was never afraid of me."

"What's there to be afraid of?"

I laughed once without humor. "Plenty, as you well know." I looked up at him, trying and failing to smile. My words came out in a whisper, a secret confession. "I'm sad that you're leaving."

"Me too, a little. But I think it's for the best."

I nodded, trying to convince myself he was right. "Sure."

"You've had to rely on me a lot since we met, and I'm glad I could be there for you. But you're ready to stand on your own. You need to build your own life here, Gwen. And you can do that better if I'm away."

I kept nodding, probably looking deranged. With a heavy inhale, I withdrew my hands and changed the subject. "I met Garreth and Elana earlier. My whole family is gifted, it seems like."

"Garreth is a good kid," John said. "And Elana would be a good friend for you. She's very clever and isn't afraid to be blunt."

"I've noticed. The question is whether or not she *wants* to be my friend."

He smirked. "Just give her time. She'll come around before too long. Then she'll be your staunchest supporter."

My heart sank when I thought of Elana in that vision, cursing Sasha. Cursing me. "I hope so."

And as the thought passed, I noticed again that strange sensation of a presence. Just like the other day in my room with Josephine, there was something—some*one*—that shouldn't be.

I turned quickly, staring into the dark street behind us, but there was no one there.

John shifted as well. "What is it?"

My eyes roamed over the empty street. They kept falling on one spot in particular.

There. That's where it came from.

John stood and peered into the shadows. "Is someone there?"

And then came the voice of a small girl, a voice I recognized from my nightmares. It was faint, like it had been whispered from across the room, but it was unmistakable.

"I found you..."

I tumbled off the low wall and clutched at John's arm. "Who said that!" I called out, stupidly.

I knew who it was. I just didn't want to believe it.

"What do you hear?" John asked, alarmed. He half held me up when my right leg buckled under me.

I couldn't quite get a fix on her, but I knew she was there. I groped for John's hand and pulled him back into the roots of my mind.

"Shh," I said over his questions. *Do you feel it?*

He stilled and listened through me.

It was obvious when he felt her. His grip tightened on my

hand, and his breath stopped in his chest. His gaze zeroed in on that empty spot in the street.

"What is that? Who is that?"

A breathy giggle came in answer, like a delighted little girl who had just won a game.

John heard it this time, but only because I did. We both stared in horror at the empty street as the presence faded into nothingness.

John and I stood in silence, holding each other up in our shock, waiting to sense her again. But Sasha didn't materialize in the empty street. She had really and truly disappeared.

"What does this mean?" John asked, staring into the darkness.

"I don't know."

PART FOUR
AN ARCHER
IN THE FIELD
FOUR YEARS LATER

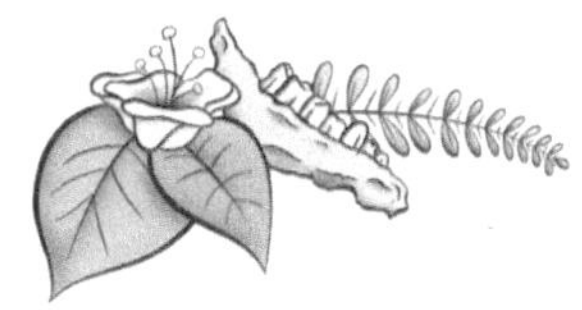

TWENTY

I ran my fingers over the entry in the ledger. This had to be it. Maybe not the answer to everything, but a signpost, at least. Finally, I had found a new piece of the puzzle.

I picked up the heavy volume and hauled it across the room to the low table I had commandeered over the years. The Greathouse library was open to everyone, under Wallace's watchful eye, but this area had come to be mine alone. It was tucked back in the far corner under a huge window, which gave excellent light. The table was low to the ground, forcing me to sit on the floor to use it with ease, and fat armchairs surrounded it.

It was arranged for comfortable reading, but it had become my workspace.

I lowered myself to the floor and pulled an old literature book toward myself from a nearby pile, opening both books side by side to compare.

"I should have guessed you'd be here," Josephine said, making me jump.

I barely glanced up as she crossed the room and settled into one of the armchairs.

"Look what I found," I said, passing the book to her.

"An old schoolbook?" Josephine marked the page with a finger and turned the book around to read the spine. "*All Things in Balance.* Is this the one with the prophecy handwritten in the corner? *Beware, beware the Crone.*"

"Yes, that's the one. It's medieval literature, mostly history and mythology of the Old Kind and the World Mothers and Fathers. Spirits, giants, merfolk...you know. But the point is, this proves that the prophecy is much older than any of us thought before. This book is from nearly three hundred years ago."

"It's held up very well to time," Josephine said, passing it back.

"You're not impressed." It was a resigned statement, not a question. Jo was never impressed with my research anymore.

She shrugged. "I still think anyone could have copied the phrases in the book at any point between the time it was bound and now. Who's to say this is proof of anything?"

"This," I said, handing her the ledger next. "I just found this ledger, which was kept by a scribe back in the court of Queen Lily. Look at the handwriting. How he made his Bs. It's identical."

Josephine studied one, then the other, while I barreled on.

"This scribe copied the prophecy into *All Things in Balance* around two hundred years ago. And, and! He was Ambic! Maybe *that's* where the prophecy originated. All the way to the New Ambic Islands. And look. It's complete. It has all four verses. It's rare to find all four together like this. You almost never see the lines about the dead place. '*The fates, the gods, the laws of man, there none dare to go.*'"

Josephine nodded. "Which is why you've been holding on to this book like a magpie for more than a year now."

I accepted the ledger back from her with a stubborn expression. "I'm not obsessed."

"You are the very definition of obsessed, Gwenna," Josephine said with an indulgent smile. "I still don't understand why you can't let go of this prophecy about the Child."

I sat back on the floor and leaned against the armchair behind me with a sigh. "It's about me, Jo."

"It's not, though. We stopped this prophecy from coming true. It's been over for years."

"But what if it's not?"

My sister studied my face for a few seconds. "You haven't felt her for a long time, right? Sasha, I mean?"

I nodded.

"How long has it been since the last time?"

"Nearly a year."

"And you're sure it's not some kind of aftershock? Some kind of symptom? A result of seeing that horrific vision back when you first arrived?"

"I used to be so sure." I lowered my eyes to the cluttered table. "It was so real. And the fact that she heard me, Jo. Sasha heard me speak. She felt me, just like I've been feeling her."

"You used to be sure?"

I looked out the window, uncertain. A huge apple tree stood just outside, ancient and bent with time. It was only just spring, and a few early leaves had begun to unfurl. In a few weeks, it would be alight with lacy, white flowers.

"Do you—" She hesitated. "Have you considered going back into that vision? To see if she feels you again?"

I shook my head decisively and began stacking books on the table with muffled *thwumps* of colliding covers. "No. Absolutely not. I won't risk her noticing me again."

"Right." Josephine nodded, lips pursed. "Gwen, I'm sorry to change the subject, but I did come find you for a reason. Have you forgotten what day it is today?"

"Of course not. How could I? Johnny's already reached out to me twice today to make sure I knew when they'd arrive."

"Then why aren't you ready?"

"What's there to get ready for?"

"You're not going to come out and greet him when they get

here? He hasn't been home since last summer. Since the Games, practically."

I leaned forward and rested my forehead on the table, arms over my head. "I have work to do."

"Horse shit," Josephine said with uncharacteristic vulgarity. Clearly, she was dreading this visit just as much as me. She came around the table and hauled me to my feet. "Go wash your face and put on something decent. John isn't the only one coming home. We all have to be there to greet our aunt. They'll be here within the hour."

I allowed her to drag me from the library, but I wasn't happy about it. "She's the one I want to avoid."

"Necessary evils," Josephine said.

There was commotion down the streets long before the two dark carriages rolled up to the Greathouse. We had plenty of warning, even without John's frequent telepathic updates. My family filled the front steps, along with several servants and Cynebald the general, who was deep in conversation with Kerric.

Four years before, I had been the one arriving. Now I stood on these foreboding steps, just another one of the crowd.

Nanette came and put an arm around me in greeting as Garreth ran by with one of his friends, both boys taller than me these days. When Garreth passed, I sent a sharp command to his brain. He didn't expect it, but he grew stronger every day. So, instead of doing a perfect cartwheel as I had coerced him to do, he simply stumbled. Garreth recovered easily with a smooth somersault.

"Very manly!" Nanette said appreciatively.

He came up, laughing. "Nice try, Gwenna!" he shouted before running off with Charlie.

"Garreth, get back here!" Elana called. "They're almost here!"

But it was too late. Even as Elana yelled after her son, the carriages began rolling into the crowded courtyard.

Aunt Heidi had never been one for unnecessary frills. Her carriage was simple and small, only just big enough to carry Heidi herself, along with her serving woman. She brought a string of merchants and their carts with her, as usual, hauling mostly barrels of salted trout for sale in our warehouses.

Several soldier escorts rode on horseback before and behind. I recognized most of them from previous visits, but I couldn't help scanning their faces while they moved through the crowd, searching for one in particular.

I spotted John right away, with Dan riding alongside. They rode with the rear guard, a long owl feather pinned onto John's cloak, which fluttered in the wind. He looked just the same as the summer before, when I'd seen him last. Tall and commanding, though his hair had grown a little longer.

John saw me the same instant I found him. At first, his eyes widened in surprise, but his expression melted into a lopsided grin of greeting.

"John's looking well," Nanette said in my ear, waving at him with her whole arm.

He laughed as he dismounted, though the sound of it was lost to the crowd.

"Yes, he is," I admitted with a carefully neutral expression. My heart had kicked up a bit at the sight of him, which was concerning. But I couldn't deny Nanette's opinion of his appearance.

He had always been so handsome. But more now than I remembered him being last summer.

Kerric led the way down the steps to help my Aunt Heidi out of her carriage, but he paused long enough to embrace John and slap Dan's back on his way.

Heidi's handmaid, Clara, stepped primly out behind her, her black hair loose in the brisk wind. I grimaced at the sight of her. It had been too much to hope that Clara had decided to stay home this visit. She would be tormenting the kitchen staff within the hour.

John came to Josephine next. He picked her up in a huge hug, both of them giggling. When she found her feet again, she reached up to tug at his hair.

"You need a haircut," she said.

"What do you expect me to do?" he asked. "You weren't in Silda to remind me all winter long."

"Look at this!" Josephine ran her fingers through his hair, combing it in front of his face to cover his eyes. "How could you not tell for yourself?"

John laughed and ducked away from her, shaking his hair back before turning his gaze on me. "Hello, Gwen."

He didn't hug me. He didn't even shake my hand. But he didn't have to. I flicked the owl feather on his cloak with one finger.

"You still have it."

"An old friend gave it to me last summer."

He meant me, of course. I had given it to him the night before he left. I hadn't been able to say a damn thing, with my chest clenching so hard, hating every time he rode away. But I had been able to pull the owl feather out of my hair and press it into his hands. That said enough.

My chest constricted for a different reason now, though. "You've grown shorter since I saw you last."

That got a laugh out of him, but he didn't have time to reply. Sinead came bounding up the steps, crammed herself between us, and rammed into her brother. The whole crowd devolved into laughter, greeting, and exclamations.

"Hello, Aunt!" Josephine said when Heidi topped the stairs, moving with considerably more grace than Sinead had.

Heidi hugged and kissed my sister warmly, then forced herself to embrace me as well. I allowed it with a polite pat on her back but stepped away as soon as was acceptable.

She was a tall woman, with a liberal amount of gray streaking through her brown hair, despite her relatively young age. It was pulled tightly back, as usual, which did her handsome face no favors.

Aunt Heidi hated me. At first, I had been severely disappointed. After being so welcomed by Josephine and Kerric—by most of Valheid, in fact—I had been excited to meet my mother's sister.

But that excitement quickly turned to bitterness when, just a few months after coming back home, Heidi visited and turned up her nose at me. Quite literally. And aside from a single, hissed "Witch!" in my direction during dinner, she refused to speak to me at all.

Kerric had taken her into his study and berated her mercilessly, or so Josephine told me later. I retreated to my bedroom for the rest of the night, angry and confused.

But we couldn't avoid each other forever. And over the years, we had come to an understanding: We would stay out of each other's way as much as possible. And when we were forced into each other's company, polite civility was the best we could do. And so far, it had served us both just fine.

"Hello, my dears," Heidi said without looking at me. "It's so good to be home again!"

"Yes!" Josephine took her arm. "Come inside and out of this ruckus! We weren't expecting you to set out for another two weeks, Aunt."

"With this warm weather, how could we not come early? As soon as the pass cleared, I ordered the carriages prepared. I wanted to be here in plenty of time before the Spring Festival! I want to help in any way I can."

"There's no need for that," Josephine said.

We passed into the great hall, surrounded on all sides by people greeting and embracing each other, then moved to a smaller alcove on the left, where we were safe from the worst of the commotion.

"Gwenna and I have everything under control. Everything is planned and ready."

"Nonsense, dear!" Heidi waved one hand and shifted her back toward me. "You'll have so much to deal with this year, what with your wedding this summer. You can't do it all on your own."

I caught Jo's eye over Heidi's shoulder at this snide comment, but my sister resolutely refused to engage.

Our aunt continued without pause. "I was just telling Clara on the way here that all the garlands will need mended and hung and the supplies inventoried. When is Aristeidis coming again? In time for the festival, I hope? Oh, Garreth! Come here, boy, and let me look at you!"

With Heidi's attention caught, I saw my opportunity to slip away. I edged toward where Dan and Sinead carried on a frantic conversation full of hissing and laughter, but Garreth caught me. He took my arm as he approached Heidi and patted it affectionately, forcing me to stay put.

"Hello, Aunt Heidi!" He kissed her once on the cheek, never letting go of my arm.

There would be no escaping now.

Garreth knew exactly what he was doing, the little rat. I was surprised he had the guts to provoke me. Maybe he didn't think I'd be brave enough to retaliate in front of Heidi.

"You have grown so tall since I saw you last year!" Heidi said, but I wasn't paying attention.

I busily picked at Garreth's mental shields, searching for any cracks.

We had been practicing hard these last four years, working to build up his abilities to protect his mind. Together, we grew in strength. Every time he kept me out of his head, I had to figure out a new way in, finding with each attempt that my sibylline abilities were stronger and more subtle than any of us had realized.

But he always found a way to get me out again. Sometimes, it took extreme effort on his part, but Garreth always succeeded in the end.

In the early days of our lessons, it had been like breaking a soap bubble with a stick. One prod and the whole shield collapsed. But once he felt it, he understood it better. Soon I had to poke harder at shields like egg shells, which cracked and shattered. Then he began constructing his shields with bricks and stones. These had cracks, if I could find them. For one terrifying week, he discovered how to devolve into gulpy molasses that exhausted me to wade through.

He was a very visual person, often using those specific words to discuss his strategies: brick, crack, molasses, darkness, thorns, wire. His strength ran deep, and he was clever. Garreth used every trick he had to slow me down and keep me out.

Recently, I'd taken to trying to catch him off guard, like earlier on the front steps. His friends mocked him for being so clumsy, not realizing he was forever dodging my silent tricks.

He got better at it every day. Faster.

And Garreth was ready for me now. He had caught me in a cage I didn't want to be in, grinning like a smug fool while he spoke with his great aunt. But Garreth knew I had claws, and he was ready for them.

So, when I went digging into his mind, I found every trick he had: walls of stone and mortar, molasses coating every crack, darkness over everything. There was no avenue to slide through, no way to even find a crevice to exploit.

It was very good. I was quite proud of him.

But if I couldn't slip in, I would have to use brute force. With a pleasant, slightly distracted expression, I heaved everything I had at Garreth's mental shields.

He stumbled on his words, but his shields held. He shored them up while I gathered myself for a second blow.

"Are you all right, my boy?" Heidi asked, putting a hand on his arm.

"Yes, of co-course," he grunted.

Garreth scrambled inwardly to build back his crumbling walls.

"You don't look well. Josephine, why don't you take him to talk with Gregor? No, I won't hear any arguments, Garreth. You look like you might be sick any moment."

Josephine understood immediately what was happening. She gave me a pointed look, reassured Heidi, and silently called out to John all at once.

She tended to sic John on me when I made trouble. When he was home, at any rate. He was the best option for distracting me, though sometimes Jo's efforts backfired and he just egged me on.

I had to work quickly, before he made it to us from across the room.

"Yes, Garreth," I said. His shield splintered enough for me to wedge myself through and take hold of his life string. "Maybe you should go lie down."

I had him now, though my mental grasp was tenuous at best. Garreth wriggled and writhed to get out of my grip, but I was able to force his body to dry heave once in a tremendous, echoing gag.

"Garreth!" Heidi cried out when he doubled over, retching.

He finally shoved me off, both mentally and physically, but the damage had been done. Heidi was all over him, bustling Garreth off to coddle him, and I was finally free.

I smiled pleasantly after him, and he bowed once in mock defeat, allowing himself to be dragged away.

"Was that really necessary?" Josephine asked, doing her best not to laugh.

"Probably not," I said. "Oh, hello, John. You've just missed poor Garreth. He's not feeling well, so Aunt Heidi took him upstairs."

John laughed once. "Poor bastard. What'd he do to deserve that?"

"Nothing!" Josephine said, swatting me.

"He knows what he agreed to!" I replied. "He knew exactly what he was getting himself into by coming over here."

"What did he agree to? To be abused at every opportunity?"

"No, I—" I cut off when Clara's face appeared behind Josephine's shoulder. She glanced away when I noticed her, just another person in the crowded great hall.

Josephine raised her eyebrows, questioning.

I opened my mind to her. *That maid is snooping behind you, listening.*

Josephine sighed. *Already?* "Gwenna, why don't you take John upstairs and show him what you've been working on?"

"More research?" John asked, taking my arm.

He steered me away from where Clara leaned against a wall, chatting politely with one of the soldiers from Silda. His hand was so warm, and my heart kicked up again. I didn't like to think about what that meant, so I shoved the feeling away into the darkest corners of my mind.

"When I can find the time." I forced my gaze away from Heidi's snoop and toward the stairs.

"Found anything good?"

"I don't understand what she has against me," I said in a low hiss as we climbed the stairs.

"Clara?"

"No, not Clara. She doesn't matter. She's an annoyance, but she's just a tool. It's Heidi that worries me."

"She has always been opinionated, that's true."

"Don't start your politics with me, Johnny. What is she doing here so far in advance of the Spring Festival?"

The noise of the main hall died away when we turned a corner. With a quick look around, he steered me toward the library at the end of the hall.

"Not here, Gwenna. Come on."

Twenty-One

The library was empty. There was no one inside, not even Wallace. Everyone had gone downstairs to meet the arrivals and greet old friends.

As little as Heidi liked me, her people were always happy to come here, and our people were always delighted to welcome them. Several of her entourage had been born and raised here in Valheid. And, of course, there were always messages and regards sent from friends left behind in Silda.

They all had friends or family members either in the Greathouse or in the town, and everyone else was just glad to have the excuse for a celebration.

John shut the door behind us, and I moved toward the cluster of armchairs that had become my own.

"Tell me what's on your mind, Johnny," I said.

"You're sure there's no one around to hear us?"

I confirmed it with a nod. "There's no one here. Not even Wallace."

"The pass wasn't clear, Gwenna," he said, his expression somber. "Heidi received word from some traders that came through Silda two weeks ago that the snow had almost completely gone, so she ordered the journey moved up. Right away, she said. But the pass wasn't clear. We had to break two feet of snow with a crust of ice an inch thick. The carriages barely made it through."

"Why didn't you turn back?"

He threw up his hands. "Hell if I know. Dan and I tried four times to convince her to go back and wait a few more weeks. Maybe send a team to clear the road. But she insisted we press forward."

"See? This is what I'm talking about, Johnny. There is something wrong here. I can't put my finger on it, but something has its hand on our lives. Josephine just tells me I'm obsessed, but I'm not. I'm telling you, something is wrong."

"What's made you think that?"

"Aside from getting impossible visits from Sasha, you mean?"

John took a step forward, his hand outstretched, alarmed. "You heard her again? When? Did you see her this time?"

"No, no. Nothing for a year. Nothing since that last time in my room."

He sat in the nearest chair, resting his head in his hands. His hair had gotten so long it curled around his fingers wildly. Many people had much longer hair than this, but he had always kept his so short. It was a strange version of him. I found myself wanting to reach out and touch it, the way Josephine had done on the front steps, but couldn't.

Instead, I knotted my fingers together.

"So, what else has there been?"

"I don't know," I said, looking away. The piles of books and scrolls on the low table drew my eye. These were safe to stare at. "Little things. Things that seem innocent on their own, but all together—"

"What things?"

"There's the big things. The attacks from raiders have continued steadily for years. Like the one when we met. Small raids. Occasionally, a farmhouse burns down. Those are easily explained, though. Just crime. But it's the little things that worry me. The petty fights that people have. Nanette says she lost an entire herd of cattle to disease last spring. Happened overnight. We've had five different families abandon their farms outside Valheid over the last few years. Their neighbors go looking for them one day, and they're all just gone. And now this. Heidi gets some report that the pass is clear and insists on coming now. Why?"

"You think someone is pulling strings?"

I shrugged. "I don't know. Maybe it's all coincidence, but I can't seem to let it go. It's like pushing on a sore tooth. On their own, these things are just isolated events. Nothing. But if you put them all together, plus Sasha, plus this wedding that Authe Ida sued for...There are too many events, Johnny."

"And what makes you think any of it's connected?"

"That's just it! There is no connection! Not one common factor. And that's why Jo thinks I'm obsessed."

"That and the research, I suppose." He picked up one of the books from the table, knocking several pages of notes to the thick rug with a flutter.

"It's the only thing I can think of to do." I pulled out the ledger and *All Things in Balance*, passing them to John.

"The prophecy?" The set of his mouth was eerily similar to the one Josephine had worn earlier that afternoon.

He gazed down at the verses scrawled in the margin, and not for the first time. I had shown this to him twice before. Both instances, I had come away feeling even less sure than before.

"That prophecy was about me, John. About Sasha. There has to be a reason she's cropping up now."

"The reason she started cropping up was because you made yourself known to her that first day, four years ago."

"But that's exactly what I'm talking about!" I knelt before him, rifling through a pile of notes. "She's not real, right? She *can't* be real. She was a vision. An alternative version of me. The life I could have had but didn't. She never happened." I couldn't find the page I was looking for and gave up. "So how could she have heard me?"

He held my gaze, shaking his head.

"Jo thinks it's an aftershock," I continued when he didn't respond.

"She's said as much to me before."

"She thinks it's in my head."

"I know."

"Do you think it's in my head?"

John stared at me for a long moment.

"You do?" My heart sank as the words broke past my lips.

"I don't think you're crazy."

"That's not what I asked," I said, getting up and retreating to the window.

"Just listen to me. I don't think you're imagining things. I felt it that night, that first time. I heard her myself."

"And?"

"The point is that there is no clear answer here. I don't know what to think about Sasha or about your connection with her. Is she real? Maybe. Is this all some recurring hallucination? Maybe."

I covered my face with my hands. How could he say such a thing?

"Gwenna..." John came over to me.

I took a step back, but he wasn't having that. He gripped my upper arms and made me face him.

"Look at me. Come on. Look at me."

I allowed my hands to fall and peered up at him. His hands burned on my arms. I clenched my fists in front of me to stop myself from reciprocating.

"I don't know what this is," he said, "but I think you're right to be concerned. Maybe it's nothing, but maybe it's something. We've all seen things we can't explain since you came home. In this strange world, you're the strangest thing by far. All the rules we had before, all the explanations we knew, you've defied them all."

He took my face in his hands then, making a blush creep up my cheeks. He was standing too close.

"I've never doubted you, Gwen. And I'm not going to start now."

I nodded a little before pulling away from his touch, breaking the moment. He let me do it, a little frown between his eyebrows.

I cleared my throat, looking out the window instead of at him. "So, I suppose you didn't find anything in Heidi's collection? No mention of the prophecy?"

John shook his head. "Heidi doesn't have a Wallace to curate a collection like this. Most of the historical texts that Silda ever had were sent here already. She had very little to look through."

"And there was nothing in Purgo?" My voice was steeped in resignation. "Or in Mairn?"

"No. Nothing."

"When do you go to New Ambia next?"

"Gwenna—"

"But I really wish I could go myself. Look here. Look at this ledger." I snatched the volume off the table and flipped to a random page. "See the Bs? This scribe must be the one who copied the prophecy into *All Things in Balance*. This is proof that the prophecy dates back to Queen Lily, at least, and he was Ambic. Maybe its source is in New Ambia? You wouldn't know to look for something like this. Maybe there was something... maybe something that didn't seem related. When you go back—"

"I'm not going back."

That stopped me in my tracks. I stared at him, my mouth slightly ajar.

John inhaled deeply and avoided my gaze. It took a long time for him to find his words, like back in the early days, when we had first met. With a flash, I remembered a moonlit night, sitting on a low wall overlooking a bean field.

"You make me stumble," he had said back then.

"I'd thought to stay home for a while," John said finally. "I've been traveling for years. I—" He shrugged.

"For how long?"

He shrugged again. He was so flustered, which set me to blushing again.

"Indefinitely."

"So, you'll be here for the Spring Festival next month?"

He smiled a little, amused. "I suppose so."

"They've made me the Chalice this year."

His eyes narrowed on me, the fluster suddenly replaced with a sharp tone. "What?"

It was my turn to shrug.

"You're the Chalice? With the grease paint and the kissing? And the—" He gestured at his own chest, clearly referencing the costume the Chalice wore.

Spring was a time of renewal, and the Chalice was the World Mother of fertility and passion. The costume was not conservative.

I nodded.

He crossed his arms. "Why?"

"Jo thought it was a good idea, since she's leaving this summer. She said it would be a good way to cement my position here with the people."

"Your place here is plenty secure."

"They're afraid of me, John," I said. "They're my friends, and they love me, but there's always this concern, this reverence at the back of everything they say and feel. They set me apart. I think Josephine is right on this. I want to do it. It's an honor to be chosen."

"And there was no one else?"

I huffed in exasperation. "Did you not believe me when I said I wanted to? Of course, there were other women who wanted to be chosen, but it fell to me. I was happy to accept. It's already been announced."

We stared at each other, both of us incredulous for entirely different reasons.

"So, you'll be there?" I asked.

"I don't know."

"You just said five minutes ago that you would be here for it."

"I don't think I can watch you kiss every person in the city in one night, Gwenna."

"It's not me! It's the Chalice!"

"It's you! It's—" John cut off and deliberately lowered his voice. "It's you."

"Are you trying to say you've never kissed a Chalice before?"

"Of course I have, but—"

"And you're standing there, acting like I haven't done the same?"

"Damn it, Gwenna!"

"You said yourself that vision wasn't going to rule us!" I hissed. "You said that to me, and then you left!"

He glared at me, and I glared back.

"I *had* to leave," he said, his voice dangerously low.

I shook my head. Not at him, but at myself. Of course, he'd had to leave. It had been best for both of us, and it was his duty, besides. I'd known it then, and I knew it now. But the words just kept pouring out of my mouth in a torrent.

"But now you're staying?"

John nodded.

"What if I said I wanted you to come to the Festival?"

"I won't kiss you."

"You don't have to."

We devolved into glares once more. We had come up here to talk about my research. How had we gotten derailed so easily? In four years, we'd never once brought up that damn vision we had shared.

It struck me then that I wasn't that girl anymore. I was older now. Old enough that the idea of wrapping my arms around his neck thrilled, rather than terrified. Soon, those visions would start coming true. Too soon.

"I'm going back downstairs," John said. That frown seemed permanently in place between his eyebrows. "I still haven't had a chance to speak with Kerric."

He didn't wait to see my nod of acknowledgement before he turned and strode toward the door, leaving me in the muffled silence of books and dust and pride.

Twenty-Two

Leland arrived only a few days after Heidi had settled in. He always came weeks in advance of a festival, trying to make every night a small feast while more and more guests arrived.

"This is why we set aside so much," Josephine said to me one afternoon. We had gone over lists with Margery, the head cook, and were strolling down the covered walkway outside the cookhouse. "He just loves to consume as much of our resources as he can while he's here. Get his money's worth, I suppose. At this rate, I'd almost rather do without his hops and grain."

"What if we requested more from him in tithes?"

Jo stopped and leaned against the stone wall, appraising me. "How do you think he'd respond to that?"

A mental picture came to me of his round face turning downward while still managing to simper.

"Not well."

"Exactly." She bounced away from the wall and continued walking. "It's not worth the headache. Plus we'd probably lose what we *do* get from him. Not to mention the men he sends to train with Cynebald for the Guard. As it is, we have enough to feed him and his entourage for a few weeks a year. It's a high price, but it's one worth paying. Barely."

"If we had Margery water down the soup while he's here, maybe he'd lose the taste for it and not stay so long."

Josephine laughed out loud and tucked my arm under hers. "Poor Margery's pride wouldn't survive, I think!"

"You're right. It's a bad idea," I said with a grin. "Plus, we'd be stuck eating it too."

"Exactly. Look, there's John and Paul. I wanted to ask them about the north field."

She pulled on my arm, and we both stepped out into the weak sunshine that shone down on the bustling courtyard in front of the Greathouse. The cold air bit against the exposed skin of my chest and forearms, but the breeze had begun to carry the scent of grass instead of snow.

At the sight of John, however, a bout of nerves drowned out the excitement of approaching spring. The men led mules in the direction of the stables, both mud-splattered and sweating despite the chill. I tried desperately not to lock eyes with John, but it happened anyway, just like always.

It was worse when he immediately looked away.

Josephine didn't seem to notice. "Just the two we needed to see. Please tell me you've dealt with the northern field."

"Not yet," Paul replied. "We're working on it. It's been left fallow for five years now."

"I've had Bernard complaining to me every day this week," Josephine said. "That field is the responsibility of the Greathouse, and he says hogs are tearing everything up and knocking down his fences."

"I'll go talk with him, let him know what's going on." John hauled on the stubborn mules even before he finished talking.

"Better yet," Josephine said, leaning after him. "You can go with Kerric and the rest of the hunters tomorrow and bring home some of that meat. We could use it, with all the guests arriving every day."

John's mouth soured. He still wouldn't look at me. "I've got ten men working on clearing that field, Jo. I can't just leave them to do it alone while I go off hunting."

"What's got you in a mood? Of course you can. Tell them they'll each receive a roast after it's been processed."

"I'll stay and direct the work," Paul offered to John's back while the latter continued to haul the mules along. "I'll deal with it, Jo. I promise. I'll see you both tonight at dinner. Save me a seat, Gwen."

I gave him a small wave and a nod, stepping aside when one mule brayed and lashed out with a whippy tail.

I stared after them both, eyes screwed up against the sun. "John's not happy with me," I said by way of explanation.

"Why?"

"Because I'm the Chalice this year."

It was her turn to stare after him. "Can you blame him?"

"I'm not promised to anyone. Even if I were, it wouldn't matter."

"It's not unheard of for a Chalice to take the role to heart. It started out as a fertility rite, after all."

"Again, what difference does that make?"

"None whatsoever." Josephine turned back toward the house. "But I can understand why Johnny doesn't want to think about you kissing other people, much less sleeping with them. Promised or not."

"I wish I never saw that vision."

"Don't be so sure about that," she said with a laugh.

"Either way, we have other things to think about right now." I sighed. "Leland will demand the best tonight."

Meals were held in the dining hall, where the Greathouse fed anyone who worked or lived there. Usually, it was simple fare: soups with coarse bread and ale. But when we had visitors, the kitchens outdid themselves.

The heavy tables were laden with beef, winter peas and cabbage, dark bread, dried fruits, and tureens of Margery's best onion soup, rich and full of flavor as usual. Mead flowed, and laughter shook the heavy beams that crisscrossed overhead.

I saved Paul's regular seat next to mine at the head table. Usually, John would have come to sit nearby as well. He was home so rarely, and he always made sure to get close enough for conversation.

But that night, he remained at the far end of the hall with his uncles and Dan, all of them still covered in mud from the day's work. Shortly after I found my seat, he looked up and gave me a friendly nod. An olive branch.

I smiled back. Maybe a little too readily. I wished he would come sit at our table, but I'd take the nod and be grateful. I'd have given anything to end this standoff between us.

Unfortunately, not even Paul could save me from my aunt, who positioned herself directly across from me that evening.

"I imagine you're not looking forward to this summer," Heidi said, her tone overly polite over her mug of ale. A thick lock of dark hair had come loose from her usual prim bun, and I couldn't stop staring at it.

"Why do you say that?" I asked.

"Because Josephine is leaving, of course. Getting married to that Metaxas boy."

"He's no boy, Aunt. He's past thirty."

She waved a hand dismissively. "What will you do with yourself? Once she's gone?"

I forced my eyes away from her stray hair and turned my attention to my plate. "I'll miss her, of course, but I'll be running the house. Jo has been teaching me what's expected."

"Oh. My dear." She speared a potato with her fork. "What an impossible task."

"Gwen is doing very well," Paul said.

"Of course she is," Heidi replied with too much sincerity. "But to run a house you did not grow up in? Josephine has been doing this since childhood."

Somewhere in the back of my mind, I knew she was baiting me on purpose. Maybe I hadn't grown up in Valheid, but I'd lived there for four years, and I'd been helping my sister run it all that time. Heidi knew this as well as anyone, and yet she needled at me.

And of course, I responded exactly as she wished: with too much fire.

"What alternative is there?" I asked, putting down my fork. "Whether it's an easy endeavor or not, it's fallen to me."

More than one head turned in our direction, Kerric's included. Heidi raised her eyebrow just a hair, which made it even harder to lower my voice.

"I am still learning. That's fair enough." I turned back to my plate. "But I am learning, Aunt Heidi. This is my home, and I will run it, as is my place."

"Of course, dear," Heidi said in an empty tone. "I have every faith in you."

"Heidi, are you tormenting my sister again?" Kerric asked from the end of the table.

A few people laughed, which had clearly been his goal.

"Of course not!" Heidi responded jovially. "Gwen is just a little over excited, that's all. We were discussing her plans for running the house once Josephine has gone off south to the sea."

The smattering of laughter at the table petered out.

"I'm not gone yet, Aunt!" Josephine said, dragging the mood back up by her fingernails. "I hope you're not counting the days, Gwenna!"

She was handing me a lifeline, and I wasn't so far gone to miss it. "Of course I am! I can't wait to be rid of you!" I raised my mug to toast her, and several others joined me, all of us laughing again.

"Oh, very good!" Leland called sycophantically from Kerric's left side.

This was another lesson. It was the job of the lady of the house to keep the peace, even with the Heidis of the world at your table.

"Heidi, tell us about the improvements you've made to your trout hatchery," Kerric said.

I caught his eye while Heidi launched into the details and mouthed a sincere "Thank you" to him. He gave me the barest of winks.

"You're going to have to work on that," Paul said to me in an undertone.

"I know," I said, forking a piece of fruit.

He sipped from his mug, grinning at me. "Who's that Garreth is talking to? That blonde girl?"

In the crowded hall, it was impossible to lay eyes on Garreth, so I had to cast out with my mind to find him. He sat with the usual brash of teenagers, joined by a few faces I didn't recognize. The blonde in question was closer to woman than girl, wearing a blue, linen dress meant for warmer weather than this.

"I don't know. Is she from Leland's party in Mairn? Must be. She didn't come with Heidi."

"Poor kid's going to have some heartbreak this season," Paul said, tucking into his food.

We watched them for a few minutes. Garreth gesticulated wildly to his rapt audience, telling a vigorous tale of adventure, no doubt. Everyone burst into laughter, Garreth included, when my nephew nearly slipped out his chair in his gusto.

"Would it be too mean to test him now? When he's so distracted and nervous?" I asked.

"Definitely," Paul said.

"Should I make him pick his nose or faint?"

"Pick his nose," came Paul's immediate response.

I gripped my fork a little more tightly in concentration, but I needn't have bothered. Garreth's shields were little more than paper and straw right now. He wasn't concentrating at all. If I moved quickly, I might actually get his finger all the way inside his own nose.

He felt me coming at the last second. His reflexes grew faster all the time, but he really hadn't been prepared, which was exactly the point of these exercises. So even though I sent his finger in motion toward his right nostril, Garreth aborted the action halfway through and ended up socking himself in the face with a limp hand.

Everyone at his table burst into laughter again, including the pretty blonde.

Paul snorted once into his mead, earning a pointed look from Heidi. I adopted an innocent expression, and Garreth turned to glare at me from across the crowded hall, incredulous. Heads turned toward the source of the laughter, assuming the young people were simply enjoying the party to the fullest.

But Garreth continued to face my direction, his expression melting to confusion and alarm. What was he looking at?

Everything happened all at once.

I allowed myself to cast out across the whole room and take a brief stock. Something was out of place, but I didn't have time to examine it. Whatever it was—or whoever it was—stood a good distance behind me, near the kitchen staff entrance.

Garreth launched himself out of his seat, running between people and across tabletops in a mad dash that baffled me. He kicked over plates and goblets, and their owners cried out in complaint. Gone was the laughter from his face. His eyes narrowed with purpose, his mouth set in determination as he scrambled toward me.

Then John's voice, unmistakable over the din of the crowd, bellowed, "To arms! Kitchen door!"

Heidi and Josephine, along with most on their side of the table, wore sudden expressions of shock and fear.

Kerric attempted to scramble away from the table, but his heavy chair slowed him down. He slammed his weight against the cumbersome thing, forcing himself up.

I took in all of this in under a second, then turned to face the presence behind me that had alarmed the room.

I had been so caught up in Garreth's shields that I had missed it. I hadn't noticed the man who didn't belong.

But I saw him now.

He wore plain clothing, dirty but well made for living rough. The man had no gear or bags, only a dagger in one hand and a sword at his belt. He sprinted forward at top speed, eyes on me alone, knife raised.

He was a mad bull trapped in the dining hall, and he was charging me.

TWENTY-THREE

I didn't have time to get all the way out of my chair. Didn't even have a moment to think or scream. I could barely comprehend what was happening before he was on me, knife careening toward my chest.

My body reacted out of pure fear and panic. Vision faded into white nothingness, and all feeling and orientation disappeared. Was this fainting? Had I passed out?

But I couldn't have passed out. I was still thinking.

There was a heavy thud and scrape when my chair went flying. The dagger embedded into the table right where I had been sitting half a second before.

But I wasn't there. Instead, I stood about five feet away, still but panicking.

My heart thudded away in my chest like a galloping horse, and my brain went completely silent while the scene erupted around me.

Half the room fled, and the other half charged. The man bellowed a wordless cry of frustration when Paul deftly knocked his hand away from the knife, which stood quivering in the wood of the tabletop.

At the same time, Garreth reached the table after his mad scramble across the room and hurled himself at my attacker, latching arms and legs around neck and torso. This sent them off-balance, and they both went down.

Kerric dove into the fray, along with two guards from other houses, and John crashed up to the chaos, barehanded and focused. He scanned the struggling pile on the floor.

It hit me that he was looking for me in that mess. I *should* have been at the bottom of that pile. The jolting realization set my brain to working again.

I'm here, I sent to him.

His wild eyes found me immediately. "Stop them!" he shouted over the din.

I nodded. Yes. That's exactly what I should do.

Since my brain had resumed operation, it was easy enough to halt every person in the fight. Only Garreth continued to move once everyone else had gone stone still. We could hear him grunting and struggling to disentangle himself, even over the panic and shouting from the rest of the room.

Garreth gave up pretty quickly. "Will you please help me out of this?" he asked of anyone who might hear.

John bent and started hauling men up. One at a time, I returned their movement so they could get up and dust themselves off. Each of them cast horrified glances at me in turn. I met every glare, one after the other, wondering which would be the first to condemn me for invading their minds. Which one would be brave enough to make me answer for myself?

At that moment, I couldn't tell if I would apologize or be defiant, and I desperately didn't want to find out. In the shock of the attack, it was near impossible for me to think. There was no telling how I'd react.

But no one spoke. They all looked away and tended to themselves. My own inner war was deferred.

Garreth got to his feet as Kerric and Paul bent to bind the man who had attacked me.

I already knew it was too late, but I let them discover it for themselves.

Someone had brought a knife to the defense and had stabbed the attacker in the throat. Blood spread in a wide, gruesome pool while the crowd gathered around. The immediate danger had passed, and now everyone just wanted to see.

"Search the kitchens!" Kerric shouted. "Cynebald! The house and grounds."

"I'll organize a search of the town!" Editha, one of the captains, shouted from the back of the crowd. She stalked out of the room, trailing several soldiers with her.

"Are you okay?" Josephine asked. She held me before her, looking me over from top to bottom.

I nodded. My hands were shaking and numb, just like that horrible night in the woods all those years ago.

"I knew for sure you'd be hurt!" Her voice was high-pitched and cracking. "He went right for you!"

I continued nodding while she worried over me, but I comprehended very little of it. Now that the danger had passed, the adrenaline crashed over me. A dull roar in my ears drowned out everything, and all I could think about was how I had to stay in control of this panic or someone might get hurt.

Something crashed into me, and I was smothered with a dirty work shirt wrapped across a thick male chest. John's arms went around me and crushed me to him. At first, my hands hovered behind him in surprise, but then they went around his middle in a desperate grasp for solidity.

"You can give it to me if you need to," he said into my hair.

I shook my head against his shoulder.

"You're so fucking stubborn," He squeezed me even tighter.

And just like that, as I breathed in his familiar smell of sweat, smoke, and horse, the panic began to leach away. I huffed a humorless laugh into his shoulder and tried to focus on slowing my heart.

They found no trace of the man who had attacked me anywhere in the Greathouse or in the town. No baggage or rented room had been abandoned. There were no campsites or covered up fire pits. Whoever he was, he must have walked into Valheid and come straight to the feast hall to make his move.

"He can't have been alone," Cynebald said that evening in Kerric's study. Kerric, John, Josephine, Heidi, and I had come to hear the report for ourselves. "He must have had accomplices to help him disappear so completely. Someone to account for any possessions and cover up his presence here."

"They came now by design." Kerric rapped his fingers on his desk. "Travelers are only just beginning to arrive. Just enough to blend in, not so many as to complicate things."

"It was planned. That's for sure," Cynebald agreed with a sharp nod of his head. "And if he did have companions, it's possible they will make a second attempt."

Kerric darted his eyes to me, but Heidi cut him off before he could comment.

"We can't be sure Gwen was the target. She may have simply been in the wrong place at the wrong time."

"We do know she was the target," Josephine said. "He went right for her."

"Maybe she was simply the first person he saw," Heidi said.

"We can't make any assumptions here." The edge in John's voice caught my attention.

"John's right," Kerric said. "No assumptions. We know nothing, and we have no way to get any answers, with the man dead and gone. All we know for sure is an attempt was made on my sister's life. Gwen, you've been threatened. I can't take that lightly."

"What does that mean?" I asked.

"It means you will be under guard from here on out. No more riding alone. No more going into the town without an escort. Not until we can be sure the threat is passed. We may want to get someone else to be the Chalice as well."

Josephine covered her eyes with one hand.

"I hardly think that's necessary," Heidi said.

"For once, I agree with my aunt," I said. "First of all, I wasn't alone tonight. I had more able-bodied protectors around me at dinner than ever. It didn't stop him. Secondly, I am not helpless, as you well know. In fact, I am probably the most capable person in this room. In this house, even."

"I know you can stop anyone, but you didn't tonight, Gwenna. He got past you when you were distracted."

"He got past me, true, but he still wasn't able to hurt me. I was able to get out of his path."

John stood up from his usual seat by the window. "I would like to hear more about that, actually. How did you move so quickly? You were in your chair one moment, that knife inches from your chest. The next thing I know, you're yards away. How did you do that?"

"I don't know," I said, biting my lip.

"You don't know?" Kerric asked.

"It was instinctual." I shrugged, my pulse rising. Words were pushing to my mouth, but I couldn't speak them aloud. How could I tell them what I suspected? What I remembered? That tonight was not the first time that I had moved in such a way?

Not even I understood it, and I was desperate to get up to my room to test my theory.

Josephine stared at me, eyebrows drawn together.

I shook my head, still shrugging. "I don't know. I just got out of the way."

Kerrick rubbed at his eyes, clearly exhausted. "You're not inspiring much confidence, Gwen."

"I don't want a guard," I said. "And I will be the Chalice as planned."

"I agree," Josephine said. "There is no need to give in to fear. Gwen will be safe enough at the festival. In fact, she'd be safer than most. She'll be visible and surrounded by people all night."

"Fine, you will be the Chalice," Kerric conceded. "But I stand by my decision that you don't go out on your own."

"But—"

"That's the end of it," he said, cutting me off. "Gwenna, I mean it. I want someone with you at all times. Someone who can handle a blade. Do you understand me?"

"Even in my room at night?" I asked sourly before I could stop myself.

"Damn it, Gwen! Don't test me on this! That man got into my house and made it within six inches of my family. In fact, every member of the household is under the same order. We will take every precaution. Josephine, Gwen, you both will carry a knife from here on out, and do not go out alone. Heidi, I suggest you do the same. And we will be doubling the watch from now until after the festival. That's the end of it. Get out, all of you. Cynebald, stay back, please."

We all filed out of his study into the still crowded great hall. Heidi said a stiff good night and moved toward the stairs. Her maid, Clara, appeared as if from nowhere, along with one of Heidi's guards. They followed her up and out of sight.

"Gwen," someone said.

We turned to find Garreth approaching us. He had cleaned himself up quite a bit, but a fair amount of my attacker's blood stained his clothes. Garreth had grown so tall over the last four years. I sometimes forgot he was only eighteen. He seemed so young, but that was how old I had been when I had first come to Valheid.

That was how old I had been when I'd become a murderer.

I hadn't felt young then, and Garreth didn't seem to feel young now.

"You're all right," he said, more of a confirmation than a statement. "Good. I'm glad. That means I can be pissed with you."

"What? Why?" I asked, affronted. The conversation in Kerric's office still chafed a bit, and I desperately wanted to get to the quiet of my room. I needed to think.

"No more surprise coercion," he said. "No more."

I rubbed the heels of my hands into my eyes. "Can we discuss this tomorrow?"

"No, now." He followed as John, Josephine, and I moved toward the stairs in Heidi's wake. We were all exhausted.

"I can't think about this right now, Garreth."

"There's nothing to think about!"

"Okay, fine!" I burst out. The noise and bustle fell away as we climbed the great staircase. "The answer is no. The lessons continue."

"I don't agree." He threw out his arms in a defiant shrug. Garreth had no difficulty in keeping pace with me. "You no longer have my consent."

"Well, that's sort of the point, isn't it? I don't need your consent."

"Gwenna," John said, his voice low.

"I don't!" I lashed back. "If he wants me out—" Then I remembered that Garreth was the issue here, not John. I turned back to my nephew. "If you want me out, then keep me out. It's as simple as that."

We reached my door first. I turned the handle, but Garreth braced his hand against the door frame so I couldn't open it and escape. Josephine and John slowed to a halt, unwilling to interrupt again.

"It's a violation!" Garreth hissed.

Blood boiled under my skin. "Of course, it's a violation! That's the point!"

"But that's just it, Gwen. There is no point. Why are we pursuing this? My shields are strong enough. You are the only person who can get through, and even you have trouble these days!"

"I have trouble, sure. But I can still get through."

To prove my point, I slammed into his shields. His hand blocking the door slipped a few inches, then stabilized. He really was getting exceptionally strong.

Garreth took the small victory and ran with it. "See? I've learned everything there is to learn. I am strong. We can continue regular lessons, but no more surprise attacks. No more!"

"The surprise coercion is the most important now. You have to be ready at all times. That takes training and vigilance. That is what you are still learning."

"But why? What purpose can there possibly be?"

"Because!" I stopped and took a steadying breath, glancing over at John and Josephine. I kind of wished they weren't here to witness this, but really, it didn't matter anymore. I adopted my teaching voice and leveled my gaze on my nephew. "What are my rules?"

"I don't see how—"

"What are my rules, Garreth?"

He rolled his eyes. "No coercion. No listening in. No lying. What does this have to do—"

"Listen, Garreth. No one should have the power that I was given. No one. But I have it. I am a bomb waiting to go off. I have rules for myself, and I follow them to the letter so that no one gets hurt. No coercion. No listening in. No lying. Not ever."

"I know that." He sounded a bit more like the teenager he was.

"But what happens when someone threatens Jo? Or your mother? Or Sinead? Or anyone else I care about? What happens then? What do I do when we need information from a man to save someone we love and he just won't give it up? It would be the simplest thing in the world to just dive in and take it. Should I do it?"

Garreth didn't answer this time, which was understandable. There was no right answer.

"What do I do when there are assassins in my house, threatening my family? Should I listen in to every person in the city to find them?" My voice rose again.

"Maybe!" he spat back defiantly.

"Should Kerric ask me to do that? Should I offer it?"

"Maybe you should!"

"So, you're saying it's right for me to invade the privacy of every person in this city on the off chance that one of them is guilty? Just because I was threatened? Who am I, Garreth? I'm no one. I'm no better than any of the rest of the people in this city. And neither is Jo, nor you. None of us is worth it. Because once I allow myself to break that rule, it will be easier to break it next time. And even easier the time after that. And the next. Until there are no rules. Until this heinous power of mine goes unchecked and I become the monster I was born to be!"

His words failed him.

John, Josephine, and I had never shared the horrific vision of Sasha with anyone aside from Kerric, but Garreth had probably guessed over the years. Whatever he assumed, I had just confirmed it.

"I need you, Garreth," I said. "I need you for that day when I start making compromises. When I start breaking the rules."

He stared at me. "But—"

"I hope that day never comes," I pressed. "I hope this is all for nothing. But one day I may hurt someone for the greater good. When that day comes, I need you to stop me. Because you're the only one who can."

Josephine gasped. "Gwenna."

Garreth glanced up at her. Understanding hit him, and he recoiled. "No. Absolutely not."

I stared at my nephew, feeling only coldness.

"That's ridiculous," he insisted. "Even if you can't control me, you can control others to protect yourself."

"That's why you train in the practice yard," I said. "If you want me out of your head, keep me out. The training continues."

I moved his hand physically, opened my door, and slipped inside.

"Gwen..." John pushed past a stunned Garreth. "We need to talk about what happened tonight."

"Not now," I said. "Tomorrow."

My hands shook on the door handle. These were things I had known for a very long time, but I had never said them out loud before. Garreth was still so young. He didn't deserve this, but what alternative did I have?

My nephew was still staring at me, horrified. Josephine took his arm and led him away. I couldn't bring myself to look at him.

"He'll be all right." John watched their progress down the hall.

"I know," I said to the floor. "He's strong enough to do what's needed. He proved that tonight when he tackled that man."

John smirked once, then turned a serious expression on me. "You have an awfully grim idea of the future."

"I have to be careful."

"I'd stop you before he has to," he said.

"No, you wouldn't."

"No, probably not," he said. "When's the last time you went hunting?"

"Two weeks ago."

"Come with us in the morning to the north field. We'll talk then." He pulled a sheathed dagger off his belt and held it out to me.

"I have a blade," I said. "I have six."

John pushed it into my hand and turned my braid over so the feather tied into the end showed right side out. "Well, now you have seven."

I took the weapon from him, mostly just so he would go. It was small, a comfortable fit for my hand. The handle was of a deep hickory with a steel pommel and crossguard. It had no ornamentation and was fitted with a plain, leather sheath, probably cowhide. It was exactly the sort of practical thing I'd expect him to carry.

John paused halfway out the door. "Are you sure you're okay?"

I nodded and squeezed his arm. "I'm just tired. I need to think about some things."

"What things?"

"Goodnight, Johnny." I pushed him gently into the hallway and closed the door.

I stood for a long time, leaning against the wood, clutching John's hickory dagger in my shaking hands. John remained on the other side for almost a whole minute, probably debating whether or not he should press the issue. But finally, he turned and walked back the way we had come.

I had to wait until he left to ensure he didn't hear anything that would alarm him. The whole time he hesitated and for many minutes after he had gone, I stared at the window across from me. I could see nothing but darkness outside the thick, wavy glass, but I knew what was below. An empty lane that ran between the Greathouse and the bakehouse, two floors down.

It was the last thing I wanted to do, but I had to know.

I had to be sure.

With a deep breath, I stalked across the room and thrust the window open.

Twenty-Four

The full moon lit up the night. Without the reflective barrier of the thick glass, the lane was clearly visible below me. Someone had left a cart full of hay down there, a few feet to the left of my window.

With great determination, I set one foot on the wide sill, then the other. It was a big step up, but not so much that I had to strain. I stood there in the chill night wind and strapped the hickory dagger to my belt, just in case.

The incident at dinner had alarmed me more than anyone in the Greathouse could know. How had I gotten out of the way of that man's knife?

When I was young, back in the Sacred Wood, I had long wondered how Theo could appear and disappear as if by magic. She had taken me with her, passed through the void separating our world from that dead place she called the Sanctuary.

And then I did it myself.

In my fear, I had fled Theo and her Sanctuary and returned to my own world.

The question of "how" had niggled at me consistently for the past four years. How had I done it? I didn't remember deciding or acting. It just sort of happened. More than once, I had stood in the silence of my bedroom and tried to slip out of the world, just like I had done back then. I had been afraid at first, but my need for answers drove me on.

But time after time, I failed. I didn't move an inch.

Until tonight.

The feeling had been just the same. Whiteness, disorientation, a sensation of nothingness. I had done it by instinct out of self-preservation. I had slipped between the worlds to reappear five feet away, out of danger.

If I put myself in enough danger now, could I do it again? Was this the key I had been missing? It was a whole new world of possibility, a gift far greater than any I already knew. And until tonight, it had stayed just out of reach.

I gripped the edge of the window frame and stared at the moonlit lane below. A fall from this height wouldn't kill, but it would cripple me. This was insanity.

No, there was no room for hesitation. Only real risk would force this other ability, this instinctive self-preservation, to work again.

And so, before I could think, I set my jaw and jumped.

Instantly, I knew I had been entirely mistaken.

The ground rushed at me in startling clarity. I could see every stone, every blade of crushed grass, one stubborn wildflower blooming too early at the edge of the lane. My stomach leaped into my throat. At first, I felt like I was hovering, but then the ground rushed at me. I stifled a scream and threw out my hands to brace my landing, but it never came.

When the panic reached a tipping point, it happened.

Whiteness overtook everything, and I lost the ground. An invisible current buffeted me into the void, directing my path through the nothingness.

But then it passed, and I hit the earth with a breath-stealing thud. I lay gasping in thin, pale grass, which clung to dry dirt. It took a moment before I could look around properly.

This wasn't the lane under my room. I had jumped out of my window and landed in another world.

Huge, gnarled trees rose above me, their sparse leaves still as stone in a windless, gray sky. Everything was silent. There were no insects, no scurrying animals, nothing.

It had worked. I'd done it—had passed through the void. But instead of simply moving out of the path of danger, I had fallen out of the world completely.

With a jolt, I sat up. This was the dead place. The Sanctuary.

Panic sent my heart beating again, but I gasped it down. This had not been my intended destination when I jumped out of the window, but I didn't want to leave again, not yet. This could be my chance to get the answers I had been looking for.

This place was important. It was part of the prophecy of the Child and Crone. In another life, it would have been my home and would have kept me young for decades.

It would have ruined me.

Suddenly, I felt a presence behind me.

I whirled to face Theo and leaped to my feet. My knees were bent, ready to run. I drew on every trick I had learned from Garreth, clamping shields of stone and glass over my mind. Theo was powerful, true. But I was stronger.

Beware, beware the Child.

"Well, hello," she said in a hoarse, dry voice. "I wondered when you'd find your way here."

Theo looked just the same as the last time I had seen her. She wore identical, threadbare clothes and had the same papery skin. The feathers and bones still rattled on her staff. It had only been four years, so it wasn't strange that she hadn't aged. But her clothes, so close to falling apart back then, should have been in the rag bin by now.

I said nothing. This was something Kerric had taught me:

Allow the opponent to fill the silence with information, not the other way around.

"Still nothing to say to me? Even now?" Theo asked. "You're talkative enough among other people."

"People I trust," I said.

"You should be less trusting, child."

"But I should put my faith in you?"

She smiled half-heartedly but let it pass. "To what do I owe the honor of this visit?"

"Chance."

"Chance, is it? Didn't mean to come here, did you? Came by accident?" she asked in a tone of blatant disbelief.

"Yes."

She raised one bare eyebrow. "Is that a fact? You're stronger than I guessed."

"What is this place?"

Theo appraised my wary stance for a few seconds before replying. "Why do you want to know about the Sanctuary? You've made your home in the world, among people. Have you bedded your man yet? Will you marry like your sister? Like the *civilized* people by the sea? What do you care of this 'dead place'?"

She emphasized the last two words in such a way as to make it clear she knew how Josephine and I referred to it. Theo wanted to be absolutely sure I knew just how little I could hide from her. It was blatant intimidation.

"If you know so much about me, then you'd know why I ask," I spat back. "There is much I don't understand about myself, about the life I could have had. About the prophecy between us."

"Does it haunt you?"

I did not reply.

"It's not too late, you know," she said thoughtfully. "It's not too late to help me, to help those like us. This place"—she spread her arm wide to encompass the silent, dead wood around us—"it gives the gift of time. We have all we need. We can stretch across kingdoms, generations, time itself, and bring about the change that is needed. Safety for the sibylline."

"You've said as much before. But I'm not convinced you know what you're doing. You haven't improved the world much, so far as I can see."

She narrowed her eyes at me. "You live in peace and security among people who know what you are, do you not? Such a thing was not possible even fifty years ago. Trust me. I remember the persecution all too well. There is a reason I named this place The Sanctuary."

I clamped my mouth shut and again said nothing. She was pulling me out of my depth, and we both knew it.

Theo took advantage of the toehold she had gained. "And trust me when I say your place in that city is tenuous at best. And your Jo is sending herself into a lion's den. How do you think those people in Bluewater will react to a sibyl amongst them? One married to the lordship? One who will give them telepathic heirs?"

A cold stab of fear ran through me. Theo was very good at this, at her "whispers." She named one fear after another, corralling me.

"This is what I work for, child! And you can help me. Together we can make Authe Ida safer for Josephine and her children! We can make it safer for the hundreds like her living in hiding."

"This is not why I'm here!" My shouts sounded strange in the silent wood. The thirsty earth robbed the air of all noise. "I want to know what this place is! I want to know how I got here! How I moved here!"

Theo stared at me, incredulous. "Isn't it obvious? It is a shame you did not come to me as a child, Sasha! I could have taught you so much!"

"My name is Gwen!" I hissed.

"It wasn't always," she said calmly. "I've seen visions of her, did you know?"

Again, my mouth clamped shut. This was too much. I had gone too deep. It was time to leave, but I couldn't make myself go.

She was taunting me on purpose to keep me here. I shouldn't listen. But it was working, and I was allowing her to draw me in.

"I used to see visions of us practicing together here in the Sanctuary. You would have been powerful, stronger than you are now. You'd have had the training and the time you needed to become a true force in this world. You are a shadow of what you could have been."

"I am not her! She never happened. I am not that abomination!"

Theo stopped, and I sucked in my breath. I had said too much. She had loosened my tongue. I shouldn't have come here. Clearly, she had not seen what Jo had shown me. She had not seen how Sasha would overpower Theo and ruin all her plans for acceptance.

"Why do you say it like that? 'I am not her?'" she asked. Her eyes narrowed, and her tranquil tone disappeared. She became a rat scurrying after the scrap of information I had let slip.

I took a step back in fear when she advanced on me. "Don't touch me!"

Theo reached for me anyway, with claws for hands, her eyes alight. "She heard you, didn't she? She heard you in a vision! I knew it! I have heard myself before, only once. I thought I'd imagined it. It never happened again. But I knew it!"

She gripped my arms, shaking me slightly. I tried to back away, but she held tight with her gnarled fingers. Her manic smile twisted her lined face into a grotesque mask.

"They are real, aren't they? The visions? They're not echoes. They're real!"

I ripped my arm out of her bony hands, my heart racing. On instinct, I drew John's hickory dagger and brandished it at her, but it didn't matter. In the same instant, the whiteness overtook me again, and I was hurtled through nothingness.

With a wave of nausea, I found myself brandishing the dagger at the empty air in my own bedroom, the window open on my right. My breath came in ragged gasps, and I dropped the blade with a clatter.

But this horrific night wasn't over yet. My eyes fell to a spot of empty air by my bed, and a little girl's delighted laugh filled the room.

No.

I sank to my knees and covered my ears, but I still heard it. "Go away," I said.

The laughter dropped away, but she was still there. I sensed her moving closer, though her feet made no sound on the floorboards.

"You can't tell me what to do," said Sasha's smiling voice.

I bent further until my forehead came to rest on the floor in front of me, my hands still clamped over my ears.

She was right. I couldn't tell her what to do. So I wallowed inside my own mind and closed it all up in shields of thick glass and iron. If I kept my focus inward, she became muffled and distant.

All I could do was wait her out.

TWENTY-FIVE

"What's bothering you?" John asked the next morning.

We rode side by side in the northern field, seemingly alone. The rest of the hunting party had spread out, disappearing in the fog and the overgrowth. The early morning sunlight wasn't strong enough to chase away the chill. The hoof-beats and the voices of the others floated to us in the mist as they passed.

It had been a productive hunt so far: two hogs taken and two more spotted when they ran from us. Usually, I would have been giving chase as good as any, but that morning I couldn't muster the energy.

"I didn't sleep much last night," I said after a long moment.

Editha appeared as if from nowhere and bolted past us in a thunder of hooves and flying mud. She threw a determined grin at us and slipped between the young trees ahead.

"She'll get one today if it kills her," I said in a desperate attempt to redirect John's attention.

It didn't work.

"What was keeping you up? Was it the attack or Garreth?"

"Both, I suppose." Even though I hadn't had a thought to spare for either subject all night.

"Garreth will be fine. It was a shock for him, but he'll get his head around it."

"I know."

"And there is no guarantee that any other attack will be made or that you were even the target last night."

"I know," I said again.

"But you're still worried?"

"No, I—" It was so hard to lie to him. It always had been. I shouldn't have been lying anyway.

"What?" he asked.

I should tell him everything: how I had escaped that man's knife the night before and how I'd jumped out of my window afterward. John should know I had spoken with Theo. It all tried to come out at once, but it only jammed up in my mouth.

Instead, I pulled on the reins. "I'm going back to the Greathouse."

John's hand was fast. He leaned out and grabbed the nearest thing he could reach, which turned out to be the hem of my wool coat. His horse followed the lean of John's body and stepped closer so he could grip my reins and stop me from leaving.

"What aren't you telling me?" he said over my half-hearted protests.

I covered my face with both my hands and focused on breathing for a second. There was no getting away from this. He wouldn't believe me. No matter what Theo had said last night, I still wasn't sure myself.

"I think she's real, Johnny."

"Who?"

"Sasha. I think she's real."

"You're Sasha."

I shook my head, my face still covered. "No. I mean the vision we saw and the voice we heard. She isn't just an echo. She's real."

He watched me, appraising. "What brought this up? Did you feel her again?"

I nodded miserably into my hands. "She was in my room half the night."

John let go of my reins and sat back in his saddle. "She's silent for almost an entire year, and now this. And you're sure it's not just a sort of vision? Are you sure you're not having premonitions or seeing the past?"

"She responds to me, John! She hears me! She answers back!"

"Stranger things have happened, Gwenna. The fact that she seems to hear you does not make her real! How can she be? She's you!"

"She's not me!"

"She is! She is you! You cannot be in two places at once, Gwenna. You can't. It's not possible."

"How do you explain it, then? How could I possibly be interacting with something that isn't real?"

He hesitated for a moment, clearly afraid to say what was on his mind. "I have a theory."

I waited with halted breath for him to continue, but still he paused.

"What is it? Please."

"Maybe it's like a dream," he said finally.

My gaze grew hard. "A dream?"

"Don't look at me like that, Gwen. Yes, a dream. I don't mean it's nothing. Clearly, it's not nothing. But we don't know what dreams are, really. What we do know is that truths can appear to us in dreams but distorted. Maybe these episodes are visions, but distorted like dreams are. Whatever your gifts are trying to tell you, maybe your own fears are twisting it around and making it unclear. Giving them the appearance of yourself as you could have been.

"I know there are parts of yourself that you are afraid of, Gwen, and Sasha is the embodiment of those fears. Maybe that's what you're seeing and hearing. But I know one thing for absolute truth: There is only one of you. She can't be real. Not like you are."

The misty silence fell around us once more, and rain began to drip through the trees. I had been so sure of myself just a few moments before, but his theory made sense. I was torn between fear of the little girl who haunted me and the desperate desire to believe John, that she was just a phantom, a product of my own second sight.

"There's more," I said softly. "Last night, after you—"

But an inhuman scream drowned out my words.

My horse's mane twitched horribly and flashed red. She vaulted me up and backward. I scrabbled at my horse's bloody neck, desperate for anything solid to hold on to, standing up in stirrups that were suddenly at the wrong angle. Then she came crashing down, only to launch upward again, this time unseating me violently.

There was no time for panic or reaction. No time for anything.

One second, I teetered over the backside of what now seemed like an absurdly large animal; the next, I slammed into the ground and cracked my skull on a rock.

"Shh, Ms. Josephine," someone said. Mary's voice, smooth and familiar. "Just lay still."

The more Josephine tried to focus on it, the more it slipped away. Like a dream within a dream.

Josephine hurt everywhere. Joints, head, jaw, chest. It felt like a nasty illness, the kind that sapped all energy and spiked fevers. But it wasn't as bad as the cramping in her abdomen. And none of it upset her more than the mess of blood between her legs.

Faces swam into focus around her: Heidi, Clara, Mary...She lay in a carriage, tucked in tidily on the seat. The other women mopped her forehead and whispered fervently with each other. Heidi was crying and hissed at her maid in a panic, but Josephine couldn't make out their words. It was so hard to focus on anything.

Josephine hated the blankets they had wrapped her in. She should be cozy and warm and dry, but she wasn't. Josephine was wet and sticky with the hot blood soaking her thighs and the padded seat beneath.

Voices carried in from outside the carriage, but Josephine couldn't be bothered to place any of them. None of it mattered. Not anymore.

Josephine!

Her eyes popped open. Had they been closed? The interior of the carriage swam around her. Clara leaned down and tried to bring a cup of water to her lips, but Josephine turned away from her and reached out for the voice in her head.

John? Did you find Gwen?

Yes! She's alive! We're coming.

Josephine! I'm coming! Hold on just a little longer! It was Gwen. Her inner voice shone like a bright flame in the darkness.

Clara tried again to push the cup of water on Josephine. "Just a little more, Miss Josephine," she said while Heidi looked on with watery eyes. "Just one more sip."

Consciousness came back in stages. First was the pain. It dragged at my skull like jagged glass. Then came the light rain pecking at me. The sharp, cold sensations pushed away the last dredges of the disturbing vision. I could still feel Josephine's helplessness, her hopelessness, her agony...

But now I was back in my own body, in my own mind. Just a

moment ago, I had been having a conversation with John in the morning mist and had been thrown from my horse.

And what of my horse? The poor mare had been injured, though not too badly. Where had she run off to?

Where was John? He had been right with me when I fell. Did he run off to find the person who had shot my horse? What else could have caused that unnatural twitch of the mane and the sudden swipe of blood across her neck? Someone had fired an arrow, and once again, I had probably been the target.

My head hurt too much to move, and hot blood soaked into my hair. No one seemed to be coming for me, but I desperately needed help. I closed my eyes again and reached out with my mind.

John hadn't gone off to find the archer. He lay unconscious in the dirt six feet away from me. A quick mental check confirmed he was unhurt, only sleeping. I had probably put him out by accident again. It was very likely no one had any idea there was an archer, which meant the danger had not passed.

Dizzy, I reached out further in all directions. The rest of our hunting party still gave chase to the two hogs they had spotted just before Editha had passed us in the woods. I had only been uncon-scious for a few seconds. Three had heard my horse's scream of terror and were circling back to check on us.

But they wouldn't make it in time.

There was only one other person in the area: a woman kneeling on the rise to my left, behind an elder tree already dotted with tiny white flowers. A stranger. She had found a better vantage point to see me where I lay in the bloody scrub. The woman had already nocked her next arrow, drawn back her string, and lined up her shot.

I lashed out in a panic. There was no time to think, only time to act. I clamped down on her consciousness with such force that it shattered. The woman collapsed, and her arrow lobbed half-heartedly from her bow when she went limp.

In the blink of an eye, she was dead. I had accidentally severed the link between mind and body in my panic.

I closed my eyes on tears of anger and regret.

Murderer.

"Gwen!" John's voice clawed its way into my muddy head. "Gwen! Are you okay? What happened? Oh, fuck, your head!"

His face swam over me as I cried in the increasingly muddy underbrush. The rain pelted harder in a steady drizzle. I shivered from the cold but also from the pain and shock.

"What happened?" he asked. His gentle fingers found the blood soaking into my hair.

"John! Gwen!" Another voice cut through the fog. Kerric's horse loped into view, followed closely by Garreth and Editha. "Are you two all right? We heard a scream!"

"It's Gwen!" John answered over his shoulder as the others approached. He eased me up into a sitting position, but I was so unsteady I could only lean against his shoulder. "She got thrown! Hit her head. I passed out too, but only because she did."

"Shit," Kerric hissed. He slipped off his own horse and fell to his knees in the mud next to me.

They didn't know. My horse had fled and was long gone before either of us had woken up. They wouldn't see the wound across her mane that had caused her to rear.

"How bad is it?" Kerric was asking.

John.

"Shh!" John pressed his cheek against my forehead.

The skin contact made it easier to find him in the fog. I was so dizzy I couldn't think straight enough to find the words to tell him what had happened, so I showed him instead.

"Fuck," he groaned.

"What?" Kerric asked.

"What is it?" Editha barked, at high alert.

John ignored them both and asked me softly, "Where is she?"

With a shaky finger, I pointed up the hill on our left. Editha turned immediately to look up the hill, but of course, she could see nothing from this vantage.

"Help me get her up on my horse," John said to Kerric.

"What's up there?" Editha asked, her eyes trained for any movement on the hillside.

"A dead archer." John passed me into Kerric's arms so he could retrieve his horse. "She shot Gwen's horse, apparently."

"We'll find her," Kerric said, grim. He helped me onto the horse in front of John. "Get her home. Editha, go with them. Eyes open. Garreth, with me."

John held me against him with an arm like iron around my back. Even so, his horse took off with such gusto I was nearly unseated again. I rested my forehead in the scruff of his beard as we rode through the rain, with Editha thundering along beside us.

My injury wasn't as bad as everyone feared.

"Head wounds always bleed a lot," Gregor muttered offhandedly. He closed up the wound with a few efficient stitches.

Some rest was all I needed, though the throbbing pain in my skull persisted for days.

My poor horse had fled the north field and gone straight back home to her stable. Her wound had been superficial, nothing a few stitches of her own couldn't fix. The head groom answered my worried inquiries by coming up to my room himself.

"She's being given the royal treatment and will be just fine, Lady Owl. She'll be in the low pasture for a few weeks, until her wound heals up proper."

I thanked him profusely and promised I would be down to the stables as soon as I was well enough to check on her in person.

And while I wished I were well enough to work, I wasn't. Not right away. All I could do was lie in my bed and go over, again and again, the premonition I'd had about Josephine.

She was going to miscarry a pregnancy.

When? I couldn't tell. Likely soon, if she was with Heidi, Mary, and Clara. It would probably be before she went to Authe Ida at the end of the summer. What was worse, she would be alone. She wouldn't have Aris with her, nor Kerric, John, or me.

Did you find Gwen? I would be missing. I would be so far away she wouldn't be able to reach me with her mind. Would Josephine be traveling to Aris's home in Bluewater, then? With me in Valheid, running the Greathouse like she had been training me to do? That was the plan, anyway. It all fit.

I had been looking forward to Aris's arrival shortly before the Spring Festival. He made it so easy to let go and laugh. His energy would lighten Josephine's mood, lift the house, and make all the preparations fun rather than a chore. Everyone loved his visits. But now, I dreaded looking him in the eye, knowing what was coming for him.

Why wouldn't he be with her when she was sick?

Josephine didn't understand why I wouldn't talk to her. She sat with me all through the night after my fall, but I just turned away and pretended to sleep.

"You're worried about something, aren't you?" she asked the next morning while I sat facing away from her on the bed. "You won't even look at me."

"I'm just sore." My dark hair fell over my shoulders in heavy waves. I twirled it between my fingers, agitated.

"No lies, Gwen."

"No lies," I repeated dutifully.

"Omitting the truth is the same as lying."

My mouth stayed stubbornly shut. I had omitted so many truths by that point, and I could feel them snowballing. But saying them out loud wouldn't help anyone. It would only leave me even more unsure.

Josephine tried again. "Gwen?"

"It's just the same things as always." I still did not turn to face her. "I'm worried about Sasha. I'm worried about the festival. I'm worried about you leaving. I've had some upsetting visions. And always the prophecy—"

"What visions?"

I shook my head but winced. "Nothing important. I'm just going over the same things, over and over. And I'm hurting, Jo. It's nothing, I promise."

Lie.

"If you're worried, you should talk about it. You can tell me anything, Gwenna."

I wanted to share it with her, but it wouldn't change anything. Knowing what was to come would only hurt her more. What difference could it possibly make?

I remembered what I had said to Garreth only two days before. *When I start making compromises...*

"There's nothing to worry about, Jo," I said.

Lie.

Twenty-Six

Aris arrived not long after that. I was up and about, though my head was still too sore to do much of anything.

Everyone went down to greet him when he arrived, just as we had done for Heidi. I stayed up in my room, where it was quiet and calm, and watched from the little window over my dressing table overlooking the courtyard. He had brought a whole caravan with the usual loads of goods: silks, sea salt, and barrels of citrus fruits of all kinds.

After the fuss died down, he and Josephine came up to find me.

"I see you've gone and gotten yourself laid up again," he said, wrapping me in a hug. Aris was dusty and smelled like horse, but his skin was the ruddy bronze of someone who lived and worked by the sea.

I could almost feel the salt air just looking at him.

"I don't do it on purpose," I said with a grin.

"They still don't know who's behind it?" he asked. "Jo's been catching me up on everything that's been going on. Do they think it was the same people that stormed the dining hall?"

"It must have been," Josephine said for me. "The first man left no trace. No belongings, no camp, no room rented. This archer was just the same. She had nothing with her except for her weapons."

"And we have no idea why they're targeting Gwenna? Is it because of her gifts?"

"Four years ago, I'd have said so." Josephine lowered herself into my armchair by the bed. "But you've been living here so long, Gwen. Why now?"

"Maybe they've only just worked up the courage or resources," I suggested, but it didn't feel true to me.

"I don't know," Josephine said. "We can't know. These people keep dying before we can ask them any questions."

I winced and looked away. They had carried the archer off once John and I left the field. They had buried her that same day after a thorough examination of her body. I never saw her. Not once, dead or alive. But still, I had killed her.

"I should have made her sleep. I could have," I said.

"You were panicked and injured, Gwen," Josephine said, reassuring. "I'd have done the same thing."

"Would you, though?"

"Yes," she said with a firm nod.

"Too right," Aris agreed. "But if another one has a go, try not to panic. I'd like a chance at them."

"Hell, Aris," Josephine said.

It was only a matter of time before John came looking for me. I expected him every day. Each time Mary knocked on my door, whenever footsteps sounded outside in the hall, every time Aris, Josephine, or Sinead came to check up on me, I thought it would be him.

But it never was.

Josephine said he had asked about me to make sure I was doing all right, but John never came to see for himself.

I didn't need him. After all, I had plenty of company, and everything was taken care of for me while I rested. I hadn't needed John for years. He had left Valheid to make absolutely sure that would be the case.

But still, every time the door opened and it wasn't him, my heart sank a little.

While I lay in that bed, trying to ignore the throbbing in my head, all I could think about was how his neck had curved around my forehead, his arm tight around me, and the heat of his chest as he raced me back to the Greathouse in the rain. John had been terrified and focused and worried, and I had felt it all.

I was in love with him. It had been creeping up on me the last year or two, so slowly I'd barely noticed it. I had tried to ignore the erratic tapping of my heart every time he came into view and would chastise myself whenever I noticed the curve of his thigh or the breadth of his chest. The warmth and comfort of him was friendship and familiarity, or so I tried to tell myself.

But it wasn't. It never had been.

I'd known to expect this ever since that night in Barano, on the front deck of a little, rain-battered inn. Ever since we'd shared that damned vision and all paths before me disappeared but one. Only John.

Would I still feel this way if we had never seen that vision? Would I have fallen for someone else? Paul, maybe? A life with him would have been simple and peaceful. There were also several young men in the town or in the barracks who had caught my eye over the years. Would I have pursued those options further? Or would I have stayed alone, taking lovers but no partners, like Kerric had always done?

None of that mattered, though. It never had. We had both always known what was coming for us. And now that it was upon me, I was afraid of it. The fact John stayed away made me think he felt much the same.

When he finally did come find me, I was in the library, sitting in an armchair next to my sprawling pile of books on the low table. The apple tree outside had burst into full blossom, and the sweet floral scent wafted over to me on the breeze. I had come for a change of scenery, though I still didn't feel up to research. The wingback armchair was comfortable and familiar, and the books were old friends.

"What are you thinking about?" he asked.

I jumped, not having realized anyone else was there. Instantly, my face reddened, and I looked away. Having now admitted my feelings to myself, after ignoring them for so long, I was shy of them.

He must have noticed my anxiety, but being John, he took it all in stride. "Does it still hurt?" he asked, easing himself into the chair across from me.

"A bit," I said, eyes on the apple tree outside. "I'll mend."

"Two attempts on your life in as many days. Are you worried?"

"Are you?"

His mouth turned up in a crooked smile. "No. I'm more worried you'll kill yourself by accident."

I pressed my half-formed smile into my knuckles, still refusing to look at him.

"Your hair is so long," he said. "I didn't realize."

I chanced a glance at him. John wasn't looking at my hair. He studied his own hands.

"Braids pull on my stitches," I said.

"You always wear it up. And you've got no feathers. I don't think I've ever seen it loose before. Aside from—" He cut off and fell silent.

I fidgeted in my armchair. We both knew what he had stopped himself from mentioning. We had seen quite a lot of each other in that shared vision. This only confirmed my suspicions. He had been mulling over the same things as me the past few days.

"Speaking of which," he went on finally.

"John," I tried to cut in, but he talked over me.

"Speaking of which," he said, a little louder. "I'm sure you noticed, as I did, that the visions are starting to come true. You and I on that horse, in the rain, covered in blood. We've been there before. Do you remember?"

I buried my face in my hands. "Of course, I remember."

He dragged his chair closer to mine, and I pressed further into my wingback. John ignored this gesture and leaned forward.

"Gwen, I can't tell you how terrified I was to wake up and find you bleeding out there. I thought you were dead."

I couldn't help but scoff lightly. "I can't have been dead. What about our destiny?"

"Not all visions come true, and you know that. I want this one to be real. I'm ready for it. Aren't you?"

It was so like him to just say things outright.

"No," I blurted without thinking.

"That's not true and you know it." John took hold of my upper arms in a coaxing stroke. "What is it that's holding you back?"

I shrugged and flung one hand out absently, then crossed my arms over my chest. "There's no one thing," I mumbled. I couldn't tell if I wanted him to move away or come closer.

"Is there someone else you care for?" He asked it very carefully.

"No, but that's just it, John! There could have been. There have been others. But I knew from the beginning that they would all come to nothing. Every path was taken from us. From me and from you. It isn't fair."

"I don't give a shit what's fair. I thought I made it clear to you when we first saw that vision that it meant nothing. It doesn't have to mean anything."

"How can it mean nothing? You saw it the same as me. You felt it. How can you say it is nothing?"

"I don't mean this is nothing." John stroked my arms again. He squeezed, gentle, clearly stopping himself from drawing me to him. "What I mean is, we don't love because we saw the vision. We saw the vision because we love each other."

I shook my head, but the words wouldn't come.

"Tell me what you're thinking. Good or bad, I want to know."

When I still could not form my thoughts into words, he continued.

"I know you love me, Gwenna, sure as I know I love you. If that damned vision taught me anything, it taught me that. I saw it. I felt it. And I know you did too. Whatever has tangled you up, I know it will sort out with time."

Again, doors slammed around me. One by one, the options disappeared.

"Let me ask you this," John said. "If we hadn't seen that vision, would you still be hesitating? If you didn't already know that you and I would be forever, would you want me then?"

I considered this for a long moment, tried to ignore the vision and consider my feelings separately.

Yes, I had been missing him over the last few days while I convalesced. He had always been a confidant, even when I thought myself to be crazy. After the attack in the dining hall, only his embrace had been able to calm me. And the past four years had been a chaos of excitement and disappointment as he came and went.

I had barely touched him since that day in Barano four years earlier. I couldn't bear it. But I'd wanted to.

What was stopping me now?

Nothing.

I slid off my chair and wrapped my arms around his neck in a tight hug. It startled him, but he embraced it immediately and came down onto the floor to kneel with me. His beard scruffed against my ear as I hugged his neck. John buried his face into my loose hair and held me against him like he'd never let go.

The solidity in his arms soothed away every anxiety, and the words finally came.

"I do love you." I breathed into his hair, which had grown too long. I ran my fingers through it the way I had been imagining for days. It was soft and thick under my skin and smelled like smoke, sweat, and earth. "We should have been allowed to discover it for ourselves, but we weren't. I know my next path is you. I wish I didn't know it, but I don't regret it. But John, the path I'm on now hasn't ended yet. Not quite yet."

"Gwenna, please."

"In ten days, I play the Chalice," I said, holding firm around his neck. "I won't do that if I'm promised to someone."

He tensed up, gripping me tighter somehow. "You're still going through with it?"

I chuckled and turned my eyes to the ceiling. "It's a great honor to be chosen, John."

He released me then, but he was reluctant to let go of my hands. Neither of us could look the other in the eye.

"Ten days," he said.

"This path ends with the festival."

His hands were rough and stained, with nails bitten too short for comfort. I couldn't take my eyes off the sight of them wrapped around my fingers.

He must have liked how it looked as well, for he drew my hands to his mouth and pressed a kiss to my fingers. My stomach swooped deliciously at the feeling of his lips on my skin, and I sucked in a startled breath.

I wanted to take his head in my hands, to claim that mouth myself, but not yet. The time wasn't quite right.

He met my gaze, eyes hard. "I won't kiss you," he said.

"I know."

TWENTY-SEVEN

In the past, I would have canceled lessons with Garreth in the days before a festival. So many things needed extra attention. Crates and barrels would have to be unpacked and inventoried, livestock slaughtered and prepped, and washing done. The kitchens ran day and night to prepare food and heat water. We brought on extra help from the village to take care of the many visitors, and everyone needed their hands held.

And on top of all the preparations, everyday work needed to be done, now that the snows were finally melting. Shearing and sowing and weaving and trading and building. The city was alive with activity.

And the closer we got to midsummer, the more I felt the weight of it all on my shoulders. While Kerric dealt with the politics of Derehan, it was Josephine and I who kept the gears of Valheid running. And soon, it would fall to me alone.

More people arrived every day. Tensions were always high when the crowds got thick. Even though the general spirit was a happy one, guardsmen were alert and ready, especially in the evenings, when beer and whiskey flowed freely in the streets and public houses. More than once, they had to intervene when some petty argument got too heated, and the guardhouse served as an excellent place for the over-indulged to sleep it off.

Usually, I would put aside my routines so I could devote all my attention to helping and learning from Josephine how to make sure everything went smoothly. But this year, my sister had decided *she* would be the one assisting *me*, rather than the other way around.

"So you can get a feel for the full responsibility before I go," she said matter-of-factly while I fretted over lists, casks, and the inevitable handful of careless helpers.

But in light of the argument with Garreth a few nights before, I dug my heels in and carried on with lessons as usual.

He noticed.

"Can't this wait until after the festival?" Garreth asked, arms crossed and bitter. "I'm supposed to be patrolling right now."

"Editha knows you have extenuating circumstances," I said with a set expression. "She'll accommodate you."

"And why are they here?" He jerked his head toward John and Sinead, sharing a bench at the foot of the table, and my sister, who sat at the head. We held our lessons in Garreth's apartment, as usual. His rooms were grander than my own, but not by much. He was his father's heir, after all.

This room he used as his office. As a child, Garreth had studied with his tutors at this table. But now, he mostly used it as a surface to collect books, belts, and bows, with one corner kept clear to use as a workbench for fletching arrows.

He never bothered to clear it off when I came for lessons, and today was no exception.

"They are here because you cleverly found a hole in our education last week," I said. "You pointed out that I could simply coerce others to disable you, even if you kept me out of your own mind."

"We're volunteers for the slaughter." Sinead grinned madly. She tossed her thick braids over her shoulder and rubbed her hands together.

"May the Old Kind save you, Sinead," Josephine swore, but the other ignored her.

"This should be fun!" she pushed on. "I've never been coerced before. What does it feel like?"

Sinead's hand rose up, and she neatly inserted her finger into her left nostril.

John snorted with a poorly concealed humor.

And of course, because John had laughed, my own mood soared. After our conversation in the library, a huge weight had been lifted. Now that we had spoken the words aloud, every worry and disappointment I'd harbored seemed so childish and far away. This man was my favorite person, and soon our life together would begin in earnest. Everything was falling into place.

The romance of it hadn't been stolen after all.

I turned my attention deliberately away from John, whose smile broadened when he found me grinning back at him.

"I am going to attempt to control the others, and you are going to try and extend your shield to them," I told Garreth. "I picked these three specifically. Jo is sibylline, like me, but John is only a passive telepath. Sinead is ungifted entirely. Between them, we should get a good idea of what is possible."

Things did not go well. Not nearly as well as I had dared to hope.

"He can't extend his shield at all," I told Kerric that evening after supper. Josephine and I sat with him in his study, taking advantage of the rare opportunity for the three of us to speak in private.

"Should he be able to?" Kerric asked.

Josephine shrugged. "There's no 'should be' about it, I'm afraid. We're all figuring this out as we go."

"He's the only one that can keep me out," I said. "And I was desperately hoping he'd be able to protect others as well."

Kerric slid his eyes over to Josephine, and they shared a look.

"I'm not being paranoid," I said sourly. "Even if my fears are unfounded. Even if I never cross a line, even if—" I hesitated over the name, like always. "Even if *she* is just a figment of my imagination, there is still Theo. There may still be other unknown threats like Theo. It is worth being prepared."

"That's true enough," Kerric said.

"There is one positive," Josephine said, clearly desperate to placate me. "I was able to shield Sinead's mind from Gwen, though only for a few seconds. And with John's help, I was able to hold the protection even longer."

"Which got me thinking," I said, when Josephine gave me an encouraging gesture. "Then I tried shielding Sinead's mind, and Josephine couldn't get through at all."

"So even though Garreth can only protect himself, we can protect others."

"And we can improve our skills with time." I refrained from pointing out that if I was the threat in question, then none of this mattered. They would have responded to such a statement the same as always, and the exchange wouldn't be helpful.

Kerric watched us, eyebrows raised. "So overall, a good lesson, then?"

"Yes, even if it wasn't in the way we hoped," Josephine said. "Any new information is a step in the right direction."

"Speaking of information..." Kerric's voice was too light, and I instantly went on edge. "There have been some complaints about Heidi's maid, Clara."

Clara tried again to push the cup of water on me. "Just a little more, Miss Josephine."

I shook my head to clear the upsetting premonition away. Just the mention of Clara's name was enough to drag it to the surface.

"There are always complaints about Clara." Josephine's voice served better to drive away the ghosts than my determination alone. "Who has she been pestering now?"

"Everyone," Kerric said. "Complaint after complaint. 'She wants to see my inventory lists.' 'She follows me around.' 'She demands to be left alone in the storeroom.' 'She sneaks out after dark.' 'She threatened me just for asking what she was doing.' 'I caught her coming out of my room.' It's endless."

"So, talk to Heidi about it," Josephine said. "She threatened someone? That *is* an escalation."

"I won't read her," I said, ignoring Josephine's suggestion.

Kerric's gaze darkened.

"Nobody asked you to," Josephine said.

"He was about to ask it. If he was going to speak to our aunt about it, he would have just done it. He's bringing this up now because he doesn't want her involved." I turned to our brother. "Do you suspect Heidi to be behind Clara's actions?"

"I've spoken to Heidi about this in past years, but the pattern continues," Kerric said. "Either Heidi is exceptionally poor at managing her people, which I'm sure we can all agree is not likely, or she's allowing it. Or maybe even asking for it. Gwen, if you could read her thoughts, we could put all this to—"

"No." The word fell flatly between us.

Kerric froze, his last words half formed on his lips. Josephine pursed her mouth and said nothing.

Finally, he tried again. "You won't even consider—"

"No. And I'm ashamed of you for asking it." My heart thumped in preparation for a fight, but with great determination, I stopped myself from saying anything worse.

Kerric was very like me. We were both stubborn and hard-headed as goats. His chest rose and fell with the effort it took to not dress me down. He was my elder and my lord, and he was not accustomed to being refused.

"Josephine has helped me in this way many times in the past," he began. "Especially back when Eustis Metaxas was in power. The bastard used to send spies across the southern border to cause havoc, and they were very hard to deal with. So, we'd ask a few leading questions to get them thinking about the incident in question, and Jo listened in as they constructed their lies. But this time, I feel greater skill may—"

"Then ask Jo to do it again!" I said too loudly. "You already know my opinions on that disgusting tactic, but at least with her, it will only ever be listening in!"

I had to leave. There was no way in hell this situation was going to improve if we both remained in the same room. Already, Kerric swelled in his chair, ready to give back as well as he got. And I was so worked up that it would devolve into shouting almost immediately.

In a haze, I found myself stalking out of the door, which slammed behind me despite my best intentions to de-escalate. Faces turned toward me—various servants, guards, and visitors. Aunt Heidi herself was walking by, arm in arm with Leland the Pest. They both stopped to stare, and Heidi raised one eyebrow, as if to say she was supremely unsurprised by my behavior.

"Come, my dear," Leland said to her in his high, melodious voice. "Let's walk outside, where it's quieter."

"Excellent idea," Heidi replied. "It's getting a little crowded in here, isn't it?"

The pair turned and headed toward the front doors.

"Yes, you're right. Very crowded."

I watched them go, bemused. What an odd pair they made. It had never occurred to me that Heidi would ever take a partner. She was so severe it was difficult to think of anyone wanting to spend much time with her.

I shook my head. That was unfair to Heidi. She didn't like me, true enough. But that didn't make her a wholly bad person. If a little companionship made her happy, then all the better.

Mary caught my eye next as she moved across the main hall toward the door leading down to the kitchens. I called out to her, mindful of all that still needed to be done before the festival in two days. Plus, as Michael had always said, there was nothing better than work to soothe the mind.

"Miss Gwenna! There you are!" Mary called in relief. She veered in my direction. "We've been looking for you everywhere. Do you remember that delivery of plum cider we were expecting last week?"

"Twelve casks? Has Carl still not arrived?"

She shook her head. "They sent a rider to inquire this morning, and he's just got back. Andrews farm is deserted. Just like the others. Animals everywhere, crops rotting in the field…Cynebald is probably on his way up to see Kerric about it any minute."

Shit. That was one meeting I desperately wanted to butt in on, but I didn't dare so soon after shouting at my brother.

Josephine.

She responded immediately. *Yes?*

"Miss Gwen?" Mary asked, but I put a hand on hers to halt her question for a moment. She understood and fell silent.

Cynebald is on his way up to speak with Kerric about the Andrews farm. Will you stay and hear what's going on?

What happened?

The general himself appeared from a sheltered doorway across the hall, expression grim as usual, and strode in our direction. The axe he habitually wore on his belt shone in the failing light coming through the open front doors.

He's on his way in now. The farm was found deserted. I want to know what's going on.

Cynebald disappeared into Kerric's study before I finished the thought, and Josephine didn't have a chance to respond.

"What do we have to replace the plum cider?" I asked Mary, my eyes on the door.

"Margery thought of a light sangria using last year's wine. I was just on my way to give her this updated inventory of the cold stores."

"I'll come with you," I said.

Twenty-Eight

The Chalice was the World Mother of fertility, renewal, and passion. She was the embodiment of our baser natures, and every year, we did our best to celebrate them all night long.

When I was little, growing up in the Sacred Wood, Michael and I would remember the World Mother by roasting duck eggs and dried plums on the fire, staying up late telling stories, and dancing to the music of Michael's finger drum.

But here in Valheid, "little" would have been blasphemy. In the center of the market square, we would light a great bonfire whose flames would rise almost as high as the second-floor windows of the Greathouse. Interspersed through the crowd would be groups of musicians playing drums of every size, from tiny finger drums like Michael's to great basses the size of a steer.

The kitchen staff laid out platters of food on rows of tables: perfectly boiled eggs seasoned with mustard and chives, cinnamon tarts and last year's dried plums, cold sausage and great wheels of strong cheese. Jams and jellies were ladled out; any berry or fruit which had once held a seed was made into a spread for Margery's best crusty bread.

And though the traditional plum cider was sorely missed, sangria, ale, and wine would do the job well enough, along with several cases of rum Aris had brought with him from Authe Ida, as a goodwill gift from his father.

Because I was playing the Chalice this year, I didn't go out to start the festivities with Josephine and Kerric. Instead, Sinead and Mary stayed with me in my room, watching and joking while the bonfire was laid out and people began overflowing the square below my window.

The women had brought with them the little trunk holding the Chalice costume. When they opened it, the room was bathed in the scent of rose oil, which had been used to treat the leather skirt before storage every year.

Without a word, I stripped down to nothing. Sinead passed me the leather skirt and helped me tie it securely in the back. Then together they used the soft woolen band to wrap around my chest. There was no shirt.

I hadn't expected to feel so exposed. My body began to tremble with nerves and anticipation. Sinead noticed, but she only winked and grinned wickedly at me. Her frivolous attitude helped with my anxiety, and I returned her grin.

Though there wasn't much clothing, there was plenty more in the little trunk. The women drew out strand after strand of bells, little bones, shells, feathers, and animal teeth. These were draped around my neck, tied to my wrists and ankles, wrapped around my bare waist, and woven into the elaborate tangle of my hair.

Every part of me was meant to draw attention. The bells rang, the bones and shells clattered, and the feathers fluttered. With every movement, I was a cacophony of noise and life.

Mary came with the little pot of grease paint next. It hung from a beaded chain to be worn around my neck. It hung heavy below my breasts, thumping against a strand of bells around my waist.

She pulled out the cork and passed it to Sinead to be set aside.

Next she dipped her fingertip into it, which she used to paint great swaths of dramatic black under each of my eyes. Mary dipped into the paint one more time and used her blackened finger to draw the symbol of the chalice on my forehead, just under my hairline. A simple curved line—the bowl of a goblet. The representation of a womb.

As was traditional, we had all kept our silence from the time the chest was opened. Now, Mary broke that silence.

"Bless me, Lady Mother."

With a ringing, rattling movement, I picked up the paint pot from where it lay against my stomach. I dipped my trembling finger into the paint and rose to draw the chalice on Mary's forehead too. The bowl-shaped symbol was wobbly, and I willed my hand to stop shaking.

"Bless you, child," I recited, the bones clattering in my hair. I leaned forward noisily and we kissed each other lightly on the cheek.

"Bless me, Lady Mother," Sinead said next.

I repeated the blessing with her. The chalice, the kiss.

When I pulled away, Mary grinned, bouncing on the balls of her feet. Sinead was hardly less excited.

"Let us go down, Lady Mother," she squeaked. The giddiness in her voice greatly tarnished what was meant to be a solemn recitation, and it pulled a smile out of me.

"May the peoples of your womb be blessed, Lady Mother!" Sinead said with extra bravado, swinging her arms toward the door to lead me out.

The Spring Festival was no portentous occasion. It couldn't be. These young women, like everyone else in the city, were ready to let loose their inhibitions and enjoy the night. With the ceremony over and the days of work and preparation done, it was finally time to play.

"Let us go down, my children." My heart still thudded heavily in my nearly bare chest, but their squeals of delight when they turned to wrench open the door were good for the soul.

They preceded me through the nearly empty Greathouse. A few stragglers spotted us while we moved down the stairs. They whooped and chided their friends to move faster to beat us outside.

I hesitated just before exiting the big double doors. Even through the anxiety about kissing so many people, about being so exposed all night long, one other thing jangled my nerves.

Would John be out there? I had told him the festival was all that stood between him and me. A thousand different things might happen tonight, but I couldn't let myself get lost in that forest of fear.

With a deep determination, I stepped out into the night.

It was dusk. Drink flowed, and people danced to the rhythmic music of the drummers. It took a moment for word to spread that the Chalice had arrived. Excitement moved through the crowd like a great wind through tall trees. People cheered and reached out to touch my arm, my hair, or one of my feathers when we passed.

For the first time in four years, not one single person seemed to care what I was. Tonight, I was just the Chalice. I wasn't overly gifted, wasn't a bomb waiting to go off or an unnatural phenomenon. I was just me.

It felt wonderful.

Mary and Sinead led me up to the bonfire, where Kerric, Josephine, and Aris waited in a little knot. They turned to greet me when I stepped up to them.

"Bless me, Lady Mother," Kerric said with an easy smile, though his voice was barely audible over the drumming and the crowd. It seemed that no matter what our argument had been before, it didn't matter now.

I found the pot hanging from my neck and painted a clumsy chalice on his forehead with my finger. He presented his cheek to accept my kiss and gave me one in return, and then he passed me the torch.

With one encouraging glance from Josephine and one giant smirk from Aris, I turned to face the crowd. I thrust the torch high into the air, and the crowd roared.

"May all the peoples of my womb be blessed!" I shouted into the din.

I lowered the torch to the pyre, and the bonfire leaped to life, causing those of us standing too close to step quickly backward.

"Bless me, Lady Mother!" Josephine cried with a laugh after we recovered from the excitement of the bonfire.

I painted her chalice and kissed her. She dragged Aris forward.

"Bless me, Mother!" he shouted, gamely.

I laughed and blessed him next.

"Bless me, Lady Mother!" I didn't know this man.

The crowd shifted and writhed with the rhythm of the drums. It didn't matter who he was. He was one of the many people of the womb. So I painted his chalice and kissed him lightly, same as the rest. He whooped and twirled away to dance.

And then came another, and another, and another. An endless stream of revelers asking to be blessed. Some I knew well; others I didn't. I found it extremely hard to kiss Leland, but I managed it. Just the lightest brush possible and then away before his perfume could overpower me. And Heidi primly presented her cheek to me next. She didn't kiss my cheek in return.

It didn't matter. I wasn't me. Everyone was blessed because I was the Chalice.

I painted chalices for them all, kissed each of them. It was a night of touching and moving and letting go, and I found it to be the easiest thing in the world to do. We were all one family together, one celebration, one life.

After a while, the blessings slowed down, though they never stopped completely. There was always someone else who needed a chalice and a kiss. But after a while, I found time to dance and eat.

Sinead and Paul dragged me over to join their group by the fire, and we all danced as a single many-limbed creature, with the drummers beating out our pulse.

Even though the night air was cool, sweat coated our skin. Shirts were quickly abandoned, by women as often as men. Others joined us and left again, all of us moving to the endless, irresistible beat. Occasionally, someone would come up to me with a bare forehead, and I would bless them without stopping the dramatic swaying of my hips. Then they would dip me back and land a kiss somewhere on my face until I laughingly shoved them off.

As the night drew on, everyone got drunker and bolder. More than once, I had to pull away before a light kiss on the cheek became something more intense. But by then, nearly everyone had been blessed, and they were searching for kisses elsewhere.

Getting drunk had never been an option for me. So, while everyone else had an endless supply of energy, I began to feel the night wear on. I extricated myself from a stranger's arms with care and slipped out of the mass of dancers. After a quick mental search, I located Josephine and Elana near the food-laden tables.

"There you are!" Josephine called when I approached.

Elana handed me a cup of sangria, and I drank it down, reaching for a cinnamon tart at the same time. "Having fun?" she asked with a grin.

Her chalice mark had gotten smeared at some point in the night. A swipe of black stood out on the back of her wrist, where she had rubbed it partly away.

"Yes!" I shouted. "But I'm getting tired."

"You're not allowed to get tired." Elana laughed. "You're the Chalice. You're here 'til dawn."

I groaned good-naturedly. "I'm going to need a little more to drink in that case." I reached for another tart.

"Look who came!" Josephine slurred, pointing. From out of nowhere, Aris barreled into her from behind and buried his face in the curve of her neck. Josephine ignored this and shouted, "I told you he'd come! I told you!"

Aris found her mouth, finally claiming her full attention.

I turned to where she had pointed, and my heart jumped into my throat. John leaned against the low wall bordering the square. He watched the dancers crowded around the bonfire, his expression tense. He still wore his work clothes, though he seemed to have made an effort to wash his hands and face.

My heart swelled in my chest at the sight of him. Maybe it was the wine. Maybe it was the laughter and the singing all around me. It could have been because I had been playing the part of the Chalice all night, spreading joy and boldness to everyone I met. Whatever it was, for once, I didn't hesitate.

I won't kiss you. Fine. That was fine.

"Hold this," I said, handing my sangria to Elana.

She smiled, adding its contents to her own before stacking the cups.

John noticed me coming through the crowd.

As the Chalice, I drew everyone's attention. That was the point. Between the jingling anklets and the bells in my hair, I was audible, even over the din of the dancers and the roar of the fire. Revelers stopped me more than once, asking to be blessed. I obliged them, drawing the little black chalice on their foreheads, kissing them, and spinning them off to join the crowd.

He watched it all with furrowed eyebrows. John stood motionless against the wall, his eyes traveling audaciously over the bare skin of my midriff while I walked toward him.

"You came," I said, once I was close enough to be heard.

"You asked me to."

I couldn't smile, though I wanted to. Something lingered in the air between, something bigger than a smile, but I didn't know quite what to do with it. So, as usual, when I didn't know how to interact with someone, I fell back on ritual.

With a rattle of beads, I dipped one finger into the little pot of grease paint hanging around my neck. All my fingers were black to the second knuckle by now, so it didn't matter anymore which I used. I reached up and drew a graceful chalice on his forehead, just below his hairline. He let me do it, taking in my own elaborate face paint. Heat flooded my face as he stared at me.

Then, because I had been doing this all night long, I leaned up to kiss him on the cheek.

He jerked away from me before I could touch him, however. It was just an inch or two, with a sharp intake of breath, but it was enough to stop me stone-cold. We locked eyes, neither of us daring to move at first.

"I've been watching you," he said, when I sank back to my heels.

"Have you?"

"It's good to see you laugh and dance. You don't get to do that very often."

"Would you like to dance with me?"

His mouth twitched with indecision.

I took his clean hand with my filthy one and pulled him toward the bonfire. He didn't stop me, which I took as encouragement enough. When we reached the mob of dancers, all of them drunk and alive with the heavy beat of the drums, we didn't know what to do with each other.

But I still gripped his hand in mine, and he held tight as well. My heart began to hammer. My fingers burned where he touched them, and I wanted to feel that everywhere.

I pulled on his hand to make him step closer. Bodies heaved and pulsed all around us. The fire cast strange shadows over John's face when he came near, making him appear wilder and fiercer than anyone there. His eyebrows were clenched in a frown, his mouth drawn. He darted his eyes down toward my midriff again, but this time, it was because I had placed his hand amongst the strings of beads and bones on my bare waist.

I began to swing my hips in the familiar rhythm I had been

using all night long. My body knew how to move, despite the tension called up by John's hand on my bare skin. I turned in his embrace and leaned back against his chest, always moving to the drums.

Dance with me.

He relaxed behind me and finally began to move.

John knew how to dance as well as any of us in Derehan. We all learned at a young age. Even I had been taught, by our little fire in the hollow, to ride the pulse of the music and *dance.* It was a part of who we were. We were wild and free, and we loved it.

When he danced with me, truly danced, everything else melted away. There was nothing but the two of us. Feet stomping, hips rolling, chests heaving. There was no tension, no romance, no nothing. We were just two sweating bodies lost in the movement, marveling at how well we responded and reacted to each other, reveling in the sensations of skin sliding across skin.

I could have danced with him for the rest of the night. It could have gone on for the rest of my life, and I never would have tired. But after a while, John lost the rhythm a bit. He moved a little slower, then a little slower still.

His gaze grew dark, darting from my mouth to my eyes and back again.

My sense of the rhythm stumbled too. My heart beat out of sync with the drums. It hammered in my chest, and for the first time in hours, I remembered I wasn't far from nude.

And for the first time ever, that thought excited rather than embarrassed.

His fingers were iron bars on my hips. He took half a step to close the distance between us. My chest heaved in anticipation, setting all the balls rolling in my little bells. When he finally kissed me, it was open and wild and free. No hesitation, no awkwardness of a timid first kiss. It was confident and matter-of-fact.

This was inevitable, and it was glorious.

And as he possessed my mouth right there, in the mass of

dancers, I finally lost all sense of control. John stepped right into the sphere of my mind, right among the roots, and we became one mind together. I tasted like cinnamon tarts, and beer lingered on his breath. My mouth was soft and pliable. He loved the feel of my arms tight around his neck and my fingers in his hair, the glide of lips and tongues and teeth.

He was on fire, and so was I.

Couples and groups had broken off from the main party to find shadowy corners or deserted alleyways wherever they could. Tonight was the time to enjoy flesh and sensation, and no one held back.

The first three places we stumbled to were occupied, but finally, I was able to locate an empty garden shed just around the corner. John hauled the door shut behind us a little too roughly and shoved a light stool against it. The barricade would be nothing if anyone tried to open the door, but neither of us were thinking straight.

He lifted me onto a creaking workbench, scattering hand spades, empty pots, and netting. And because I wore nothing beneath the little leather skirt, the only barrier between us was his own work pants. That barrier was removed in half a second, and then it was done. We were connected. And for the first time in my life, I finally understood what a fulfillment sex could be.

It wasn't just pleasure; it was a completeness. We were whole and mended. Before, I had only been myself, but now there was us. It was a rightness I hadn't known existed in the world until now.

And knowing it was John I clung to and kissed, John who worked inside me, John whose waist my thighs clamped around, that was enough to turn me to liquid gold in his arms. It didn't matter that we were rutting in a dirty old potting shed or that anyone walking by could hear us. Tonight, this was exactly the right thing to do. Anything less would be blasphemy.

"Be my woman," John gasped afterward. He held my face

between both hands and kissed me over and over. "Take me as your man and have no one else."

"Yes." I breathed into his kisses.

"Promise yourself to me," he said with a smile. "Say it again."

"I promise." I took his mouth. "And you. You have to say it too."

"Gwenna, I promise myself to you." He kissed me everywhere: my neck, my jaw, my lips. He breathed his oath in my ear. "You're my woman, and I'm your man."

"You're my woman, and I'm your man," I repeated breathlessly.

He stopped and looked at me, a teasing expression on his reddened face.

I giggled. "You know what I meant!" I said, pulling him close.

We both grinned and laughed and kissed again. We would never stop. There would never be enough.

The door slammed open, sending the flimsy stool flying across the shed, and two young men locked eyes with us in the doorway. We all froze in shock. John did his best to shield me from view, with his own pants around his ankles.

"Out!" John yelled over my surprised giggles.

"Pardon!" the first man said. "As you were!"

"The Chalice? Nice!" the second crowed.

"That's the Owl!"

John grabbed an empty terra cotta pot and threw it at the closing door, sending shattered ceramic flying in every direction. Both men laughed hysterically and went off to find some other secluded corner.

John's glower immediately softened at the sound of my laughter. I tugged on his shirt and pulled him back where he belonged.

TWENTY-NINE

I don't know what I had been so reluctant about. John had been a fixture in my life since the day I'd met him, a magnetic north constantly dragging my compass in his direction. But now, he had become part of the very fabric of my life, and I'd finally found that feeling of home I had been searching for since arriving in Valheid four years earlier.

Very little changed, but somehow, everything was different. In the few days after the festival, with the Chalice costume cleaned, leather conditioned, and stored away in the little trunk once more, the city and the Greathouse resumed its normal pace. The visitors left, and the market stalls which had swelled out into the city proper were once again neatly contained in the three market squares.

Margery took two days off from the kitchen, which was her routine after a festival, and the Greathouse resumed its quietude.

John went about his usual tasks, and so did I. Life continued as normal. And though everything was the same, it was all somehow better. Knowing I would see him in a few hours, that he was mine and I belonged to him, that his things were slowly migrating to my rooms, that he'd be there at night without fail—it made all the difference. We weren't alone anymore.

Not that I'd been alone before. I had friends, family, and a life with purpose. But having him meant my heart grew even more to accommodate the new and glorious whole.

After a couple of weeks, when he'd usually take off for Mairn or Authe Ida or New Ambia, he stayed, just like he had said he would. Kerric appointed Dan to take his place as emissary, and John joined his uncles in the leatherworks guild. He came in for dinner every night, smelling like burnt leather, saddle soap, and lye.

"Do you miss it?" I asked one night while he shucked off his work pants.

"What?"

"The traveling?"

John shrugged and began running a soapy cloth over his chest and arms by the basin in the corner. "Sometimes. I think I'll miss the people most. I have friends everywhere now. Good friends."

"You won't miss sleeping under the stars along the road?"

His beard twitched with a predatory grin. "Not with a soft, familiar bed waiting for me every night."

I smirked when he started toward me, still dripping and only half washed. "You won't get bored with the same bed every night?"

"Not with you in it," he said, crawling up on the sheets.

I backed away, laughing. "You're getting the bed all wet!"

He scooped me up and buried his face in my neck. "Good!"

Aris would stay two months with us, then he and Josephine would travel to Authe Ida for their wedding at midsummer. In light of the premonition I'd had about Josephine being alone and ill on the road, I convinced her to allow me to come with her for the ceremony. It was only ten days by the road circumventing the Sacred Wood, but ten days could be a long time in the wrong circumstances.

And because I was to go, John also insisted on coming, likely for similar reasons. Not only his best friend, but also his woman would be off traveling and gone for only the Old Kind knew how long.

"I can't say I'm disappointed," Kerric admitted to me in a low voice one night over dinner. "I'm sending six men to escort her, plus Heidi and her men, but I'll feel better knowing you and John will be there."

"You mean you'll feel better that John is there?" I asked.

"Yes, that's true. He has proven his abilities on the road more than once. But I'm glad you'll be there too."

"Why?"

"Because you're going to Authe Ida, to Bluewater. I don't trust Metaxas, especially not in his own city. And even though I know you refuse to use your abilities, I believe you would for her."

I stared at him, a little taken aback.

"If you had to," he said seriously.

And to my deep disquiet, I couldn't tell him he was wrong.

PART FIVE
A JOYFUL DEATH

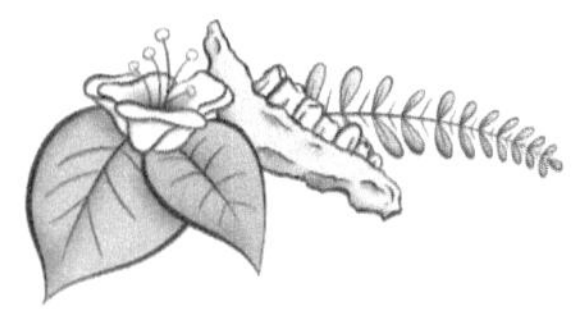

THIRTY

Two months passed in a flash. It was one of the happiest times in my life. All my favorite people in one place, with no Heidi and no Leland to spark my temper. It had been a good season, with busy markets and promising signs of a plentiful harvest to come.

And every night, I lay in John's arms, wondering at the security and warmth I had found. That vision between us, however it had plagued me before, faded into a distant memory. It was something to laugh at and dismiss, which was exactly what we did.

Before I knew it, we were having a bittersweet farewell feast for Josephine and Aris. Margery outdid herself once more, and we all ate, drank, sang, and told stories about Josephine as a child. Everyone agreed wholeheartedly that marriage was silly nonsense but that Aris was a good man for our Jo.

As planned, Heidi arrived two nights before we were scheduled to leave. The Greathouse became a confusion of packing, sorting, lists, and tearful reminisces right up until we rode away.

It wasn't my turn for goodbyes, but I still teared up when Josephine hugged Kerric farewell. They grasped each other tightly, whispering words meant for just the two of them in that great crowd of well-wishers and escorts. When she finally broke away, Jo's eyes were red, and her face was a mess. She gave my hand one quick squeeze when she passed on her way to her horse, which Aris held for her.

"Take care of her," Kerric said, hugging me next. "And be safe, Little Owl."

I nodded, brushing away my own tears.

"We'll send a rider as soon as we arrive," John said, passing me my reins.

"I'll be looking for it." He turned and embraced our aunt next, then helped her up into her carriage.

We were a large party moving out of Valheid. Heidi's passenger carriage also held Clara and Mary, who would be assisting the group on the long journey. We also brought a covered cart full to bursting with Josephine's possessions and supplies for our trip.

With four of Heidi's guards, six of ours—including Dan as emissary—six Authe Idan soldiers who had come with Aris, John, and me, two vehicles, eight spare horses, and a stray dog that followed us out of town, we would be moving slowly.

"It usually takes ten days to make this journey," John said brightly from his saddle. "But with all this, it could take more than two weeks."

"No wonder so many cut through the Sacred Wood," I said.

Josephine and Aris raced to the front of the party, clearly delighted to be on their way to a new life despite the farewells.

"Are you glad to be back on the road?"

John turned to me, eyebrows narrowed. "This isn't the first time you've brought this up. Are you worried I regret my decision to stop traveling?"

"It was your life for a very long time," I said.

"That's true. It was. And I'm grateful for those experiences. But I have no regrets, Gwenna. Not one." He gave me a broad smile, then slapped the back of my mare. "We'd better get going, or they'll leave us behind."

We moved at a decent clip and arrived at Barano by midday. We stopped there for Dan to speak with Governor Cornelious and to change the horses. John and I slipped off from the group, promising to catch up as quickly as we could, and went off south to Mariah's house.

From the first glimpse, I could tell something was not right. The house was cold and empty, the door hanging open on its hinges.

"Oh no," I said, stepping inside.

The remains of a dinner prep rotted on the butcherblock, the knife resting as if it had only just been set down. Someone had been looting. Drawers sprawled open, with their contents strewn about. Nothing of significant value had been missed.

"Where could she have possibly gone?" I asked.

"She can't have told anyone. We'd have heard she was gone." John righted a small table and stared down at the knife on the butcher block. "This is the same knife she used on your leg that night."

"Is it?" I peered closer at it. A small paring knife, sharp but plain.

"There's no one around?" he asked.

I shook my head, dread tying my stomach in knots. "No. This is a dead place." I swallowed hard and pushed back the tears threatening to fall. "There's no point in staying. Let's catch up with the others."

Despite my determined bravado as we loped away, I still looked back at the empty windows. My friend was gone. She had been gone for a long time, it seemed, and I hadn't known. And there was absolutely nothing to be done about it.

We were able to stop in towns every few days to resupply and change horses, but more often than not, we had to halt early in the evening and camp near the road.

Heidi begged Josephine to sleep in the relative comfort of the carriage, but my sister refused. She snuggled up to her man by the fire instead. Something told me she wouldn't be sleeping rough again for a very long time. Authe Idans weren't wild like us.

As much as John claimed to prefer my soft bed, his mood wasn't dampened by the hard ground and the bugs flitting by the torches. And even I found it to be a peaceful, nostalgic way to rest.

"I used to sleep in the trees sometimes in summer," I whispered to him one night as our companions snored around us.

"How?"

"The trees are bigger in the Wood. The boughs were wide and flat, and I was very young," I said with a breathy laugh. "I could sleep anywhere back then."

"My father used to take me into the mountains in high summer to live rough for a week at a time," he said. "My mother thought we were insane. 'We build houses for a reason!'"

I laughed a little louder this time, loud enough to be heard over the chirping racket of the cicadas, and got shushed by someone on my right.

"*Shh!*" John hissed to me, mocking, which set us both to giggling like children up past their bedtime.

The woods were a mysterious depth on our left every day. Four years earlier, five men had come barreling out of those trees with an unconscious teenage girl to find Paul waiting for them with a cart on this very road.

I had no idea where we had exited the woods that night, no way of recognizing when we passed it on our way. Somewhere in there, four days' walk in the right direction, was the Hollow. Michael's bones would be long scavenged and gone, but our hut would still be there, in its circle of protective stones. My blanket would be on my bed, my favorite book still on the stool next to it.

If John or Josephine noticed I was withdrawn at times, neither said anything about it.

I hadn't liked from the beginning that Mary and Clara came with us. Everything about this journey was adding up to the premonition I had seen. Josephine might well have been pregnant already, whether or not she had told anyone or even knew about it herself. In my vision, it had been Heidi, Clara, and Mary tending her, sick in the carriage.

But I was here, and John was here, and so was Aris. She wasn't alone. Josephine was well and happy. That premonition might take place years from now or not at all. I'd had plenty of premonitions in the past that had come to nothing.

"Did Kerric ask you to read Clara after I left that day?" I asked my sister over our simple lunch of dried bread and squirrel stew.

She screwed up her face in deep thought and swallowed a bite of heavy bread. "When?"

"Before the festival. He asked me to read her, and I yelled at him for it."

Her eyebrow shot up in a wary expression. "Oh, right. No, I never did."

"Why not?"

She shrugged and took another bite. "He asked me to, but I decided you were right to object. It's not right to go spying in others' heads, especially of our own people. So Clara was being especially suspicious. So what? It came to nothing anyway, and I'm glad I didn't invade her privacy."

I nodded and looked over to where Clara talked with one of the guards from Silda. Her dark hair was caught up in a tidy knot on the back of her head, her clothes simple and practical. There was nothing to give concern in anything she did or said. She was just a serving girl and companion. Nothing more.

But on the sixth day, something happened to cement my worries in stone.

"There's a rider coming," I called to John over the jangle of the horse tack.

"Where from?"

"The south."

We had finally begun the curve to the south, signaling we had reached the western border of the Sacred Wood and were nearing the northern border of Authe Ida. In a day or so, we would turn eastward and begin the final leg to Bluewater in the southeast.

John urged his horse faster, and I followed him to the front of the group to speak with Dan and Aris.

"Who is it?" Aris asked me.

"He's coming from the direction of Authe Ida. He'll be here in a few minutes. You can ask him yourself."

It turned out that Aris knew him. When the rider came into view, Aris let out a shout of greeting and sped off to meet him. We couldn't hear their words from such a distance, but they embraced, slapping each other on the back and laughing audibly.

"This is Tadeas," Aris said to us when they approached the group. "Tadeas, this is my woman, Josephine."

The tall, blond stranger twisted his mouth a little at what he perceived to be foreign terminology, but he didn't interrupt.

"And this is her sister, Gwenna, and you may recognize John. Their aunt is in the carriage. This is Dan, the new Derehani emissary."

Tadeas greeted us all politely and even shook John's hand. "Good to see you again," he said.

"You as well," John replied.

He turned to me next but caught his breath before speaking and abandoned all other greetings.

I'd say he's heard of me, I thought dryly to John, who responded with little more than a tight expression.

Tadeas pivoted to Aris instead. "I bring word from your family to speed your journey home, Aris," he said.

Aris shrugged and spread his hands, encompassing the unwieldy mass of vehicles, horses, and supplies. "We're moving as fast as we can, my friend."

Tadeas shook his head and gripped his friend's shoulder. "No, I came to bring you ahead of the group. Your sister is not well. She's asking for you to come."

Aris's cheerful expression died away. "Which one?"

"Amanda Rose."

"What's wrong with her? Is it serious?"

"A fever turned bad," Tadeas said. "No one saw it coming. It may already be too late."

Aris turned to Josephine, who took his hand. "You have to go," she said. "You can move much faster, just the two of you. We'll be right behind you."

"No," I said sternly.

All eyes turned to me and silence fell.

"Gwenna—" Dan began, but I interrupted him.

"No. Don't go."

"I have to," Aris said, eyebrows drawn.

"Why not?" Josephine asked over him, her authoritative tone the mirror of my own.

I stared from one to the other. What difference would it make to tell them?

None at all.

I pictured my sister sick in the carriage, not dead. Only the pregnancy would be lost, if she was even pregnant at all. There was nothing to prevent it or make it better. If he left and I was right, then she would be without her man during the ordeal. But if I made him stay and it came to nothing, he might never see his sister alive again. It would be my fault.

"Why not, Gwenna?" Josephine asked again. "What aren't you telling me?"

But I kept my mouth stubbornly shut. There was nothing to be said now. She knew I had foreseen something. There would be no pretending otherwise. All I could do was refuse.

"No lies." Josephine reached for the bare skin of my forearm, but I jerked away, stepping behind John and gripping the back of his shirt with both hands to steady them.

I didn't want to put him in the middle, but he bore it with a grim expression and didn't object.

Tadeas's gaze bounced between us with a look of pure

incredulity, as if he wasn't sure if he should be taking our odd conversation seriously. I glared at him once. He immediately grimaced and stopped staring.

"You refuse to tell me what you saw?" Josephine snapped at me through John's bulk.

I didn't answer, though I held her gaze just over the top of my man's shoulder.

"Then I can only assume it means it won't make a difference. If you won't give me a reason he should stay, then you are giving your blessing for him to go." She turned to Aris. "Go."

Aris turned from her to me and back again in an odd reflection of Tadeas's confusion. "Jo, are you sure?"

"Yes, I'm sure." She did not look in my direction. When he hesitated again, with Tadeas bouncing on the balls of his feet, Josephine let out her breath. She squeezed his upper arms and looked him in the eye. "Go, Aris."

He set his mouth and nodded, kissing her once before setting off to prepare.

They were gone in under ten minutes, disappearing down the road in a hot haze of dirt kicked up by their horses. Josephine, Heidi, and I stood together, watching them disappear around a bend.

"Will I see him again?" Josephine asked me quietly.

"Nothing I saw suggests you won't," I said.

She nodded once, eyes dry, and turned away.

Heidi looked over at me, expression set. This was my mother's sister, and sometimes, when she held her mouth in just the right way, I could see Josephine in her face. This was one of those times.

The expression lasted only a second before she sniffed at me.

"You'll be the death of her," my aunt said.

I opened my mouth, ready to bite back at the injustice of those words, but she turned and followed my sister back to camp, leaving me to fume and grumble.

I could only hope I had made the right choice.

THIRTY-ONE

It started early the next morning. Josephine woke up half the group by vomiting at the edge of camp. I assisted her myself, bringing cool water and a clean cloth to soothe her. It seemed to help, and she was able to sleep a few more hours before the sun came up.

She rode in the carriage that day, too tired and uncomfortable to manage a horse. We had to stop four times that morning to let her be sick in the brushy ditch, and at lunch, we decided to quit early for her sake. We made camp, and I sat with her all afternoon and evening, only leaving when Mary or John was there to keep her company.

It was just nausea and discomfort. There was no miscarriage, only what appeared to be food poisoning. No one could figure out what had caused it. Josephine had been eating the same travel rations as the rest of us.

"Is this what you saw?" Josephine rasped out that evening. She lay curled up on the carriage seat, sweating in the balmy summer heat.

I sniffed and wiped my own damp brow with the short sleeve of my shirt. Mary had brought out a little chest with ointments, soothing teas, and bandages, which had been packed for our journey.

"He should be here," I said, feeling vindicated and closing the lid too roughly. We had used up all the ginger lozenges, not that they had helped much. The little glass jars rattled in the box when I stuffed it back under the seat.

"I'll be all right," she said dismissively. "You said yourself I would see him again. A bit of vomiting won't kill me."

I nodded and decided against telling her what might still come. It wouldn't make any difference.

She wasn't better by morning. If anything, she had grown worse. We couldn't move on. Josephine spent the entire day in the carriage, unable to keep down much more than the broth Clara kept simmering on the fire outside. She took sips of it when prompted, then fell back on the sweat-soaked cushions.

Josephine lapsed in and out of sleep all day long, and I was left for long stretches of time to desperately wish I hadn't allowed Aris to leave. When I exited the carriage in the early afternoon to find some food for myself, I instead found John and Mary whispering near the edge of camp.

"What's going on?" I asked as I approached.

Mary turned her harrowed gaze to me. "How is she? The same?"

I nodded and repeated my question. John passed me his water skin.

"Mary has been hearing rumors," he said while I drank.

"What kind of rumors?"

"They're blaming you," she said in a hushed voice. "They all saw you try and stop Aristeidis from leaving the other day. They saw you argue with Miss Jo."

The water skin fell from my lips, and I stared at her, incredulous. "Who is saying this? What, do they think I poisoned her? My own sister?"

John put a calming hand on my arm, and I remembered to keep my voice down.

She shook her head. "It is Heidi's men and the Authe Idans that Aris left to escort us the rest of the way. They are saying things like, 'That Owl has put the evil eye on the lady,' whatever that is. And that they shouldn't speak to you or make you angry or they'll be next."

I snorted. "That's ridiculous!"

"It doesn't matter if it's ridiculous," John said.

Mary shook her head emphatically in agreement. "Any time I or Dan or any of the others defend you, it gets worse. They mock us. They told me I was bewitched and nothing I could say would convince them."

"It's the beginnings of hysteria," John said.

His eyes held mine for a long moment.

"Remember the fear of men," I quoted softly.

"Exactly."

"What are they going to do?"

John crossed his arms over his chest. "If Jo improves soon, which I expect to happen, it will come to nothing. We can only wait. If we act too soon, it would be seen as an admission of guilt."

"She can't be sick much longer." Mary took my hand. "Food poisoning doesn't last more than a day or two. She'll improve by bedtime. You'll see."

John nodded, but his expression remained stony. He was aware I had seen something that had scared me, and he could tell it hadn't yet come to pass.

I looked between the two of them, wishing Dan were here as well. These were my friends, my family. I squeezed Mary's hand and took John's as well.

"I will run," I said, realization dawning.

John shook his head sharply. "No. If you run, they will see it as confirmation. You cannot run."

"Miss Jo needs you," Mary said.

My mouth tightened into a thin line. "You misunderstand. This is not me making a plan. It will happen. I will run. And Josephine will be alone. Promise me, both of you. Promise me now that you will not let her out of your sight until I get back."

John tightened his hand to a vise-like grip on my fingers. "Don't run."

"I will." I tried to put as much comfort and confidence into those words as I could. "There will come a time, very soon, when I will have no choice. She will be alone."

"Miss Jo won't be alone, if I have to stay awake three days together," Mary said solemnly.

"Go be with her now. I'll relieve you in a little bit so you can rest before I go."

She nodded and took off for the carriage.

"Gwen, please. Don't go." John's voice was tight. He took my face between both of his hands and pressed his forehead to mine.

I leaned up to press a kiss to his mouth. "I come back," I whispered.

"Don't leave."

There was nothing more to be said about it. I didn't want to go, but now I understood why I hadn't been with her in the premonition. Something would happen, and I would be forced to flee.

But I would come back, that much I knew.

"Find Dan and the rest and tell them to hold their peace," I said. "No more defending me. I won't have them caught in the middle when this goes sideways."

He took a deep breath and nodded.

I quirked my mouth up in a humorless smile. "I suppose I had forgotten how hard it is in other places. Derehan has become a bubble of safety for the sibyls."

He nodded his forehead against mine. Then he took a deep breath, let it out, and set off to speak to Dan.

Now that I had been made aware of the situation, it was impossible to miss. Attention followed me everywhere. I did my level best to avoid eye contact, to lessen the perceived threat, but it was impossible to do completely. More than once, I would look up and someone would glance away quickly. Everywhere I went in the camp, silence fell, as if conversations were halted as soon as I approached.

It was easiest to sit inside with Josephine, where there were fewer people to stare at me. But when night came, Heidi herself shooed me out to get some rest.

"I'll sit with her," she said, taking my spot at the front of the little carriage.

I sent Mary in as soon as I was out, and Heidi didn't turn her away. John was on watch, so I sat next to Dan, who passed me a bowl of stew in silence.

Sleep was hard that night. Every noise sent my eyes flying open. There were only five other Valheid guards that we trusted, and they all agreed to stay awake and alert in shifts so I could get some rest. Two months ago, I had kissed and blessed every one of those men. They had seen me become a woman under Josephine's guidance, had lived in the same city with me for four years. They knew these rumors were preposterous.

But they were Derehani, and they remembered the fear of man. So they kept watch for me.

The time came sooner than I expected.

I had barely slept, waiting for dawn to come. Because if Josephine was able to rest well and improve, the danger would pass. For her *and* for me.

But it was to be exactly as I had foreseen it.

I woke with a sharp intake of breath when a hand clamped over my mouth. John's hand. The sudden stab of panic abated when I sensed the familiar brush of his mind. He knelt next to me by the fire. The night was quiet and dark, but the twilight of pre dawn already crept into the eastern sky.

When he was sure there was no chance I would cry out, he removed his hand from my mouth and pressed a finger to his lips.

What is it? I asked silently.

Something's wrong, he said. *I'm not sure what it is. Some of Heidi's men and the Authe Idans aren't bedding down. They're gathering themselves together.*

My frown deepened and threw out my thoughts. Five minds, alert and determined. They were strapping on weapons and gathering ropes.

Bonds.

They're preparing to capture someone, I said with rising dread. I gripped his arm in alarm. *They're coming for me.*

John nodded, his suspicions confirmed.

It's time for me to run.

There was no hesitation at all, no doubt in his eye or his mind. *No, we run. Together.*

Sure enough, he already wore his cloak and boots. He had his knife fastened tight to his thigh, and the strap of a bag was just visible, looped over his arm.

He was ready to take me and run. He was ready to abandon everything, run with me into the wild, and risk it all.

I shook my head. *No.*

There is no other option. He gripped my hand and hauled me up.

I let him do it as I glanced around for my own boots.

No, John. You have to stay with Josephine and make sure she stays safe. There, my boots were just to my right. I bent down and grabbed them, along with my cloak, which I had been using for a blanket.

John took the boots from me and carefully led me away from the other sleepers.

I am not leaving you to fend for yourself alone in the wild.

A small smile pulled at my eyes. I put a comforting hand to his cheek. John leaned into it, sharp worry etched over his brow.

I lived my whole life alone in the woods before you stole me away, I reminded him. *Come find me. When all is safe, come and find me. I know how to stay hidden, so listen for my call.*

Gwen. He left the silent plea unfinished.

John knew I was right. We could not trust Heidi or the Authe Idans, when Josephine was so ill in her carriage. Who knew what nonsense they might do in their fear?

The air was much colder away from the heat of the fire. I gently eased my cloak open so I could put it on but stopped when two men approached us out of the dark. Both Heidi's men—one named Gerrald and the other Rowan. They were acquaintances, only speaking to me when absolutely necessary, but I had known them for years.

"You there," Gerrald said to me, clearly unnerved.

They hadn't expected to find me awake and alert, much less with an intimidating companion. They all knew John well enough to be wary of his strength and dexterity.

"What is this?" John demanded, feigning ignorance. He stepped in front of me in a not-so-subtle protective stance. John gripped my hand behind his back, stopping me from running until the right moment. "It's barely morning. Go back to your watches."

"We're not on the watch," Rowan said. "We're here to bring the Owl to our lady."

John didn't back down. "If you're not on the watch, then you should be asleep. We have another long day tomorrow. Heidi can speak with the Owl in the morning."

If I have to fight them, I will lose any power to help Josephine after you're gone, John said to me.

I can muddle them, but only for a few seconds, or else they'll feel me. That way, it will look like I ran on my own.

I could have done more, and we both knew it. I could have held them and all the others asleep or incapacitated for as long as I wanted. I could have forced them to do anything or nothing.

But even if that were a reasonable choice, even if I wanted to hold them in thrall continuously until Josephine improved, what then? Their opinions of me would be confirmed, and I would be condemned as a witch, an evil that must be dealt with.

John knew better than to even suggest it, which only made me love him more. Because even if it were a reasonable path, I wouldn't take it.

Gerrald spoke again, mustering his courage. "Our lady wants her confined."

"Confined?" John didn't have to feign his indignance now. "Why?"

Dread filled me as their thoughts moved. *They plan to kill me immediately and claim I fought them as an excuse.*

John tightened his hand on mine behind his back.

"Come now," Gerrald said. "You'll have to speak with Lady Heidi afterwards. She'll explain it all."

He took a step toward us, a rope in his hands, but that one step was all he managed. I slipped into both of their minds and scrambled them about. It was the most I could do without creating suspicion.

They both hovered stupidly for a few seconds while the confusion cleared from their minds. After a few blinks, they looked around and found me gone.

Before disappearing across the road and into the woods to the south, I had given John's hand one final squeeze. I had abandoned my cloak on the ground and fled.

John faced the guards alone, still clutching my boots in a trembling hand.

Thirty-Two

I had a head start, but that was all. For the last four years, I had lived in a city, so though I knew the woods as an old friend, I had lost the feel of it. The leafy ground cover was slippery and soft, no good for running. Buried amongst the leaves were fallen branches and stones, which dug into the soles of my bare feet.

I pressed on, pushing through brambles and sneaking under branches to put as much distance between myself and the camp as I could.

It didn't matter. I was on foot. Before long, my pursuers came charging after me on horses, with bridles thrown on in haste.

John! I called. *Are you with them?*

Yes. Which way are you going?

I ducked to the left, and now I'm hiding behind a large boulder about fifty yards from camp.

"To the right!" came John's voice distantly over the jangle and stomp of horses.

They wouldn't be able to move too fast in the dark and without saddles, but they were moving quicker than I could. If

John could keep them off course, then maybe I would be able to slip away.

But they didn't heed him.

"No, no!" another man called. "I saw her head this way!"

Run! John said, but I was already up and moving.

"There!" someone shouted. The white of my loose shirt moved plain as day through the black trees and approaching dawn.

The chase was on. I ran for what seemed like hours, though it couldn't have been long at all. The increasing glow to the east helped me judge my direction, and I pressed forward.

The Lily River cut through the jagged earth a mile or two east of the camp, well west of where the Hollow lay in the Sacred Wood. It was a last resort and the only landmark I knew in that part of the world.

I dove through the thickest undergrowth, knowing the horses could not easily follow me through. John led them in the wrong direction more than once and bought me precious seconds, but it was not easy to miss me in the growing dawn. They always found my trail again.

Even though I occasionally was forced to muddle someone who got too close, I could never quite get away. And I dared not do more for fear they would realize I was coercing them.

This could not continue.

My feet were a bleeding mess, and my chest heaved and ached with the strain of drawing breath. My legs wobbled beneath me, but I pushed on. I glanced around every tree, every boulder, searching for a bolt hole or a likely branch to climb. But there was no place for me to hide while the eyes of the soldiers were on me.

There was no choice. It would have to be the river.

I was close. A clearing was just visible through the trees ahead, where the giants parted for the gorge and the wild river below. The soldiers were right behind me, their horses frantic with the chase.

There was no stopping me now. I sprinted directly for the

river, entirely heedless of the slapping branches and the cutting stones.

One soldier closed in on me, with John on his right. John rammed his horse into the soldier's, seemingly by accident. The man slipped dangerously to the left and cried out in alarm. His horse stumbled with the shift in weight and dropped back.

John came charging behind me. *Gwen! Head east! The river is ahead! It's too far down!*

I ignored him and cleared the treeline. Another soldier broke out of the woods a little east of us and raced full tilt toward me.

I ran for the cliff.

The low, grumbling roar of a waterfall shook the earth as my destination grew nearer. I had judged my direction accurately. We had emerged from the trees just where the river delved even deeper into the gorge it had carved into the earth.

If I had been still at that moment, I would have heard the birds singing in the early morning light. The gentle rustling of the trees in the breeze would have soothed me. The rumble of the nearby waterfall would have excited me. It was a beautiful area, wild and free of human impact. If I had been still at that moment, I would have found peace at the cliff's edge.

Instead, I ran for my life. Men on horseback were in hot pursuit, and my aim might very well kill me.

But there was no stopping now. I broke from the trees at full speed, with John and the other two close enough to touch me. One man tried, but his grip wasn't secure, and I was able to wrench myself free.

"Gwenna! Stop!" John's voice sounded from right behind me, but I did not look back. "Gwen!"

The edge came up faster than I would have liked, but there was no room for hesitation. With one almighty leap and a grunt of effort, I floated over a hundred feet of empty space.

For just an instant, everything was clear.

The waterfall was only twenty feet from me, and it immediately drenched me in the clear spray. The feeling of stillness did not last. My stomach felt as if it had been wrenched from my body when leap changed to fall. The wind whipped past me, and I went down, down toward the river.

John's cracking voice followed me into the gorge—one long wordless cry of shock and disbelief.

The raging white water loomed closer and closer, and I began to doubt the sanity of my plan. I still had not crossed over into the dead place, and I began to believe I wouldn't at all. I braced myself for the crushing end, biting through my lip to keep from screaming.

And then, it stopped.

I landed with a gentle thud on sparse, dry grass with a shocked gasp, and my eyes popped open. Absolute silence replaced the roar of the river, and instead of the soft gray light of dawn, a sickly brown glow filtered through the gnarled trees of the Sanctuary.

I rolled over onto my back, breathing hard. My long, wet hair stuck to my face and arms in tendrils, and my shirt and pants had been ripped and torn during my headlong dash through the woods. My feet throbbed with the pain of multiple cuts and bruises, but that was not my first concern.

I was no longer being pursued, but I was not safe here either.

"What now?" said a raspy voice behind me.

I lurched to stand and faltered. My feet weren't just cut and bruised. They were striped with multiple serious lacerations. I bled freely into the dry dirt, which seemed to drink up the blood as readily as seawater in sand.

"What did you do to yourself?" Theo asked casually.

"I had to run for it."

"Oh? Folks aren't so accepting as you thought?" She limped closer, favoring her right leg and leaning heavily on her staff. Theo stretched out a hand to me, where I knelt in the bloody dirt. "Come on, and we'll set you right. Can't have you bleeding to death."

I hardly thought that would be a danger. The injuries weren't that bad. But she was right. I needed attention. Standing would be extremely painful, much less walking or running again. Adrenaline alone had carried me the final leg to the river. I had barely felt the hurt at the time, but now it lanced up my legs in pure agony.

"Where are you taking me?" I asked.

"To my place." Theo shook her hand impatiently at me. "I can set you right. I have medicines."

I frowned. The last thing I wanted was skin-to-skin contact with this heinous old woman, but I couldn't just sit there. And in all the times I had confronted her, Theo had not been able to best me. Not even close.

Plus, if Sasha was any guide, I was far stronger than Theo could ever be.

I took her hand, and in a blink, we appeared somewhere else. It was the silent dead place, but we were in a different location within that realm. Before us stood what was unmistakably Theo's home.

Rather, it was a well-established camp.

There was no shelter, for there was no weather here, but she had collected an assortment of small furniture next to a cooking fire and plenty of worn carpets to make a cobbled-together floor. It was all very tidy, right down to the neatly made straw mattress on the low-slung bed frame near the fire pit.

I said nothing while Theo helped me sit in one of two squat chairs near the smoldering fire. A half-empty bowl of stew sat on a table next to me. Clearly, she had been eating her supper when she sensed my arrival.

Theo started rummaging through a trunk across from me and quickly pulled out a little metal tin. It had a tight-fitting lid with a worn pink flower with seven pointed petals. Painted over the flower was a familiar rune in gold: the trivara. It was the symbol of the maiden, mother, and crone.

"This is something you won't have seen before," she said with pride. Theo eased herself down on the rug in front of me and pried off the lid. "It's called Athorum. I got it in a country far from here in the west, across the Arigua Ocean."

"I wasn't aware there was such a place." I picked up the lid and studied the flower and trivara rune. Blossoms like this didn't exist in real life, but the illustration was certainly beautiful.

She shrugged and began massaging the smelly stuff on the bottoms of my feet. Whatever it was, it worked very quickly. Almost like magic. Maybe it *was* magic. Pain sang through my feet at first contact, but it stopped almost as quickly. She pushed torn skin back in its place, and it seamed together, with pink, new scars already forming.

"Of course you weren't." Theo picked up my other foot. "It's too far. Authe Ida doesn't build boats big enough to carry the required supplies. It would take months and months to get there."

"Then how did you get there?"

She dropped my left foot and wiped her hands on her threadbare apron. The old scars on the back of her left arm caught my eye with the movement. There were three of them in parallel lines, faded and soft with time.

"Same way you got here, you halfwit."

As soon as she said it, it made perfect sense. Halfwit indeed. Because when that man had come at me with a knife in the dining hall, I had disappeared from one place and appeared in another. What difference did it make if I moved six feet or six leagues?

"How do you move in that way?" I asked.

Her lips twisted up in a sneer. "What in the hell are you doing here? You made it perfectly clear last time that you wanted nothing to do with me or this place. What do you want?"

"I don't want anything," I said honestly, taking the cloth Theo offered me to wipe off my feet. "I had to escape them in a way that wouldn't make them suspicious."

"So, running barefoot over stones?" she asked with heavy sarcasm. "How did you get here, if you're so unclear on the method?"

"I had to jump from a high place. I jumped into a river. And before, I had to jump from my window."

She let out a barking laugh. "Ha! I did that once! A long, long time ago. It's an effective way to fake your death, to be sure."

That thought hadn't occurred to me in the intensity of the moment. Would they all think I had died? Would John?

"I have to get back."

"And what? They'll welcome you back with open arms? Why were they chasing you anyway?"

"They accused me of poisoning my sister."

Theo laughed again. One loud, barking, "Ha!"

"It's not funny."

"It's incredibly funny, considering it was her aunt who did the poisoning. And she blamed you!"

I stood abruptly. "What?"

"Didn't you know?" Theo asked, still laughing while she put the little tin of Athorum in its trunk. "Heidi of Silda has been trying to kill you for months. This is just her latest attempt. When her assassins failed, she decided to make you guilty first. Then your death would be mandated by law."

"You're lying." Blood boiled in my ears, and my breath stopped altogether.

She shook her head, grinning to herself as she picked up her half-eaten stew, now gone cold. A layer of solidified fat floated on top, which she broke up with her spoon and ate with apparent relish.

"If you say so," she said, her mouth full.

"How could you possibly know Heidi poisoned Josephine? It only just happened!"

Theo slurped up a bit of stringy meat. "Haven't you noticed? There's no time in this place. All of that happened years ago. Everyone was talking about it. Heard it from at least a dozen different people. I went into their minds and saw it myself. Bet you can't guess what happens next! Do you want me to tell you?"

My heart hammered so fast it hurt. A buzzing in my ears drowned out the horrible silence of that place. Heidi, our own blood, was using my sister to get to me. And I had *left* Josephine in her care.

"Lies!" I snapped.

"Don't take my word for it!" Theo threw up her hand and slung fat off the end of her spoon. "Go back and read her. The reports were quite clear. There was no doubt she was guilty. Her and the serving woman."

Yes, I needed to get back, and fast. Maybe it wasn't too late to stop my vision from coming true after all.

"How do I move like you do?" I demanded.

She eased herself onto the other low chair and stared up at me, appraising. A dribble of broth shone on her chin. "You simply will it, child. Just make it so."

"How?" My stern voice seemed to make the dead trees shiver. "I've tried that before. Nothing happens."

"You do it the same way you call up a vision. The same way you walk into another person's mind. It's all the same skill applied in different ways." She laughed once, incredulous. "Haven't you realized that yet?"

Well, that was a stupid. What an incredibly...odd way to think of it. The same skill? How could moving through the void be the same as entering another person's mind?

"You mean, move the mind and the body will follow?"

"What? Did you think your body controlled the mind instead? What makes us sibylline is the ability to *move the mind*, you idiot. Move it to other people's heads, move it to other worlds. What's the difference?"

I glared at her for half a second longer, then turned away and stalked off on feet that were hale and strong once more.

She called after me. "See? This is what I could have taught you! Think how much more powerful you could be! It's not too late! There is still much to learn."

The memory of Sasha, covered in blood and sneering, sent shivers down my spine. I already knew what sort of power Theo would encourage me to use. Whatever Theo wanted to teach me, the cost wasn't worth it.

I continued walking and did not look back.

A little way off, I stopped, eyes closed. All I could do was try.

But where to go? In the vision, Josephine had heard John's voice. I had been with him.

We're coming.

Before, I had moved on instinct, out of self-preservation. Now I had to do it on purpose.

I thought back on all the times I'd attempted such a movement over the years. I had failed every time. But back then, I had seen it as moving my body through the world.

Maybe Theo was right. Maybe it wasn't moving my body, but moving my mind in the same way I did to see visions, to let John in, to listen in on other minds. I needed to move my mind out of the world and into the void, then reinsert it somewhere else. And where my mind went, my body would follow. Just like it had when I'd jumped out of my window.

There was no putting it in words, but Theo had been right. In the great tree of my mind, there was no stretching out of branches. Instead, there was a slight shift. Like picking up the entire sphere and setting it down somewhere else.

Move into it.

I slipped into the void between worlds and focused on the sensations that were left to me. No sight, no sound, no feeling, but there was current. It swept me through the void, almost indistinguishable from the emptiness. But it was there.

It pushed me back to the real world, right where I wanted to go.

THIRTY-THREE

I knew it had worked before I opened my eyes. Sound existed again: water dripping, wind rustling leaves, birds chirping in a sunlit drizzle. A little way off, a branch broke and clattered to the leaf litter below.

"Gwen?"

My eyes flew open.

John, glorious, rain-soaked, and heartbroken, strode toward me in the gentle rain. Already, I was soaked again. It had only been twenty minutes, maybe less, since I had jumped into the Lily River and crossed over, but John's pale face had grown haggard and tired. Dark circles stood out in sharp relief under his eyes, and his mouth twisted in a grim scowl.

Could I have been gone longer than I thought? It was impossible to tell in the overcast woods.

His long strides ate up the distance between us. He caught me up in a bone-crushing hug, taking my feet clear off the ground. "Are you real?" he asked into my hair.

"Of course I'm real."

He held my face between both hands, studying me. "Don't

you ever"—he shook me gently for emphasis—"do that again." Then he wrapped me back up in another hug.

"I won't. I promise."

"I thought you were dead," he said, his voice cracking. "I couldn't feel you anymore. Everyone kept saying you were dead."

"I'm sorry." I wrapped my arms around his middle. Sympathetic tears sprang to my eyes. I had hurt him. Badly. "I didn't know how else to get there except to jump. I understand it better now. I won't have to do that again. I'm so sorry, John."

He held me far enough apart to look me in the face. "Get where?"

"To the dead place." I told him everything in a rush, including all that I should have mentioned before: my theories on how I avoided the attack in the dining hall and what I had tried later that night.

Coldness hardened his features when I spoke about endangering myself for the sake of an experiment. "You jumped out of your bedroom window? Are you insane?"

"I thought that was the only way at the time. But John, there's more."

Learning that Heidi might have been behind all the attacks on me, including this one, was the final straw. He was the one seeing red this time.

"We have to get back now." John pulled me by the hand in the direction of the setting sun.

"How long have I been gone?" I asked, trying once again to judge the time by the hazy sky.

"A day and a half." He held a branch aside for me.

I tugged him to a stop and gaped at him. "How long did you say?"

"A day and a half," he repeated, perplexed.

"I was only gone twenty minutes, John. Only twenty minutes, by my count!"

He returned my stare for half a minute at least, then, unable to find any response, said nothing at all. John pulled on my arm and continued walking.

"Who is with her? How far is it?"

"Mary and Dan are taking shifts. I was with her all night. We haven't left her alone with anyone we don't trust. Not for a minute. And thank the Old Fathers for it. But Gwen, I don't know if it's safe for you to go back there. No safer than when you left. We're outnumbered, and Josephine is worse. She miscarried in the night. We didn't even know she was pregnant, though something tells me you knew."

I glowered ahead. The wet leaf litter disappeared under our feet.

"The last time—" The words died in my throat. With a great swallow and determination, I tried again. "The last time I acted on one of my visions, the last time I used my abilities to interfere, I killed someone."

John remained silent beside me, his breath coming fast as we hurried through the woods.

"So I made the rules. No lying, no listening in, no coercion. And I stuck to those rules religiously." I dared to look over at him, trudging through the drizzling rain. "I've known this was coming for three months. I saw it when I was knocked unconscious in the north field. Later, Kerric asked me to read Clara. Looking back, I think he may have wanted me to read Heidi as well. I refused. On principle alone, I refused to act."

"You weren't wrong to refuse," he said matter-of-factly.

"I don't think there is any such thing as right anymore. Our own aunt did this, John. She is our blood. Even if she hates me, how can she dare hurt Jo?" I shook my head, stepping high over a fallen tree in our path. Wet leaves stuck to my bare feet. "You say it's not safe for me at camp, but you've got it wrong. It's not safe for *them*."

A menacing half-grin appeared on my man's face. It was

response enough. He wholeheartedly approved of my new perspective.

We were only about a mile from camp, just far enough for John to get some solitude and rest. When we drew close enough, he called out to Josephine, using the same words I had seen in my vision.

Josephine!

Her response came quickly. *John? Did you find Gwen?*

Yes! She's alive! We're coming.

My turn next. *Josephine! I'm coming! Hold on just a little longer!*

When we drew close, I took stock of every mind in the camp. There were four of Heidi's men, the Sildans, and six Authe Idans, plus Heidi herself and Clara. We were indeed outnumbered, but that all came to nothing as soon as I approached.

"It's the Owl!" someone shouted when we came into view.

"She's alive!"

"Gwenna!"

The few expressions of relief and welcome were drowned out by alarm and purpose. Gerrald and Rowan approached me, along with Baron, the leader of the Authe Idan guards. All three were amped up and excitable, shaking with adrenaline.

And all three stopped in their tracks less than two steps later.

It was satisfying to reach out and hold three people at once, and for a moment, I wondered how many I could control together. I had never allowed myself to consider this scenario, much less try it, but now I had been presented with more than enough justification.

No. It was bad enough I was breaking the rules at all. I must not allow myself to go further than absolutely necessary. My abilities stretched before me, with no boundary in sight, calling out to be released. If I let myself go, where would it end?

So instead, I wholly ignored them and stalked right past the frozen men to the carriage. One other guard made to move, to protest and detain, but he stilled, much to the confusion and fear of their peers.

It was the easiest thing in the world to take their bodies from them. And it felt wonderful, like stretching after sitting cramped for too long. If I'd had time to stop and think about it, that good feeling would have scared me a little. But right then, in the heat of the moment, I only allowed myself to relish this little taste and let go of the possibility of more.

The carriage door wrenched open with more violence than I intended, and all its occupants jumped.

Mary sat in the back corner, mighty relieved to see me, and Josephine lay groggy on the bench. Clara eyed me, wary and ready to bolt at the first sign of danger. And Heidi...

My aunt glowered at me, tears streaking down her cheeks, an expression of pure hatred on her not-quite-beautiful face. She was preparing to dig her heels in, brokenhearted and guilty as she was.

"Out," I said to them all with quiet menace.

None of them moved. Clara's knees bent, and she leaned toward the opposite door, even though she would have had to trample Mary to exit by that route. Something told me she wouldn't hesitate.

"You don't give orders to me," Heidi spat, though her voice was weaker than I expected. She held up her dignity with willpower alone.

"You're right." The anger was shocking in my chest. It pulled my lip up in a snarl I no longer cared to hide. My heart pounded, and my entire body shook.

Somewhere in the back of my mind, I knew this was dangerous. I needed to rein myself in immediately, or I would do something regretful very soon.

Too late.

It was too tempting to push my abilities further, to see how far they could go. And now I had an airtight excuse. They deserved this. And even if they didn't, I wasn't inclined to care. I was pissed off and powerful. More than that, it was right for me to feel that way, so I was free to embrace it.

"You're right," I said again. "I have no need of orders."

Clara and Heidi relaxed immediately, causing Mary to flinch and stare at them in horror. The two women climbed out of the carriage, calm, no hint of their abhorrence showing on their empty faces.

But I felt it, clearly as I felt my own rage. They no longer belonged to themselves. Their bodies were mine now, extensions of myself, just like the men who stood frozen mid-step behind me. Every breath, every movement, every blink. They were my own bodies. I could move them as easily as my hand. Their terror was my terror, their hatred my hatred.

It was so easy. So much easier than with Garreth. And glorious.

"Mary, please stay with Josephine for a while longer," I said, my eyes on my aunt's blank expression.

Mary swallowed hard, nodded once, and sat down, watching us through the open carriage door with eyes wide.

I looked from Heidi to Clara and back again. Where I shook with rage, they stood at peace.

"Gwenna? What is this?" Dan approached me warily, looking to John for reassurance.

"This is an interrogation," I said, not looking away from Heidi.

She returned my gaze, a picture of serenity.

"Tell them what you did, Aunt."

I released her upper body, holding her feet and legs so she could not move away. She did not waste the opportunity to spew her filth on me.

"You are an abomination!" Her voice burst out of her in a wobbly scream. "You are unnatural! An evil that must be removed! Look at what she is doing to us! Look at the invasion! It's disgusting!"

I halted her words for her and found myself screaming back. "You want to see an abomination?" I stared Heidi down from just inches away. It was an idiotic tactic for intimidation, but it felt good to puff up in front of her, to be bigger, assertive, dominant. "Then look at this woman...This woman who would poison one niece so that she could blame another! Her own blood! Deny it! I beg of you, deny it!"

My words triggered the thoughts I wanted to read in Heidi's mind, memories I wanted to see.

Heidi recalled speaking quietly with Clara over several occasions, instructing her and hearing reports, suggesting elder leaves as the best option. Very low doses would make Josephine sick but not kill her. Readily available in any stretch of woods. Easy to conceal.

Clara's mind was just as helpful. She thought of a vial of the toxic extract, adding just a few drops to my sister's water every few hours. And when Jo began to miscarry, Clara had consoled my aunt. *It is a necessary sacrifice.*

My blood began to boil when their thoughts confirmed Theo's words. And with satisfaction, I used Clara's hand to fetch the vial of toxin from her apron pocket. She held it up for all to see.

I released Heidi again, expecting her to hurl more insults, but she merely broke. Her face crumpled, and she wailed in great, heaving sobs.

I let her do it.

"You murdered my sister's child," I said over her weeping. "All for what? To get to me? To blame me?" I turned my attention to Clara next, needing to confirm the rest of their sins. "And what about you? My brother begged me to read you months ago, but I refused. Because it was wrong. And yet all this time, you conspired to kill me with your mistress. Two assassins, two attempts on my life. And now this!"

Again, Heidi's thoughts bent to a secret meeting with two hired killers, arranging to have me disposed of.

I returned Clara's upper body to her. She dropped the vial of toxin, which broke on impact with a rock, and immediately began a stream of lies. "I'm innocent! She made me do it! She ordered me to, threatened me if I didn't! She's evil, Miss Gwenna, my lady. I had no choice. Please, help me!"

"That's enough," I said over her, taking her body once more.

Heidi continued to sob, finally able to get out a few strangled words. "I didn't know she was pregnant! I didn't know! She was only supposed to be ill for a few days, then recover. I was assured it would cause no lasting damage."

I advanced on her again, my rage a cold stone in my chest. "You think that excuses you? You tried to have me murdered on two occasions and then resorted to this trickery to have my brother condemn me instead. And you think ignorance of a pregnancy makes you innocent?"

She looked me full in the face, her own blotchy, running with tears and snot. Her pride shone through once more. "I regret the baby," she said to me with a cold voice. "But I was right to try and get rid of the devil that stands before me."

A hand closed around my upper arm, and I was hauled roughly away from Heidi. My bare feet skidded over the rough ground when John moved me aside.

And with one viscous swipe, he slit Heidi's throat.

Blood welled from the cut, spilling over in a waterfall of gore. It soaked the front of her linen shirt. Heidi stared at him in shock. I gazed at her, dumbfounded.

My control on Clara and the objectors slipped. Swords were drawn, and shouts rang out. The Derehani guards were fewer, but they were big and intimidating, and thankfully, they were enough to stop Heidi's men from advancing right away.

Clara tried to run, but Dan sprang into action. He clamped his arms around her from behind in a bear hug, pinning her to the spot. Dan yelled over Clara's blood-curdling screams, and slowly, the words made their way into my fogged brain.

"Heidi Moore! By the power granted to me as emissary by

Kerric Moore, Lord of Derehan, I find you guilty of three attempts of murder upon a member of the ruling family!"

Heidi fell to her knees, ashen-faced and silently crying, and stared up at Dan as he pronounced her guilt in a rush. She was unable to speak or breathe over the burbling wound in her neck.

"By virtue of your own confession, you are guilty! I condemn you to death by the hand of John of Valheid, to be carried out immediately!"

She passed out before he finished speaking and was dead seconds afterward, sprawled out on the ground in a wide pool of blood soaking into the dirt. The only sound was Clara's hysterical screaming.

John stood there, his lip curled in a sneer of satisfaction and disgust. His chest heaved, his bloody knife gripped in a steady hand.

I couldn't stop staring at Heidi's dead body. She was gone. It was just a pile of meat that had been walking and talking less than a minute before. It had a human face, but everything human about it had been wiped away.

Dan was talking again. I didn't look up. Clara had devolved into gut-wrenching whimpers as Dan repeated the sentence, this time condemning her. John stepped forward, and the cries were cut off with a sound of choking and dripping. Dan finally released her, and Clara slumped to the ground next to her mistress, falling into my field of vision.

Two piles of meat.

I looked to the carriage. Mary and Josephine had been watching the whole scene play out from the darkened interior. When Josephine met my eye, she gave no hint of what she thought or felt. She simply turned away and lay back down. No approval, but no condemnation either.

John glared at the bristling guardsmen who faced him, blades out, unsure of what to do. Dan's quick thinking had made this official business. Justice. The Authe Idans had no jurisdiction on how the Derehani emissary meted out justice on his own people. And though the Sildan guards had been loyal to Heidi and their home, Valheid and Kerric's own emissary were a higher law than she could have ever been.

And she had confessed. They couldn't deny she was guilty. They had all heard her admit it. And Clara, despite her paltry lies about being forced, had also admitted to being a party to the crimes. She'd had the poison in her pocket.

"Weapons away," Dan said to everyone present. "Now. This is over. Weapons away."

Slowly, hesitantly, everyone obeyed.

John spoke next, his bloody knife still gripped tightly in his right hand. "There have been some rumors lately about Gwenna Moore, known as the Owl. She left two days ago to spare you all from having to deal with you in other ways. But she's back now and won't be leaving again. If anyone here is uncomfortable with her presence, you're welcome to fuck off and go home."

His voice cracked at the end.

No one said a word in response.

Thirty-Four

Every single Authe Idan soldier left within the hour. They all avoided looking at any of us while they packed up their things, claimed a healthy portion of our supplies, and took off to the south. We could find our own way to Bluewater, they said, and left.

The Sildan guards ended up staying. They couldn't claim we had been wrong to execute Heidi and Clara, and with their mistress gone, they had only Dan to answer to.

That night, I sat with Josephine in the carriage, just the two of us. Mary and I had helped her get cleaned up with plenty of warm water and fresh clothes. We tore out the cushion she had soaked through with blood and burned it. In its place, we laid folded furs so she would be comfortable during recovery.

Josephine was feeling much better, having gone without a dose of the elder toxin for a full day. But the miscarriage had left her in pain and extremely fatigued, and she was still dehydrated from all the vomiting.

We sat in silence for a long time. I tried desperately not to picture the blood welling from Heidi's neck over and over again. I tried not to imagine the ruined blankets we had peeled away from my sister just a few hours before.

"I didn't mean to fall in love with him," Josephine said into the dark, making me jump a little.

I sat on the floor of the carriage, with my back against the seat where she lay, but I turned to face her more comfortably.

"What?"

"When I agreed to this, I didn't mean to love him." She adjusted her position on the hard furs and found my eyes in the darkness. "I could tell he was a decent man, and I expected to go off and have an adventure and maybe a family, and see the world."

I took her hand and held it.

Josephine smiled a little to herself. "But he was so earnest. And the way he danced that first night all those years ago...I couldn't help it." Her fragile smile faltered, and her next words were strangled. "I was going to tell him about the baby on our wedding night."

My fingers tightened on hers. She sobbed into the pillows, grieving for the child she would never meet.

"I'm so sorry this happened to you," I said through my own tears. "I'm so sorry I didn't read Clara when Kerric asked me to. I could have prevented this."

She shook her head, unable to protest properly around her grief.

"And I let Aris go, and then I left too." It had all been my fault. I hadn't poisoned her, but it had been in my power to prevent it, and I hadn't.

They had probably waited until Aris had left before giving the first dose. Maybe Aris had been called away on purpose, for this very reason. How deep did this conspiracy go?

Josephine continued shaking her head. "This is not your fault. This is Heidi's fault. And Clara's. I also chose not to read them, remember? I also could have stopped this from happening."

"I saw you miscarry months ago, Jo. I didn't tell you."

Pain flashed across her face. "Did you know it was preventable?"

I shook my head. "No, I had no idea. I only saw you alone. With them."

"Then there is nothing to be sorry for. You made noble choices, Gwenna. And you helped me make noble choices. And sometimes, bad things happen anyway."

"I'm so sorry."

She nodded and laid her head back down with a sigh. "Me too, Little Owl." Josephine squeezed my hand. Her tears started up again, but softer this time. "I want to go home."

We were a solemn group while we packed up camp the next morning. The men buried Heidi and Clara just off the road. A large stone marked the shared grave. I made myself stop and visit it before we left, to say goodbye and forgive them. They had done terrible things, but justice had been served, and it was over. I would not carry this weight home with me.

Mary and I took turns riding with Josephine in the carriage, and we made good time, considering the cumbersome vehicles. We stopped only when we had to for the sake of the horses.

On the third day, Josephine was up and alert but still in no condition to sit in a saddle. She remained in the carriage, with her arms resting on the open window and her head cradled on her crooked elbow, just watching the woods slide past.

I rode with her that morning, so she was the first to notice me sit up with relief on my face.

"He's coming. Aris is coming up the road!" I threw open the door and hung out of the swiftly moving carriage. "Stop! Every-one, stop!" *John! Stop the men!*

Only our driver heard me. John reined his horse in and called out an order, and the others slowed to a halt.

Josephine stumbled from the carriage before it had come to a full stop. She faltered a little, gazing back along the road where I pointed.

At first, there was nothing to see. Only dust and sunshine. But then a dark speck appeared and grew steadily larger. One rider galloping as fast as he could in our direction.

With a whimper of relief, Josephine took off toward him. She wasn't quite up to the exertion, but she hurried as fast as she could bear, eyes streaming.

Aris threw himself off his horse well before he met her and ran the last few steps, enveloping her in a tight hug that brought them both to their knees in the dusty road. My sister hadn't made it too far away from the group, and we all meandered after her, stopping far enough to give them space. We all watched their reunion and heard him worry over her, take in her ashen complexion, her sadness.

It was difficult to watch, like tearing open a half-healed wound. Josephine poured out everything she had suffered, clinging to his neck and sobbing. His piercing blue eyes met mine over her shoulder.

Josephine didn't blame me, but for one heart-stopping minute, Aris did.

And then he closed his eyes, buried his face in her shoulder, and let her cry.

It took a long time, but finally, the pair of them came back to us.

Aris had returned with news.

"I met my soldiers on the road, the ones that abandoned you." He said the word *abandoned* like a swear. "They told me everything that had happened since I left and begged me to come home to Bluewater with them, but I'm done with that place."

"Why? What happened?" Dan asked.

"My father has betrayed us." Aris held Josephine up, with one arm around her, and faced us with a grim expression. "When I arrived home, all my family was well. There had been no illness. It was a lie."

I closed my eyes, dreading what was to come. This confirmed my fears that Heidi and Clara had only been a small part of the menace around us. So many little things, too small to matter on their own. But all together?

"It's been him. This whole time, it's been him sending raiders into Derehan. Even when we first met, Gwenna. That ambush when we first met you. That was him. My own damned father sent soldiers after us from Bluewater."

John scowled, incredulous.

"But why would he do that?" Dan asked, just as dumbfounded.

"To speed an alliance, apparently." He jerked his head in my sister's direction. "To make you think you needed his military to ensure protection and peace. But he was the one sowing all the discord!"

"But why go to so much effort for a marriage alliance?" I asked. "What could Bluewater possibly gain from this?"

"I don't know." Aris started walking toward the camp, pulling his horse and Josephine with him. "I imagine he saw it as a toehold to gain power in the north. I didn't stick around to ask many questions once I learned his next move. We haven't got a moment to spare. We have to get back to Valheid as soon as possible."

Aris told us everything in a rush as we remounted.

"He's been hiring mercenaries to bring violence to Derehan all these years, and now he's gotten together little less than an army. Six thousand men and women from all over Authe Ida, all trained to fight and kill as a profession. And he's sent them to Valheid. They're on their way, even now."

"But why?" Dan asked, his voice stern.

"To ensure Josephine doesn't back out. To make Kerric grateful. He wanted Valheid threatened so that Bluewater's army could come and save the city. He'd be in after that. He sends the threat, then saves us from it."

"This is the stupidest thing I've ever heard," John said with a growl.

"It is quite unusual for him," Aris admitted. "I had a hard time believing it, but I saw the army with my own eyes. It is something my uncle Eustis would have done, were he still alive to govern Bluewater. My father has gone mad."

"I'd believe it of either of them, Authe Idan savages!" muttered Gerrald from the back of the group, just loud enough for us all to hear.

"How far away are the mercenaries?" Dan asked.

"I can't be sure, but it won't be long. I saw them myself as they left the city. They likely passed through the eastern part of the Sacred Wood, a shorter road than ours. We have to warn Kerric. I can only hope we get back in time."

"I can ride ahead." Dan mounted his horse while he spoke. "I can make it much faster without the carriages."

"I'll go." My voice was stronger than I expected.

"No, Gwenna," Dan said. "Stay with your sister. I'll go."

"Dan, please. You don't understand. I can get there faster than any of you. Aris, is there anything else to report?"

He shook his head. "No, that's all. Six thousand mercenaries. They arrive from the south any day now."

I nodded, then leaned up to kiss John. "Explain to them for me?" I asked him.

He nodded once, mouth tight.

"I'll be back as soon as I can." I let go of him and stepped back.

They all just stared at me, unsure what the hell I was doing.

I closed my eyes.

Like picking up my mind sphere and moving it right out of the universe. Making it happen. Passing through the veil to Kerric. Finding the whiteness between the worlds.

"Gwen?"

My eyes flew open. My brother, Cynebald, and the two captains, Editha and Graham, stared at me in shock. I stood in Kerric's study, the dusty air of the roadside still sharp in my nostrils.

"How did you get in here?" Kerric rose to his feet in alarm and glanced at the closed door. "Why are you back so soon? Where's Josephine?"

"It's good you're all here," I said to the room, moving to the table to sit down. "I have a lot to tell you."

Their expressions grew progressively more grim as I spoke. When I got to the part about Josephine, Heidi, and Clara, Kerric roared in fury. The entire house heard it. The alarm rippled over my senses in a wave.

He yelled question after question, demanding to know her reasons, her methods, and what punishment had been done. I told him about the miscarriage and how Heidi had been behind the attempts on my life. Kerric outright threw his inkpot at the wall.

"She stood here in this very room and pretended to know *nothing*!" he fumed. "She let me fret and strategize. She actively tried to kill her own family! In this very room and she said nothing!"

The others were horrified and disbelieving, but none dared speak out.

Kerric boiled with rage. He approved of John's action, and he nodded, absentminded, when I explained how Dan had justified it. I had expected a bigger reaction from him on that score. Clearly he was too angry at the moment to realize the enormity of what Dan had achieved with just a few well-chosen words quickly spoken.

"But that is not the reason I came here today," I said finally. "Aris caught up with us just now. He brought news of an army coming, Kerric. An army of mercenaries. Six thousand, he said. Marching out of Bluewater."

"There are no mercenaries in Bluewater." Cynebald gripped the handle of his axe.

I resumed talking, telling them the news Aris had brought from his father and the Authe Idan mercenaries. And while I spoke, coldness doused Kerric's rage.

"We have no army," he said softly.

"We will fight to the last body to protect this city," Cynebald said, and the two captains voiced their agreement. "Every guardsman will fight, and we'll draft every able person from the city to stand with us, as is their duty."

Kerric nodded, staring at me. "They march directly north?"

"Yes. That is Aris's best guess."

"They'll pass through Mauland and Silmere...and Barano at minimum. They must be warned."

"Every city has its Guard," Editha said. "We can call them to come form the militia."

"That will leave the towns defenseless," I objected.

We all turned to Kerric for his decision.

"You traveled here in an instant?" he asked. "Can you move anywhere like that?"

"It seems I can."

"You will go as far south as Mauland, and to every town between here and there," Kerric said. "You will tell them to evacuate to the wilderness and to send every guard they can spare to Valheid. Tell them to empty their towns and hide."

"They won't listen to me. They'll laugh me out of their halls. I will appear out of nowhere and tell them a ridiculous story about an army being sent by our allies! It's absurd!"

"Everyone in Derehan and beyond knows about my sister, the Forest Witch," Kerric said. "They know I trust you."

I narrowed my eyes, dubious.

"Just give them a little show. No one can doubt you speak the truth," he said.

"Kerric!"

"Fine!" He threw up his hands. "When you travel, can you take someone along with you? Can you take John? Everyone knows and trusts John."

"I haven't tried. But Theo once brought me with her to the dead place, so I suppose it's possible."

"Go now," he said. "Try to take John with you and go south. And we will send messengers to the settlements around Valheid itself."

I nodded once, squeezed his hand, then stepped back. If they gasped, I wasn't there to hear it.

John's face came to mind when I slipped between the worlds, so when my sight returned, he was who I saw riding toward me. He rode at the front of the caravan, dust flying under the hooves of so many horses. His shout halted the group when he spotted me standing, still as an old tree, in the middle of the road, like I'd been there forever.

"How did it go?" John asked when he got close enough.

I waited to tell them the plan until everyone was gathered close enough to hear, They all agreed it was the best move to make.

"Are you willing to try to come along with me?" I asked John.

"Hell yes." He passed his reins to Gerrald next to him.

It was a little more difficult with John. Rather than slipping between the worlds, I had to drag him along. But it was doable.

My man didn't seem to enjoy the sensation very much.

"Hell. It's like your breath stops," he gasped after the first time, but he didn't complain otherwise.

We slipped from town to town, spreading the news. It all went quite smoothly. Even though they were stupefied by the news we brought and our method of traveling so fast, they listened.

We were too late for Mauland, though. When we arrived, smoke filled our nostrils. The air was filled with crying and calling out all around us. The attack was long over. The survivors were already cleaning up with dead expressions.

"They didn't come to kill," said Celine, the governor of that city. "They were clearly just passing through and raided us for supplies. We tried to defend ourselves, but there were too many of them. They took everything that was left from the last harvest. All of it. The storehouses are empty. We have nothing to get us through to the next reaping. Just what people had stored in their larders."

I stared around at the destruction. Most of the town remained untouched, save for a few broken windows, but a couple of buildings had been burned and were still smoking. Most of their Guard had been either injured or slain. They had nothing left to give.

"The mercenaries are marching on Valheid soon," John was saying to Celine. "We have to deal with them first. But as soon as the danger is past, we will send relief."

"I'm sorry we didn't make it sooner," I said.

We hadn't *known* sooner. The mercenaries had gone through Mauland the night before. There was no one to blame for this but Milhail Metaxas.

When we finally made it back to the caravan, I was beyond exhausted. Dragging John through the world was more draining than I realized, and by the time we were done, I could barely stand.

"You should go back to Valheid and sleep in your own bed," Josephine said after I climbed into the carriage next to her.

I shook my head. "I'd rather stay with you."

Over the next few days, as our group made their way back home, John and I went all over Derehan, not just to those in the path of the incoming mercenaries, but everywhere, calling in the militia. I slipped back to Valheid a few times to check in, and by the second day, the guardsmen had begun to arrive. They moved quickly, bringing few supplies and only what weapons they could carry.

On the third day, John asked if we could go see the invasion force with our own eyes. "Can you take us somewhere they can't see us? But where we can see them?"

In answer, I held out my hand to him.

We appeared on a craggy hill south of Silmere, overlooking a vineyard. Hard, green grapes already dotted the leafy trellises. Below us, a black mass moved, crushing the fields under their merciless boots. Behind them lay a dark scar of trampled earth.

The damage to this vineyard was massive, though the buildings appeared to be abandoned. Thankfully, the farmers had fled in time.

I had expected to find vast swaths of men, like we heard about in stories of great wars. Fires, beasts, and a sea of dirty bodies.

But that wasn't the case.

Six thousand wasn't so great a number from this height. The mercenaries took up most of the field, from one end to the other, but only because they were so spread out. They walked and rode almost casually, with carts studding their number here and there, lugging supplies and weapons.

"How bad is it?" I asked.

John inhaled a long breath before answering. "Bad enough. I don't think this army is meant to conquer, only to damage. There aren't enough of them. But they will do damage."

"Aris must have been right, that this is just for show. To make us think we need his father's resources."

John's mouth tightened, and he raked his hand through his hair. It stuck out at odd angles. "It's such a ridiculous thing to do. This must have cost him dearly to purchase. What benefit could he possibly gain? We have nothing in Derehan that he could want. Nothing worth all of *this*." He spread his hand wide to encompass the sprawling group.

"The only thing he's asked is for Jo to marry Aris."

"His way into the north," John said. "But we have nothing. We don't have mines or trading routes or armies. Only farmers and superstition."

"And he was getting the marriage. He was getting what he wanted! Why do this now?"

"He must have thought Jo might try to back out once she got to Bluewater," John said.

"Does he know she's gifted?" I asked.

"We've been very open about that since you came home four years ago. He can't *not* know."

"Then maybe he was afraid she'd read him. Maybe now he's done pretending."

"It's still so ridiculous. I can't understand it."

Below us, one of the mercenaries strolled close enough to spot us if she glanced in the right direction. She was tall, with her temples shaved and her blond hair braided high in dirty swaths on the crown of her head. The mercenary looked bored, like she was wishing she hadn't agreed to go on such a long march after all.

"Little things," I said softly. "On their own, easily explained. But all together—"

"Hmm," John mumbled in agreement.

"I'm afraid there is more to this that we haven't yet seen."

The woman passed below us. She didn't look up.

"Can you stop them?" John asked.

Yes, if I did it right. If they were funneled to me a handful at a time, I could stop them. I could even have done it from where I stood, tired as I was, and they would never even know I had been there.

I could create a pile of carrion right here in this vineyard. They would turn on each other as my puppets and start falling, a few at a time. They would realize it was happening without understanding why. Some might flee, some might try to find someone to fight, but they would all die.

And I almost told him so.

It was the drugging call of my abilities, wanting so badly to be used, that held my tongue. It made me afraid.

"There are too many," I said. The cowardice tasted like cold slime on my tongue.

John took my hand and squeezed. "Then let's go back to the caravan."

THIRTY-FIVE

Our group finally arrived in Barano the next morning and home to Valheid by dinner. The city had swollen once more with extra bodies but without the air of festivities in the alleys and public houses. The markets were closed and boarded up. The militia camped just outside the city wall, and the stink of so many bodies living too close in the summer sun hit me hard.

Inside the gates, the city was eerily quiet. Valheid had evacuated, the same as the southern towns. Those too young or weak to fight fled north toward Purgo, where Nanette had agreed to make space for them as best she could. If it were winter, it would have been a desperate situation. But with the summer heat and the streams still swollen from the spring thaws, they were safer in Nanette's fields, sleeping under the stars, than they would have been at home.

Council members were thin on the ground. Most were needed to lead their people or secure their lands and shops, so only fifteen attended that first meeting. After a few minutes of rest and washing, Josephine, Aris, John, Dan, and I joined them, bringing the total to twenty. Less than half our usual number.

It would have to do.

It was to be a concise meeting anyway, and I said very little. Talks of battle and strategy and blood. Cynebald led the discussion, assigning tasks and taking suggestions decisively, but it didn't matter. An air of panic threatened to burst the dam at any moment.

"We stop them at the wall for as long as we can," he said. "They will be funneled in by the mountain pass at first, but they will get around us quickly. We will have to be prepared—"

"This is going to be a slaughter," someone said down the table.

"There aren't enough of them for this to be a slaughter," John said. "Only six thousand. We have just as many, and we're fighting in our own home."

"It will be bad, but we won't fall," Nanette agreed with confidence.

"That's all well and good for you to say, Nanette," called a high voice from the back. Leland the Pest. "The city may not fall, but hundreds of our people will."

A general growl of approval swept through the room.

"What about the Owl?" Leland asked, while he still had the majority of the room behind him.

I jerked my head up. "What *about* the Owl?" I asked sternly.

"With your considerable abilities, you should be near the front lines. You can kill people from a distance, can you not? You can make them kill each other. It's reasonable to think you would be able to save us all from this horror. No one else needs to fight at all if we set you up right."

Silence met his words. No one spoke, not one person.

They all looked to me, everyone but Kerric, who stared at the table. Even John and Josephine watched me, wary, clearly hoping for any miracle I might be able to provide, though they wouldn't ask for it outright.

"I won't do it," I said.

"Why not?" Cynebald asked.

"Because it's wrong!"

"It's no more wrong than our soldiers taking lives with their bare hands," the general said.

"The two aren't comparable! It's not the same thing!"

"How is it any different?" Kerric asked in a soft voice, meeting my gaze.

I stared at him, at a loss for words. After all these years, after all the explanations and persuasions, my own brother still did not understand. The pressure of their wanting beat at me. I could understand why they wanted this. After all, I had already considered it while watching the invaders marching through that vineyard.

I could do it. I could save them all.

And deep down, in the darkest part of me, I wanted to try. Just to see if I could. Not to save anyone, but to explore how far my abilities stretched. To recapture the taste of power I had found when I questioned Heidi and Clara.

But it was *wrong*. The action would be wrong, and my motivations would be even worse.

"I will be down there, fighting with our people," Kerric continued when I couldn't speak. "I will be down there, making a monster of myself, asking my people to do the same. If Jo were trained with a weapon, she would be down there with us. I would expect this of my own sister. And I expect it of you."

"Kerric, it's not the same," I said on a breath, begging him to understand.

"It's your responsibility to defend the city and the people, same as the rest of us," Cynebald replied.

Kerric put a hand up to silence the general. This was his point to make as my brother.

I stared around the room. They all thought I was being a coward. Deep down, I agreed with them because I could *easily* sacrifice my own well-being to protect them all from the horrors of battle. I could protect every single innocent life.

But it wasn't right, damn it!

"I could kill all of them," I said quietly to the room. "Not all at once, but I could do it. I could stand at the gates to the city and drop them all as they approached, a few at a time."

"So, it can be done!" Leland said with a note of victory. "There is no need for the militia at all!"

Faces turned to me, just waiting for me to confirm it.

Anxious, I tapped my finger on the table. How could I explain this? Would it be possible for them to see beyond their own self-preservation?

"Johnny, if you were in a battle like this, how many could you kill before it ended?" I asked.

"Ten or so, more or less," he replied.

"And you, Cynebald?"

"The same. Maybe more." Cynebald held his head high. "If I didn't fall first."

"Ten or so," I repeated, then turned to my brother. "You are willing to ask each of these men to take ten lives, Kerric. A steep cost for defending their home, but one that's reasonable to pay. Expected, even. Ten lives apiece. Do you really think it's the same thing to ask me to take six thousand?"

Kerric held my gaze, and I thought he finally understood what he had been asking me to do.

"I do not belong in this fight any more than I belong in a war between two anthills," I continued. "Those people coming to attack us...What right do I have to decide that they deserve to die? They are just soldiers doing what they were paid to do. It is chance alone that I was born here, among you people. What if I were born in Authe Ida? What if I were one of them?"

"You're *not* one of them!" Kerric said.

"And I'm not one of you either!" I shot back. "I love you all, and this is my home. And you are my family. But I will never be the same as you! I can't be! I am the only one like me to exist, probably ever. No one should have this power. No one. Not me, not Derehan, not anyone. It isn't right!"

"Gwen—" Kerric began, but I spoke over him.

"But I do have this power. And I could kill every person in this room right now. I could make you do horrific things to yourselves and to each other. What's stopping me? It's not because I know you or care about you. It's because *it's not right!* It's because no one, not you or anyone else, deserves to have that end. No one deserves to be reduced to nothing. Because killing you all would be *nothing* to me."

The entire room stared at me, horrified. Even Leland's simpering expression had been replaced by fear.

"And if I did this thing now, if I killed them all for the greater good, then it would be that much easier to do it again next time. And even easier the next. The only thing stopping me from becoming a true plague on this earth is my morality, and you're asking me to compromise it. Give me a blade and I will defend this city to my last breath. But I will not allow you to wield my abilities as a weapon!"

I fell back into my chair, my breath coming heavy, and waited out the silence.

Finally, Kerric said, "There are very few left in the city who need defending, Gwenna. If you will not fight on the front lines, then I ask you to be their last defense should any of the mercenaries break through. That will be your duty."

He held my eyes for a long moment. It wasn't a question. It was an order to accept his compromise.

I wanted to tell him no, that I should evacuate to Purgo that night and remove myself from the equation entirely. But it was reasonable. It was honorable, and it was right. If I could fight, then I had a responsibility to do so, whether I wanted to or not. No one else had any choice in the matter, so why should I get one?

"Yes, I will do that," I answered softly.

John took my hand and squeezed.

I could feel Leland's eyes on me from the end of the table. That man had wanted to use me as a shield, and he had immediately convinced the entire room they were entitled to use me in that way, regardless of the consequences.

They were wrong to ask it of me, and I was wrong to tell them no. I should be sacrificing myself for all these innocent lives. That's what a good leader would do. Wasn't it? An able person would do something wrong for the greater good. Right?

There was no such thing as right anymore.

THIRTY-SIX

I checked on the approaching soldiers every few hours. They came steadily, encountering a few emptied towns along the way. The army helped themselves to whatever supplies they could carry and cared nothing about breaking down doors to get them, but they didn't go out of their way to cause destruction.

They were coming for Valheid. The army had a specific purpose, and nothing was going to deter them.

By the end of the second day, they entered the pass south of the city. They had been marching for weeks, but they were strong and well fed, and they had been trained for this.

Cynebald led the militia into the field south of the wall. They would keep the fighting out of the city as much as they possibly could. I was to stay at the Greathouse with the fifty-two civilians who had remained behind to help in those last days. They all gathered to wait in the main hall, with me standing alone in the shadow of the great double doors.

"Just leave the doors open," Kerric said to me before he left. "If they get past us, there's no point in encouraging them to cause more damage. You'll need to take them out as soon as they approach."

"I can handle any man that gets past you from here. They'll never make it to the Greathouse."

He shifted his weight from one foot to the other, his leather armor creaking, and clenched his fist on the hilt of his sword. "Jo told me once, only once, about the vision she showed you on your first day home. And, of course, she couldn't bring herself to give many details, but I got the gist of it."

He took my arm and squeezed, but I could only stare out onto the empty courtyard.

"You are not that person," Kerric said.

"Everyone keeps saying that." I sighed. "I can't tell if it's just because nobody wants to consider such horrific things or if you're all deluding yourselves. But Kerric, that *was* me. It *is* me. That's the entire point."

His hand fell to his side, but he didn't argue.

"I'm a monster in a cage," I said quietly. "There is no lock. There is only me, desperately holding the door shut."

John appeared in the stairwell with Josephine. Both looked stern.

"It's time," she said. "Editha has spotted them at the pass."

I reached with my mind and confirmed it. They would be within bowshot soon. How far had they been instructed to take this? Kill a few, then feign defeat and leave? Or would they carry on and on until they were forced to back down? How much of a show was Metaxas seeking to put on?

Kerric hugged Josephine and me tightly, then turned to stalk toward the southern gates.

John said nothing, only stood before me with his brow furrowed. I took a crow feather out of my hair and tied it into his with practiced fingers. He never did get that haircut, and his loose curls had almost reached his shoulders by now. I grasped his head in my hands and pressed our foreheads together.

After a moment, he pressed a kiss to my mouth, and then

turned to follow Kerric down the main street, his steel flashing in the sun.

Josephine put an arm around my waist, and we watched them go.

"It doesn't make sense." She shook with anger and fear. "Why send this army now? Milhail Metaxas had his intermarriage. He had his alliance. Why take such a step as this? Why now?"

"Maybe it has nothing to do with any of those things."

"Then why?"

I had no idea how to answer that question, so I didn't even try.

The first blow hit me hard. An arrow shot by the Authe Idans struck a Sildan guard in the arm. A breath of hesitation descended on both sides, then hell broke loose in a wave of rage and violence.

I huddled in the open doorway, hands over my head, as life after life was extinguished on both sides. We had the advantage, with archers lining the city wall and mounted soldiers mowing through the invaders, but it was a catastrophe.

"I should be down there," I whimpered. "I was wrong. I should be down there. I can stop this."

"No, we need you," Josephine said through gritted teeth. She was monitoring Aris, Kerric, and a dozen others.

The crowd of silent civilians watched us from inside the great hall. They held each other, unable to do anything but wait for bad news.

If I left them, they might all die. They each had weapons, of course, but mostly little blades and a few cooking knives or hay forks.

Another death. Another, another, another.

"I can go a little closer and thin them out." But I still couldn't make myself move forward. Tears fell freely down my face.

I should have left for Purgo. I still could. I could wink out of there and remove myself from the situation.

But the innocents behind me could die. They relied on me. I had promised to protect them.

"Stay here," Josephine said. "You're doing right. Stay here. Stay with us."

She was trying and failing to help me stay sane. Josephine was trying to keep me on the path I had chosen.

But I shook my head. "There's someone coming."

Josephine looked up, but the woman was still around the corner and out of sight. She had slipped past the line at the wall and was moving up the main street with a purpose.

"Another," I said. "A woman, then two men. They're getting through."

The first woman came into view through the arched entrance to the courtyard. It was the same woman, the blonde with braids I had noticed in the vineyard a few days before. She didn't seem so bored now.

She spotted us standing in the open doorway and turned toward us. We would be easy numbers for her. Easy glory, so far as it was counted in Authe Ida.

I broke away from my sister and stalked toward the woman, shoulders hunched, arms out in a placating gesture. "Stop! Stop and go back!"

As much as I felt the need to help in the battle, I still hesitated. This was *wrong*.

And a very small part of me understood the truth: Once I started, it would be too easy to keep going.

The mercenary paused for a half a second before sizing me up. I was just a young woman in comfortable pants and a linen shirt. Hair in a practical braid, feathers fluttering in the wind. I had only John's walnut dagger on my thigh—a small threat compared to her twin blades.

Small, not intimidating. Even less of a threat was my sister behind me on the Greathouse steps.

The woman grinned and continued in my direction.

"No! Please don't make me!" I screamed, desperate.

The woman ignored me. She kept coming, blades out, blood dripping from their curved edges.

"Gwen!" Josephine's voice cracked on my name.

The woman stepped through the archway and into the courtyard. Time raced by, and my options disappeared with every deliberate step she took. I couldn't coerce her to leave. As soon as I let her go, she'd just come right back. And if I put her to sleep, she would simply wake up.

The mercenary was halfway across the courtyard. Josephine screamed. I cried, defeated.

She was only a few paces away.

"Please!" I whimpered.

She raised her blade, her muscles rippling under the tight, sun-bronzed skin of her arm.

Quick and clean.

With only a little adjustment, her arm betrayed her. One of her swords plunged into her own abdomen instead of mine.

Like the thief in the woods. Like the archer under the elder tree. The woman collapsed mid-step and crumpled at my feet, bleeding from a fatal wound.

Josephine's screams stopped with a gasp. I couldn't look down at the woman on the cobbles in front of me. Tears streamed down my face.

That was three.

Murderer.

"Gwen! Two more!" Mary called from the doorway.

The two men I had sensed earlier were running toward us. They had watched their comrade fall and were coming to deal with whatever threat I posed.

"Please!" I sobbed as they approached the courtyard. "Go back!"

They ignored me and kept coming. This time, I didn't wait for them to get close. There was no talking them out of this.

I slumped and turned their blades against each other.

Five.

More people gathered in the entryway with Josephine, watching me in shocked silence.

Another man approached up the deserted main street. The line at the wall was breaking, and more were coming through.

I didn't even look up at him. Didn't call out. He fell in front of Anders's Milliner Shop a block away, one of his own arrows jabbed into his neck.

Six.

My eyes were dry now. There was no point in tears anymore.

None of my companions saw the man and woman approaching from the east. They had gone down a side street and weren't visible from where we stood.

But I felt them. And I killed them. My friends didn't even know they had been there.

Eight.

Pain. Blinding, breath-stealing agony stabbed through my middle. It was slicing and poking and pushing inside my gut, where such things should never happen. It was a physical wrongness I couldn't get my mind around. Something was *inside* me, breaking me.

My scream was instinctual. I would have vomited if my stomach muscles were still able to contract that way. But when I looked down at my hands where they clutched at my gut, there was no blood. No weapon, no wound.

"Gwen?" Josephine called. "What's wrong?"

"John," I whispered.

Dread filled me in a sickening wave. It was *John's* blood. *John's* broken body. With a wrenching tug that knocked me to my knees, the blade was hauled out of him. Somewhere out there, John was bleeding out in the street.

"Gwen?"

I turned to look up at her with a horrified expression. She

stood amongst our friends in the open doorway, all of them concerned but too nervous to venture out and check on me.

This was my family. My home. And these people had come to hurt us for no goddamn reason. They had come, and I could stop them.

All doubt left me.

All reservations gone.

I was going to stop this right fucking now.

"Gwen?" Josephine asked again when my expression hardened. "What's going on?"

I turned away from her and stalked toward the main avenue. All I could think about was John. The wound was minimal, but he was bleeding badly. There was very little time and so much still to do.

John was the goal. But I had to finish this battle first.

"Gwen!" Josephine's call pitched upward into a scream.

Three more mercenaries had appeared from the east, over the low wall of the courtyard.

I didn't turn or acknowledge them, just took them out simultaneously.

Eleven.

I couldn't abandon my friends at the Greathouse, but there was no way in hell I was staying put while my man lay dying. With determination, I cast out a wider net around the Greathouse. Already, there were six others around the property I hadn't noticed. In two quick swipes, they fell.

Seventeen.

Yes, I could maintain this as I went.

It was like looking out over a vast field. Every life stood out so clearly I couldn't miss them. I worked outward from the Greathouse for a few seconds, jogging down the street, finding every life moving through the city and putting it out. It was systematic and cold, and soon, there was no one left to threaten my defenseless friends at the Greathouse.

Energy surged through my body, like taking off soggy, too-tight boots at the end of a long workday. It was the first life-giving breath after being too long underwater. For the first time, I had turned my back on the cage of rules and found no boundaries to hinder me.

Gwen, don't come. John's inner voice was strong. *Don't come here. I love you. Stay where you are.*

I blocked him out. There was no saving me now. The beast inside, the monster I had trained so carefully all my life, was finally free.

Free and trembling with rage and anticipation.

I came across several more enemies on my way down the street. They all saw me as easy prey, a quick kill, but it was the other way around. They didn't get a chance to recognize the irony of it.

Blood spattered the cobbles as I passed the entrance to Turly District. Shouting, clashing, the screams of horses and men came at me long before I made it to the wall, but I was numb to it all in my joy. Bodies lay everywhere. This was a horrific scene, but right then, I didn't care.

Kill, kill, kill.

One after another, they dropped, leaving Derehani soldiers baffled at the sudden victory.

I was getting into the thick of it now. John lay a block away, outside the leatherworks he loved so much. Everyone had already discounted him as fallen, and nothing threatened him now except time.

Many dangers lingered between us, but those were easily dealt with.

Shouts rang out when people noticed me moving through the melee, but the fighting quieted. Bodies fell one after another as I passed. Life after life after life...Each one was satisfying but not quenching. With every exertion, my energy grew and grew to a dizzying pitch.

I must have been a terrifying sight. A young woman, already

spattered with crimson from flying blades, hands steady at her sides. Simple clothing fit for housework, hair dripping with blood, chest heaving in delight. My face was open in ecstasy, and I extended myself further.

There was no end to my reach. I was free.

This was hard, but I was good at it. It felt wonderful to stretch myself, flitting from one mind to the next in rapid succession, like dancing. If they were mid-swing, I would simply nudge them so their blade landed in their own gut or in their comrade's neck.

How much could I accomplish at once? How many could I coerce to act individually?

Many. Dozens.

My face was a mask of dreadful satisfaction. Gore spurted across my front. I had allowed a woman to get close enough to threaten me, just to see if I could make one of her commanders gut her in time. I delighted in forcing his hand, in taking away his deepest inhibitions.

Soldiers lurched around me, and I moved through them like it had been choreographed. Blades swung, and ichor coated the streets. My puppets continued fighting each other even with fatal wounds and broken bones.

"Gwen! Stop!" Kerric's voice cut through the din, easily distinguishable as the fighting died down. All our men had become still, staring in horror while I directed our enemies to slaughter each other.

There were still so many to kill, so many threats to wipe away. I couldn't leave a single enemy to harm my people. It was wrong—at a distance, I knew it—but again came that relieving sense of justification.

They deserved this.

But Kerric was right. No time for playing. I needed to kill and move on. That would be a new challenge. How far could I go from my physical body?

My consciousness swept through the streets. The shocked

screaming spread in a wave outward from where I stood. There were a few dozen Authe Idans in the city itself, but most of them were congregated close to the wall or outside in the fields.

John was just visible a few feet away. He gaped at me, eyes hard. *Stop!*

"Gwenna, stop!" Kerric commanded. "That's enough!"

He came at me, but I took his body as easily as anyone else's. I halted him in his tracks and took his voice.

Now I could ignore him.

I wished I could see the effects of my work in the neighboring blocks and outside the wall, but I didn't want to move far away from John. There were only mere minutes before his time was up.

So, I closed my eyes and looked through the eyes of others.

All throughout the city, Authe Idans fell, most of them to their own blades, all with shocked expressions as their hands betrayed them. I was a dancer, quick and precise. I was a weaver, too fast to detect the exact movements of skilled fingers manipulating the weft.

It was my masterpiece.

Bodies fell, and when one man died, I used the next to see my work. The horrors swept through the streets and beyond. Beautiful, gothic death. All at my will.

This is what I was born for. This was my purpose, and I was so good at it.

"Gwen! No!"

Garreth was harder to stop than his father had been. He raised his hand to crown me with the hilt of his sword, and I only just managed to force another Derehani soldier to hold him back. Careful not to hurt him, only restrain.

"You told me to stop you!" he screamed at me. His voice cracked as if he was still a child. He fought against the man holding him. He fought so hard I drew two others to help restrain him. "You have to stop!"

Almost. *Almost* done. Just a few dozen more and it would be finished. Complete. Satisfied.

I continued sweeping death down the streets, catching any stragglers as they retreated. They ran full tilt from the city, and I flexed in preparation to see how far I could stretch my mind away from my body.

"Gwen!" John's voice was a bare croak. He tried not to cough on the blood in his throat, for fear of tearing his wound further. "Gwen, please."

His was the only voice I couldn't ignore. Disappointed in a job not quite finished, I opened my eyes to look at him.

He lay just a few paces away, draped on top of another body. His entire midsection and both hands were glossy with blood. The feather I had tied in his hair was soaked in it. His skin was ashen, and his eyes were half closed.

Shit, was I too late? Had I gotten so caught up in death and purpose that I had let him get too far gone to save?

With a gasp, I leaped at him. The instant my skin found his, I dragged us both through the void to the Sanctuary.

THIRTY-SEVEN

We landed awkwardly in the dusty grass near Theo's camp. The old woman was nowhere to be seen. Off whispering at someone, probably.

It didn't matter. I knew where she kept the little tin of ointment she had gotten from some unknown land on the other side of the Arigua Ocean. My blood-soaked fingers slipped on the clasp of the trunk, sending a stab of pain through my hand when my skin scraped along the metal latch.

I swiped them roughly on my pants and on one of Theo's rugs to dry them and started rummaging through the trunk. I tossed out other items I might have paid more attention to if I'd had the time to spare: a necklace, a book, a pendant, cooking utensils, a wooden dish, and cotton gauze. But it was all thrown aside until I found the little tin with the pink flower and gold trivara painted on top.

Inside, the precious Athorum salve that would heal any wound.

The same one Theo had used to heal my feet the last time I'd been there.

"Just hold on a bit longer," I told John, leaning over him. I ripped his leather armor aside and slathered the precious stuff into his wound, digging my fingers in deep and wincing at his groan of pain. Then I heaved him over onto his side so I could salve the exit wound on his back.

"Just breathe," I said.

John said nothing. He was past speaking. It took all his effort to keep pushing air in and out of his lungs.

When I was finished, I laid him back down as gently as I could. His skin was pale as paper and cold to the touch. And even though the Athorum seemed to be stopping the bleeding, I couldn't find his thoughts anymore.

He had passed out.

"John?" I cried, slapping his face with bloody fingers. *John! Wake up!*

I checked the wound. It had sealed up to a rough, pink slash that appeared weeks old. But still, I could not wake him. Had I been too late?

Desperate, I closed my eyes and pressed my forehead to his. His life was almost gone. I could barely see it if I didn't look directly at it. The merest whisper still connected to his body in a faint, glimmering filament.

It was a freshly spun thread too thin to hold the weight of a spindle. Sinead had taught me to break threads like that, then I could rejoin it to the fiber supply and replace the break with a stronger thread.

But this thread could not be broken. I had to shore it up instead, twisting my own life with his like strands of shining flax.

I wrapped my life around his and held on tight, giving more of myself to this task than I had in the battle just moments before. All sense of time was lost. I stayed deathly still until finally, *finally*, a gentle breath tickled the loose hair around my cheek.

"Johnny?" I whispered, peering into his expressionless face. When there was no answer, I checked his wound again. Only a puckered, pale scar marred the flesh of his abdomen.

"What did you do?"

The harsh voice rang through the silent trees, making me jump and whirl.

Theo stood amid the mess I had made of her things, livid. She found the Athorum tin where I had dropped it and glared at me. "Did you use all of it? Do you have any idea how rare Athorum is?"

"He was going to die!" The adrenaline of the past few minutes crashed into me, and tears began to pool in my eyes.

Had it only been minutes?

"What did you do, you idiot?" she spat at me. "You are supposed to be correcting the imbalance! What did you do to get in this state?"

She gestured wildly at me, at the gore soaking my clothes and hair. The blood of hundreds of men and women. Thousands. People I had forced to kill each other, needlessly gruesome.

I remembered the looks on Kerric's face. Garreth's. Josephine's. They had begged me to stop, but I hadn't listened. I had been enjoying myself too much.

And now that I had been sated, now that the craving had been fulfilled, I recognized the horror of what I had done.

"Gwen? What happened?"

I turned to John, my eyes watering and my throat closed. He slowly sat up, uneasy, looking around at our surroundings.

It had been a nightmare. That was all. It hadn't really happened. We would go back, and it wouldn't be as bad as I remembered. I had run to John to save him. That was all. I had run through the streets...Defended myself, maybe. But that was all. I couldn't have done the rest.

"Gwen." John's voice was sterner now. He'd caught sight of Theo and reached for me, too weak to move much. John had lost a lot of blood. Too much.

"What did you do?" Theo screamed at me. Tears pooled in her

eyes, and her mouth twisted up in anger or grief or confusion...I couldn't tell.

"There was an army!" I said, voice cracking. "They came to kill us."

"What army? Who sent them?"

"Metaxas."

"Gwen, stop talking." John grabbed my arm and pulled me closer to him, dragging me awkwardly through the dry, dead dirt. His eyes never left Theo, brows drawn tight together. "Get us out of here."

Theo stood a little straighter, as if suddenly remembering herself. "Milhail Metaxas doesn't have an army!" she screeched, advancing on us. "Milhail Metaxas is supposed to be fostering peace!"

"Gwen, let's go home."

I looked up at Theo, tears coming in earnest. "Why am I like this?" I asked her.

"Because you are weak!" Theo stood over me, an ancient and terrible priestess for a god I did not know.

"No!" I whimpered.

She gazed down at me in disgust. "I wanted you to be the best of us! But clearly, you're unworthy. If I had gotten to you earlier, this could have been avoided!"

I had a flash of that vision, the me I could have been in another life—a life with Theo. Sasha had been covered in blood then, just like I was now.

"No!"

But no matter how many times I protested, I couldn't change the truth. I was and always would be that monster. Josephine might have saved many innocent lives by sending me away as an infant, but she hadn't saved me.

"Gwen, take us home!" John gritted out. "Now!"

"Yes! Go home and fix this!" Theo's voice broke again. "You made this mess. Now clean it up!"

"Gwen!"

His hand wrapped around my wrist in a firm grip that bit into my skin.

"Gwenna! Now!"

John's voice was so commanding, so authoritative, that I obeyed on instinct.

It was exactly as I remembered. The blood, the bodies...They lay slumped over each other in haphazard heaps. Most of them were the Authe Idans, but here and there was a familiar face or the crest of a Derehani household.

I fell to my knees the moment we appeared on the street in front of the leatherworks. John went down with me. He was too weak to walk unaided, much less hold me up too.

We seemed to have arrived mere seconds after we had left. Everyone stood in exactly the same place as before. Not a single step had been taken in any direction. Kerric cried out when he saw us and ran to lift me bodily from the street.

Darkness invaded the edges of my vision. At all costs, I could not let it spread to others. I had to lock myself back in that cage.

It was all I could do, in my panic, to wrap myself up in the sphere of my mind and let the blackness blot out the horror of what I had done.

I woke in my bed some hours later. Someone had changed my clothes and washed away the blood. I lay in a clean night shirt on soft blankets.

But I wasn't alone.

An unfamiliar guard stood by the door, and Josephine sat on the armchair near the window, the one overlooking the alley by the bakehouse. Her face was drawn and serious, but when she felt me wake, it flashed with fear.

She sat up, staring me down. Her mind was impenetrable. If I wanted—if I really wanted to—I could get through it, but it would be very hard. My sister was not weak.

It was easy enough to confirm my suspicion of why they were both there. Josephine was shielding the guard's mind with everything she had.

He was there to kill me if I needed killing, and she was there to make sure I couldn't stop him.

It was a kindness that they'd found someone who didn't know me. It would have been easier for him to do it.

"That's not necessary," I said with a croaking voice.

Josephine cocked her head to one side but did not lower her shielding. "You scared us, Gwen."

My throat constricted even further, and I squinted against a pounding headache. "Where's John?"

"He's in Kerric's rooms, recovering."

I hesitated to ask my next question, terrified of the answer. "Who else was killed?"

"Plenty," she snapped. Josephine rose to her feet, and the guard took a step forward, alert. "I hate that you had to do this, Gwenna. But if you were going to do it anyway, why didn't you do it sooner? Why didn't you kill them before they even got to the city?"

Her voice cracked near the end, and her face broke a little. The guard tightened his grip on his halberd.

"Who, Jo?" I asked in a small voice.

"Derrick. Stephen. Maryanne. Editha. Paul." She broke off on Paul's name, but she forced herself to keep going. "Plenty, Gwen. Plenty more. Dozens of people who won't be going home tonight. Because of you. Because you didn't want to be responsible."

Her words sucked the breath out of me. Stephen? Editha? Paul?

I gaped at her when she finally broke down. With a sob, she turned and stomped through the door. The guard followed her with one wary glance back at me.

Paul?

I didn't try to leave my room. Could barely even get out of bed. I just lay there, cold, unfeeling.

Paul was dead? Where? How? Had it been quick? Where was his body? Had he been alone?

Just like Mariah, it had happened without me knowing. It didn't feel real.

Mary came in with a lunch tray at some point, but I couldn't eat. It wasn't until John stepped quietly in that I even sat up.

He appeared shrunken and wan in the doorway. His face was a mask of exhaustion, but the usual brightness had come back to his eyes. He was healing quickly.

I quailed under his steady gaze, and no words came out. He crossed the room and hauled me into his arms with a sigh like relief.

It was a shock to be surrounded by warmth after being cold and empty for so long. If the memory of my rampage weren't so fresh and clear, I might have believed myself to be frozen forever.

Don't think. Just don't think about it. You did what you had to do. Just don't think about it.

"Gwen?" he said softly.

Don't think about it.

I couldn't lift my eyes to face him. "Hm?"

"Gwen, look at me." John set me gently away from him, but I couldn't look up from his chest.

"Look at me," he said again.

Don't think. Don't think. Don't think.

He put his hand under my chin and turned my face up.

His expression was worried, anxious, relieved, afraid—all at once. For the first time, he was afraid. Not of me, but for me.

The instant I met into his eyes, I cracked. I couldn't dam the thoughts anymore. They came spilling through a fissure in my own will and poured into me. I thought of that thief in the woods all those years ago, of putting people to sleep against their will, of Paul and of Editha, and of all those men the day before. So many. Too many.

"I don't—" I started. The tears came too fast. My throat closed up.

John took my face in his hands and waited, his own eyes watering.

"I don't know..." My voice sounded thick with the force it took to speak. Finally, with great effort, I managed to whisper it. "...how many I killed."

The dam broke. I broke.

John pulled me close, and I sobbed into his chest. I clutched at him, desperate to make this feeling stop, wanting to reclaim the emptiness.

But it wouldn't stop. It came in waves, one after the other.

Murderer.

Monster.

Thing.

The thief.

The archer.

Paul.

Editha.

Stephen.

Soldier after soldier after soldier.

Murder.

Manipulation.

My knees gave under me, and we both sagged to the floor. John was still too weak to hold me up, but he refused to let go. He enveloped me in his arms and hauled me into his lap. I pressed my face into his shirt and wrapped my arms around my head.

Monster.

Murderer.

Manipulator.

Thing.

Wave after wave of self-hatred crashed into me, dragging sobs from my tight throat.

"I don't want to kill anyone!" I gasped in a high-pitched wail. "I don't want to be that person!"

"I know," John said into my hair. His voice was just as strained as my own.

"I didn't ask for this! I don't want it!"

He squeezed me tighter, and I just cried more.

It took a long time. At one point, I was sure I would never feel normal, never feel like a person again. Was I even still a human at all?

It took a very long time, but John held me all through it all. Until, just like that, I took in a deep breath. Then another.

I opened my swollen eyes. I had ruined his shirt completely. I scrubbed at my face, feeling wet and uncomfortable now that the tears were slowing. John seemed close to tears himself.

"Don't tell me I had to do it," I said, my voice hoarse.

"I wasn't going to."

"Because I didn't have to do it. I didn't have to kill them. Not like that." Maybe I did have a few tears left after all, but I didn't collapse again.

"If you didn't—" he began, but I interrupted.

"No, I mean I could have done it clean. The way I did with the archer in the north field. It would have been just as easy," I said, all in a rush. "But I didn't, John. I didn't. I massacred them. I did it without even thinking about it. I'm a monster, and I enjoyed it! I felt so free! Jo didn't save me at all. I'm still that *thing*."

"*Shh*," he said, desperate, but he couldn't stop my tide of words.

"It'll never be over. Because I am the Child, John. Don't you see? I will always be that monster. I will always kill people. Those soldiers, they won't be the last. Don't you understand? Next time,

I won't think then, either. I'll just kill and kill and kill! And no one, not one single person, could ever stop me!"

"Gwen," he pleaded.

"You wouldn't be able to stop me! Josephine couldn't. Theo couldn't. Garreth might keep me out of his own head, but not for long. I have the ability to make anyone do anything I want!"

"But you don't!"

"But I could! I could make you stand up right now. I could make you take your dagger and kill me right now. I could do it!"

"Maybe you could!" he said. "Maybe that's true. But you won't!"

I wanted to. Just then, I wanted to so badly. I wanted to end my own wretched existence, to rid the world of me, to prove him wrong. It would be easy. Just make him stand up and threaten me. Just a little. Just enough.

But I couldn't. I couldn't make John a puppet any more than I could force my own hand to turn that dagger on myself.

I clutched at my head. My hair fell in loose snarls all around me, and I grabbed at it, glad of the dull pain when I pulled too hard. This I could control. I deserved it.

"You are not the Child, Gwen," John said firmly. "You are not. Maybe you could be. Maybe you would have been in another life. Maybe you still have all the same skills, but you are not her. You will never be."

"How do you know?" I asked through clenched teeth.

"I know because you are grieving for yourself and for the soldiers you killed. You killed them on a battlefield, just like the rest of us, but still, you grieve for them. You can cry. You feel remorse. That Child we saw in the vision, that Child that you fear, she stopped being capable of remorse decades ago. That's the difference. That's what makes her evil, and that's what proves you are not."

Remorse. Yes, I felt that. It tore through me like a scythe.

"Maybe you didn't have to kill those men that way," he continued. "But you did. You made a choice in battle, and now it's over. We can't change it. But don't forget why you did it. Tell me why you did it, Gwen."

"For you," I whispered. "To save you. To save my people. To stop the fighting."

"You did it for love. If you were a monster, you couldn't love us enough to fight for us."

The things he said made sense. I couldn't argue with him, but I wasn't ready to agree with him yet either.

"You're not innocent, Gwen," he said, a note of finality in his voice. "But that's okay. None of us are."

I didn't know how long we sat there on the floor, putting ourselves back together, piece by piece. It was Kerric who finally put an end to it. He thrust my door open without knocking and glared down at me with hard eyes.

"Let's go," he said sharply.

"Where?"

"There's a council meeting."

I stared at him in shock. They would allow me in after all I had done? Just that morning, Josephine had been ready to have me killed.

"Now, Gwen. You've wallowed up here long enough. Let's go." He turned and left just as abruptly as he'd come.

The council chamber was silent as Kerric and I found our seats at the head of the table. No one spoke. They barely even looked at us. Most of them were still covered in blood and mud, though all armor had been discarded. John sat, deflated, in his chair next to mine, and Josephine's face was stone. She wouldn't look at me.

As usual, Kerric began with practical matters. Decisions were made about caring for the wounded, the allocation of supplies, and relief for the sacked towns in the south.

Then followed a lengthy discussion about what to do with the thousands of bodies littering the city and the fields outside the wall. There were too many to bury. Too many to burn. They would foul water sources and spread disease.

Finally, Leland suggested in a somber tone that we make use of the old plague pits a few miles east of the city. And if we set to work now, a new one could be dug before it was too late to move the bodies. Whatever was left could be burned.

I stared at my clenched hands and said nothing.

A tense moment of silence descended around the room. Finally, Kerric spoke as if he had to wrench his jaw open to do it.

"An answer must be made."

A general mumble of agreement went around. The councilors sounded angry, vengeful.

"We have no army," Garreth said. "We can't spare anyone to respond in kind."

"I can take a letter," Dan offered. "But that's such a weak gesture it would be laughable."

"We can't do *nothing*," said Mark by the door. "We may as well invite him or someone else to invade us."

"I'll go." I spoke very quietly, but everyone in the room heard.

"What are you going to do? Go there and murder everyone so there's no one left to attack again?" asked Mark with an angry snarl.

I stood. My knees sent my chair skidding backward. Josephine stood up as well, her eyes steady on my dark expression, but she waited.

"I did not want to kill them!" I said with a shaking voice too loud for the room. "I told you I did not want to do this thing! But you kept me here! You—" I broke off.

I trembled with a new sensation. This anger was a relief after the hours of lonely grief. I was furious with everyone: with myself, with Metaxas, with every person in that room.

"I don't need to kill anyone else," I said. "I can just show them. I can show Metaxas what I have done. I can show anyone else who is with him. It will be enough to make it clear that Derehan is protected."

The room fell stagnant with mutinous silence.

"You said an answer must be made." I turned to my brother. "But you're wrong. I've already made the answer. Metaxas simply doesn't know it yet. I'll go there and tell him."

"And what exactly will you tell him?" Leland asked from his cushioned chair. "I have dealt with Milhail Metaxas myself. He is not a man to be convinced of anything."

"He's right, Gwen," John said. "The harder you push, the more stubborn Metaxas gets."

"My father does not learn," Aris added from his seat next to my sister.

"You did," I said. "Before you came here, you didn't think the sibyls were real. And now here you are, promised to one."

I gestured toward Josephine, whose stony stare still hadn't wavered from my face. She continued to watch for any sign I might crack again, gripping Aris's hand like a lifeline.

"The people of Authe Ida have an ingrained narrative, Gwenna," Aris said. "We grew up with bedtime stories about the mindwalkers, but that's all it is to us. Just stories. It's not real. It would take much more than a vision to convince anybody. They would explain it away. He would just try again."

"Derehan remembers, but Authe Ida has forgotten." said Mark.

A grumble of agreement met his words.

"Well put, my boy," Leland said with a pompous nod.

"What about when the remnants of his army return to confirm my story?"

"He will try again, Gwen," Aris insisted. "He will buy a larger army. He will try again."

"I still don't understand why this army was sent in the first place," John said. "What we need is an interrogation, not a response."

"Yes, Gwen," Dan agreed. "You should go there and make him confess, the way you did with—"

He cut off, but everyone knew he meant Heidi. My jaw tightened at the memory of that hateful morning on the road. It had been the day the first crack appeared in my self-control.

"Fine," I said abruptly. "I will go to Bluewater and confront Metaxas. I will find out why he did this thing, and I will show him the results of it. John will come with me to provide credibility. Aris, I will need an audience. When is your father likely to be in a crowd?"

"He takes supper with the entire household. Much like we do here."

"Good. He thinks we're wild things up here, but he doesn't know what wild means. I plan to show him."

THIRTY-EIGHT

Sinead brought the Chalice costume to my room that night and set the trunk near the wall right by the door. The bells inside jangled noisily, the sound only barely muffled by the closed lid. She stood up and studied my wary face for a long moment.

"You're sure about this, Owl?"

"I'm not sure about anything, Sinead. But it won't stop me from trying."

She pursed her lips, then nodded. Sinead turned and left the room without saying anything more.

I went over to the trunk and opened it, filling the room with the overwhelming scent of rose oil. Just as before, there wasn't a lot inside. The Chalice didn't wear much by way of clothes, after all. I pulled out the leather skirt and the soft wool top, both carefully cleaned and stored only a few weeks before. It felt like years since John had peeled these off me and laid them ever so gently on my chair. I hadn't spared half a thought for them since.

And now I was planning on taking these simple clothes, these symbols of our first coupling, and defiling them with war.

I closed the trunk with a snap and moved abruptly to sit by the window.

How had I gotten here? How had all this happened? Sometimes, it felt like only a few weeks had passed since I'd been happy and oblivious in the Sacred Wood.

What would Michael think if he saw me now? If he knew what I planned to use my abilities for? If he knew what I'd done with them already? Would things have turned out differently if he hadn't lied to me? If I'd known more about what I could do and where I belonged? If I'd known when to break the rules and when to keep them?

I would give anything to talk to Michael again. To shake him and make him explain why he had lied to me and kept me in the dark. But he was lost to me in the depths of time.

Haven't you noticed? There's no time in this place. All of that happened years ago.

Theo's voice came unbidden to my mind. A week ago, in the dead place, she had said something huge.

There is no time in this place.

When I had jumped into the Lily River, had I landed in the future? Was that even possible? I had overlooked those words in the rush of learning about Heidi's treachery. But now?

I stood up, my hands shaking with the possibility. Just like learning to jump between the worlds, maybe all I had to do was try?

I closed my eyes, picked up the metaphorical sphere of my mind, and passed through the timeless void between the worlds. Before, I had appeared before John or Theo simply by thinking of them. But now that I looked for it, I recognized the current for what it was: time itself. It eddied and flowed, pushing me along a predetermined path.

But I had a specific place to go. A certain time.

Like wading up a stream, it took effort, but I had always been strong. I pushed through the current with deliberation, and when I opened my eyes, daylight filled a familiar room.

Tears sprang up the second I realized where I was. Our little hut nestled in the protected hollow in the Sacred Wood. The familiar smells of earth, dried herbs, grease, and mildew filled my nostrils. My chest swelled with nostalgia. There in the corner, my cot, with my favorite book on the table next to it. Right where I had left it.

Birdsong came in through the open windows, and two half-drunk cups of tea sat cold on the low table next to me.

I remembered those cups of tea. Michael had poured them for us after the first time Theo had taken me into the dead place. He had told me lies about her while we sipped them. Chamomile and lavender—his favorite recipe.

"Who are you?"

I turned to face him, wary. Michael perched on his cot, the same one he had retreated to after I'd accused him of lying all those years ago. He stared up at me, blue eyes narrowed under his bushy eyebrows, hands gripping the edges of his cot.

The sight of him floored me. There he sat, like it was any other day. I supposed, for him, perhaps it was. My heart stilled in my chest, and my eyes burned hot with unshed tears.

Where was the other me, then? Outside? Sewing a pair of fur boots and pretending everything was okay?

A quick glance out the window confirmed it.

A younger version of me sat under the willow tree, her attention fully absorbed on her task. She was so small, just a wisp of a girl wearing scraps of leather. Her hair floated around her head, like a cloud of black tangles with feathers stuck in at odd angles. A mess.

The sight of it pulled a smile from my lips. This was how I'd looked the first time John had seen me. No wonder he'd been so conflicted. I really had been just a child. A wild thing.

"Gwen?"

I turned back to Michael, but words wouldn't come. He appeared exactly the same as I remembered. Thin and wiry, with white hair and beard softening his wrinkled face.

"Is that you, Little Owl?" He braced his hands on the edge of the cot, levering himself upward to stand before me.

He looked me in the eye for half a second more, then pulled me toward him for a firm hug, like the father he had always been.

The familiarity of it was too much for me. I had been so angry with him for so long, but really, I had missed him. I wrapped my arms around his thin middle and sobbed. "Hello, Michael," I said into the wisps of his hair.

He held me at arm's length. "You've grown up. How long has it been for you?"

"You knew this too?" I demanded. "You knew I could move through time?"

He quailed, mouth opening and closing as he tried to find an answer. Michael didn't need to bother.

The smoldering anger came rushing in, fast in the wake of my relief and happiness to have him back again. "You should have told me that!" I said, desperate to keep my voice low so the other Gwen wouldn't hear us from outside. "Why didn't you tell me anything! Why, Michael? Why did I have to learn everything too late!"

"How long has it been?" he asked again.

I scrubbed away the tear running down my cheek. "Four years. Four and a half."

His mouth pulled down into a frown. "And I wasn't with you?"

I clammed up, unsure of what I should and should not say to him. "I shouldn't have come here," I said, but I couldn't bring myself to leave.

He took both my hands in his own and squeezed. "I am an old man, Gwenna. If my time is coming, I won't fight it."

Another tear escaped my eye. "No. I don't know if it's possible to change my past, and I don't want to find out. I came here to ask you why you kept me in the dark my entire life. Why, Michael?"

He tilted his head to the side, eyebrows raised in sympathy. "If you have learned what you are capable of, what you can do, then you know why I kept that knowledge from you."

My gut twisted with anger and fear. With self-loathing, hope for the future, regret. With everything that might have been if I had been better informed.

"No, I don't understand!" I snapped. Angry tears rolled down my cheeks. "Maybe if I'd known how far it went, I wouldn't have slaughtered all those people, Michael!"

He recoiled, but my words didn't slow.

"Maybe I could have stopped the Authe Idans from coming at all! Maybe I could have saved Jo's child! But no, you told me to lock it away. No coercion, no listening in, no lies. That's what you told me!"

"Gwen—" he began, but I cut him off.

"This is *your* fault! Because I tortured myself to keep those rules. And all for nothing. I became the monster anyway! *Your* fault!" I jabbed a finger at his chest, but my anger wasn't enough to hold back the heartbreak, and a sob escaped my throat.

Michael gathered me to him when I properly broke down.

"You should have told me!" I cried.

"*Shh*," he murmured, stroking my head as if I were still a child.

And for the first time in a long time, I really felt like one. I allowed him to hold me while I sobbed, a different kind of embrace than John could give. This was my home, the only parent I had ever known. This was my childhood and my innocence, still there underneath the blood and regret.

After a long moment, Michael's soft voice broke the silence. "I did not know how much to say. If you knew you could travel anywhere with half a thought, you might go into the world before you were ready. If you knew about the possibility of moving through time, you might see things or tamper with events that are better left in the dark. If you knew you had a family, you might have sought them out and met a city that still remembered and feared you. There were too many ifs, Little Owl. Too many dangers for a child with no obstacles."

I sniffed and pulled away. The younger me still sat outside under the willow tree, her hands busy with the half-finished boots.

"I planned to tell her when John comes to get us," Michael said softly. "I don't want her going to Valheid unprepared. But..." He trailed off, reconsidering. "But I suppose that doesn't happen, does it?"

I shook my head, my focus still outside under the willow. My heart felt emptied out. "It's comforting to know now, though. That you were going to tell me."

"I don't know what kind of life you've had these four years," Michael said. "I hope it was a good one. I hope you can find peace. But Gwenna, you must do it on your own terms. You must find the balance. Your abilities are a part of you, always. You cannot pretend they don't exist, just as you cannot cut off your own arm. Find the balance."

Outside, the younger me stood and began gathering up her tools.

"I have to go," I said.

"Find the balance, Gwen." He took my hand. "And find peace."

"I am a weapon, Michael. I can never have peace."

"You are not a weapon, child," he answered sharply. "You are a person. Your abilities give you heavy responsibilities, but nothing more. If a hard choice must be made, make it and move on. You can only do your best."

I nodded, squeezing his gnarled hands in my own. "Okay. I'll try. I have to go before she comes back inside."

"I love you, Little Owl," he whispered.

I backed away from him. The younger me stepped onto the porch, her bare feet silent on the uneven, creaking boards.

"I love you too, Michael," I said as quietly as I could so she would not hear. "Thank you for my childhood."

His bright eyes watered, and he smiled a goodbye.

Young Gwen grasped the handle, and the door rattled in its frame.

I disappeared before it opened even an inch.

John didn't come to bed until late. I didn't have the heart to tell him about Michael, not yet. It felt too fragile. I wanted it to be mine only, just for a little while, so decided to tell him once everything was over.

He slept, and I lay nestled against his broad back, wishing it were time to go. How did he sleep so easily when the next day might go so badly? Maybe he was just used to it. He'd had plenty of bad days, plenty of battles. This was just another day for him.

Time continued to drag by. Hour after hour, I stared into the darkness of my room. I took to silently counting John's breaths to stop thinking about what I would say the next day. I made it up to 244 when he actually spoke aloud, causing me to jump.

"Go to sleep," he mumbled.

"I can't."

"What are you counting?"

I frowned into the darkness. "You heard that?"

John rolled over to face me and wrapped his arm around my waist. "You were focusing very hard on it. It worked itself into my dream, so I was counting blades of grass in a field."

My mouth quirked downward. "I didn't realize I was sending you anything."

"Hmm."

"Johnny?"

"Hmm."

"Tell me everything's going to be okay."

He opened his eyes. I could only just see the glint of them in the dark, but it was enough to prove he was looking at me.

"It's all going to be okay, Gwenna."

I nodded, mostly to convince myself he was right. I tucked my head under his chin and closed my eyes.

And I must have slept because I woke to the first watery sunlight of the morning. My room was a little gray, not quite fully lit. But it was enough. Finally, I could get up.

Still, time dragged by. We weren't to appear in Authe Ida until late that night, when supper was in full swing. I wouldn't need to start getting dressed until the evening.

I filled the day with work, mostly outside in the fresh air. The bean fields required hoeing, and the wheat fields after that. Marsha Brandan needed help washing the fleeces she had sheared the week before, so I rolled up my sleeves and packed them into suint baths, one after the other, to ferment.

It helped pass the day more quickly when I was working hard and listening to the gossip of other people laboring beside me.

And then time began to rush forward. Dinner came and went before I could blink. And then somehow, I was up in my room with Mary and Sinead, opening the Chalice trunk. Mary piled strand upon strand of bells, bones, shells, beads, and feathers on my wrists and ankles.

Sinead, her face an unusual mask of grim determination, spent half an hour teasing and braiding my hair into wild elegance, more feathers and bones tied into it for good measure. Mary's hand shook just a little when she raised the brush to apply the grease paint under my eyes and on my forehead, but she did it flawlessly.

When I finally looked at the result in the mirror, I barely recognized myself. Gwenna was gone, and only the Wild Thing was left. Even with my drawn, sad face, I was fierce to look at.

"Is it enough, Little Owl?" Mary asked, stepping back to take it all in.

"Almost." I looked down at my hands. Something wasn't right.

At the Chalice Festival, my fingers had been black to the second knuckle. "I need some mud."

All three of us went downstairs and outside, drawing every eye on our way. The bells and bones rang and clattered with every movement I took. They followed me straight outside to a mud patch near the back door, which never quite seemed to dry out. I plunged my hands into it and rubbed mud all over both of my feet and ankles. I wasn't careful about it. Dirt got everywhere, up my arms, splattered across my skirt.

While I did this, Sinead stepped to the herb garden and yanked off two large twigs of rosemary, which she added to the jumble of my hair.

"For luck," she said in a low voice, the sharp scent hitting my nose.

I swiped the worst of the mud off my palms. When it was done, I turned and faced them both. "Thank you," I said.

Mary shook her head. "No, thank *you*."

I nodded. In a burst of nerves or insanity—or maybe it was the true spirit of the Chalice taking over—I opened the little pot of grease paint around my neck, dipped one finger in, like I'd done a hundred times before, and drew a little chalice on Sinead's forehead. Then I did it again for Mary. Both accepted the blessing, though it was not the Spring Feast, and held their heads high when we went back inside.

We found everyone in the Council Room, as planned. The room fell silent as we came in, looking for all intents and purposes like a goddess and her two priestesses.

John stood with Kerric at the head of the table. My man was not wildly dressed. In fact, he was very respectable in an embroidered wool shirt and bandolier. His knives were polished to a high shine, and he even wore a single silver ring on his right hand. He was the very picture of an ambassador in a foreign court.

And when we stood together, we only served to make each other more extreme. Compared to John, I was a true savage. Next to me, he was a respected politician. Neither of us could be ignored.

"Are you ready?" John asked.

I made my way noisily to his side and nodded, producing more ringing from the bells in my hair. I rubbed my hands together, not liking the feel of the mud drying on my skin. A glance out the window told me it was finally time. The sun was just starting to set in the west. Would it look different descending over the sea instead of the mountains? Would I even see it?

"Don't forget," Aris said from my left, "you'll have to break him. You will never convince him that he's done wrong or that you are right. He will never agree to compromise in any way. You must break him. At the very least, you must convince him that Derehan is a lost cause, not worth the effort."

"I remember. Thank you, Aristeidis."

"It's time." John slipped his fingers through mine.

"We're in your hands now," Nannette called from across the table so everyone could hear her. "We trust you to do what's needed, and we are grateful to you."

A murmured assent went around the room. I turned and faced Kerric, but neither of us could find the right words to say. He only nodded once, and I took that as his blessing.

I nodded to myself, to the room. "Okay. It's time."

Ready? I asked.

I'm ready. John said.

One, two, three.

It must have been a shocking sight for all those we left behind. One second, John and I stood amongst them. The next, we had simply gone. Not even the slightest ringing of a bell remained behind as evidence that we had been there. I had left only a few muddy footprints.

But to us, it was even stranger. In the space of a single blink, our entire world had been swapped out. We stood in total silence in the dead place. John's breath came heavy for several seconds.

"Are you good?" I asked.

He rubbed his face as if he could wipe away the nausea and nodded.

"I'll give you a minute to feel better. When we arrive, we have to be still as stone. I don't want them to notice us at first. I want them to wonder how long we'd been standing there."

His breathing slowed. "That's a good strategy."

I smiled. "You ready?"

"Hell yes."

I gripped his hand in both of mine.

One, two, three.

PART SIX

THE WILD THING

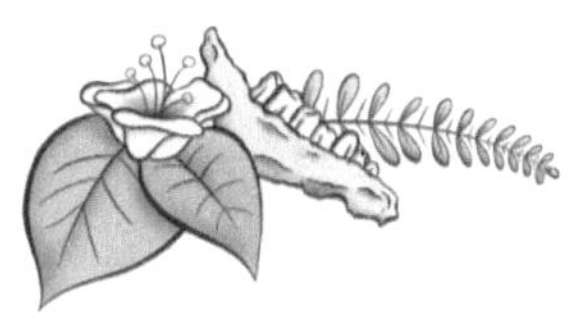

THIRTY-NINE

Sound returned first. After the silence of the dead place and the nothingness between here and there, it was piercing. Music, laughter, footsteps, spoons scraping bowls, glasses clinking, and over it all was the warm hum of voices. Dozens of voices. Maybe more.

When the awareness of sight came back, the room became less noisy. I began to see women walking by, not just hearing their heels on the stone floor. The clinking glasses held bright, bubbly liquid. The voices came from every side, with people gathered and mingling.

It had been a delicate transition. I hadn't done this much before, and I had never needed to consider crowds. What would have happened if I had appeared in the same space where someone else already stood? Was that even possible? And the fact that I had never been to this place before, never seen it with my own eyes, didn't help.

So I had focused on the idea of Milhail Metaxas. The threads of his life had bloomed before me through the currents of time and space. I'd followed them to the room where he sat, eating his supper, in a crowded hall. I'd picked out the minds of everyone in that place, and located a spot where we could appear and not be noticed. Not at first.

Don't move.

John obeyed and froze. I had to be perfectly still so not a single bell rang on my body.

How long do we stay like this?

It won't take the room long to see us. Follow my lead. We need their full attention.

John cut his eyes to his right when someone nearly walked into us. The man stopped, glared, then gave us a wide berth.

I followed him with my eyes while he approached a woman wearing an elegant string of pearls in her hair and a shimmering coral pink dress. He said something to her and pointed. She turned and glowered at us as well. Her friend, wearing twice as many jewels and half as much clothing, pivoted to look next.

These people were not so different from us. They were not so prim and proper, not so high as I had expected. Where I wore feathers, they wore shells. Where we were dark, they were golden, like Aris. They were not close to the earth as we were, but close to the sea.

Even so, I did not fit in. John was acceptable here, but I certainly was not. I was a dirty rag of a woman covered in feathers and bones, leather and mud. Black smeared my eyes, and my hair was more knots than bells, which was saying something.

I wasn't close to the earth; I *was* the earth.

Though Metaxas wasn't visible from where I stood facing John, I could feel him a short distance away on my left. He sat at the head table, talking with a man on his right. Anger pooled in my gut at the thought of it.

He just sat there, drinking ale, talking and laughing and enjoying supper. Did he even know dozens of his people were rotting in a mass grave at that very moment? Did he have half a thought for the lives he had destroyed? Derehani and Authe Idan alike?

There was no point listening in now. His thoughts dwelt on his conversation, but that wouldn't go on much longer.

Silence rippled around the room as more and more people noticed us. The time had come at last.

Quickly, I gathered every mind in the room. Most of them were aristocratic or middle class, at least. Servants moved about with trays and pitchers. Only a few guards stood near the doors, but many of the attendees were military men. The ornamental knives in their bandoliers were plenty sharp. I had to have every risk under my control. I allowed them all free movement for now, but I stood ready to draw their puppet strings tight at the first threat.

Gwen?

Let them make the first move.

The room went quiet. Even the musicians stopped playing. The crowd of people had backed away from us and clustered near the walls, leaving a wide empty circle, with only John and me at the center. They all stared, open-mouthed, at us—the perfect, attentive audience.

"What is this?" a voice boomed from my left.

Metaxas.

Thoughts flitted through his mind at the sight of us. We were outsiders, foreigners, and my appearance was abominable to him. He didn't know what to make of the bones, bells, and dirt.

My blood boiled. My fingers flexed on John's hand, drawing from his well of calm. We both remained still as stone.

"John of Valheid. Is that you there?" Metaxas's voice fell heavy, the confidence of a younger brother who had received power late in life. "I wasn't expecting visitors from Derehan. When did you arrive? And who is this you've brought with you?"

John finally moved, but only a little. He turned his head so he could more easily meet Metaxas's eye. His tight grip on my hand shook in obvious anger, and his expression was ice.

"Come now, man!" Metaxas said. He stood up and scraped his chair noisily against the floor. "Cat got your tongue?"

No one laughed.

"I've brought my lady to see you, Metaxas." John's voice rang out clear on the heels of Metaxas's words. No one present would miss a word. "She wishes to speak with you about our proposed alliance."

"Your lady?" Metaxas snorted softly.

I kept my awareness tuned to his. At any moment, he might think something useful to me. Something damning. But right then, the only thought that crossed his mind was that I didn't deserve the word *lady*. He wasn't wrong. I was more of a forest witch than anything.

Metaxas brushed that aside and said in a kinder tone, "Come, man! It's a feast! Join us for dinner and ale. Bring your lady and sit at my table."

This offer was met by further silence. John returned Metaxas's gaze with venom.

This was perfect. If we refused to speak, it forced Metaxas to be the one searching for words. He tried to think of any way to get us out of the room and away from his guests, and his irritation washed over me. We were embarrassing him.

"Come, John. This is not the place for politics. We'll prepare rooms for you after your journey. We can talk in the morning."

Silence.

The revelers stood frozen around the room, their eyes tracking between Metaxas and us. Now we had everyone's full attention. Now was the time.

Metaxas took a step to move around the table, but my voice stopped him.

"I know what you're thinking, Mihail Metaxas." My singsong voice bounced off the high plaster ceiling and reached every corner. I put as much confidence and bravado into it as I could muster.

It was his turn to fall silent. But it didn't matter. I didn't need a response.

"You're thinking, 'How did a woman wearing so many bells get into the middle of my hall without making a sound?'"

To illustrate my point, I turned toward him at last. The dozens of bells in my hair rang softly with just the movement of my head. I let go of John's hands and shifted to face Metaxas fully. The bracelets, anklets, and bells sang out into the quiet room. Bones and shells clanked against each other. The feathers danced as the air moved over them.

Everything about me was meant to be noticed, but not a single one of them had seen me come in.

John's mouth quirked up a little. *You're so fucking dramatic.*

Thank you. I latched onto his approval and held on tight. This was going to work.

Metaxas stared at me, lips parted, eyebrows drawn. He was a very lean, powerful figure of a man. Tall as an oak and still strong despite the gray at his temples. He wore expensive but plain clothing. Linen, probably, and leather similar to our own back in Valheid. A sword hung at his waist—the only adornment.

"A lady, eh?" he said finally. "That must mean you're the one they call the Owl. Kerric Moore's lost little sister." *The sibyl*, his thoughts said. *The reader of minds.*

Then, to my intense irritation, he began repeating that phrase deliberately.

The reader of minds. The reader of minds. The reader of minds.

He was well prepared for someone like me. Metaxas knew how to hide his thoughts. This was not going to be easy.

I swept an exaggerated bow in acknowledgement, which set the bells to ringing again. My heart pounded in my chest. The urge to rush him with my bare fingernails pulsed through me, but that wouldn't solve anything. I needed to play the part. Distract him. Get him to think, or better yet, to speak.

"They said you grew up wild," Metaxas said. *Wild, wild, grew up wild.* "I suppose they weren't wrong."

"No indeed, my lord." I plastered a smile across my face.

"What is it you came to say that can't wait until morning, my lady?" Metaxas twisted his mouth on the words "my lady," and he resorted to repeating those words over and over to himself. *My lady. My lady.* It was smoothly done. Not one errant thought crossed his mind.

The others were of no help either. Perhaps they knew nothing of Metaxas's plot against us, or they were too afraid to think of anything besides my alarming appearance.

"Only this," I said, my smile broadening. "I came to inform you of the death of your army. I killed them in battle two days ago...after they sacked several of our southern towns and attacked Valheid."

His eyebrows shot up, and his words came out on a half-swallowed laugh. "You killed—?" For the briefest of seconds, his thoughts flashed to the commanders he had sent northward, but he changed direction immediately. "I don't know what you mean, my lady. I sent no men to Derehan. Not for war or any other reason."

He gestured to one of the guards at the end of his table.

"Take the Derehanis upstairs and keep them there until I can come deal with them appropriately. I apologize to my guests! Let the meal continue!" *Continue, continue, continue, continue.*

Again, echoing silence met his words. His guards did not move to apprehend us. The musicians did not pick up their instruments. Not a single guest took a step or said a word.

Metaxas glared around at them all. He had no way of knowing I held every person captive where they stood. I had taken their voices and their feet so they could not move or interrupt. They could only clutch at each other and watch.

They would feel it, though. There were too many for me to hold them with subtlety, so each person felt the vise-like grip of my mind on theirs. Fine. That was fine. Let them feel it. Let them fully understand what was happening and who they were up against.

"Bale!" Metaxas barked at his guardsman. "I said, escort these guests upstairs."

Bale turned shakily toward his lord and bowed his head in silent apology.

"Bale! Neo!" Metaxas marched right up to where the guard stood at the end of the table, then to another by the door.

They flinched away from him, unable to follow orders. He shook the arm of a woman seated nearby. She yanked away and covered her head with her arms.

"They won't answer you," I said. "No one will. You are alone now, Metaxas. They are eyes and ears, nothing more."

He turned and glared at me. His eyes flicked to John. "What is this? What is happening?"

John returned his gaze. "My lady wishes to speak with you, Metaxas."

His poisonous eyes landed on me once more. "You. You're doing this to my people. Release them immediately. This is an invasion."

"Yes!" I smiled again. "Yes, an invasion. That's what this is. An answer to the one we received two days ago."

"I say again, I did not send any men to Derehan!"

His rage echoed through the hall, making everyone flinch where they stood. It wiped the smile from my face, leaving only fire behind.

Metaxas moved to stalk around the table and toward me, his hand reaching for his sword, but he only made it one step before he stopped as well.

I glared at him, and his eyes widened in fear. His thoughts took on a frantic note, but his control remained steady. *Can't move. Can't move.* His mouth worked, but no sound came out. That pleased me.

Yes, I wanted him afraid. I wanted him to see who I was.

I would break this man. I would get the information I wanted. It would simply take time.

FORTY

I cocked my head to one side, a wolf stalking its prey. My next trick required more distance, so I began to walk. John stood, arms crossed over his chest, and watched me.

I took my time strolling toward the crowd, where it had gathered near the wall, and walked among them carelessly, bells ringing, bones clanking. They leaned away from me and clutched at each other. I had no thoughts for them now. My eyes stayed fixed on Metaxas.

"I wonder, Metaxas," I said. "There is a song in Derehan. We all learn it as children. Have you heard it? About a Crone?"

I released his voice so he could speak again. He only glared at me and spat on the floor.

"Now, now, Metaxas," John said. "That's not polite. Answer the Owl's questions."

Metaxas's thoughts soured further, but still he did not waver. *Bitch. Can you hear me, bitch? Fuck you. Fuck you.*

"Have you heard the song?" I asked again with more force.

His taunts were nothing, and it wouldn't do to reveal how closely I was listening in. Not yet. So far, he had no confirmation that his misdirection was even necessary. Eventually, he would slip up.

His mouth twisted, as if on something sour. "Something like 'Beware the whispering Crone? She tells tales to draw you near?' Is that what you mean?"

"Yes! That's not exactly right, but you get the idea. Tell me, do you know the next verse too?" I stepped between two women, my eye still on the lord. My feathers ruffled against them, and they closed their eyes, leaning as far away as their rooted feet would allow.

"Something about a Child?" he said through gritted teeth.

"That's the one. 'Beware, beware the Child, who has no need of tales.'"

I raised one hand in front of me, palm down. The action was echoed by everyone in the room except for John. Hundreds of steady hands hovered in the air before their quaking owners. Even Metaxas, who was purple with fury, lifted his hand as instructed.

"'She'll turn your hand and smile,'" I continued, flipping all our hands palm up as one. A soulless grin stretched across my face.

Then I slipped out the world and back into it again directly behind Metaxas, close enough to whisper in his ear. For the barest of seconds, when I moved, I lost my grip on the room. Chaos spilled around. People fell, called out, and ran for each other and the doors. Metaxas got his sword halfway out of its scabbard.

Finally, he faltered in his internal chanting, but it was of no use to me. He was too overcome by the sudden freedom and immediate recapture to think of anything I cared to know.

Stillness fell once more when I regained control. People sprawled across the floor. Others came to rest pressed against the doors, still closed.

"'The Wild Thing unveiled,'" I hissed into Metaxas's ear, loud enough for everyone to hear.

He jumped and tried to turn, to stumble away, but with his feet rooted to the floor, he only managed to lose his balance and collapse on the table in front of him. A roasted chicken and several cups upturned, sending mess and chaos flying. He lay there shaking, his breath coming in huge gasps.

I shook too. The wildness was coming to the surface. It had only been a show before, but now it took over. I grabbed two fistfuls of Metaxas's shirt and hauled him upright again. He towered over me, but he was terrified. Metaxas gripped my wrists too tightly, trying to free himself.

Vaguely, I could tell he was hurting me, but I didn't care. It didn't occur to me to take tighter control of him and protect myself. I was an animal. All I could think of was more, more! More force. More intimidation. *Break him!*

I twisted my mouth into a snarl. "Would you like to see what I did to them, Metaxas? Your army of mercenaries?" I shouted into the silent room.

He flinched but could not break away. Metaxas beat at me with his fists, blows landing on my arms, shoulders, and face, but he could not pry me off.

"I'll show you what they did! And I'll show you how I retaliated!"

John appeared behind him, prying Metaxas's hands away so he couldn't hit me anymore. I barely noticed and continued screaming into Metaxas's face. The bones and bells rattled around my neck.

"I'll show everyone here what you did and what you cost them!"

And with an almighty roar of effort, I took one hundred thirty-six minds fully captive. I had to sacrifice control over their voices and feet, but I had won their senses. They would see, hear, and feel only what I gave them, and I had only nightmares to share.

If I hadn't been so enraged, I wouldn't have been able to do it. I wouldn't have been able to relive that horrendous afternoon when the Authe Idan soldiers sacked my home.

The people saw a different me. Not a forest witch, but a tidy, respectable young woman with only a few feathers in her hair and without a single speck of mud. They watched while I hovered in the Greathouse courtyard with Josephine. Felt my pain when John was stabbed. Felt my fury as I moved through the city. Watched as the soldiers became the grotesque puppets of a young woman insane with rage, joy, and satisfaction. Followed in horror while they gutted themselves and each other.

They felt my gratification as if it were their own.

The people were imprisoned in that nightmare with me, witnessing my enemies fall to my rage. They knew how helpless they were against me.

I was a monster. I was inevitable.

When the vision ended, I released them all. Only Metaxas remained under my control. He would not be leaving. Not yet. I glared up at him, tears dragging rivers of black makeup down my face. The party goers screamed and shouted in panic. They trampled over each other in their haste to find the doors.

With resignation, I took their feet once more. The show wasn't quite over. I couldn't allow them to leave.

"Do you see now, Metaxas? Do you understand?"

Metaxas's face mottled with anger. He shook uncontrollably, even as he struggled against John's firm hold on his arms.

"How dare you?" he said through clenched teeth. "You little bitch. How dare you come into my home?"

"How dare you come into mine!" I screeched.

My fingers curved into claws. I clutched at his face and took full control of his entire body. Every breath, every blink, was a gift from me. But still he frantically held onto his thoughts. *Fuck you. Fuck. Fuck.*

"My people are dead because of you! I became this monster because of you! And for what? For a little more power? For your pride? Speak! Why did you do this thing!"

Blood welled from under my fingers where my nails pierced his skin. It dripped thickly into his heavy beard, and he gritted his teeth in pain and determination.

With great effort, he forced the words out. "For you."

For you. For you. For you.

I drew my eyebrows together and shook my head. "What?"

"I did it for you! Because you refused to just fucking die! Why won't you just die, you abomination!"

And then it happened. He slipped. For half a second, he remembered composing a letter to an ally. He wrote it in his bedroom late at night, several months before, when the air blew cold over the sea and whistled past the shutters. Metaxas had pulled a heavy quilt over his lean shoulders and gazed with righteous anger at the word on the paper, still shining in wet ink: *abomination.*

That was all, just a single second of an old memory. But it was enough.

I stared up at his maniacal grin. Realization washed over me. I released his face as if it had burned my skin. My bloodied hands shook, and I backed away.

He seemed to think he had won something because he stood suddenly taller, even though John still held his arms fast behind his back.

"And I would do it all again!" he shouted, triumphant. "Anything to remove you from this earth. You are a plague and a demon! You said it yourself! A monster—"

I took Metaxas's voice then, leaving him to gape like a fish out of water, and found John's grim expression.

"An abomination?"

John let go of Metaxas when I resumed control. "Heidi," he said through gritted teeth.

"You were in league with my aunt." I turned back to Metaxas.

His face twisted in confirmation. *Get out of my head, you bitch! Get out! Get out!*

"You incited her to attempt violence against her own blood.

She murdered my sister's child. Your own grandchild. Did you even know? You must have. Your men returned to you afterward. They would have brought the news."

He opened his mouth, and I allowed him his snarling voice. "Good. I'm glad the mutt was killed. And it wasn't my grandchild. Aristeidis ceased to be my son when he left this house two weeks ago."

"But why?"

Around us, the astonished faces of the highborn Authe Idans of Bluewater looked silently on, mesmerized by our display. Were Aris's sisters among them? Which ones?

They weren't so different from us, really. Just men and women going about their lives. They had come to supper in this version of a seafront Greathouse, like any other day. Even now, across the silence of the room, the steady, rushing sounds of the ocean floated through the windows.

This was a beautiful place. If things had gone as planned, Josephine and I would have arrived as guests by now. She would have been married and getting settled. I would have seen that endless horizon of water with my own eyes.

"Why did you sue for marriage if you didn't want Josephine to bear your heirs, Metaxas?" My eyes remained on the open window. I couldn't see the shore from here, only a stone courtyard. But I could hear it.

"I didn't know what she was. Nobody knew until a few years ago. When you cropped up, alive, and ruined everything. And your country became a cesspool of demons and witches."

"And so, you conspired with my aunt to have us killed?"

"I wouldn't have pushed Aristeidis into it in the first place if I had known!" he hissed. "Release my people and begone, witch. You have made your point. I have killed some of your people and paid for it tenfold. Go in peace and leave us be!"

"I'm not finished with you yet!" I shouted. A wave of fear

spread outward amongst the people in the wake of my fury. "I still have questions, and you are not making sense!"

"Derehan was always a haven for sibyls," John said. "More than one Authe Idan has sought sanctuary with us over the years. If you hate us so much, why would you want to ally with us in the first place?"

Metaxas clamped his mouth shut and said nothing. *Get out. Get out. Get out. Get out.*

The old woman.

"What?"

I flicked my head to the right, where the errant thought had come from. One of the servants clutching a pitcher of wine stared back at me, wide-eyed but steady, from his spot near the wall. He was young, not much older than myself, and as gold as Aris ever was. His thoughts jumped instantly to fear at being noticed.

"I, I didn't—" the man stammered. "I didn't say anything."

"She's reading your mind!" Metaxas screamed at him. "She's a witch, you idiot! Can't you see it? Think of nothing! Or repeat something in your head!"

"What about an old woman? Did you see her?" I asked the serving man.

He shook his head, casting confused and defiant eyes at his master, who continued to chastise him.

"Guard your thoughts, man! Give her nothing! Or you're for the whip!"

John moved toward the man, a picture of authority and grace. Even compared to the Bluewater lords, who were taller and grander, John's posture demanded absolute attention. "Look at me, friend. What's your name?"

"Hollis."

"Do you know me, Hollis? I was the Derehani emissary for many years."

"I know you, sir."

John nodded once in acknowledgement, then pointed at

Metaxas. "That man sent six thousand of your countrymen to my home in order to kill us. He has attempted three times to kill members of the ruling family of Derehan by conspiracy. These are acts of war. You understand what that means?"

Hollis nodded, his fair hair shining in the candlelight.

John put a hand on the man's shoulder. "Listen very carefully. We do not want war with the city of Bluewater or with Authe Ida as a whole."

Hollis's brown eyes switched over to where I stood, watching, and images of me covered in blood and delight flashed across his thoughts.

John turned him back with firm pressure on his shoulder. "We do not want war," he repeated. "The Owl defended our city, and she would do it again."

He straightened and addressed the entire room at that point.

"She would do it again!" he said, more loudly so everyone heard.

I shifted my weight from one foot to the other and refused to meet any gaze that fell on me. My head began to ache with the effort of holding everyone, listening, staying ready.

"That is why we are here, to make sure you all understand that Derehan is defended." John turned back to Hollis. "We are here to make sure that never happens again. Your master has been lying to us and to you all. We only want to understand where this aggression is rooted. Does that make sense?"

Hollis nodded again, and once more, he thought of the old woman.

I jumped at the opportunity. "Did you see her? The old woman? Was she here?"

He remembered speaking with another servant, hearing others gossip about a meddling old woman. "I never saw her here," he said. "But there has been talk among the servants that the master meets with an old Derehani woman. And I think—I think I met her once. Years ago, by the sea. She said to me...She said...The truth. I'd tell the truth. And I'd never know..." He swallowed hard, looking a little lost.

His thoughts flashed through his memories. Theo's face by the sea. She squeezed his shoulder and said, *"But now you know. Your honesty will be greatly appreciated."*

But this Hollis person hadn't seen Theo in the capital. He hadn't witnessed Theo and Metaxas conspiring. This wasn't proof enough, but now I knew what to look for.

I turned back to Metaxas, who was resolutely chanting in his head.

"What's he thinking?" John asked. "Was it her? Was it Theo?"

"He's being very rude about my appearance." I said, but my attention was drawn away by other thoughts in the room.

Hollis hadn't seen the old woman, but the others had. Images of Theo slipping through a door, half-remembered echoes of her rasping laughter...The memories fluttered in and out of people's conscious thoughts. Until one word caught my attention:

"Eustis?" I said upon an exhale, and every eye jumped to my face.

"Get out of my house!" Metaxas screamed.

I glared at him. "Hush. I'm thinking."

He fell obediently silent, not that he had a choice, and instead returned to his internal chanting.

"Eustis?" John asked, stepping closer. "Eustis Metaxas? The former lord of Bluewater?"

An unamused smile spread across my face, and I held Metaxas's gaze. Finally, the pieces were all coming together.

"Eustis Metaxas," I repeated, "who mysteriously disappeared five years ago, allowing his younger brother, Milhail, to seize control. Thus ending the lynchings in Bluewater and triggering an alliance, which sent Aristeidis north to Josephine."

John's expression resolved into understanding. "I think we're done here," he said, taking my hand.

"I think you're right." I enjoyed the purple tint to Metaxas's face as he struggled against my hold on him. "We have an old woman to find. But first—"

I turned and stepped onto an empty chair, then directly onto the feast table, using John's steady grip for balance. To make room for my bare feet, I kicked the remains of a casserole to the floor, my anklets of bone jangling.

"I apologize for interrupting your supper tonight," I said, addressing the whole room. "But I came here to make one thing very clear, and I needed as many people to hear my message as possible. As John said, we do not want war, but we are defended. Any attack on Derehan will be responded to in kind."

To illustrate my point, I made another push through the growing ache in the back of my skull. Every person in the room, Metaxas included, drew weapons. Those who didn't have blades instead broke glassware and pressed the sharp edges against wrists, wrapped sashes around their own necks, laid tines of forks against soft flesh, or simply pushed fingertips against their own eye sockets.

Their fear and desperation ratcheted up to a fever pitch when their own hands betrayed them but every one of them stopped just short of actual injury.

I looked around, my face a bleak mask. It would be so easy, so satisfying, to just make them do it. They didn't have to kill themselves, only damage. They would deserve it, after what had been done to my people. Metaxas especially.

John squeezed my hand in a silent reassurance, and with a relieved sigh, I came back to myself. These people did not deserve this. And even if they did, I was not qualified to judge them. I had already meted out my justice. It was time to go home.

"You all fear me," I said. Weapons dropped to the floor all around us. "Good. You should fear me. But don't let that fear rule you. I certainly won't."

"Derehan remembers." John squeezed my hand again to signal he was ready.

Forty-One

I could not imagine the chaos that ensued after we blinked out of existence. Many people probably fell over or fled. There was likely screaming and panic when my hold on them released. They might not have quite understood, in the pandemonium, that we had gone so completely. Perhaps they searched for us through the grounds and surrounding city, or possibly they were simply grateful to be free of me and let us go without chase.

My thoughts were entirely on Eustis Metaxas, Aris's missing uncle who should have been lord of Bluewater. Perhaps that was why, when we emerged from the nothingness between worlds, Eustis was who we found ourselves looking at.

Or rather, what was left of Eustis.

"By all the gods," John said breathlessly. "What is this?"

I stared at the impossible scene laid out before us. We had come into Theo's Sanctuary, but now I believed, more than ever, that our own name for it was more fitting: the dead place.

I had no idea how big this place was. Perhaps as large as the world of the living. I had only ever seen Theo's bivouac and a random stretch of dry trees. This spot was little different: windless, brown, and silent. The canopy of trees blotted out the gray sky, and the ground was free of brush. Only dead leaves and sparse, dry grass.

And bodies.

Hundreds and hundreds of corpses littered the ground, as far as the eye could see in all directions. Perhaps thousands. They did not rot, smell, or degrade. There was no blood, no scavengers, nothing. Every face was as fresh as if they had died only seconds before. They might have been sleeping, every one of them, save for the odd positions they lay in.

And directly in front of us rested Eustis Metaxas. He looked very much like his younger brother: tall, lean, angular. His body sat crumpled against the base of a tree, his face turned upward to the empty sky. His expression was relaxed but still held the vestiges of confusion. His brows were drawn together, his mouth turned slightly down in a frown.

"I think we've found all the people who have gone missing," I said softly.

"There are so many?" John swallowed hard and ran a shaking hand down over his beard. His voice went very tight. "Did Theo do all this?"

"I assume so, but only because we're here in the dead place. She's the only other one I know of that can get here."

"There are no injuries." He stepped between bodies and looked closer. John turned the face of a middle-aged woman to view her more clearly. "How did they die?"

My headache pounded against my skull. "I don't know."

John dropped the arm of a nearby body and stood up straight. "So, she killed Eustis. She made him disappear. Are you thinking the same as me? It was a deal to give power to the younger brother?"

I nodded. "It all makes so much sense. Eustis hated the sibylline, and with Milhail in charge, the lynchings stopped. Plus, he sued for peace and a marriage alliance with Derehan. It suits her goals perfectly. A more tolerant world."

"And when you and Jo began living openly in Valheid, he went back on the deal."

"It was too much for him. He won't lynch us, but he doesn't want us in his family. He was raised in the same house as his brother, after all. The same prejudices."

"Except he would have you assassinated," John said in anger. "And Jo too. And half the city."

"Hm."

"What do we do now? I'd say you've neutralized the threat from Bluewater, but this—" He waved a hand to encompass the slaughter around us. John turned back to me, then froze at the sight of my expression. "Gwenna? What are you thinking?"

"I'm thinking this has to end. Now."

"And how do you plan to do that?"

I reached for his hand, but he jerked away.

"I'm taking you home," I said.

"And then what, Gwenna?"

"And then I'm going to kill her." Why was he suddenly being so difficult? Didn't he understand the urgency?

"How?" He burst out a humorless laugh. "The Crone has been walking the earth for centuries. She can move like you do. She has some unknown way of killing people without leaving a mark." He gestured at the carnage surrounding us. "What in the hell are you going to do to her?"

"I'm stronger than she is! I'll overpower her!"

"How? Tell me how! When she jumps in and out of this world too fast for you to catch her? She's been doing this for generations, Gwen. You may be stronger, but she has more practice. More skill. Do you really think you can protect your mind, get into hers, keep up with her, and do the job all at once?"

I floundered. My eyes fell on bodies no matter where I looked.

I didn't like how right he was being. I just wanted to act! I wanted her dead!

"I don't have to get into her mind!" I said and fumbled for the walnut dagger he had given me all those months ago. It took several seconds of rattling bells and bones to unclasp it from its sheath and brandish it.

John wasn't convinced. His patronizing expression said it all.

"What other option do we have, Johnny?" I gestured with the shining dagger. "Look at what she has done."

A dry, chilled laugh echoed between the silent trees, and we both swiveled to face the source.

Theo stood about twenty paces away, watching us with a lowered head and hunched shoulders. Her ratty cloak hung lifeless from her thin frame. "As if you're any better!" she spat out. "You killed an entire army in a matter of minutes. At least I paced myself a bit!"

I wrapped John's mind up in my own so she could not get to him and backed toward him, tripping over Eustis Metaxas's prone body. John caught me and hauled me against him, his hand tight on my upper arm.

"So timid?" Theo said with a cackle. "Not thirty seconds ago, you were ready to run me through! All talk, eh? No action?"

"Your time is over, Theo," I said with as much bravado as I could muster. "This is between you and me now."

"No. I don't think so. The job isn't done. I'd like to kill Metaxas for going back on our deal. I'd like the boy, that Aristeidis, to be lord of Bluewater, and I'd like him to take lovely Josephine with him."

I made half a noise of protest, but Theo's raised voice overpowered me.

"We were supposed to have a known sibyl ruling two of the greatest city states on the continent! You in Valheid, and Josephine in Bluewater. That was the deal! We were supposed to have a little blasted progress!"

"But Metaxas turned on you," I said. "He wasn't as compliant as he led you to believe."

Theo raised a crooked finger at me. "You will forget what you saw here. You will look the other way and go home!"

"And if I don't?" I asked, more angry than defiant.

John's hand tightened on my arm, a silent warning to maintain control.

"Then what's one more generation?" Theo asked. "I've waited this long. I can bide my time a little longer. I'll just wait until your sister pops out a few children. I'm willing to bet at least a handful of them will be gifted. The sibyls are strong in your family. They can be put to good use."

"Over my dead body," I hissed.

She barked out a single laugh. "Ha! Yes, my child. That's what I intended."

"I fucking dare you to try."

"If it comes to that!" Theo snarled. "But I have one other idea I'd like to try first. One that will be much faster."

"Theo!" John barked at her, a note of pleading in his tone. "Stop this! What are you doing?"

Theo refused to even look at him. She blinked out of the world, and we were alone.

And before I could comprehend that she had gone, my vision was filled with the snarling, lined face of an angry old woman. She had reappeared only inches in front of me, spitting with rage and reaching for my face.

Instinctively, I fell backward out of the world, dragging John with me, and we landed solidly in the Greathouse main hall.

My man stumbled away from me, taken by surprise. He shook his head and sucked in a huge breath.

Meanwhile, I stripped off the baubles and trinkets hung all over my body. I flung bells, bones, feathers, and belts to the floor as fast as I could. John's walnut knife, still clutched tightly in one fist, made me clumsy, but it would have been stupid to drop it, even for an instant.

We had only seconds, I knew. Only seconds before Theo might follow us. There was no time for plans, no time for anything. I had to get back to the dead place before she came to Valheid, where more bystanders, servants, farmers, guards, and councilmen were gathered to watch my noisy display.

These weren't just people. They were potential hostages.

"Gwen?" Kerric asked, emerging from a side door.

Josephine, Garreth, and Nanette came out behind him, worry etched across their faces.

"There's no time!" I called. "Garreth! Jo! Be ready! I don't think she'll come here to make a show, but be ready just in case. I don't know what she's planning!"

"Gwen?" John asked, but I lurched away from his outstretched hand.

"I have to end this," I said, pleading for him to understand.

"Who is coming?" Josephine asked, her voice raised in alarm.

More people gathered as I hauled the heaviest strings of beads over my head. It snagged in my tangle of hair, and I wasted no time in ripping it out. The pain barely registered in my adrenaline-fueled state. The beads clattered to the flagstone floor.

"She won't come here, Gwen," John said.

"She wants me dead! She said so! I can't risk her coming here, where she can threaten everyone else."

"You can protect us better if you're here with us!" he hissed.

"Who are you talking about?" Kerric called in a heavy voice. "How did it go with Metaxas?"

I looked from my man to my brother, to my sister, to my friends who gathered around me, almost as silent as the dead place.

No, not silent.

Outside the open windows and doors, life continued in the warm summer air, unaware I was even there. People laughed and talked, and animals brayed. Somewhere, someone was working construction. Hammers rang out in sharp staccatos and echoed over the cobbled streets.

This place wasn't dead. Not yet.

And then my eye fell on a young woman near the back wall, a serving girl with a full water bucket in one hand. She reminded me of Hollis in Bluewater, not in appearance, but in expression. Concern but not fear. She stood straight and unafraid, watching my display like everyone else.

And over her shoulder, a lined face appeared, shrouded in white hair and a ratty, gray cloak. The face split into a satisfied smile when our eyes met.

"No!" I cried, half raising my hands in a useless gesture of alarm.

But it was too late. Both Theo and the serving girl blinked out of existence, bucket and all.

FORTY-TWO

Everyone in the room swiveled to follow my gaze, and several guards on duty drew swords and bows. But they saw nothing to worry them. It was just an empty stretch of wall.

"What is it?" Cynebald asked from the doorway to Kerric's study.

"She's here! She was here!" I turned in all directions, a single bracelet of bells ringing on one arm, but Theo was nowhere to be seen in the echoing main hall.

"Who?" Kerric asked.

"Theo," John answered.

"Everyone, join hands!" I called. "Now! Do it now! Quickly! She'll come back!"

No one acted fast enough. A rumble of confusion and worry spread around the hall. A few reached for their neighbor's hands.

Josephine, grim-faced and stern, was my best ally. She and John began herding everyone together, shouting instructions. "Skin to skin! Everyone! Here, take his wrist. That's good enough."

Most of them didn't seem to understand the severity of the

situation we were in. All they saw was the Little Owl in a panic, and they had no idea why.

But they knew me. They trusted me. I was the Chalice and a Moore. I was one of them, and they understood what it meant to be scared.

If I was afraid, me of all people, then they should be too. Slowly, much more calmly than I would have liked, the entire room gathered around me.

I continued to spin, my mind open and searching for the old hag between the familiar faces of my people. More than once, I thought I spotted her, but she was gone by the time I looked again.

"Don't let go of each other, no matter what," I said, loud enough for everyone to hear. "She'll come back. She's up to something."

"Gwen..." John reached out to me. He held hands with Kerric on one side, and two others gripped his wrist and forearm behind him. John was as connected as anyone else.

Only I was left alone.

But the dreaded, familiar voice rasped out behind me. "Yes! Take his hand!"

I spun to face her, several paces away from John. My sister took a few jogging steps and joined the group at John's side, slipping her hand over the skin of his arm. Free hands emerged from the group and latched onto her from behind, uniting her with the whole.

Now that Theo stood in the open, everyone understood what was at stake. They all had been warned about the Crone since childhood. They knew to beware.

They cemented themselves together as one, clutching tight and standing tall.

"Very well done, child," Theo said. "I can't snatch them all at once." Her staff clicked on the stone floor, and she hovered on the spot. She tapped it over and over in apparent excitement, grinning widely.

Her smile unnerved me. What was she planning?

I stretched my shield over every mind in the house and as far as I could to those still working outside, unaware. The more people I shielded, the more limited my range became, but I had to try.

"Gwen!" Sinead hissed from behind me.

Several others reached for me. They wanted to protect me.

But I turned back to Theo, who continued to smile and watch from several yards away.

"I thought you didn't want people to be afraid. Why would you come here, to be witnessed by so many?"

The old woman shrugged. "They already fear me. I can use that. I can be the enemy and make you the hero. I had thought they feared you as well, after that rampage of yours, but look how they gather around you. It's beautiful!"

I glanced around at the crowd of silent, frightened people. Theo didn't mentally attack anyone. She didn't even test my shields to find a vulnerability.

"You're toying with me," I said.

Her thin mouth quirked upward on one side. "Very smart, this one."

"What can you possibly want? You must know your time is finally over. You've lost. Your meddling has crippled Bluewater. It has devastated Derehan. And only the Old Kind know where else you have wreaked your havoc."

"Are you going to kill me, then?" Theo stood up a little straighter and gripped her staff with both hands before her. Its gnarled wood top, with its tattered fabric and bones, hovered in front of her mouth, partially hiding the sarcastic grin.

"Yes," I said.

"So do it!" She threw her arms wide, inviting me to take my shot. "What are you waiting for, child? You didn't hesitate the other day."

"I—" My words failed me.

The animal inside me wasn't enticed by this sacrifice. It wanted to take a person's will, not be given it. There was no effort in this. And my morality had never bent toward death or destruction. It was too abrupt and final.

And more than either of these, there was still that grin on Theo's face. She had something up her sleeve.

"I'll do it if you won't," said Cynebald, striding forward. His axe spun in his hand with a deft twist.

"Cynebald! Stop!" I called.

"Stand down!" Kerric ordered from behind me.

But the general had only been a few paces away when he started. He was upon Theo in two strides, his blade raised for a clean strike.

I redoubled the shield around Cynebald's mind, but it didn't matter. Theo had no interest in his mind after all. She didn't even attempt to stop him by force or by killing him. Theo simply blinked out of the world, as deftly as I had ever done, and reappeared an instant later just behind the charging general.

She reached out a knobby hand and brushed a finger against the skin of Cynebald's arm.

And they both disappeared.

Then I understood.

This was how she had killed all those people in the dead place. She whisked a person's body through the void, a transition their consciousness could not make. Only the sibylline, like myself and John, could survive that journey. And once the deed was done, all she had to do was leave the body behind, her pile of corpses a little higher than before.

Cries of alarm rang out all around me when Cynebald disappeared. They couldn't have known, as I did, that he was dead, just another in a pile of long-forgotten corpses in the dead place. Brave, strong Cynebald, cut down so abruptly.

What was worse, the same fate had likely befallen the maid just a few minutes before, and for what? She had done nothing wrong. Theo had merely wanted to get my attention.

Well, now she had it.

Fire burned in my gut when Theo reappeared alone, back in the spot she had occupied before. Her smile reeked of satisfaction.

"Nobody touch her!" I screamed. "Do not let go of one another!"

"End this, Gwen!" Kerric said through gritted teeth.

You can do this. John's words came silently, but no less intense.

I stalked forward, the walnut dagger clenched so tight in my fist that my fingers ached. Two steps, three. Then I hesitated.

Theo glared at me, daring me to continue.

The last bracelet of bells sang when I raised my hand, poised to deal the final blow.

But again, I hesitated.

An inner war raged, and tears of frustration ran down my face.

Do it now!

It's not right!

What's one more life after you've taken so many already?

I can't do it!

But then Cynebald's words came back to me, clear as the day he had first spoken them: *It's your responsibility to defend the city and the people, same as the rest of us.*

A guttural roar gave voice to my breaking heart, and I brought the dagger down with a shrill of bells. My aim was true. I angled the blade to slip easily between her ribs and thrust with all my might.

Theo was too fast for me. My blade swung harmlessly through empty air, knocking me off balance with the follow-through.

I whirled on the spot, looking everywhere for the old woman. "Where are you?" I screamed.

People jumped in surprise at the volume and anger in my voice.

"Theo!"

"Very good!" Theo's voice sounded from the back of the room. "So, you do have it in you after—"

Her voice halted abruptly when I took full control of her. I had never tried to possess the body of a sibyl before, much less one so powerful as Theo. Her mind squirmed away from me, slippery as a worm. It took everything I had to hold on to her, and even then, my success was spotty. Her body jerked and writhed as she struggled to regain mastery of herself.

I was stronger, however.

Slowly, painstakingly, I forced Theo to walk toward me, her staff forgotten on the ground behind her, until we stood face-to-face.

"Your time is over, old woman," I said calmly.

She forced out another of her satisfied grins. "Yes," she agreed. "I've known it for a long time. Which is why I came with a contingency plan."

"What contingency?"

She barked a single, humorless laugh. "You're the hero. Don't you see, child? But what's a hero without a true villain?"

"Gwen!" Josephine's terrified scream cut through the room, followed closely by shrieks and cries from the people nearest the door.

"You want to be beloved?" Theo cried, screeching in triumphant laughter. "You'll have to earn it!"

The commotion near the door spread toward us, and the crowd broke apart from each other. Too many sounds bombarded me to identify them all. Horrific thuds, like bodies slamming into walls. Sickening cracks that sounded horribly like snapping bones.

And worst of all was the screaming.

Josephine's was the most hysterical of all. She saw before I did what had caused the alarm, and she clutched at John, Aris, and anyone else within reach. Josephine tried everything to pull people away toward the interior of the Greathouse, but she was just one woman against an immovable tide of people.

It was all her nightmares come true, all the worst things she had ever feared since the day I was born. Before, it had only been a vision. But not anymore.

A little girl, no older than twelve, moved steadily toward me from the direction of the main doors. Her long, dark hair fell straight and heavy down her back. The girl wore a plain but finely made dress of blue linen, with little yellow flowers embroidered along the hem.

She was beautiful.

The crowd parted for her like a river crashing around a stone. They threw themselves away, seemingly determined to injure themselves as they went. They flung their bodies into other people, into walls, and to the floor with terrifying violence.

"Fuck, fuck, shit." John swore behind us and hastily put all his efforts into shielding his own mind, something he'd rarely had much success with.

He and Josephine were the only two who recognized the little girl. They had seen her the day I first arrived in Valheid, in the vision that had changed the entire course of my life.

It was none other than Sasha, the girl I could have been. The girl whose childhood had stretched for decades in the dead place, indulged and warped by Theo's manipulative ideals.

Not a ghost or a vision, not a disembodied voice or a presence just out of sight.

No, she was really and truly there, not twenty feet in front of me.

FORTY-THREE

I stumbled backward, finally colliding with John and Kerric, where they remained united with most of the crowd. They both latched onto my arms. My strength redoubled when I connected with them. I cast a wide net over every mind in the room once more, but it would do little good. With large numbers of people to protect, I was encumbered. She only needed to reach further.

"You're not real!" I said with a shaking voice.

Sasha laughed, a melodic peal of delight that rang out of her like music. It was the same laugh that had haunted me for the last four years. "Of course I'm real! Same as you are!"

She looked around at the crowd with delight. They presented a whole new audience, a new batch of toys to play with.

"You can't be real!" I insisted. "You're me! We can't both be real!"

Sasha came level with a whimpering Josephine and frowned up at her, disapproving. "Come now, sister. No more tears. I think you've been spying on me for quite some time, haven't you?"

Josephine could not answer, only cringed as far away from

Sasha as she could. Aris clutched her close to his body, not knowing how to protect her but determined to do it anyway.

Sasha only tisked and moved past her, coming steadily closer to me. "We'll talk later, Jo, dear. First, I'd like to speak to this one."

Her words sounded almost comical coming from the mouth of someone so apparently young. But this was no child. She had lived for decades already. In the vision where we had first encountered her, Kerric had been an old man. Sasha must be at least fifty.

But the memory of an old, injured Kerric brought another recollection to mind: a single man in that vision who had resisted the terror before us.

Garreth.

He stood across the room, his expression stern with concentration. Even now, he continually shored up his mental shields, brick by metaphorical brick. He had gone nearly cross-eyed with the effort of it.

Above all else, Sasha must not notice him.

"You don't belong here," I said, dragging my eyes away from my nephew. "Go back to where you came from. To your world, or whatever it was."

"You know? I don't think I will," Sasha replied, her voice light.

I raised one hand, the walnut dagger balanced on my open palm. My bracelet of bells rang a cheery note that did not match the pounding of my heart. "Look, I mean no harm to you. I only ask that you leave us in peace." I lowered the dagger to the ground and slid it across the floor away from me.

It skidded over the flagstones toward Garreth, who stopped it deftly with his foot.

It was an empty gesture, and we both knew it. Neither of us needed physical weapons. Sasha continued speaking as if I hadn't interrupted at all. And to my desperate relief, Garreth seemed to have gone unnoticed.

Garreth had his own blade, of course; he never went anywhere without it. But now he understood what I wanted from him, and now he didn't need to worry about the noise of unlatching its sheath. He needed only to pick up my dagger from the floor.

Sasha continued speaking, to my great relief. "I've been talking extensively with your Theo. There was another in my world, you know. The Theo I grew up with. But this isn't the same old hag, is it?" She frowned sympathetically at Theo, who I kept rooted to the spot with as little effort as I could spare. Sasha continually poked and prodded at my shields. She hadn't gotten through yet, but she was only playing so far.

"Oh yes? And what did you talk about?" I asked.

"We wondered how many worlds there might be."

Sasha stopped about five paces away and studied my face. She looked lazily up at Garreth's mother, Elana, who stood abreast of her at the front of the crowd. Sasha made a halfhearted attempt to gain Elana's mind, but I deflected her.

"There's my world," Sasha continued, her gaze running over each face in turn.

I scrambled to keep up with her, protecting mind after mind in a fevered race.

"And there's this one. Plus the Sanctuary you know. We wondered if my Sanctuary and yours were actually the same place. It would be very difficult to tell."

"Have you seen other worlds?" I asked through gritted teeth.

I tried containing her mind instead of protecting everyone else, but it was like trying to hold a raging fire in my bare hands. She flared out unpredictably and with force.

"I'm starting to think I have. And so have you. And our dear sister. What if our visions weren't just visions? What if we were spying on other worlds? Alternatives to our own?"

I gaped at her when the hugeness of this thought struck me.

"There could be countless worlds," she said. "All results of slightly different choices throughout history. There could be millions of me out there. And millions of you. I wonder if anyone else has figured out how to travel between them? Probably. If I could do it, then surely someone else has."

On my left, a sharp snapping sound, followed by a horrified scream, signaled a hole in my shields. Someone had been forced to break their own finger.

I clung to John and Kerric behind me. Garreth began to move toward Sasha. His mind was so well-shielded I couldn't even feel it anymore. Could Sasha? The little monster wasn't stretched so thin as I was, and she had decades more practice.

"It's an interesting thought," I said vaguely, chasing Sasha's focus around the room.

Mark lurched toward the woman on his left, reaching for her neck, but I severed Sasha's control before he could do any damage.

Sasha barely reacted, only moved on. She seemed to be enjoying this dance. I was probably the first real challenge she had ever encountered.

Behind her, Garreth inched forward. He gripped John's knife in one practiced hand, his feet rolling smoothly from heel to ball.

"This is quite fun, isn't it?" Sasha said.

Garreth stood only four paces away.

"I wonder which one of us will tire first?" Sasha asked.

"Me, probably." Tears of frustration gathered in my eyes, and someone else cried out in pain.

Sasha moved on again, faster and faster.

Three paces away.

"I wonder, is Leland of Mairn still alive in this world? He was a dear friend of mine. Very supportive. Of course, he got old and died ages ago. Poor man went senile. But you're all so young here."

Two paces away.

"He is still alive," I said. "He's an ass."

"Shame, shame. That's not nice."

Josephine went rigid next. I screamed my anger and helplessness when Sasha finally bested me.

My sister moved her hand steadily toward her own face, one finger pointed directly at her right eye.

Aris gripped her arm, and Josephine struggled against him, seemingly desperate to get her finger into her eye. She tried with her other arm. Aris stopped that at the last second.

"Come on, Jo," Aris begged. "Fight her."

Tears streamed down Josephine's face. Sasha only laughed.

"Stop it!" I screamed at her. With a heave of effort, I severed the link.

Josephine relaxed against Aris, but Kerric took her place. His fingers began traveling toward his face instead. John released me and fought my brother's considerable strength. It was all he could do to pry Kerric's hands away from his own eyes.

"Brother dearest! It's so good to see you again!" Sasha sang from behind.

"Stop!" I screamed. "Stop it!"

The silence following my outburst rang in my ears. Kerric aborted the action against his own face and stood unencumbered, master of himself once more.

John's gaze fell behind me, his expression desperate.

I turned, only to be met with a grisly sight.

Garreth stood over the beautiful little girl, his hand red to the wrist. He had sunk the walnut dagger into Sasha's side, and blood oozed out around the handle.

Sasha gazed up at Garreth, comprehension coming too slowly. She lashed out at him with the wildness of an injured animal, and finally, his shields began to crumble.

There was no time. It would take mere seconds for her to get through and kill him with half a thought.

I launched forward, wrenched the dagger out of her side, and plunged it into the vulnerable place where her neck met her shoulder. The blade hit bone and slanted off to the side a little, but I had hit my mark. The blade came free of her body with a sucking sound, and blood gushed out of the wound in an unstoppable stream.

Her focus rested solely on me. Sasha could not speak or breathe, but she could look. She stared at me with the eyes of a child. My own eyes. This was the face I'd had growing up in the Sacred Wood. The face Michael had known.

Behind me, Theo laughed. Her voice went hoarse with the effort of it. "Yes! Yes! Well done! You've saved them all!"

I watched Sasha turn gray and collapse into the ever-widening pool of blood around her. She was not me, but she was at the same time. And she was gone.

With a final effort borne from exhaustion and defeat, I turned to Theo next. She wasn't fighting me anymore. Theo just held her head high as I approached.

"It's time," I said.

"I know."

I jabbed the knife into her neck, the same as I had done to Sasha.

"Fuck," John said on a shocked sob.

The room spun around me. No one moved. No one could quite believe it was over. The only sounds were the echoing whimpers of pain from a handful of spectators around us.

Only fifteen minutes. That was all.

Fifteen minutes ago, this house had been busy, going about a normal day. Then I had frantically appeared, followed by Theo. And now I stood over the body of a child and an old woman, my right hand soaked in blood, and Garreth's likewise.

"Drop it," Josephine said in a wobbly voice. She came up behind me and put a hand on my arm, causing me to jump violently.

I turned to her, desperate for any kind of order in this chaos.

"Drop the blade," she said. "It's done. It's over."

I obeyed her. The walnut dagger clattered and bounced on the floor. Josephine pulled me backward, away from the expanding pool of blood.

My gaze fell on my nephew. His expression was a mirror of my own: horrified and shocked.

It had been his first murder. He was only eighteen years old, and he had just driven a knife into the body of a little girl. It didn't matter that she was older than any of us. It didn't matter that she had been a monster. He had done this violent, abhorrent thing, and it would haunt him for the rest of his life.

I broke away from Josephine and wrapped my arms around Garreth's neck. He didn't reciprocate, but he let me embrace him.

"You did right," I said in a strangled voice. "You did exactly right. You saved us."

Garreth shook and trembled under my touch, and his breath came in ragged gasps. He did not answer me.

Elana came up behind me and took Garreth in her arms. "Come away, son," she said in a hard voice.

He responded to his mother better. Garreth turned and allowed her to lead him away from the evidence of what he had done.

The crowd slowly came alive around us. People shouted orders, Kerric and Aris at the head of everything. They began locating the injured and herding everyone out of the great hall.

Josephine stayed, and John came to me as well. He bundled me up in a tight embrace, and his familiar warmth was enough to break the dam. The tears came in a choking torrent, and I clutched him to me.

John said nothing while I cried into his chest. He simply stood there, held me tight, and let me do it.

FORTY-FOUR

Derehan and the city of Valheid had seen more violence and death in three days than they had known in a century. After sacking six towns during their journey north, the mercenaries had killed sixty-two men and women in the outskirts of the city. An estimated fifty-five hundred Authe Idans had been forced to kill themselves and each other by the rage of an Owl. Then, before the city had had time to recover, a demon had come among the survivors.

While just four died that day, the rest of the city would spend the remainder of their lives looking over their shoulders and wondering. They only partially understood where Theo and Sasha had come from or what their abilities and motives had been, so the fear would remain forever.

And when the full truth of what John and I had discovered in the dead place became known, the Derehani people began to grieve in earnest. For weeks after Sasha's death, people came to me, asking about their loved ones who had disappeared over the past few years.

"Would you look for them, Little Owl? Could you tell us if they're in that place?"

Sometimes, I found nothing, only bones or graves in the world of the living. Twice, I found the missing person alive and well in some other town. Those pieces of news were easier to deliver.

But more often than not, I found a timeless corpse under the dry, brown trees of Theo's Sanctuary. No one could say what they had done to offend the Crone, but at least their families finally had closure.

They all thanked me for my trouble, but those meetings invariably ended in weeping.

My tears had all been spent. I only shed a few for Mariah, who I found open-eyed and at peace in the dead place. When I brought her back, I had her buried in the Barano cemetery alongside her family, who had gone before her.

Several weeks passed before the evacuated citizens of Valheid came home. Some never did, choosing instead to stay in the wilderness or in smaller communities, where they felt safer.

As a means of distraction, I threw myself into the country's recovery. There was an endless amount of work to be done. Aside from the hundreds of bodies still awaiting disposal, there were buildings to repair, relief to be sent to the southern towns, and a city full of people who still needed to eat and maintain their livelihoods.

And then there was Garreth.

After two days withdrawn in his rooms, he finally emerged. He seemed mostly unscathed and went about his duties as usual. But the shadows under his eyes never disappeared, and he seemed to have forgotten how to smile properly.

Garreth sat quietly next to his father at mealtimes, and only Elana could get any kind of response out of him that hinted at the boisterous young man he had been before.

"He'll be all right in time," she said to me one night after supper, though her expression was drawn. "He's been training to fight since he was a boy, but he was never meant for it, I don't think."

"He's always been very good at it," I said.

Elana nodded, her bright red hair flashing in the light of the brazier. "He handled the battle well, but what happened with *her*? That was different."

Across the room, Garreth leaned back in his chair, watching a young woman playing a fiddle, his expression blank. He kept his shields solid and tightly controlled at all times, now. I could barely even feel his mind, and I did not attempt to break through to see it more clearly. Something told me I wouldn't have much success anyway.

"I killed a starving thief when I was his age." I ran my fingers along the faint scar on the side of my neck. "He had a knife to my throat, so I took his life."

Elana said nothing, but I had caught her attention.

"Paul told me to think of other things, to pretend it never happened. But that didn't work."

"How did you get past it?" she asked.

The fiddler pulled a slower, solemn tune out of her instrument, and Garreth's expression flickered.

"I didn't. I probably never will," I said. "It's strange. I hate what I did that day, when the Authe Idans came. I was... monstrous. But I regret what happened with the thief so much more. I could have made him sleep. It would have been easy, and it would have saved my life just as effectively. He was hungry and desperate. He was only doing what he had been trained to do by poverty, and I killed him for it."

Elana took my hand in hers and squeezed. "Remember the fear of Man," she said in a whisper.

My vision blurred in an unexpected swell of tears. Yes, I would remember my fear that night in the woods. And I would always remember the horrific lesson it had taught me, the lesson Michael had tried and failed to teach me using words alone.

The fear of mankind was the most destructive force in the world. And the fear of the Little Owl was more devastating still.

~

That night, John and I went upstairs earlier than usual. It had been a very long day hauling supplies and clearing debris from the battle site in the outskirts of the city. The pyres for the bodies of my victims had finally burned down to smoldering ash, and fresh, spring showers were doing much to wash the blood from the streets.

I undressed and rinsed my face in silence while John flipped through the inventory books for the Leatherworks Guild.

"What?" he asked.

I turned to face him, water dripping from my elbows. "I didn't say anything."

"You said my name."

"No, I was—"

I fell silent when he caught sight of something behind me. His expression of horror sent a thrill of alarm through my body, and I twisted around to see what it was.

Me. It was me.

Another Gwen stood silent and broken near the bed.

She wore the Chalice costume, the leather skirt torn and ruined. A wound on her thigh leaked blood down her leg, and her face was a mess of grease paint and tears. Only a single bracelet of bells remained on one wrist, trembling out a steady ringing.

"What is this?" John asked. "Who are you?"

The other Gwen sobbed once, then advanced toward him. She crossed the room in four limping strides and wrapped herself around John's middle.

He held his arms up and away from the woman who embraced him. John looked up at me, his face torn between concern and confusion.

I said nothing, only watched. Was this a Gwen? Or was it a Sasha? Her mind was entirely cut off from me. It was strange to feel, from the outside, the metaphorical glass sphere that guarded my mind. Where Sasha had been a ball of fire, this Gwen's mind was cool and contained.

"I know you're not him," she said into John's chest. "I know you're not my Johnny. I know, but I—" She broke off and sobbed again into his shirt.

John's brow lowered and drew together. We both understood at the same moment what this must be.

Sasha had said it herself. How many of us were there? Millions? More? If every vision we saw was an alternate universe, then the number was more likely to be infinite.

And if Sasha had mastered how to pass from one universe to another, then it was likely another one of us had learned to do the same.

John relaxed his arms and returned her embrace. He hugged her like he hugged me when I grieved—firm and possessive. She sobbed again and clung tighter to him in response.

"What happened?" I asked in a soft voice.

The other Gwen finally loosened her grip on John, but she couldn't bring herself to pull away completely. She gripped his shirt in trembling hands and stared at his chest in defeat.

"Has she come here yet?" she asked.

There was no need to ask who she meant. "Yes."

"How many died?"

"Sasha didn't have time to kill anyone, but she injured twenty-two. Theo killed Cynebald and a serving girl called Rowena."

The other Gwen nodded and rested her forehead against John's chest. "You managed better than I did."

"How many were lost?" John asked.

Gwen shook her head. "It doesn't matter. I only wanted to see you one last time. I shouldn't be here."

She held his face in both hands and studied his expression.

"Thank you," she said on a breath. "For everything." Then she rose up on her toes and kissed him.

He did not pull away from her.

Finally, she turned to me.

"This will never be over, will it?" I asked.

She frowned, breaking a little more inside. "I don't think so."

I nodded. If she had been Josephine or Mary, I would have held my hand out to her in comfort, but I couldn't bear the thought of touching this doppelganger.

"Remember the fear of Man," I said in a desperate attempt to share the small measure of comfort Elana had given me a few hours before.

She dipped her head once in acknowledgement, then she was gone. Aside from the blood stains on John's shirt, she might have never been there at all.

FORTY-FIVE

Peace came slowly to the valley where Valheid nestled with its farmland.

We received an envoy from Bluewater three weeks after that night in our room. They brought a message from Milhail Metaxas with an official apology and requested that Aris come home with Josephine, as had originally been planned.

"No," was Aris's immediate answer. "If my father wishes to see me, he can come to Valheid."

The Bluewater emissary, a man called Theron, eyed me warily during the conversation with Aris. I vaguely recognized him from my visit to Metaxas's feast hall, and clearly, he recognized me.

The next morning, Josephine stood with her man at the large window on the second landing and watched while the Authe Idans rode away with his message.

"Are you sure?" she asked, putting her arm around his waist.

"Absolutely," he said, with a grim twist to his mouth.

His expression melted into his usual impish smile when he looked down at her. He bent down and scooped her up, eliciting a surprised squeal from her.

"Come, woman," he said in a serious tone. "We have things to do." And he carried her up the stairs, blatantly ignoring the raised eyebrows and laughter from the rest of us.

Elana was right to have confidence in her son. Garreth slowly returned to himself, one day at a time. Kerric pushed him to pick up his former routines with the Guard. And although he resisted at first, Garreth responded well to the athletics, the camaraderie, and the familiar.

One hot afternoon in late summer, we passed each other in the courtyard.

"Doing well?" I asked him in greeting.

"Well enough," he answered with a smile.

His cheerful expression floored me. It was the first real smile I'd gotten from him in months. I had nearly accepted the idea he might never be easy with me again. But there he was, the real Garreth. Still there after all.

We continued past each other without saying anything further, and he headed down the road toward the barracks. I watched him walk away for a few seconds. He waved to a friend and stepped off the road to chat for a moment. My heart swelled at the sight of it.

Someone bumped into me—an errant brewer's boy, running through the courtyard without watching where he went.

"Sorry, Miss Owl!" he called back to me, then hurried off around the corner.

Mary witnessed the incident, and she veered closer to where I stood. "Ornery little brat," she said in passing with an indulgent smile.

I laughed and looked around at the people going about their day. An immeasurable sense of lightness filled my heart.

Darkness would never truly be gone. The dead place persisted, and an idea nagged at the back of my thoughts that another Sasha might someday find her way to me. Despite all this, there was good to be had, here and now, in the real world. In my world.

This was my home, and these were my people.

For them, I would not be afraid.

The Story Continues

with Book Two: The Giant Singer

If you enjoyed this book, please consider leaving a rating or review. With your support, I can keep daydreaming for a living.

You can find convenient links to all the popular review sites on my website: annacackler.com

THE SIBYLLINE SAGA

The Forest Witch

The Giant Singer

The World Mother

The Old Kind

THE GIANT SINGER
THE SIBYLLINE SAGA: BOOK TWO

Eoghan and Nora are on an epic quest to wake up the legendary Giants and save their war-torn country. But this straightforward mission is only the beginning, and soon the stoic Eoghan and fiery Nora have a new goal: stay together, no matter what.

This epic second installment of The Sibylline Saga appears at first glance to be an isolated event, but the ripples of Eoghan and Nora's choices spread further than they can ever know. This is more than just a quest story. It's a tale of faith, determination, and abiding love.

The World Mother
The Sibylline Saga: Book 3

With her family by her side, Gwen sets out into a world beset by great stone Giants, guided by ancient prophecy, and nearly torn apart by the delusions of a World Mother.

In this breathtaking conclusion of The Sibylline Saga, Gwen must confront the truth of who and what she is – or risk losing everything.

THE OLD KIND
A STAND-ALONE ANTHOLOGY
IN THE SIBYLLINE SAGA

A grieving flax spinner descending into madness. A fiery rebel stuck between land and sea. Two sisters, divided by faith and determination. An immortal man, and the ravens that watch him from the trees. The Old Kind lurk at the edges of these stories. Almost gone, but never forgotten.

These four stand-alone tales – THE GLASS WHEEL, BLUEWATER, STARSONG, and RAVEN'S END – explore the overlooked corners of the Sibylline Saga universe. These are stories of hope and healing, where the bond between sisters, the bravery to truly feel, and steadfast love can conquer all.

Content Advisory

This book contains scenes that may be distressing to some readers. Below is a list of these topics, drawn up to the best of my knowledge at the time of publication. A regularly updated list can also be found on my website: annacackler.com

If, while reading this book, you come across any sensitive topics that need to be added to this list, please reach out to me at anna@annacackler.com and put CONTENT ADVISORY in the subject line.

~

Mild-to-moderate gore and violence (no body horror), control of another person's body via coercion (supernatural mental ability), death of a parent, miscarriage, brief mention of harm to children and animals (harm occurs off-page, but the effects are briefly mentioned). There is a love scene on the page, but it is not explicit.

ACKNOWLEDGMENTS

I am so grateful to everyone who has helped me make The Sibylline Saga a reality. I could not have done this without the network of support from both family and from new friends I've made along the way.

Many thanks to those of you who helped me name the Athorum: Gerry Robinson, Jim Meeks, Ashlyn Van Benschoten, Sallie Montuori, and Bear C. It was so fun to brainstorm with you all the ways this mythical cure-all came to be.

I'd also like to thank my many early readers, who helped me polish the series: Zhade, Elizabeth Plass, Brittney Willbanks, Enos Evans, Pam Cemen, and Carla Evans. I couldn't have done it without your feedback and encouragement.

And thank you so much to Lyndsey Smith at the Editing Forge for her tireless work in giving this series its final polish.

There are three other people who have supported me through the ups and downs of being an author. It began with my mother, who told me stories every night and shared her love of books with me. Thanks, Mom, both for the excellent start and your ongoing support and encouragement.

Thank you Chelsea for listening to me ramble and vent with infinite patience. You say you envy my confidence, but that's all fake. You kept me sane when I was barely keeping it together.

And thank you to Kevin, my very best friend and the best husband anyone could ask for. I can't express how much your support and your faith in me has meant.

This series has been an absolute labor of love that began when

I was just a teenager. I am so incredibly proud of it and of myself for getting this far. And I'm can't wait to see what comes next, because this is only the beginning.

About the Author

This part of the back matter is supposed to be so professional and polished and distanced. "Anna Cackler received a bachelors in writing at blah blah blah blah."

But at this point, I am completely out of fucks to give on the matter. I have done every step of this process myself (aside from some volunteer readers and one professional editor). I've had to learn how to write, how to draw, how to make covers, how to connect with readers, and how to construct a story in a profession that changes in fits and starts every other year and is flooded with unsolicited advice online.

And now I'm at the end on my own merit, and there's no publisher or agent or editor to tell me I have to do this any specific way, so screw it.

Here I am. First person POV in an About the Author. Exhausted. Completely over it.

Because if I can't be real with you here, then what's the point?

I did get a Bachelor of Arts in Writing from the University of Central Arkansas. There wasn't a creative writing major at the time, so I had to make do with just "writing." That meant I took classes in fiction, novel writing, and "workshopping" (beta reading). But I also took classes in academic writing, audience, technical writing, and even creative nonfiction. That last one didn't really work with my brain, I don't know why.

This was a long time ago, though. This was back when self publishing was brand stinking new. This was back when my professors would say things like, "Don't even THINK about self publishing your book on Amazon or whatever. You'll ruin your career. No publisher will ever touch you again if you cheat like that."

Yeah... that bit of wisdom didn't age well, did it? Looking back, it really smacks of, "Nobody's gonna buy the cow if you give the milk away for free."

But I'm really happy about my strange collegiate education otherwise. I learned some things in my Academic Audience class that have hugely impacted how I communicate with my fiction readers. And the Technical Writing class really ingrained in me the idea of context. If you don't create the context on the page, then it doesn't exist, and your reader's in the wind.

I am so grateful for that early foundation in writing skills. But I'll be honest, I took that foundation and used it to learn 10 times more later on. I have learned so much from my fellow writers, some friends, others internet friends, by reading for others and discussing their stories and my own. I've done more than one obsessive deep dive into how a certain book or television show communicated the most minute theme or detail (you can find my insane rants on my blog). And I am convinced to this day that Merriam-Webster Dictionary doesn't have the faintest idea what a trope is in the context of fiction.

All that is to say... I've learned a lot, mostly by doing.

My first versions of The Forest Witch were flipping awful. So bad. I wrote it when I was fifteen and had no idea what the heck I was doing. That's why the plot structure is so wacky. Yes, I'm aware the plot structure is wacky. But I'm leaning into it. Don't yell at me. I'm basically just a giant ball of anxiety in size 12 shoes. There's no room in here for more shit feelings.

Gwenna was originally named Jana. She was a mute and kind of a bitch. The mute thing was directly drawn from Daughter of the Forest by Juliet Marillier, which inspired me to begin writing seriously. The bitch thing was mostly because I was an angsty teenage a-hole at the time. I mostly grew out of that.

I never finished that early draft. It just sat idle on my computer for a good 15 years. During that time, I went to college. I grew up. I married my best friend, and we had a couple of kids. I wrote a couple of rom coms, and one erotica. There was some fan fiction that I never published, and about 40 kergillion half started stories that never got off the ground.

But then one day I was digging through my old files and stumbled across what was then called Fireflies, with its sad little mute bitchy FMC. And it had such GOOD bones. Wacky bones, but good bones. I changed her name to Gwenna (because you can't have a Jana, Johnny, and Josephine all in one story). I gave her a voice and a heck ton of agency. I wrote it all over again from scratch.

I changed the name to The Hollow, then to Little Owl, then to The Witch of the Silent Wood. And then, because that was way too long to fit on the front cover, The Forest Witch.

And now, twenty years after I first started writing it, it's in your hands. It's real. And I might just cry about that a little.

There are a lot of things about me that are probably more appropriate for the back of a book like this. More serious things. More practical things. But at the end of the day, I'm just a woman. I'm pushing middle age even though I still feel like a high schooler (except everything hurts). I've got a one-eyed pekinese dog asleep on my desk right now. Pretty sure she just farted.

I'm still married to my best friend, and our kids are in high school now, which is weird as hell. They're both really cool people, though, which I'm grateful for. One of them is a programming genius apparently and the other one is getting really REALLY hard to beat at backgammon. I can't wait to see what they do. They're barely at the beginning of their lives, and I might cry a little about that too.

I feel like when I finally publish this book, something magical will change in my life, but it probably won't. I'll still miss trash day most weeks, and there's still more laundry to do. Always with the laundry omg.

But one thing will change: this book will finally exist out in the world, somewhere besides my own daydreams. And that's worth something. That's real.

Anyway...

Well I don't know how to end this now, so I'm just gonna go. Okay love you bye.

~

www.ingramcontent.com/pod-product-compliance
Lightning Source LLC
Chambersburg PA
CBHW030043130726
47901CB00007BA/1743